The Broken Home Boys

A 1960s Santa Cruz California Novel

ROD GLASGOW

For Pam
my lifelong adventurer
of the heart
soul
and all the cool places
on this earth.

Prologue

June 1969

Two boys sat beside an old man in a small truck so ancient that a chrome strip bisected the windshield. Feeble wipers pushed water back and forth across the flat glass, each stroke briefly revealing a two-lane black road stretching away to a silhouette of low mountains in the distance.

They had been poking along for nearly three hours until the light had faded, and a drizzle had swelled into a steady rain.

Between the man's initial "Where ya going?" to a recent "It's still a ways," he had replied with little more than grunts to attempts at conversation.

Festus, as the younger boy thought of him, had driven the whole way hunched over the wheel with his two hands nearly touching. Underneath a wide-brim hat that must have doubled as a dog's chew toy, a short, patchy, grizzled beard framed sparkling eyes and a near-toothless mouth. He smacked his gums regularly and irritatingly often.

The boy in the middle was fourteen. His friend next to the door was fifteen. In the enforced silence, they kept their thoughts to themselves. They were nearing the end of a long, dangerous day, glad to be in the old man's truck. If only he would drive faster.

After traveling hundreds of miles, they were somewhere in the remote rural sparseness of Northern California—and refuge was still far away. The first boy was tired, and the rhythm of the blades answered the rhythm of the gums to push him down into a heavy sleep after total dark descended.

A screech of brakes and a jab from his friend woke him.

"This is as far as I can take ya."

The rain had progressed from solid to torrential. The boys peered through distorted windows at the raindrops' frenzied dance on the asphalt. It appeared they were at the end of a Highway 101 off-ramp. All was black except for a few distant lights and one car's yellow beams slashing through the falling walls of water drenching the highway.

"Here?" the 15-year-old asked in a voice competing with the battering on the roof.

"Yep, gotta get home up thataway." He pointed a limp, crooked finger toward a barely visible side road.

The two kids looked at each other, faces half-lit by reflections from the headlights and half-darkened by dismay. Then the older boy gazed again at the rain, visibly swallowed, met the other boy's eyes, and shrugged *whatever*. They grabbed their bags from behind the seat, thanked the man, and stepped out into the cold and wet.

1

April 1964

It was taking too long to eat Sugar Frosted Pops. Duncan Findlay, age 9, sprinkled more sugar on his bowl of cereal and watched as his beloved Nana poured boiling water onto her Lipton tea bag.

"Did you like the train ride?" she asked her daughter's son.

He slurped a big spoonful and swallowed. "It was great," he said, waving his spoon in the air. "There were windows in the ceiling and I could watch the stars and Keith and I had our own bed."

Nana smiled. She wore a calf-length black dress with embroidered white flowers splashed across her right shoulder. A neat woman, her favorite saying was *A place for everything and everything in its place.* Cataract-milky eyes looked at Duncan through thick glasses as she dipped the bag up and down in the steaming water. "You sure got up early. Everyone else is still asleep. We are the early birds."

Duncan lifted the bowl and gulped half of what remained like a whale ending the lives of a swarm of krill. "Uh-huh," he said.

Only a week before his mom had announced that the family was moving to Scotland. First, they would visit Nana in Santa Cruz, California, for two whole weeks. Then, it was off to New York, where they would board a huge ship to cross the Atlantic Ocean.

Just a few days ago their train had pulled out of Moorhead, Minnesota. As it had clap-clap-clapped along many miles of tracks, what burned in Duncan's mind was that he would soon see the great Pacific Ocean. Before they left, he had read about it and pestered his mother with questions about that massive sea that covered a third of the world.

Their train had pulled into Oakland the night before, and after a long taxi ride, they rolled up to Nana's house on Soquel Avenue. He remembered little of their arrival, being mostly asleep, and was carried up to bed in Nana's attic.

Although he loved his grandmother and had not seen her since he was what he thought of as little, he had a desperate urge to get outside. Rescue came in the form of his mother entering the tiny kitchen just as Duncan poured the rest of the bowl down his throat.

"Good morning," she said.

"Morning, Ava," Nana replied.

"Hi, Mom, can I go play?" rushed past his lips, sounding like HiMomCanIGoPlay.

Ava Findlay turned toward her oldest boy, sitting on the edge of his stool. Her eyes were framed by lush waves of dark hair, plump, rosy cheeks, and the charcoal-toned smears of too little sleep. She wore the same wrinkled gray skirt and pink blouse she had arrived in.

"OK," she said.

"Thanks, Mom!" he said as his feet hit the floor, and he headed for the door.

"Whoa, take your coat; it's still cold out."

Smoothly, he zagged into the living room, snagged his light blue jacket, and made for freedom. He had the glass-paneled door wide-open and the screen door halfway when Ava said, "Don't go too far."

"OK," he shouted after the screen door slammed back from its spring. He went down the few wooden steps at the rear of the house and ran down the long, steep driveway to the quiet residential street at its foot. Perhaps if his mother had had some coffee first and had not been so tired from her journey, she might have remembered to give him more specific instructions. The hazy order to not go too far meant, to Duncan, that he could go anywhere he wanted to.

For a moment he stood on the concrete pavement soaking in sunlight as warm as a new friend. But basking would have to wait; he was on a mission. He strode the short block to Soquel Avenue and made a right turn, heading down the hill to the next street. Very few cars were out, and no one was walking, but an old man stood on the corner.

Duncan sprang into a run.

Pulling up five feet short behind the gray-bearded man, he boomed, "Where's the ocean?"

The man flinched, dropped the matchbook he was opening to light the cigarette dangling off his lips, and turned to look down at the short, brown-haired boy. "What?"

Remembering his manners, Duncan pulled a long breath and said, "Excuse me, sir. Can you tell me where the ocean is?"

The man's eyes were bleary and red-veined, the beard raggedy and mottled gray and white. He bent down to pick up the matchbook and slowly lit his cigarette while peering at the kid like he might be an apparition.

Duncan wondered if the man had heard him, for he squinted and puffed, squinted and puffed, but said nothing. Maybe it had something to do with the fact that they were standing on Ocean Street. He took another drag, fingered his beard, and looked around as if this might be a Candid Camera gag.

The man's light went green. He shrugged, still said nothing, but pointed south down Ocean. Then he headed across the street toward the river.

"Thank you, sir!" Duncan called.

Seeing no cars nearby, he darted across against the red light. He dashed past the gas station toward the crest of a slight hill and expected to see the great sea just beyond. Instead, standing there kitty-corner to the 7-Eleven, he saw the road stretch down from the rise, lined with cute little houses and a scattered procession of tall palm trees like exclamation marks promising great discoveries just ahead.

Santa Cruz was a town on the edge of huge changes. No resident could likely have seen the approaching cultural tsunami and population surge. 1964 Santa Cruz was a sedate beauty languorously nestled on the north side of Monterey Bay. It was a town for retirees and merchants who cashed in on the summer crowds that swarmed over the hill from San Jose. The Valley escapees would fill motels with signs proclaiming surf and sand and beach. They jammed Ocean Street and screamed as they rode the Giant Dipper. But when the school year resumed, the town returned to its calm, quiet, and boring self. The downtown would continue languishing with its 1930s to 1940s architecture and hodgepodge businesses.

The city politics were so conservative that only a few years before, the police had shut down a rock 'n' roll dance at the Cocoanut Grove, sending two hundred frustrated teenagers home because they were engaged in 'suggestive, stimulating, and tantalizing motions induced by the provocative rhythms of an all-Negro band.'

They hadn't seen nothin' yet.

Tsunamis were coming, a set of epic waves whose tops could only have been seen by true visionaries: sex, drugs, rock 'n' roll, massive antiwar protests, rebelliousness, environmentalism, women's liberation, long hair, patchouli, and an assertion of liberal thought that would freak out people who had never gotten their freak on.

UCSC was only a year from being built in the hills overlooking the town. It would prove to be a Trojan horse of cultural change, a stallion penetrating the virgin minds of the time. The university would open the way, and behind it would come thousands of hippies fleeing the Summer of Love in Haight-Ashbury—a cultural episode quickly corrupted by infiltrators, opportunists, tourists, and the natural consequences of romanticizing mind-altering drugs.

Santa Cruz was a town of that unique beauty that exists before one becomes self-conscious about being beautiful. It was that sublime beauty that so enchanted Duncan. The very air seemed alive, surging and sparkling inside the membranes of his mind. It was air full of exquisite scents: salt, fish in the bay, beds of kelp, seals sunning themselves, eucalyptus trees and sunbaked sand.

With no ocean in sight, Duncan continued past the bungalows with their low-fenced yards and casually landscaped shrubs and enjoyed the pallet of blue and pink and yellow pastel paint adorning them.

It can't be far, he thought. But after a half-mile the street that promised an ocean ended, crossed by another street and blocked by a wall of rocks and dirt beyond.

Left or right?

He went right because two cars turned that way. Soon he came upon a bridge and a sign that declared: Beach. The houses gave way to little shops and motels, windows filled with T-shirts, swimwear and knickknacks. Looming before him was an incredibly tall wooden roller coaster. But where was the ocean? A sign proclaimed Santa Cruz Beach Boardwalk. Up the stairs he ran and saw past the wide expanse of brilliant sand the ocean spread out in a broad circular bay, its far side barely visible.

He hesitated in the middle of the concrete Boardwalk. To his left, as far as he could see, were rides and concessions, but they all looked closed. To his right there were more rides and a long, covered promenade. Only a few people could be seen strolling.

He turned in a circle, awed by wonders that put the fairs back home to shame. He ran to a domed building and gawked through the window at a carousel with its herd of wooden horses, each adorned with colorful wraps and large faux gems.

He ran toward the huge roller coaster but froze at the rhythmic murmurs of waves caressing the shore. They called to him like Sirens beckoning: *Come play with us.*

He flew down the steps to the beach and then more slowly through the soft, giving silica grains. He stopped just feet from the swash, dazzled by thousands of winking sun flashes glancing off the water.

He stripped down to shorts under his pants in less than a minute. His dive into the bay was a clumsy belly flop as a wave tripped him. The shock of the cold water was like a slap. He leapt up to stand waist-deep in the sloshing foam.

Duncan did not care that it was cold. He swam. He splashed about. He whooped and hollered, got knocked down by surprise waves and laughed with joy every time. He ran about the beach and chased dour seagulls that grudgingly flapped away at the last moment.

After an hour of this he noticed a man walking on the mostly deserted mile-long beach. The man was slowly approaching, waving a pole back and forth, his eyes intent on the ground.

Duncan dug into peculiar wet sand that sprouted hundreds of little air holes after each backwash. He jumped at finding a gray-shelled crawling thing in his hand. "Eeyah," he said, throwing it down.

Someone laughed and said, above the noise of the surf, "They're called sand crabs. They won't hurt you." The man with the pole, ten feet behind him, looked kindly and amused.

After a moment, Duncan asked, "Sand what?"

"Sand crabs."

"They live under the sand?"

"Yes."

"Kinda like worms?"

The man thought about it. "Yeah, pretty much. I guess they eat stuff waves bring up."

They looked at each other for a while—the boy in tan cotton shorts and the man with his fisherman's cap, long blue shirt and jeans.

"Why do you wave that pole around?"

The man lifted and looked at it as if to confirm which pole the kid was asking about. "This? It's a metal detector."

"Metal detec...?" He stumbled on the word.

"Yeah. It helps me find anything metal buried in the sand."

Duncan saw a brown plate-sized disc attached on the end and a wire coiling up to a small box near the handle.

"Why?"

The man hesitated but seemed to take his meaning. "Folks drop all kinds of things here: coins, rings, watches, necklaces." He reached into a canvas bag hanging off one shoulder and pulled out a pocket watch dangling on a chain. "Found this early this morning just over there." And he pointed up the beach toward some cliffs.

"Wow."

"I think it's silver," the man said.

"Wow."

"Yeah, valuable, I think. Gotta check that it works OK." He paused and looked a bit sheepish. "Of course, mostly I find bottle caps and aluminum cans."

The boy dug a toe into the sand. The man frowned, looked around the large beach, and asked, "What's your name, son?"

"Duncan."

"Duncan, you seem alone here. Where are your parents?"

Adults asking him questions set off an inner alarm bell that suggested he might get into trouble. "Uh, Dad's in Minnesota. Mom's over there." He pointed toward Nana's house.

The man turned and may have seen several women standing behind the Boardwalk railing a hundred feet away. "OK," he said but continued to frown.

Duncan babbled in what was perhaps a child's instinctual defense mechanism, "Yeah, Dad's getting ready so we can go live in Scotland. We're visiting Nana, and then we're getting on a big ship to sail the Atlantic so we can free Scotland from the English. I'm Scottish, and Scots defeated the Romans."

The man's eyes widened at this explosion of information; his frown was gone, and safety was achieved.

"Well, that's great, Duncan." He looked back toward the women. "Do you know how to swim?"

"Puh," the boy replied, "been swimming ever since I was little."

One corner of the man's mouth lifted, and his eyes gleamed. Then his worried expression returned, and he said, "I'm glad to hear it, except the ocean isn't a lake in Minnesota. This water can grab you. No lifeguards working today either. I don't think you should try swimming unless your mother comes down here to watch more closely."

Duncan stilled. "'K," he said.

"Better just wade no deeper than up to your knees. Is she going to come down here?" The boy shrugged.

"Well, she can see you, but I'd feel better if she was close."

"I'll be careful."

He frowned again and said, "Well, you do that." Then he headed off, looking back once or twice.

Duncan grabbed his clothes and strode in the opposite direction. He found the mouth of a river that poured into the sea. He swam in its warmer waters. He climbed a cliff and looked down at another long beach to match the first one. Hunger was gnawing at his belly, but he didn't want to stop.

Finally, after more running, swimming, and exploring, he plopped down, exhausted, on his back on the warm sand. He looked into the deep-blue sky as several seagulls soared overhead and felt happier than at any other time he could remember.

How can Scotland be better than this?

2

May 1964

Duncan opened his eyes and let the bare, ragged rafters of Nana's attic come into focus. He felt the hardness of the old canvas cot he had been sleeping on and the heaviness of the thick green wool blanket embroidered US Army. He rolled onto his side and let his sleep-soddened mind get reacquainted with the place and time.

Gentle northern light shone through the sole window. His brother, Keith, only four years old, was in the adjacent cot breathing in relaxed rises and collapsing falls.

His and Keith's half of the attic was the same rough wood of the rafters. From the well-worn planks of the floor and walls to the boards of the peaked ceiling, it was the same deep red-brown, coarse, unfinished wood. Old.

It had been three weeks since he first saw the great ocean. Three weeks of fun and freedom. Weeks of being spoiled by Nana with quarters for ice cream from the shop across the street. Weeks of roaming the area, walking the streets, playing in the park, and going to the ocean, always to the great ocean.

He had played games with his sisters and once tried to fly by running down the steep driveway on wings he had built out of newspapers.

Ava had been bright and happy these past weeks. She had been so excited and determined to get to Scotland—the land of her dreams.

It was where his oldest sister, Aileen, had been born. But his mother's radiant face had recently darkened like the sun obscured by blooming storm clouds. Her eyes, once alight with joy, now flickered with the incendiary anger he knew so well.

Something had woken him. Puncturing the heavy, comfortable silence of an early Sunday morning was Ava's voice striking the air down below. In contrast were the murmurs of another, likely Nana.

He rose quietly to avoid waking his brother, walked lightly to the top of the narrow stairs, and stopped in front of the bedroom door where his sisters slept. Their half of the attic was a finished white room with a proper bed, dressers, cabinets, paintings of long-dead people dressed in blue, which hung on the walls, and windows all around that looked out upon the hillside the hospital crowned. All was quiet inside.

Stepping on the outer edges, he slowly descended the steps to the door to the living room. It was ajar, and he could look through the crack but saw no one.

The main floor of the small house had only four rooms: a great room, his Nana's bedroom, a tiny narrow kitchen, and the sole bathroom at the back of that kitchen.

The clack of a cup being set on a saucer brought Duncan's ear to the crack in the door. He listened as Ava said, "...not going; he turned the job down."

"But why, Ava?" Nana asked.

"I don't know. He rambled. I heard the clink of ice in his glass, seemed drunk already. He claimed he would never see the kids if we lived in North Uist while he was working on the Continent."

"Well," Nana started.

"Other men would do it for their families. Just an excuse, yet another excuse."

The sounds of tea sips and clacking cups occupied the heavy moments. Then, someone sighed.

"What does he expect you to do?"

"He wouldn't say. Says he's going back to Barnesville to think. To think!" she exploded and then repeated softer, "To think. I asked him to at least send money. I am almost out. We should be on our way to New York by now. He claimed he didn't have any money. I couldn't believe it. What about our savings? The tickets? The furniture he was going to sell? He wouldn't explain, clammed up. I heard him taking big swallows of something. Each time I pressed, he would only say, 'I don't have any money,' over and over. I think I sputtered; I was so angry. Finally, he would not answer and hung up on me."

"Oh, Ava."

"I tried calling back... no answer."

Another long silence followed, broken only by the pops and creaks of the old house adjusting to the warmth of the morning sun.

"What can you do?"

He heard someone rummaging, and then Ava said, "Thirty-seven dollars. I have thirty-seven dollars and four kids. No car. No job. No home. I didn't even bring many clothes. Hugh was going to bring all that to the boat. And here I am imposing on you. I don't know what to do."

"You know I'll help. You can stay here as long as you need to."

"I know, I know, but you don't have much either." There was another pause, and then he heard a rapid intake and expulsion of breath. "I hate, I truly hate to take your money. I will pay it all back, I promise."

"Did he ask about the kids at all?"

"No."

"Maybe he'll think differently after he sleeps it off. I know you two have had your troubles, but I thought he loved the kids. He'll come around."

The silence stretched.

"Maybe," Ava finally said.

The loud clatter of dishes being cleared suggested there would be nothing more. Duncan was nervous about his eavesdropping but tromped rather than crept back up the stairs. He heard his sisters moving around in their room. Keith was still asleep.

With jumbled thoughts, he lay back on his cot and stared for a long time at the barren ceiling, afraid to name what he felt.

3

Two weeks later, gathered around Nana's cherry-wood dining table, they were having a dinner of pot roast, potatoes, and Ava's favorite, artichokes. Nana and Ava were at each end. Shona and Aileen were on one side, Duncan and Keith on the other.

The two girls were older than Duncan. Shona by two years, and Aileen by four. They had heads of gently curled hair; the youngest was brown, and his oldest sister was blonde. Their cheeks were full and splashed with the natural rouge of their Scottish heritage. He would realize years later that they were strikingly beautiful. Across the table their eyes glimmered, and they occasionally whispered through cupped hands to each other, pointing at Duncan and laughing.

"Stop it," Duncan said.

That prompted more whispers and laughter.

"Stop it," he said louder.

To which they laughed and pointed. Shona stuck out her tongue.

"Stop it," much louder.

"All of you stop it," Ava said.

Duncan glowered at his sisters. They affected heavenly innocence. The three managed to be silent through a few bites of beef until Shona broke and whispered across the table, "Drunken Duncan, drunken Duncan."

Aileen laughed and joined in the refrain, "Drunken Duncan, drunken Duncan," and they collapsed in laughter.

"Mom, make them stop."

Ava seemed to stifle her own laughter but did admonish the girls. They stopped their taunting but continued to giggle.

***

Duncan had, unfortunately, earned the moniker from an escapade last winter in Moorhead. He and his friend, Todd, had been playing and, not unusually, took off to wander far down a snow-covered road. The snow had stopped sometime during the prior night. The departed storm left brilliant clear skies and harsh cold. Their little feet crunched loudly as they walked. Todd pointed at a large brown bag that was half-buried in powder at the side of the road. Duncan climbed down into the ditch to investigate. Inside were two six-packs of Olympia beer. The two boys had hauled what they considered treasure the half mile back home and hid it in a small closet under a stairwell in Todd's apartment building.

They had popped open one of the cans immediately, but it was frozen solid, and they could get little out of it.

"It's got to melt," Todd said.

"Yeah, I have to get back for lunch, or Mom will be mad."

"Let's come back tomorrow, OK?"

"OK."

The next day they were back in that closet, door closed. The cans were mostly thawed; only residues of slush floated within. They popped open two, took sips, and declared it tasted good.

Lots more sips followed, and the liking grew into sloppy love. Two more cans were opened and consumed with more gulping than sipping. The boys laughed, burped, and talked about stuff they would later be unable to remember.

Duncan and Todd were diving into their fourth beer each when Todd said, "Everything's wobbly."

"Yeah, stop moving."

"I'm not moving."

Duncan giggled. "You have a goofy face."

Todd giggled as well. "You do too."

"I gotta go pee."

"Me too, bad."

Duncan took a sip of beer as a worry nudged his mind. "Oh no," he said. "Mom will know. Smell me; do I smell beery?"

"Beery?" Todd asked, swaying while seated on a box of floor tiles.

"Yeah, do I?"

Todd leaned forward, sniffed, and laughed. "You beery."

"Let's stay here 'til it goes away,"

"I gotta pee," Todd said.

To which they fell over in laughter. Duncan tried to focus his uncooperative brain. Eventually, his bladder made the decision.

"All we gotta do is sneak in, pee, and hide," Duncan said.

"Hide? How long will that take?"

"I don't know."

"We could pee here."

Duncan thought a while, said, "No, I've peed where I shouldn't before. Mom always found out."

They parted ways and weaved toward their respective units. Walking on the sidewalk and parking lot was a challenge. It seemed to tip one way and then the other. At one point Duncan realized he was leaning against a light pole with his eyes closed, short of home. But he felt happy. *This beer stuff is great. No wonder old people drink it so much.* He belched and pressed onwards to the front door of their ground-floor duplex. The knob seemed to float back and forth in front of his outstretched hand.

He heard his sisters talking inside and hesitated. *Uh-oh, be fast.*

He rushed in, slammed the door, and headed toward safety.

Shona and Aileen looked up from their perch on the couch. "Gotta pee!" he announced and made for the hallway bathroom.

"Lunch will be ready soon," Ava called from the kitchen.

It seemed to take forever to get to his toilet refuge.

"Hey, Mom," Aileen said, "Duncan's walking funny."

"Uh-huh," she replied.

He closed the door super-duper carefully and clamped both hands over his mouth to cap his erupting laughter. The suppression sounded like a cough, blowing snot out of his nose.

Outside he heard his sisters laughing. Duncan peed for what felt like hours, and then he decided that sitting on the floor and leaning against the tub was imperative. From there, half-conscious, he tried to grasp how his head could feel like it was floating around the room while his body felt numb and boneless. He wanted to run around and play, but the thought made him queasy.

A knock on the door made him flinch.

"Hey, what are you doing in there?" Shona asked.

He didn't dare answer. A minute or two passed. Or was it twenty? A new knock came, this time insistent.

"Duncan, come out of there; lunch is ready," said Ava.

"OK, OK, be right out."

Gotta pretend not beery; Gotta get it off. He opened the cabinet. No toothbrushes, but there was a tube of Crest. He quickly squeezed a big blob of blue onto his hand and mushed it around his mouth.

He was washing it out after swallowing half when he heard Ava shout, "Duncan, come out of there, right now."

He sucked in a big breath, attempted a military posture, and walked out. Spying the dining table in the far distance, he marched forward. Shona and Aileen were already seated. Ava was bringing a bowl of chips from the kitchen.

Aileen looked at Duncan, and her jaw dropped, "What's that all over your face?" She guffawed. "Is that toothpaste?"

Shona turned in her chair, burst into laughter, and said, "Mom, Duncan's painted himself."

Ava froze in her stride, opened her mouth, and stared at Duncan, who abruptly sat down cross-legged on the carpet, bent over, and barfed.

***

His sister's giggling at Nana's dining table snapped off when Ava said, "Tomorrow, we're going to Watsonville to pick strawberries."

The heads of her three oldest children rotated to Ava. Duncan tried to work out what this meant. It sounded fun. He loved strawberries, but Ava did not look happy. Nana was exceedingly involved in cutting her roast into bite-sized pieces. Also, Ava wasn't a fun person who spontaneously went on adventures. She often tried to constrain the children's play, sometimes with odd demands, like when she told them to play in the snow but not to get their mittens wet. He and his sisters had milled around outside, trying to figure out how to comply when they concluded they had to play with their bare hands.

Duncan chose the happy option and said, "Yeah, let's go pick strawberries!"

Aileen frowned at him.

Ava looked down at her plate for a long moment and glanced at Nana, who seemed to search her daughter's face. Turning to Duncan, she said, "It's not to play; we are going to work."

Duncan mouthed *work*. Since he had never worked before, this did not mean much to him. Work was Dad being gone all day. Work was sitting in his Dad's construction trailer while men chuckled at jokes he didn't get.

Duncan wasn't getting this either, but he understood strawberries and was eager to go.

"We'll be getting up very early; we need to leave before dawn. Now finish your dinners and go to bed."

4

A va was driving her '57 Chevy Bel Air, a purchase enabled by Nana, down Highway One in the dark. Duncan and Shona were in the back, Aileen upfront. Duncan was half asleep and no longer enthusiastic about picking strawberries. He pulled his coat tighter, rested his head against the door, and looked at the towering trees lining the highway. They were big black shapes looming in the fog, wearing cloud cloaks, and their appearance chilled him. He imagined they were giants lumbering along the bottom of a great black, icy sea.

Ava was quiet and focused as the car pushed through the illuminated wall of mist. Aileen's frown was the same as it had been all morning. She had been the last to get up and had taken the longest to get ready. Her one voiced complaint was, "I don't want to pick strawberries," but it was not said in Ava's presence.

Shona was on the opposite side of the seat, leaning against the glass, as he was. She had neither complained nor enthused about this adventure. She appeared content to be going along, nothing more.

Of course, going along was natural. When Ava said, do this, do that, don't do that, Duncan accepted her dictates like he accepted the sun's heat or the Earth's pull—except when he didn't. If he had been able to think that deeply about it, this was quite often. Ava might say, don't go down to the railroad tracks, or stay away from that construction site. He would nod assent but would forget. Soon, he would be out the door running from one adventure to another, even if they were mostly in his mind.

***

It was like when he was seven, and they lived in the tiny town of Barnesville. Ava had emphasized that he must be back before dark. "There's another storm coming. Stay in the yard."

It had been a few days before Christmas, and a thick layer of snow was already on the ground. He started playing in the large front yard but soon took off wandering.

The stone wall across the street called him. It was long and old, with a fragile undulating topping of snow. He threw rocks to break down the snow barrier. In his mind he was lobbing artillery like in the movie he had seen about the battle for Stalingrad.

Their castle-like house was on the outskirts of the town, a place with less than one thousand people, surrounded by farms. Given that the light was fading and the thick low clouds were closing in fast, a journey of 200 feet would be far.

In no time at all, Duncan was over a mile away. In a grove of small dead trees, he had found the perfect stick to be a rifle, and he prowled down a dirt road, moving with his company of imaginary men looking for the enemy.

Fat whirling flakes of white filled the air. The scant light from the last of the sun, distant lights from a farmhouse, and a couple of streetlights created a magic show for him. A barren field lined with high ridges of earth and higher mounds of snow presented the perfect battleground. He set off across it, determined to take the city beyond.

Duncan's mouth spat sounds of rifles, machine guns, pistols and cannons. Ridge to ridge the fantasy battle raged. The snowfall got thicker and thicker; the wind whipped it around into great walls and wavering curtains. Sometimes, he stopped to marvel at the display, but he soon remembered the mission and took another ridge. He and his men cheered their triumphs.

After a while Duncan realized he was deeply chilled, and the snow was so thick he could usually see no more than a few feet. He was also tired. He fought a while longer as the dark deepened. The dense, dancing snowfall reflected the occasional car's headlights going down the road, and a porch light had come on over at the faraway farmhouse.

At no point did he feel afraid of the dark or the cold or the thick blowing snow stinging his face. It piled up on him and the land. He made his travails part of the arduous battle to take the city. The cold that penetrated through his coat and into his flesh, even into his bones, and the tiredness that pulled him down were integrated into his battle reenactment. It was all about endurance, brave men slogging forward to retake the city from the nasty Nazis. He and his men pushed through the piles of snow and climbed over the tall ridges of earth one after the other. Time marched, and he felt more tired and cold, so cold it hurt, but he was determined to press on. Far away, another car cruised down the same curving dirt road he had taken to get to his battlefield. Briefly, the headlights flashed in his eyes. The car went on.

Duncan advanced to the next row, pointed his gun ahead and prepared to defend against the counterattack. The air was filled with swirling flakes. He absently noticed another car's lights creeping far away on the road. As he waited for the imagined attack, he felt a great weight pulling his body down. His teeth were chattering. Snow covered him like a blanket, and he found that soothing for some reason. He decided he must rest for a while, just a little while, close his eyes and see if the blanket might warm him. The wind faded, and the flakes fell thicker.

It was so quiet, so peaceful, except he thought he heard the faint, muffled sound of his name being called. Duncan ignored this, for his men insisted they needed to rest and get warm before the next push. So he lay there, becoming part of the thickening drift, and the shouts of "Duncan! Duncan!" were like fleeting thoughts. Time passed. The cold became cozy.

Out of the black dark, at the bottom of that ocean of snow, a blazing light hit Duncan's eyes. He barely twitched. A huge shadow of a man reached down to pull him out of the drift. "Duncan, get up, boy." He was lifted, and the flashlight revealed worried blue eyes in a lined face. "Goddammit, what are you doing out here? If I hadn't, if...." The big man bundled him in his arms and ran across the field to a car drilling tunnels of white light.

The rest was like a dream. The man took off his coat and wrapped Duncan in it. He tenderly placed the mumbling, complaining boy on the front seat. It took a long time to drive a mile, with the road looking nearly the same as the fields and unable to see much beyond the hood of the car. The car heater blasted hot air that didn't seem hot enough.

The man kept saying, "Goddammit, I almost gave up," then, "thank God!"

Then he was home, carried from the car to the dining room. The man set him down in front of his father and mother, who had snow in their hair and on their shoulders. His father dropped to a knee and enveloped Duncan in a hug that went on and on, repeating, "My boy, my boy, my boy."

His mother did not hug him, but she stood nearby with a look so fierce that he thought she was angry. *Will I get the belt for this?* Then he noticed her downturned mouth, quivering lower lip, and hands clenched so hard that the knuckles were white. Something in her eyes made him think she might cry, but that was silly; Mom never cried.

***

It was not long before they turned off the highway and were driving down a two-lane road headed toward the waxing glow in the east. Clumps of tall eucalyptus trees were scattered between vast lands of tilled soil and orchards not yet showing fruit.

After a couple of miles, Ava turned off onto a long dirt road that led to a cluster of buildings dominated by a large white house. In the light of the sun that would soon crest distant hills, he could see groups of men standing around, sipping from steaming cups and talking. Cars, pickup trucks, a small old bus and farm equipment were haphazardly parked.

They stopped near the house. Ava told them to wait in the car. She walked over to a tall, sharp-faced man wearing a black cowboy hat, jeans and boots. They talked for a while. Ava gestured; the man stood straight and reserved.

When his mom returned, she motioned them to get out of the car and to gather around her. He was in front, and she crouched down before him. "Listen, this could be a hard day." She was looking at him but speaking to his sisters as well. "We are here to work, which means picking strawberries as fast as we can. Soon, that man," she pointed at Mr. Black-hat, "will give us instructions on what to do. Pay attention. I need you to do your best, Duncan. Don't eat the strawberries. I will get you some of your own when we're done."

Duncan was startled. Mom needed him to do this? She had never needed him to do anything before.

"Where's the hat I brought for you? The sun will get hot later. And, girls, don't talk to the men. We do this job and...."

"Why?" Duncan asked, feeling afraid.

"It's work we need."

"This isn't fun." He looked at the growing crowd of men in their straw hats, bandannas tied around their necks. Everything was strange: the place, the men, and even Mom too.

"I want to go home."

Ava swallowed. "We need the money, Duncan. I need you to work and," she looked up at Shona and Aileen, "I need you two to work also." Then back to Duncan, "We'll eat strawberries later; right now, be strong. OK?"

For a few moments, Duncan stared up at his mother and finally said, "OK."

The man told them how to pick: only pick ones fully red and ripe, leave the stem on, don't bruise the fruit, and gently put them in the flats, which were shallow wooden trays with a handle.

They would be paid twenty-five cents per flat and would work until 2:30.

The man looked the girls over and especially took a long look at Duncan. He frowned and said to his mother, "You sure you want your boy to do this? When the fog clears, it'll be a long, hot day stooped over in the sun."

"Duncan's tough, lots of energy, maybe too much. He'll do fine."

Duncan glowed with the praise; he liked the idea of being tough.

"And your girls? They look rather delicate."

"Tougher than they look," Ava said. But Aileen looked anything but tough. With her curly blonde hair, pale skin, rosy cheeks, and thin frame, she had more future Madison Avenue model about her than she did farmworker.

She was staring at the cluster of men waiting to start work. The Boss must have caught the direction of her gaze. "Ladies, don't worry about the men. They're Mexicans, but they won't bother you. Shy, really. Wouldn't do anything to risk losing this job."

Ava said, "We're ready to work."

"OK, but understand, those men over there are mostly experienced. They can pick six flats an hour and keep at it all day long. They don't complain. They don't take breaks except when I allow it. And I don't have to feed them much. I'm letting you pick as a favor to Sherry.

"Favor or no favor, I need you to each pick at least four flats an hour. If you can do that, I'll figure you're not wasting my time. See that field?" They looked at the long, mounded rows of green and red stretching far away. "Picking season runs just a few weeks. I can't employ any slackers. You won't pick four flats per hour today, but I will check to see if you can quickly get up to that. Fair enough?"

"Yes, let's work," Ava said.

The man nodded, and they all walked toward the fields.

"What's a Maxiken?" Duncan asked Shona.

"Somebody from Mexico."

"Oh, why is their skin so dark?"

"Because they're Mexicans." She emphasized each syllable.

"Like Negroes?"

"Negroes aren't from Mexico."

He absorbed this information, said, "Everyone here looks Mexican except for us and the boss man."

Shona stopped and studied the men moving to their rows. "Yeah, you might be right."

"Maybe they won't like us because we aren't Mexicans."

"They don't have to like us."

"I hope they do. I wonder what it's like being a Mexican."

Shona snorted. "You wonder..."

It sounded like a question, but Ava interrupted, handed them each a flat, and told them which row to work.

At first, Duncan enjoyed picking. He and Shona worked rows next to each other. Ava and Aileen worked two rows over. On Duncan's left, a Mexican man was picking quickly. It fascinated him how fast the man could check, pluck and plop the juicy-looking fruit into the trays.

He studied the man and how he worked. Ava wanted him to be strong. He had to pick fast. He looked at all the Mexican men, heads down, moving machine-like along their rows. He looked at his family and felt they didn't belong. Despite this being the Boss's farm, Duncan couldn't shake the sense that the field and the strawberries belonged to these men who worked so hard.

Ava needed him, but he was too slow, and the men probably didn't like him. He couldn't do this; he would have cried if it was permissible. The Mexican man was well ahead of him. Shona was ahead. Everybody was ahead. Mom would be mad that he was so slow.

The Mexican man had been glancing back at Duncan, which worried him. When the man stood and approached, he was afraid, but the man smiled a big, crooked teeth grin and said, "Buenos Dias, niñito."

A couple of heartbeats later, Duncan said, "Hi."

"Aquí, te mostraré."

Duncan did not understand the words, but the man reached over and showed him how to snip each strawberry using just one hand and in one motion. The man's voice was soft and gentle, and he kept smiling and nodding; his every word and gesture seemed to say, this is how you do it, not so hard. See, it is easy.

The man demonstrated over and over, piling strawberries into Duncan's flat.

Then he motioned for Duncan to do it, correcting him until he got it right. Then the man smiled wide like Duncan had won a race, said, "Bueno, bueno." And he went back to his work.

"Thank you, sir," Duncan called.

The man waved but did not look back. Duncan returned to his work, determined to catch up to Shona. He would now be so fast. Hey, maybe he could catch up to the kind man who wanted him to be here.

The fog cleared. The sun rose. Duncan caught up to Shona, but the helpful man pulled farther and farther away. Aileen was a little bit ahead. Ava was in front, but all the Mexicans were far ahead of his family.

For a few hours, he worked hard and fast as he could but saw he was only keeping up with his own family.

Soon, the heat and the monotony pressed on him until his mind drifted into a fantasy of being Superman and picking the whole field in ten minutes, amazing everyone. Once, he popped a big fat strawberry into his mouth. Shona saw him, and her eyes widened. "Don't do that."

They sweated. They picked. The sun pounded on their backs. Pee breaks and food breaks came and went. He slowed and didn't care. He looked at his mom and sisters. He had never seen them so sweaty and dirty.

At 2:30, they finally stopped. As Ava got paid, he heard the boss say, "Less than three flats per hour. Do better tomorrow."

The drive home was a blur. Duncan's hands hurt. His back hurt, everything hurt, and he was so tired he could barely move. The car stunk of their sweat. Shona and Aileen fell asleep before they reached the highway. Duncan followed. He was probably carried into Nana's. They ate dinner, but he did not remember what. Then they slept and were back on the road the next morning.

On the way, Aileen kept saying she didn't want to do this anymore. "You will do this," Ava replied, but she added, "It will get better."

It didn't get better. The second day was like the first, except Duncan didn't see the nice man. The family worked, but they didn't seem to be going faster.

His fingers were stiff, and he had begun to hate strawberries. There wasn't even any fog, so the day started hot. One of his sisters cried, but he wasn't sure which one for it was soon squelched, and they were ahead of him. Duncan looked at the dozens of Mexican men so far ahead and wondered how they did this day after day.

At the lunch break, as they walked back to their car to retrieve bologna sandwiches, Ava gathered the kids around, said, "We are not going to do this anymore. We're going home."

Her children erupted in cheers. Shona and Aileen grasped hands and danced. Duncan's shout of joy caught in his throat when he saw Ava's face fall and her head sag. She looked like she had this past November when the man in the TV announced that President Kennedy had been shot.

His sisters must have noticed too. Their cries faded as their dance skidded to a stop. Together, they watched their mother in silence, save for the caress of Spanish-speaking voices at labor in the field. Ava's vacant stare into the dirt lasted less than a dozen heartbeats. Then she glanced at her children, raised her head, and took a deep breath that lifted her shoulders and straightened her spine. The fire returned to her eyes. "Get in the car. Let's go home and wash this grime off."

5

June 1964

Would The Thing clobber the Hulk, or would the Hulk smash The Thing? Duncan wanted to know. On the other hand, Superman was up against an army of Bizarro Supermen. Would the Big Blue Guy be able to beat his strangely lovable reversed selves? He went back and forth between the two comics. Nana had given him a quarter. He could get both, but if he got just one, he could also get a scoop of ice cream. *Hmmm.*

Whispering by two boys at the other rotating wire rack distracted Duncan from his decision. He and the other boys were at the front of the Village Center Market near the corner of Ocean and Soquel. It had tall, wide windows facing south. The whisperers had black, longish hair and coppery skin. The bigger one, at least a head taller than Duncan, said something into the smaller boy's ear. They glanced at him and smirked.

Duncan scowled and smacked a comic on his leg. "What?"

The smaller boy, whose right eye was slightly lower than the other, asked, "Are you Russian?"

Duncan frowned. "No."

The bigger boy waggled his eyebrows. "Are you sure, Russkie?"

"I'm Scottish."

"So, not American. See, I told you, Randy."

"Am too. I'm a Scot, and I'm American. That's what Mom says."

"That could be," Randy said. "Dad says he's Irish-American, right Alan?"

The big boy pursed his lips, pondering the issue. "Yeah, but me and you are American American, because of Mom."

"Huh? How can anybody be American American?" Duncan asked.

Alan patted his pursed lips. "Woo-woo-woo-woo. We're Indians."

"Mom doesn't like that word," Randy said.

Duncan wondered if they were putting him on. Only a couple of years ago he had claimed to his friends in Barnesville that he was an Indian, but no one was less Indian than he.

"Our tribe wouldn't mean a thing to him."

Randy said, "Yeah, guess it wouldn't." Then to Duncan, "Where did you come from?"

"Minnesota."

"Say, you boys going to buy anything or just stand around messing up my merchandise?" asked Mr. Washburn, the tall rusty-haired owner arranging the candy display at one of the checkouts. Though the question sounded challenging, he asked it with a smile.

"Almost ready," Duncan answered.

"Us too," said the brothers.

Mr. Washburn nodded and turned back to his work.

"You want to go surfing with us?" Randy asked.

"Yeah, come surf," Alan said with an easy smile.

Duncan hesitated. Surfing was mainly a fringe sport and had not yet attained the huge popularity it would soon have, but he had seen guys riding their longboards and wished he could do it.

"I'd like to, but" he lowered his head like it was some great crime, "I don't have a board."

Randy laughed. "We don't either. We bodysurf."

"Huh?"

"Your body is the board," Alan said.

"Just swim real fast and let the waves carry you," Randy added. "I'll show you."

"OK."

"All right!" Randy said. "Come to our house; Mom will feed you, and then we'll walk down to Rivermouth."

Duncan bought The Fantastic Four and Superman. Randy and Alan didn't get anything. The boys left and walked along the line of shops toward Ocean Street.

"I should try using you as a board," Alan told his little brother.

"Try it and I'll dump you into the cliff."

When they reached Ocean Street, Randy pointed across from the hamburger joint on their right to a two-story white and yellow wood frame just a hundred feet from the intersection. "That's it."

They waited for a gap in the light traffic and then ran across.

"I don't have trunks," Duncan said.

"You can swim in your underwear," Alan said and laughed. "Or maybe go nekkid."

"Not swimming naked."

"He can wear one of my cutoffs," Randy said.

They walked down the driveway and entered a back room with laundry bins and a big metal tub with rubber rollers attached.

Duncan stopped, asked, "What's that for?"

"Finger squishing," Alan deadpanned.

"Naw," Randy said. "Mom runs wet clothes through it before putting them on the line."

Duncan wiggled his fingers. "Oh."

Alan noticed and gave him a lopsided grin, moving his eyebrows up and down. "Squish," he said.

"Ignore Buttface," Randy said as he jabbed a finger into Alan's chest. "He just likes to poke people."

They passed through the kitchen into the living room that faced Ocean Street.

"Mom, this is Duncan. Can he have lunch with us? We're going to show him how to surf."

The mother turned from gazing out the main window. She was a tall, bony woman with long black hair, strong cheekbones, thin, wiry arms, and somewhat graceless motions. Her prominent nose was mounted on a face that seemed etched with years of pain and spoke of troubles endured but not begrudged. Her white flower print dress stood out against her deep red-brown skin. Her kind eyes looked down at the boy with a trace of a smile.

"New friend, huh?" she asked Randy, continued to Duncan, "What's your last name?"

"Findlay, ma'am."

"Well, Duncan Findlay, you can call me Mrs. Kelly. You live nearby?"

He jerked a thumb over his shoulder. "At my Nana's around the corner."

She made them ham sandwiches, plus potato chips and lemonade. The boys ate and looked through Duncan's comics. Mrs. Kelly ate with them and smiled as the boys debated the hierarchical power levels of each superhero.

They changed into shorts and grabbed a few old towels she insisted they take. As the boys were headed out the door, Mrs. Kelly caught up to them and gave each boy, including Duncan, a couple of quarters for rides or treats.

Looking up from the coins in his hand into the smiling eyes of his new friend's mother, Duncan said, "Thank you, Mrs. Kelly."

She surprised him again by bending down to give him a quick hug and a kiss on his forehead, to which he blushed. "Have fun," she said and turned away.

"Woohoo!" Alan yelled as they stomped down the few steps to the street.

"Wow, Mom hardly ever gives us money," Randy said. "Better keep you around." With a big smile, he patted Duncan on the shoulder.

The edge of the low-hanging fog hovered near Soquel Avenue as they set out, but as they proceeded down Ocean, effused about surfing, Duncan's train ride story and the new bikes they wished they could have, the gray cover retreated and dissipated before them. The air was cool when they reached the beach, but dazzling sunlight shone upon all they could see: the great roller coaster, the entire Boardwalk, and the sand and waves beyond with their promises of fun and adventures to come.

6

The San Lorenzo River courses 26 miles down from the Santa Cruz Mountains, curving past tiny towns like Boulder Creek, Ben Lomond and Felton. It bisects Santa Cruz just east of downtown. In this year, its vigorous warm waters passed under bridges, providing refreshment to birds and rabbits, and finally blended into frigid Monterey Bay.

In the 1960s Rivermouth was a unique and excellent spot for surfing. As the river finished its journey with nudges against the cliffs and slipped past the narrow San Lorenzo Point, the sediments it carried fanned out to create the perfect slope for ridable waves. Without the river's warming touch, the 53-degree waters of the bay would have challenged even the torrid metabolisms of young boys.

In the future, a drought would sap the full-flowing brown waters down to little more than a miles-long sinuous pond full of reeking algae. The recently completed Boat Harbor, just a couple of miles down the coast, would have the unforeseen consequence of altering the currents such that the slope was destroyed, and sand would build up to drastically change the beach and Rivermouth. The beach would double in width and get fifteen feet thicker. Then, the defeated remnant of the San Lorenzo would not even reach the sea.

But on that first day of their friendship, the three kids could play for hours at their spot of transitory perfection.

Rivermouth also had the considerable advantages that when the waves were boringly small or the boys got too cold, they could warm up on the hot sand, find tasty food at the Boardwalk concessions, and, if they had any extra money, visit the pinball arcade or ride the Giant Dipper.

Fog hovered offshore. The waves were decent at about two to three feet. Even so, there was only a scattering of people bodysurfing.

The three boys stood knee-deep in the swash as its salty froth rolled up and back over their legs. Alan and Randy laughed at the bathers doing it wrong. A small boy got smacked down by a wave and came up sputtering.

"Don't turn your back on the waves unless you want to get your face smashed into the sand," Alan said.

A couple of young guys tried and failed to ride a wave. It lifted them and left them behind.

"They waited too long to start swimming," Randy said.

"Waves usually arrive in groups, and usually the bigger, better waves are after the first few," Alan said.

"So don't just pick any old wave to ride; look for a good one, a bigger one," Randy added.

"You want to wait until you feel the wave pulling on you," Alan said, "and then swim as fast as you can. You'll see."

Duncan listened as his eyes avidly soaked in the scene like dry sand sucking down water. The blue-gray bay showed approaching waves as straight ridges heading for the shore. The tittering of friends playing, the squeals of delight, the boom of waves, and the popping of thousands of seafoam bubbles filled his nostrils and mind.

"OK, OK," Duncan yelled above the roar of a fresh wave, "let's go." He ran a few steps through the invigorating swash, whooped and dove in.

Randy and Alan were close behind, and the three soon took positions about waist-deep, but the waves had suddenly calmed.

"Wait for the next set," Randy said.

So they bobbed together as smaller, unworthy waves lifted them each time they passed. At first, Duncan's timing was off. He started too soon, then too late, and had to watch as Randy and Alan caught their waves and swam back glowing and proud.

But soon, he got it right. The pull of the rising crest came upon him like an embrace. He felt its pure, delicious power as if it were pouring into him, saturating his muscles, bones, and heart.

And then there was the glorious moment when the wave captured him like a giant cupping his little body, lifting and flinging him forward. He rose and slid down the face as the crest collapsed at his back. He was engulfed in roiling foam, speeding beachward. The wave dissipated. He found his feet and exulted; arms raised. His newfound friends cheered and beckoned him to come back for more.

They spent that day at one with a kindly Poseidon. They baked on the hot beach, gobbled hotdogs and snow cones, flung globs of sand at annoying seagulls and laughed at each other's antics.

When the sun sank low they headed up Ocean in bare feet, sand grit on their legs and in their shorts, retelling stories of waves caught, collisions barely avoided, and making good-natured scornful observations of lesser swimmers. The three little kings of the sea chattered happily until parting at Soquel Avenue with plans to do it all again tomorrow.

7

July 1964

The golden-brown grass towered above the boys' heads. Even though no one was around, Randy whispered to Duncan, "Hey, I want to show you something." He led him deeper into the forest of grass to a spot at the steel-beamed foot of a big billboard advertising furniture. He carefully removed something wrapped in toilet paper from his shirt pocket, said, "I snagged this from home." He revealed a half-smoked cigarette.

"You want to smoke it?" Randy asked.

Duncan's eyes widened. "Sure. You ever smoke before?"

"No."

Duncan and Randy often played together in the few weeks since their first body-surfing adventure. They had wandered around downtown looking in shops, ogling bicycles and cars they couldn't buy, investigating every new thing. Once, they peered into a lowball poker room on Front Street, pressed their noses against the glass and speculated on what kind of game it was. Five old men were at a round table, very slowly playing cards. None of them looked happy, but Duncan said, "Maybe they would teach us how to play."

"Huh, you want to play that?"

"Yeah, I..." Duncan was interrupted by a florid-faced man who burst out of the door and barked, "Get the hell out of here."

When they were not at the beach or park or wandering around the town, they were reading comics from his impressive collection in Randy's room.

Randy pulled a book of matches out of his pants pocket, carefully put the cigarette between his pursed lips and handed the matches to Duncan. "Here, you light me."

It took a couple of tries, but Duncan got a match lit, brought it to the crooked cigarette, and Randy began to puff, but the match went out when it was only half lit.

"Do another one," Randy said.

Duncan dropped the match, tore off another and more carefully presented it. Randy sucked mightily; the tip glowed red, and he pulled in a long drag of smoke. His eyes went funny, his cheeks puffed out, and he exploded in a cough. In his reflexive convulsions, he dropped the cigarette, knocked the match out of Duncan's hand, and bent over to continue hacking up the fumes. Alarmed, Duncan patted his friend on the back until he recovered. Randy stood up straight but still had a green tinge to his cheeks.

"Where's the cigarette?" Randy asked.

"I smell burning."

A flame the size of two opened hands was growing next to them.

"Aeeaeh," Randy said. "Put it out! Put it out!"

Duncan tried stomping on it, but his wild strikes did more fanning than extinguishing. The flames doubled in size instantly. They jumped around the fire like drunken Russian dancers. The dry grass crackled as the flames flew up the stalks. In only seconds the fire exploded into a blooming torch, and flames licked the air several feet above the grass tops.

"Run!" Duncan yelled.

They bulldozed through the thick grass, hit the sidewalk at a sprint, zipped across the street, up the rise and headed down Soquel. Past the antique store, Duncan glanced back to see that the fire was a swelling maelstrom of angry red, yellow and black gyrating like a demon around the sign.

They fled to Ocean Street and took a sharp right to seek refuge at Randy's house. The Kelly's had an old, detached garage at the end of their driveway. They ran inside; Randy pulled the big door closed behind them. In the dark they sat side-by-side on a couple of milk crates and said nothing for a while. Only the sounds of their panting filled the dusty, motor-oil-tinged air.

Then they heard sirens.

"Oh no," said Duncan.

"Let's sneak into my room. I think Mom's gone; the car's not here."

They made it to his bedroom without running into Alan or his sister, Cheryl. Randy pulled a box of comic books out of the closet, and they lay down on the floor, pretending to read. Another siren screamed past, just outside the house.

"Oh, crap," said Randy.

Duncan's heart pounded like a woodpecker battering a pine tree.

"Will the cops get us?" Randy asked.

"I don't know. I don't know."

As time went by and no police came, Duncan's heart slowed, and soon they were truly reading their books. He was engrossed in his third comic when he heard a car pull into the driveway, followed by the sounds of Mrs. Kelly and the other two kids entering the kitchen.

The rustle of bags, cabinets opening, Cheryl giggling, and unintelligible conversations penetrated the door to Randy's room. Duncan stared at Batman, but his ears strained for any warning signs of impending arrest.

There was a quick rap on the door, and Mrs. Kelly opened it.

Duncan flinched. "Aaah!"

She flashed a small smile. "Hello, Duncan. Did I startle you?" Not waiting for a reply, she told Randy, "We're going to the new park for a picnic. Put on those old jeans, the ones already ruined with grass stains. You and Alan can wrestle all you want."

She asked Duncan, "Would you like to come too?"

Duncan looked over at Randy. During the moment that their eyes held, Duncan saw the same euphoria of salvation that he felt. Here was a chance to be far away from the scene of the crime. He turned to Mrs. Kelly, swallowed, and in the smoothest voice he could manage, said, "Yes, ma'am, that would be great."

THE BELT

Duncan's earliest memory of being beaten was when he was five years old. Ava had tied him to a white, wooden kitchen chair with a laundry line and was thrashing him with one of his father's belts.

He recalled screaming and squirming from the loud smacks and the shocking stings. Perhaps it was all his gyrations or his mother's poor aim, but the whacks of that belt ranged widely from his legs to his butt to most of his back.

The cause of that discipline was an error in aerodynamics. He and his little friends had been out in the yard playing with asphalt shingles they had found scattered on the ground from one of the nearby construction projects. To their delight they discovered that they could make them fly if thrown just right, like the yet-to-be-invented Frisbees.

He had flung one with particular enthusiasm, only to watch it arc up and curve over to plunge directly into the windshield of a passing car on the quiet residential street he lived on.

Bad luck.

The Edsel had screeched to a halt. The irate driver, a tomato-faced man in a business suit and military haircut, had chased Duncan to his ranch-style home. While Duncan hid in his room, he listened and cringed as the man roared at his mother over his offense—a menace, a threat to all drivers, could have caused an accident, might've scratched my paint. It went on and on.

His being bound to the chair was due to being an uncooperative beatee. While his mother delivered wild, enthusiastic strokes, Duncan could see his sisters in their swimsuits standing side-by-side at the entrance to the hall, watching open-mouthed.

Perhaps it was simply because Duncan's frantic motions seeking to avoid the belt looked comical, or maybe it was due to some humorous memories she was having, but when he managed to look from his sisters to his mother's face, he saw that she was smiling. She smiled as the stroke lashed hard against his ribs like a whip, taking his breath away. For a moment, just a moment, he felt cold and hurt in a place that was not his flesh.

Then the next blow came.

Afterward, his sisters comforted him in his bedroom. They studied the red stripes crisscrossing his body and concluded that the welts and bruises would take at least two weeks to heal.

9

San Lorenzo Park was a creation born out of catastrophe. In late December 1955, weeks of rain culminated in a twenty-four-hour drenching that streamed off the soil-saturated flanks of the Santa Cruz Mountains, poured into the 26-mile-long river, and overwhelmed its meager banks next to the heart of the city. Cars were swept away, buildings destroyed, and the entire Chinatown region obliterated.

The great flood was not the town's first, but Santa Cruz was determined to make it the last. With federal help and years of work, the river was bounded by a large levee. Branciforte Creek was turned into a concrete-walled ditch fifteen feet deep. Many called the job done ugly, but few argued with the necessity. The levee changed the center of Santa Cruz, and new homes and apartments would need to be built. The park was part of the San Lorenzo Project being developed on the east side of the river.

Mrs. Kelly, whose first name was Margaret, took Duncan and her brood to the park just a couple of months after it had opened in May 1964. She drove them the short distance in her beat-up Pontiac station wagon. The kids sprang from the car to explore, leaving Margaret to carry all the lunch fixings.

Duncan and Randy ran to the undulating snake, a climbable sculpture, and scrambled up its concrete humps. Alan disappeared inside a concrete dome fort to peer out from its Swiss cheese-like ports. Cheryl found the swing set and was soon flying high.

Small new trees dotted the park. The sand in the play area was clean and fresh. The grass was young and green. The day was bright and warm, and the laughter of a dozen kids tinkled in the air.

Duncan forgot his anxiety and felt no guilt or even concern for the fire he and Randy had caused.

Margaret spread the fixings for a lunch of cheeseburgers, potato salad, pickle spears and a six-pack of RC Cola to chase it down. She soon had the meat cooking on the grill.

Margaret's warmth toward him wasn't something Duncan thought much about. She readily included him in nearly everything she did with her sons. And she would correct him if he got out of line like she admonished her own boys. One time she teased him about being at her house so often.

"You sure you have a home? You're here more than there."

She had said it with a smile, but Duncan blanched anyway. He had stood frozen, deer-like, in her kitchen, feeling the rise of shameful tears. She must have seen it because she dropped to one knee, wrapped her arms around him, and said, "No, no, no, it's OK. I'm only joking, Duncan. You are always welcome here." Then she kissed him on the cheek, repeated softer, "Always welcome." But she did not let him go until he had relaxed and laughed a little.

After that, Margaret would sometimes repeat her joke if he came by late or if he was hanging out in Randy's room for hours. "You sure you have a home?"

He would chuckle, feign embarrassment, and say, "Yes...uh, maybe, Mrs. Kelly."

He and Randy were on the swings when Margaret yelled for the kids to come and eat. They ignored her, fixated as they were on their competition to see who could go higher. They swung in unison past the horizontal point where the chains went slack, followed by a moment of freefall and a sudden jerk on the downswing.

On each new downswing, they urged each other to go higher. Duncan found the freefall scary, but he wasn't going to stop.

At the start of the contest, Randy had claimed it was possible to go all the way around. Duncan had said, "No way!" Randy assured him that a boy he knew had said he'd heard from another boy who had seen it. That was enough proof for Duncan.

More intense swinging ensued, and the down jolts got more severe, but their highs only increased slightly. They could get above the height of the bar but not much more.

"Higher," Duncan said.

"Higher," Randy agreed.

"Stop that right now before you break your heads," Margaret's voice cut through their determination just as they were on the upswing again.

Duncan glanced down and saw her standing at the base of the swing, arms akimbo, glaring up at the boys. With a jerk, the chains were nearly ripped out of his hands.

"Stop right now," she repeated and waited while they slowed down.

"Let's leap," Randy said.

"Yeah, next one,"

They then flew out of their seats and landed badly in the sand but came up hooting and hollering as if they had just conquered the world.

Margaret frowned, shook her head, but allowed a smile. "Come before the food gets cold."

Cheryl was already at the table munching on potato chips and drinking an RC. She was a year younger than Randy and looked quite different from her brothers, with her straight, short blonde hair and fair skin. Her blue eyes often sparkled with some private joy, and she was prone to giggling more than any girl Duncan had met. Usually, the boys ignored her. Margaret was distributing the burgers on floral paper plates along with pickle spears.

Alan was running over from the far end of the park. Never one to miss a burger, a second one, a third, or a fourth, he made it just as Duncan and Randy were chomping on theirs.

"There is this weird huge lawn over there," Alan said. "Grass shaved to the stubs and hard as this table. Huge."

Cheryl giggled and opened her mouth wide for a burger bite. Duncan barely listened. He and Randy were busy between bites, claiming that they would go all the way around the world next time.

"Lawn bowling," Margaret said.

"Huh?" Alan asked.

"Men bowl on that lawn."

Alan's jaw dropped. He peered questioningly at his mother and then burst into laughter. "Bowl on a lawn; what kind of dorks do that?"

Margaret ignored that and said to the kids, "Everyone excited to go back to school?"

The boys stared blankly at her as if she had asked, "You eager to be locked in a coffin for nine months?"

Cheryl giggled.

"Mom! That's weeks and weeks away," Randy said.

"Not long," she replied.

"We're moving," Duncan said.

That got everyone's attention.

"You're moving away?" Randy asked.

For some reason, Alan smirked.

Cheryl giggled.

Margaret lifted a potato chip, asked, "Where are you going?"

"Finally going to Scotland, like you said?" Alan asked like a challenge.

Duncan looked down, narrowed his eyes, and said in a low voice, "No, not Scotland. Someplace in Della Vegga."

"Where's that?" Randy asked as if Duncan had declared he was moving to the moon.

"Do you mean the park, DeLaveaga?" Margaret asked.

"Yeah, the park."

Alan hooted and pointed at him. "Hah, you're going to live in a park. Hah hah."

"Shush, Alan," Margaret said. "He must mean near the park, right Duncan?"

"I guess so." Duncan had yet to look up.

Margaret reached across the table and gently touched his arm until he looked at her. "It's not far, just a few miles."

A few miles sounded like a thousand to Duncan, but her gentle reassurance gave him some hope. He nodded.

"You and Randy and Cheryl will see each other at school. Alan's nearby at Branciforte Junior. You'll visit your Nana, won't you?"

Cheryl touched his shoulder, said, "Yeah, come over then."

"When are you going?" Alan asked.

"Next week, Mom says."

The conversation turned to surfing dates, how they liked the park and whether the whole world agreed Alan was a butthole. Margaret told them not to swear. Alan threw a pickle at Randy, who retaliated with a shower of potato chips. And Cheryl made funny faces by squishing her cheeks with her hands.

Margaret leaned back, smoked a cigarette, and occasionally nudged her kids and their friend back into the corral when they strayed too far past her boundaries in word or motion. Her face shone with contentment.

As she cleaned up, he and Randy slipped away to look at the river. They hiked down the levee's barren slope of white rocks to the water's edge and pitched stones into the current.

Impulsively, Duncan asked, "Where's your dad?"

Randy frowned and hurled his rock across the river. "I dunno." Then he began kicking a clump of grass like he was determined to uproot it.

Duncan watched his friend's right foot whacking away, wishing he hadn't asked.

"Where's yours?"

"I dunno." And Duncan joined in the savage effort to destroy the offending weed.

10

CHOKE IT!

Discipline in the Findlay household varied between actual and threatened corporal punishment, which was not unusual in America at the time. The old admonition, spare the rod and spoil the child, was fully believed, certainly by Ava Findlay. She had been physically disciplined often enough by her father but never, he was told, by her mother.

The opposite was true for the Findlays. As far as Duncan knew, his father had never hit any of the kids. His mother was the one he feared.

Usually, all it took was for Ava to say, "Stop that!" or "I am going to get the belt," to make the offending child cease whatever they were doing.

Crying was not permitted. If Duncan's or Shona's or Aileen's lips began to tremble and tears formed in their eyes, they would be commanded to stop.

He remembered how his mother would bend down so they were eye to eye. She would point a finger in his face and say, "Choke it! Choke it!" sometimes followed by, "or I will give you something to cry about."

Understandably, the three kids' ability to instantly stop the impulse to cry was a bit spotty, but with a convulsive swallow, they would try.

Shona and Aileen were beaten far less often and much less vigorously than Duncan was. He assumed it was because he was a boy and boys were supposed to be tough. He also knew he got into much more trouble than his sisters.

As much as Duncan feared his mother and the specter of the belt, the truth was it had little effect on his behavior. It was only after his impulses had made him cross his latest childhood Rubicon that the *uh-oh* thought would come.

11

After the picnic, Duncan's anxiety about the fire came roaring back. During the return trip he and Randy flashed anxious glances at each other, but neither said anything. When they all got out of the car, it was clear that Margaret had had enough of her passel of hyper-charged, hyper-loud kids, and it would be best if he went home.

Home was the last place he wanted to go. He stood at the end of the Kelly's driveway, panic cork-screwing through his guts, barely able to think at all. He turned right instead of left and walked up Ocean Street like a condemned prisoner being prodded forward to his execution. At Branciforte Creek he paused on the bridge and stared into its sluggish, muddy waters but saw only horrific visions of half the town being burned down, his Nana's house gone, people hurt, and everyone yelling at him.

Panic then cooled into a lead weight of doom. For a while he could not move at all. New visions of stone-faced police officers, enraged firemen, and his Nana crying fought for preeminence. But the most terrifying vision of all was that of his mother, with lightning in her eyes, raging that she was going to get the belt.

Despite the fear, he had to see. He snuck up Branciforte Creek to May Street. He expected an adult to burst out of their door at any moment, point at him, and say, "There he is!"

Nothing immediately appeared damaged as he crept up the road, but a thick black stream flowed down the gutter. He found a viewpoint behind a car; half of the large vacant lot was now black stubble. The large wall on the east side, which formed the back of a row of doctors' offices, was singed but not burned. The smell of wet, torched grass and earth hung in the air. The sign's girders were blackened but otherwise undamaged. His heart lifted—just some grass burned. He flinched when the only remaining firetruck started up and pulled away on Soquel.

Duncan quickly walked back to the creek and took twenty minutes to find a convoluted route home to return to Nana's coming down Soquel rather than up it. Entering the house, he did his best nine-year-old interpretation of a casual, oblivious, nonchalant, I-know-nothing act. It was likely wasted on Nana, who greeted him warmly, hugged him, and asked, "Did you see the big fire?"

"A fire, Nana?"

She explained all the excitement and how quickly the great firemen controlled it.

"Wow! I came the other way."

"We were lucky none of the houses caught fire."

He hastened to talk about his time at the park. She listened with an attentive smile and gave him a cookie. He was nearly giddy with relief. He went out and looked at the burned lot again, amazed that nothing but grass was destroyed. He returned, grabbed one of Nana's The Book of Knowledge encyclopedias, took it upstairs, and fell asleep reading on his attic cot.

Shona and Aileen woke him when they returned from a shopping trip with Ava. They were laughing and chatting as they tromped up the stairs. Aileen told Duncan, "There was a big fire. Did you see it?"

"No, I was with Randy."

At dinner the girls talked about the dresses they got, and Ava said something about the car making a funny sound, but soon the adults started discussing the fire.

"Could have been a disaster," Nana said.

"Some fool probably threw his cigarette out the car window," Ava said.

"Mrs. Jenkins wondered if it was arson."

"The owners should not have let the grass grow so high. Pure negligence, I think."

Duncan blurted, "I was with Randy at a picnic way over at the park."

Neither Ava nor Nana seemed to pay much attention to his declaration, but Shona snapped her eyes on him, and he felt the x-rays of her mind. Realization soon dawned, and her mouth quirked into a little smile.

Duncan could not breathe as he waited on what she would do, but she said nothing and smoothly resumed attention to her meal.

12

September 1964

Branciforte Elementary was already fifty years old when Duncan walked down its halls on a fine day at the beginning of the school year. Its three stories of great neoclassical mass were impressive to the boy who had only known modern single-story simplicity. Somehow, it made his fifth-grade studies seem more important. Despite the fine day and the fine building, he had the new school jitters. It didn't help that the pants Ava made him wear were strange. They were used and bought at the Salvation Army store for a quarter. To his protestations, she assured him that the burgundy corduroy looked great with his red-striped knit shirt.

In the hall, looking for his classroom, he didn't see any other boys wearing pants like his. The legs were billowy and hung an inch above his shoes. The waist was high, and there were clear signs of wear on the seat and knees. He guessed his shoes looked OK; Ava had polished them, even if they were nearly worn out.

No one in the noisy chattering throng of kids around him seemed to notice Duncan until a big kid coming the other way stopped ten feet away and stared at him, open-mouthed. He was shaped like a football, with little eyes in a fleshy face. His cheeks were a splatter of freckles beneath a tangle of curly red hair.

Frowning, Duncan kept walking, but the boy jumped before him and said, "You look like a hobo."

Nervous but with a twinge of anger, Duncan said, "I do not."

The boy poked him hard in the chest. "Yes, you do, hobo."

Before he could object again, the redhead shouted, "Hey everybody, look at this, look at this. A hobo has snuck into the school. Look at the hobo!" He pointed, cackled and repeated, "Hobo! Hobo! Hobo!"

About twenty kids stopped and watched. Some laughed along or just smiled, but many appeared to wince. Duncan's insides shriveled like an ant under a magnifying glass channeling the sun. He wanted to run out of the building, but his knees were too weak to comply. It didn't last long; the kids had to get to their classes, but those seconds seemed to stretch into eternity.

With his audience dispersing, the big boy got very close, his face a sneer. He poked Duncan again. "You look like a hobo." Then he pushed him hard such that Duncan nearly fell, said, "Get out of my way, hobo."

The hall emptied. Duncan stared at the floor. The bell rang. An adult approached from the far end of the hall. He clamped his jaw tight and went to find his class.

He sat in the far back corner of the room and caught only bits and snatches of the day's lessons.

13

At first Duncan was bummed big-time that his family had moved out of Nana's. No longer was it a quick trip down the street to see Randy, to go bodysurfing, or to get an ice cream. He was far from the beach; he was far from everything.

Their new home was a small, older wood frame painted yellow with white trim. It sat at the end of a long dirt and gravel drive near the northern tip of the huge DeLaveaga Park. There were only two bedrooms and a single tiny bathroom. Perhaps it was good that it was so small since the Findlays had little to put in it.

He and Keith shared one of the bedrooms. Each had a thin, twin mattress on a low metal bedframe sans headboard, as did his sisters in the other bedroom. Ava had an old couch to sleep on that nearly filled what was supposed to be a living room. Their kitchen table was a Goodwill special; its chipped green Formica top, one extra leaf and curved chrome legs were surrounded by four vinyl-upholstered chairs. A narrow wooden porch seemed tacked on to the front of the house. A couple of worn wooden steps descended to where the driveway widened into a rough dirt oval where Ava parked her car.

But what the house lacked in charm and comfort, it made up for in location. It was near the bottom of a gentle grass-covered hill overlooking other hills, accented with sparse trees.

It was three miles to get to Duncan's school, two-thirds through the lushly wooded park. A narrow asphalt road wound around along the sides of hills, under canopies of trees, bordered by ragged bushes and the grandeur of old eucalyptus giants.

Duncan quickly fell in love with the place. Sleeping on a dingy mattress in a nearly bare house did not mean much to a kid who had recently turned ten.

It helped that Nana had given him a new Sting-ray bicycle. It may have been used, but it was new and wonderful to Duncan, and he felt like a prince when he pedaled through the park.

"I want to go show Randy my bike," he told Ava. It was midmorning; the sun was rising over the hills behind their house. She finished drying one of the breakfast plates, put it in the rack, and said without looking at him, "That's pretty far."

"Not too far on my bike," Duncan said *my bike* like he was saying *my spaceship*.

She dried her hands, turned, and smiled. "I guess you're excited. OK, but you mind the cars and be back for dinner."

He was already headed for the door.

"Stop, I mean it. Mind the cars. Don't go dashing around. Be careful."

He nodded rapidly, edging toward the exit.

"Oh, and don't bother Mrs. Kelly. She is a kind woman to let you hang around so much, but don't aggravate her. Hear me?"

"Yes, Mom."

He hesitated for the precise fraction of a second that his instincts told him would imply *I am listening,* and then he was on his bike before the screen door slammed.

"Yaaaaaayyyyyy!" he cried as he raced up the driveway's slope, and his tires spat chunks of gravel. He hit the empty road and sped up around the curve until it straightened, and he was out of sight of his house.

He was free. He eased off and rolled along with a smile that wouldn't fade. The warm sun sputtered between the leaves, and photons tap-danced over his face and arms. For a mile, he saw no one and no cars. He loudly sang a garbled version of *I Get Around* by the Beach Boys.

Sometimes he sprinted, thrilled to see how fast he could go, feeling the rush of warm air over his body. Other times he cruised at a leisurely pace, thinking of all the places he could go to on his new bike.

He was cruising when he noticed something that made him stop. Off to his left, down a short road, were tanks, big, mean-looking, tan steel tanks. The gun turrets pointed at him.

Wow!

He rode closer and paused at a single-beam barricade with a sign that ordered: STOP. Next to it, another sign declared: National Guard Armory, 149th Battalion.

Wow!

He looked around, saw no one, got off his bike, walked around the barrier through the golden grass and went up to the chain-link fence.

Cool.

Ava had told him a lot about WWII. His dad had fought in the Pacific Theater but never talked about it. He was sure these six tanks were from that war, lined up in two-by-two rows. The front four had stubby guns, but the two in the back were heftier and had much bigger guns.

He studied the fence. It wasn't very high, maybe six or eight feet, but it had barbed wire on top. That could be a problem, but if he was careful, he should be able to climb over it. He wanted to see what it was like inside the tanks or at least stand on top of one.

Suddenly, the back of his neck prickled, and he glanced around.

Nothing.

Bugs buzzed in the grass. He flinched at a vivid vision of an armed soldier charging out from the little building inside the fence and yelling at him. He jumped on his bike and pedaled fast through the grass, fleeing his imagination, until he was past the barricade and safely back on the road.

A mile later he merged onto Soquel from Branciforte Avenue. He breezed past the Foremost Dairy and Shopper's Corner. Just before the descent, he ignored the ice cream shop. He accelerated and zoomed down the hill, flying past the hospital and Nana's, going almost as fast as the cars.

At May Street he hit the brakes three times hard, popped the bike up onto the sidewalk while standing on the pedals, and continued to fly. Ocean Street cross-traffic was coming up fast, so he had to break so hard that he nearly went over the handlebars. He managed to stay upright, took the sharp right turn, then another, and skidded into Kelly's driveway.

In his imagination he was arriving in a cloud of dust and to the sound of trumpets. He jumped off, set the kickstand and ran to the back door. He knocked. No answer. He tried the knob. Locked. He ran to the front. Same.

Deflated, he returned to his bike and looked at the two-foot patch of rubber his back tire had left on the concrete. He sat on the porch for a few minutes, watched the traffic, and expected to see Randy or the Kelly's wagon at any second.

Time crawled.

Patience exhausted, he decided to search. The park was full of kids and moms, but not the right ones. He wandered over the footbridge to River Street and then down Pacific Avenue, glancing at cars and in shop windows, enjoying the ride. The Delmar Theater was showing a Jerry Lewis film, *The Patsy*. He looped back over the river, up Laurel and over to Randy's house just in time to see the family getting out of their car.

Cheryl saw him first and screamed, "It's Duncan!"

Heads turned.

As he came to a stop and got off, she asked, "Is that a new bike?"

"Uh-huh."

Randy whistled in appreciation.

Cheryl stroked the violet-colored frame. "Pretty,"

Without asking, Alan jumped on the bike and swung the handlebars left and right. "Bitchin'."

"Your mother got that for you?" Margaret asked.

"No, Nana did."

The Sting-ray design was inspired by chopper motorcycles and the new Corvette. Just about every kid wanted one.

Duncan hadn't found it odd that, although the soles of his shoes had holes, his clothes were old and worn, and he had not seen a barber in a long time, he had a coveted bike that cost over fifty dollars. And he did not dwell on the facts that the Kelly's clothes were old too, that they often ate baloney, Velveeta, corn and potatoes, and that their car blew blue smoke, or that Mrs. Kelly had a washing tub, not a washing machine. Nor that Cheryl had holes in her socks, and Alan and Randy's hair was as ragged as his own.

Randy told Alan to get off so he could sit on it.

"Go ahead and ride if you want," Duncan said.

Randy glowed and rolled toward the street.

"Stay on the sidewalk," Margaret called as she turned to carry a bag into the house.

"Yes, Mom," Randy said as he headed up Ocean.

"What a great bike," Alan said. "That knobby back tire is very cool. How does it ride?"

His was the kind of comment that presaged young men talking about their cars: Smokin' racing tires, gotta 389 under there, cool stripes, plus a 4-barrel Holley, and, what's the 0 to 60?

"Like flying," Duncan said, although he had never flown, and he surprised himself when he offered that Alan could ride it too.

Cheryl clasped her hands together and bounced up and down. "Can I ride it? Can I ride it?"

Before he could reply, Alan shook his head, said, "Are you kidding? It's a boy's bike. You're a girl. And you're too little."

The spring went out of her. She pouted and beseeched Duncan with her eyes. He looked away, out at the street.

Randy returned, singing praises of the great bike. Alan jumped on and pedaled so fiercely away that Duncan worried he might damage it, but his happiness overrode such concerns. Margaret came out to get something from the car.

Cheryl pulled at Duncan's attention with blue eyes that looked up at him through blonde bangs. Like a cat begging for milk, she asked, "Can I ride it?"

He squirmed and looked at the pavement.

"You can't ride that bike. It's not for girls," Randy said.

Cheryl frowned and stuck out her chin. Seconds ticked by.

Margaret slammed the car door and said, "Duncan, would you help me with this?"

Puzzled, he took the offered bag and followed her into the kitchen. She wasn't carrying anything. Inside, she took it from him and put it on the table. "Thanks. I wonder if you would take Cheryl on a little ride on your bike."

Duncan's mouth opened and closed. Take a girl for a ride?

"She *is* small, and it *is* a boy's bike, but she could sit behind you."

Duncan blinked a few times and bit his lip.

"It would make her so happy."

"Uh..."

"It doesn't have to be a long ride. Would you do that, Duncan?"

He looked up into warm eyes that patiently waited for his answer. It was the first time an adult had asked him to do anything.

Instructed, yes. Directed, yes. Ordered, yes. Threatened, yes.

Asked, no.

"OK," he said.

She gave him a big smile and said, "Thank you. Be safe with her, OK? And would you be sure she keeps her feet away from the spokes?"

"Yes, ma'am."

She nodded, and Duncan went back outside. Alan was speeding down the driveway, returning from his ride. Randy tossed a baseball high up in the air and caught it. Cheryl sat at the edge of the driveway, busy gathering brown leaves from the soil around a bush. Duncan walked over to her; she did not look up.

"I'll take you for a ride if you still want to."

Her face was instantly transformed, like the sun bursting out from an eclipse. She jumped to her feet, clapped, bounced up and down, giggled, and said, "I do I do I do!"

He got her seated, cautioned her about the spokes and told her to grab onto the bar at the back of the seat. He sat on the narrow front part, slowly pedaled to the sidewalk, paused, pointed the bike up Ocean, and asked, "Ready?"

"Ready!"

Before they had traveled fifty feet, Cheryl wrapped her arms around his waist. Duncan stiffened. "Hey, hold onto the bar."

"I might fall off."

He stopped, reviewed the situation, and saw she was really scared.

"Well, all right." And off they went again.

At first he had intended to give her a minimal ride, maybe up a block or so, but the magnitude of her joy was contagious. She laughed and cheered, giggled and held her legs out straight while leaning first one way and then the other to see past Duncan's arms.

He took her around a nearby neighborhood and enjoyed her squeals when he went faster or did abrupt maneuvers. They flew up and down the streets, and then he took her along a path beside Branciforte Creek. Tall trees jutted from the hillside; their branches spread wide like luxurious feathered fans. The tires crunched over a floor of dead leaves.

"Ducks!" Cheryl pointed to a raft of them lazing in the sluggish stream. He took her back through the first neighborhood, cheering and laughing with her. It had been a more than half an hour ride when he coasted up the driveway.

Alan and Randy were wrestling in the backyard. They got up from the patchy grass as Duncan and Cheryl dismounted.

"That was so great!" she said.

"Yeah, it was."

Alan approached, with Randy trailing. "You were sure gone long enough."

"She wanted a ride."

"I guess you like my sister, huh?"

Duncan squinted. "What? She's OK."

Alan lifted his eyebrows. "Yeah, but you were gone so long."

"So?"

"Must like her."

"Your mom asked me to."

"Yeah, but gone for hours. Must like her."

"Hours?! Were not."

"Must like her."

"I do not!" Duncan shouted. "Your mom made me! I don't like her!" His quick sideways glance caught her grimace of pain, like a faithful dog that had just been kicked. Her eyes brimmed over; she ran into the house.

Alan smirked, and his face shone with apparent satisfaction, about what Duncan didn't get. Frowning and shaking his head, Duncan walked to the curb.

Behind him, Randy said, "Butthole."

14

Forty minutes later Duncan and Randy sat on a cliff overlooking Steamer Lane, their tennis-shoed feet dangling thirty feet above the water. Below them, about a dozen surfers bobbed up and down on their boards as the humps of unworthy swells shrugged by.

A few surfers wore wetsuits, a mix of beaver tails and vests, but most did not. Wetsuits were a work in progress, pioneered by Santa Cruz's own Jack O'Neill, but the iterations then were difficult to put on, rather stiff, and even considered by some to be evidence of a weak constitution. Of course, paddling around and plunging into the 52-degree waters of Monterey Bay tended to soften that point of view. Every surfer wanted to extend their time riding, but without a wetsuit, an hour in the water was about the maximum they could endure before hypothermia symptoms appeared.

Steamer Lane was and is one of the most famous surfing spots in the world, but 1964 was the beginning of the explosion of the surfing culture that the Beach Boys would extol and hordes of teenagers would embrace. It was also the cusp of technological changes that would open surfing to more than just the hardy: longboards would give way to shorter and shorter boards, wetsuits would get better and easier to wear, and the surfboard leash would be invented so surfers would no longer have to chase their board down after they fell off, or worse to find it busted in half on the cliffs at The Cave.

"He was poking you," Randy said.

Duncan chewed on a thumbnail. "I guess."

"Alan likes making people do stuff."

Duncan leaned back and squinted at the sky. "Yeah?"

Randy wobbled his shaggy head and snorted, "You're funny."

Duncan sat up. "I was not funny."

Randy jabbed his belly. "Were too." Then he launched into a Duncan impersonation, waving upraised arms, shouting in a caricature of a hysterical girl, "Your mom made me! Your mom made me!" Then he guffawed.

Duncan scowled, said, "Butthole."

Randy sobered. "Shithead."

"Bug vomit."

"Cat snot."

"Dead seal guts."

"Dog diarrhea."

Duncan furrowed his brow, pursed his lips and declared, "Mile-high tidal wave of whale shit."

Randy blinked, his mouth opened as he stared across the bay like he could see the approaching monstrosity, and said, "Ewwww." Then he cracked up. "Good one."

Duncan joined in his laughter, and they were bent over howling when a sharp voice penetrated their mirth.

"Hey, you kids, careful you don't fall off the cliff!"

The two boy's heads whipped around to the speaker, an older man with short-cropped white hair.

"OK," they mumbled and turned away.

Duncan scoffed, "How could we fall off the cliff?"

Randy shrugged.

Finally, a good set rolled in, and the shivering surfers caught some waves. The boys pointed and laughed at one apparent novice who stood and fell quickly on his few attempts. But that good set offered only three footers, and then it calmed again, so the boys got bored and left.

They took the long way back to Randy's by heading up West Cliff, aiming for Woodrow Avenue. A choir of seals honked enthusiastically from Seal Rock. The day had entered a sweet spot of perfect warmth radiating off the land, entwined with wafts of rich, cool sea air that stroked over their skin. A light breeze coming off the bay lifted a flock of seagulls soaring near the cliff edges.

As Duncan pedaled, Randy asked, "Is Chuck still bugging you?"

"Naw, he's been picking on other kids."

"He's mean, just like his brothers."

"He's got brothers?"

Randy spun a story about the fearsome Putnam brothers, who had been terrorizing kids for years. While Chuck, from his sixth-grade throne, was the head bully of the fourth and fifth graders, he had even worse brothers: Ted, an eighth grader at Branciforte Junior High, and Scott, a sophomore at Harbor High.

According to Randy, Scott had even been sent to prison for nearly beating a kid to death. And Ted practically ruled his school, often dressed in a black leather jacket with dangling chains and carrying brass knuckles in a back pocket. He said even the teachers were afraid of him. All the Putnam boys were big and heavy, strong and mean.

"Stay away from him if you can."

"How come the teachers let him?"

"He's smart, careful to do it when they aren't looking. And he sucks up to them, acting the angel...until they turn their backs."

Duncan frowned. Randy was in fifth grade, too, but they only had one class together, English. They mainly saw each other at lunch or recess. "Has he picked on you?"

"Not yet."

They stopped at Graff's Market and bought a Kit Kat bar, which they split.

They rode down Beach Street, stopped and watched some boys and their girlfriends playing volleyball on the beach near the Cocoanut Grove. They were tempted to wander around the Boardwalk, maybe play games in the arcade, but the sun was sinking fast, and the candy bar purchase had exhausted their finances.

"I better get home," Duncan said.

He dropped Randy off and took the long ride back through DeLaveaga Park. As tree shadows stretched across the road, he thought about everything Randy had said. He kept seeing Chuck's round, freckled face, smirking and laughing at him, calling him a hobo. As he coasted down the driveway to his house, relieved that he had gotten home on time, he thought, *I hate Chuck Putnam.*

15

Timmy Eaton was in Duncan's arithmetic and American history classes. He was that kid that other kids called a teacher's pet, dweeb, or nerd.

He was the one whose hand shot up every time Miss Evans asked a question. He was the one who always had the right answer, got an A on every test, made the teacher smile in approval, and fellow students glower with envy and resentment.

He was the little kid in a grade of little kids. He came to school in creased slacks, shined shoes, an ironed shirt, and a well-barbered sandy-haired head.

His oval face often radiated the appearance of earnest attention. He was prone to asking incisive questions and making insightful observations while his classmates gawked and snickered. Half the time, he seemed to know as much or more than the teachers did.

He was enthusiastic during recess, joining in games and playing on the jungle gym. He was very fond of marbles and had an impressive collection in his locker, which he brought out often: Cat's Eyes, Swirls, Bumboozers, Puries, Milkies, Gooseberries and his dreaded Steelies. Duncan, like most kids, paid him little mind. He was just an oddball. Harmless. Funny. Not cool. Strange.

One recess, Willie Andrews gashed his head when he fell off the monkey bars. Timmy was the first to run to his aid, lifting his dazed and bleeding face up and calling for help.

He could be nauseating when expressing appreciation to teachers for doing their job.

Chuck Putnam led the mean kids. He and his four buddies would roam the school-yard looking for weak children to abuse. Timmy was a frequent target. They'd squash his marbles into the ground, shove him aside in the halls or order him off the swing. He would comply, and they would laugh at him. During dodgeball, Chuck and his friends would fling the red orbs like bullets at the small boy. They cheered especially loudly if they hit his head.

Timmy appeared mystified by all the hostility, clearly unable to comprehend why anyone would enjoy hurting him. He would stand there open-faced, his eyes seeming to search for an answer in the faces of his tormentors while his lower lip trembled. Sometimes he would cry. But tears were like the blood from a disabling wound to Chuck and his hyenas.

One day in early October, at the end of the first recess, Duncan turned the corner of the school building to find Chuck clutching Timmy's fine blue shirt, pulling it up under his chin and pressing the kid against a tree. Inches from Timmy's face, he said, "Where's my quarter, dickhead?"

"I couldn't get it."

"You better get it next time unless you want to get pounded."

"I don't know when Dad will give me anything."

Chuck pushed Timmy harder into the tree. "Lift it from your mom's purse."

A look of pure astonishment quelled Timmy's trembling lip. "I can't do that. That would be stealing."

The bell rang, and Timmy noticed Duncan watching behind Chuck, who noticed Timmy noticing. Without releasing his prey, the bigger boy turned to Duncan, said, "What are you looking at, hobo?"

Duncan didn't answer. He had too much going on at that moment. His fear urged him to walk away, but something else wouldn't let him. He wanted to tell Chuck to let Timmy go. He wanted to yell for the teachers. But that would mean ratting on another kid, which was the worst thing in the world.

Duncan was spared solving the dilemma by the appearance of Mr. Steinman, who startled them when he came around the corner, clapped, and said, "Recess is over. Get to your classes."

Chuck, smooth as a snake slithering through tall grass, instantly had an arm around Timmy's shoulders and began walking him away. With a smile, he said, "That was fun, Timmy. Watch out for the tree next time, OK?"

Duncan scowled at the show. Mr. Steinman squinted and frowned as if sensing the emotional dissonance. He quickly shook his head and said, "Come on, come on, Duncan. You too, you're late for your class."

16

October 1964

Duncan managed to avoid Chuck for nearly two weeks until he let his guard down one morning and got cornered behind the utility shed on the east side of the playground.

"Hey, hobo."

He turned to find Chuck and his two best friends, Greg and Denny, flanking their leader like ravens eyeing carrion. They moved quickly to trap him between the shed and the fence. Chuck stepped closer, and the ravens grinned.

"Hey, hobo, show us your shoes."

***

The Shame of the Shoes. Duncan's shoes had big holes, and he had been careful to hide that fact. Every day or so, Ava made cardboard inserts for him, but they wore through quickly.

Last Friday he forgot to be careful and exposed the soles while hanging on the gym. Chuck was right there to see.

"Oooh, oooh, look at his shoes!" Chuck had said in a voice loud enough, to Duncan, so that the whole school, maybe all of Santa Cruz, probably heard. He dropped off the bars with cheeks blazing.

"You really are a hobo." he taunted, which elicited laughter from his ravens and a few others. More taunts quickly followed:

"Do you live under a bridge, hobo?

"Eat out of a can?

"Bet you get your clothes out of the garbage.

"Do you ever take a bath, stinky hobo?"

Chuck played to his audience, and his four buddies laughed at every verbal punch. To Duncan the whole school was laughing at him, every kid, every teacher, and every person in every car driving by.

"Hobo! Hobo! Hobo!" Chuck led the chant.

Duncan ran. He ran the sixty feet to the school door like a sixty-mile gauntlet, the chanting whipping at him until the heavy door closed behind him. He hid in the boy's restroom, arms wrapped around his knees, feet up on the seat, stall door closed, suppressing his tears.

Boys came and went. The bell rang, but he waited several more minutes before daring to leave and find his class.

***

Chuck and his flankers moved closer. "Show us your shoes," Chuck said.

He didn't answer. He watched as Chuck approached, his heart fluttering like a frantic bird trying to escape his chest.

Chuck stopped three feet away and said, "Give me a quarter or show me your shoes, hobo."

"No," Duncan heard himself say.

Chuck laughed and moved closer. "He said, no, guys." They echoed his laugh.

"Quarter or shoes." Chuck lifted his chin. "Or get pounded."

Duncan shut his eyes for a moment; the blood in his skull roared like whitewater. His hands hurt from how hard he squeezed them into fists. He felt himself trembling but realized he was more angry than afraid—and he was very afraid. Then he looked into Chuck's eyes and said, "I'm not giving you a quarter."

Chuck took a half-step back, glanced at Duncan's fists and then again at his eyes. They stared at each other for seconds only. Then the big kid flashed a big smile to his flankers and said, "Ahh, I forgot, guys, he's a hobo. He doesn't have a quarter." And he pushed another laugh past his thin lips. The ravens returned pale echoes.

Randy appeared behind the crew. "What's going on?"

"Let's go," Chuck said, and as the three pushed past Randy, he added, "Bye, hobo. See ya next time."

"What did they want?"

Duncan slowly unclenched his hands, took a breath, and said, "Wanted to see," he looked away and lifted a foot so that the sole showed. "Wanted a quarter."

They looked at the three boys' retreating backs. Then, to Randy's look of inquiry, he said, "No, I didn't."

"Good, he's a mean little asshole."

"Not little." He took and released a long, shaky breath. "I hate him."

Randy stared, then said, "Yeah, me too." He offered an awkward smile and lifted his left foot to show the bottom of his shoe. "See, I've got one too."

Duncan smiled. "Yeah, but not big like mine." And showed proof.

They lowered their feet, and as the music of laughing, screaming, chattering children rebounded off the gray walls, Randy said, with a fierceness that Duncan had never seen before, "I'll fight them with you."

Duncan's face mirrored his friend's. "Yeah, we'll fight 'em together."

"Yeah, stuff Chuck's face up his butt."

Duncan giggled. "Make them give us quarters."

"Every day."

They laughed and expanded on their future battle heroics, and then Randy smacked Duncan on the shoulder, said, "You're it!"

He bolted across the wide grass yard with Duncan in close pursuit.

17

That following Friday evening, the sun was an orange blob collapsing onto a distant hill outside the dining nook where the Findlays were about to have dinner. Ava was at the stove, filling the kitchen with scents of fried hamburger, onion and Worchester sauce. Little Keith sat beside Duncan at the table, swinging his feet like dual metronomes. Aileen sat quietly at one end, allowing the golden solar glow to highlight her rosy cheeks and yellow hair.

Shona groaned as she entered. "More mince and tatties?"

Ava replied without looking up from stirring the frying ground beef, "Be glad for what you get."

Duncan liked mince and tatties, but Shona did have a point since this was the third night in a row that they would eat mashed potatoes, hamburger scramble and peas. And even though Ava made great mashed potatoes that were loaded with large quantities of butter and cream and salt, and even though the hamburger was rich and savory with lots of onion and bullion and Worchester sauce...well, even the best meal loses its allure if one repeats it too much.

Shona sat with a grumble. Ava dished the steaming meal onto the plates.

"Help your brother," she said to Duncan.

He pushed Keith's chair closer and added peas to his plate.

Each diner's plateau of spuds was topped with a stratum of saucy beef that dripped reddish gravy over the sides to surround their archipelagos of peas.

Shona poked the continent on her plate. "Why can't we eat something else?"

Ava paused her loaded fork halfway to her mouth. "Because your father hasn't sent us any money," she said.

Shona leaned her head onto one hand, frowned, and gave Asia another poke.

Aileen seemed focused on her food. Duncan pretended he was.

Keith announced, "Like tatties, not peas." And with one finger he began pushing the green balls to the far side of his plate.

Talk of their dad always chilled the room, and increasingly, Ava would blurt criticisms of Hugh. Last week, when Duncan pleaded for new shoes, Ava replied, "If I had a real man for a husband, I could get you shoes."

He didn't understand what his shoes had to do with Dad being a man, but he did gather that he would probably be walking on cardboard for a long time.

When Shona continued to force tectonic movements of her food, Ava said, "Do you think the starving kids in China would turn up their noses at this?"

Shona didn't answer but took a token bite.

The starving Chinese kids were Ava's go-to ploy to counter reluctant eaters and persistent whiners. It terminated the discussion, mainly because it was confusing. Duncan wondered what not wanting mince and tatties had to do with the Chinese. Wouldn't they still starve even if he did eat?

Fortunately, he liked mince and tatties; three times wasn't too much for him.

Out of her head-down absorption in whatever, Aileen spoke without looking up. "Mom, when are we going to get the toilet fixed? It's awful; the smell gets into our bedroom."

***

It was not the first time Aileen had asked about the hideous toilet. It had been clogged for over two weeks. They had kept using it without being able to flush until the revolting accumulation nearly reached the top of the bowl. Then Ava said they had to do their business outside behind a clump of bushes.

Being a boy, Duncan had less trouble with this than his sisters. Ava provided a shovel for when he had to do number two. He didn't like going out at night with their dim flashlight. And the times he had to dig a hole for Keith and cover up his deposits were nasty.

Keith insisted that Duncan not look and wanted him far away so he couldn't hear him. His anxiety presented lots of opportunities for teasing, like when, in mid-wee one night, Duncan threw a stick into a bush near Keith and shouted, "Hurry, Keith, a bear's coming." The frantic fleeing of the five-year-old was hilarious, but Ava chewed him out good when she had to clean the little guy's urine-soaked shorts.

His sisters, however, were mortified. "I can't do it outside," Aileen wailed. "Why doesn't the landlord come fix it?"

"Because," Ava had replied.

So, they peed outside and crapped outside, and the contents of the bowl matured in the-room-that-must-be-avoided-at-all-costs. It remained there between the two bedrooms—reeking.

***

Ava said, "It's difficult. Not yet."

"But why?" Aileen asked.

"Because."

Aileen appeared to throb with inner pressure, but she flashed her anger at her mince instead of at her mother.

***

Later, Duncan found Aileen in her bedroom and asked, "Why won't Mom get the toilet fixed?"

Her face's arrhythmic, subtle twitching suggested an inner conflict as she looked down at her brother. Finally, she said, "Because we're poor and she's embarrassed and she doesn't want anyone to see that we've got nothing—nothing but that disgusting toilet."

"Oh," He thought for a while and then asked, "Couldn't Dad get it fixed?"

"If she hadn't hounded him, always pushing pushing about Scotland, Scotland, Scotland! Not his fault."

Duncan wondered if she was going to cry or scream. "But Dad...."

Aileen crossed her arms and turned her back on him. "Go away."

***

"How was school?" Ava asked.

"Fine," Shona and Aileen answered in unison.

She wiped her mouth on a napkin and inclined her head to Duncan. "How about you?"

Images of Chuck and sounds of caustic laughter flooded his mind. "Fine," he said.

It was hard to tell whether these empty replies satisfied Ava. She moved on.

"We're going to Nana's tomorrow, and we'll stay the night."

"Yay!" all the kids cheered, except Aileen, who sulked over her mince.

Duncan's Nana, Evie McAllister, was everything a grandmother was supposed to be. She was kind and generous; she hugged him, baked delicious cakes and pies, and gave him money for treats. She smiled warmly at him and was always properly attired in dresses that came to mid-calf. He never saw her without a brunette wig or the thick glasses she needed to help with fading vision and cataracts. English tea and toast seemed to comprise half her diet. Her home was neat and clean. Glass and porcelain knickknacks filled towers of shelves in her living room.

He liked her little house and his army cot in the bare attic. Perhaps most of all, though he could not have put it into words, he loved the sense of safety and comfort she radiated. Her calm assurance buffered his often intense, sometimes furious mother. And in an even more inexplicable way, her presence lessened the painful whiplash of Hugh's baffling transformation from kind provider to despised abandoner, from good man to bad father.

But in the fall of 1964, he knew little about her beyond her simply being Nana. He didn't even know she was seventy-four. He didn't know his grandfather, her ex-husband, had mistreated her terribly with cheating and beatings. The latter mostly applied to her daughter. He didn't know she had given birth to her only child, her fiery daughter, in her late 30s. Nor did he know then of the uneasy relationship the two women had. No, she was perfect Nana, but he knew little of what she thought or felt.

18

The next morning Duncan sat in Evie's tiny kitchen, contentedly immersed in her aura as she started her morning in the usual way. He enjoyed the tap of her spoon as she stirred milk into her tea and the smell of toasting raisin bread soon to pop up. Her voice was like a song about comfort.

He heard Ava at the dining table doing something with cards, filling the air with the sharp spice of Magic Marker fumes. As usual, he was up earlier than his siblings. His sisters had been quiet behind their bedroom door as he had passed by. He had left Keith zoned out face down on his cot like a paratrooper splattered there from a skydive gone wrong.

Nana sipped her tea. "Did you have a good sleep, Duncan?"

Such questions from adults mystified him. Did he have a good sleep? All sleep was good.

Did he enjoy his time at the beach? Who wouldn't?

Do you like your ice cream? Get out of here.

Lacking the skills to resolve the mystery, he slurped the remaining milk from his bowl and said, "Yes, Nana."

"What do you want to do today?"

"Go see Randy."

Her toast popped up, and she plunked the hot slab onto a red ceramic saucer and quickly coated it in butter. She smiled. "That's nice. I hope you two have fun."

It wasn't a question, but it had the same strange flavor. He decided to let it go. His feet hit the floor, and he put his bowl in the sink. "Thank you, Nana."

He went to find Ava.

She sat at the table, holding a large postcard before her with two hands and nodding like she was admiring a great work of art. Her full, curly hair wobbled in response. On the maple surface were spread nearly a dozen similar cards adorned with big black letters.

"Mom, can I go see Randy?"

She glanced at him. "Oh, Duncan, good; I want to show you something."

He approached, and she had him sit. As he scooched his heavy chair forward, she placed a hand on his shoulder, which startled him a little since she rarely touched him.

"I know you are upset about your shoes, but I am going to fix that." Her face glowed like Tisiphone's at the prospect of a particularly exquisite torment. She lifted her hand and slid one of the cards in front of him,

"Your father," and she said father like she was saying bum or criminal or failure, "is holed up there at his mother's house and refuses to send us money, which is why you don't have new shoes. But not for much longer. My campaign is going to shame him into doing what is right."

Duncan didn't know what campaign meant, but he did understand shame. He had not yet looked at the card, fascinated as he was with his mother's oddly shining, oddly animated face. He felt his heart begin to thud heavily.

She didn't look at him as she continued, "He grew up in that little nothing town. His parents are still living in the house he was born in. He knows everyone, and they know him. I will send one of these postcards every day until he can't stand it. He'll send the money all right. He'll send it, and you'll get your shoes. See."

His attention again directed to the card, he began hard-flicking a front tooth with a thumbnail as he read the inch-high letters: YOUR KIDS HAVE NO SHOES

"Here." She shoved another one at him: WHAT KIND OF MAN ABANDONS HIS FAMILY?

And another: I MUST PUT CARDBOARD IN YOUR KIDS WORN OUT SHOES

And yet another: WILL YOU LET YOUR KIDS STARVE?

She pushed more cards before him, but Duncan could no longer read them. All he saw were black fangs. He chewed the inside of one cheek and tasted a gush of iron.

He pushed his chair back so hard it nearly fell over as he leapt to his feet. "I gotta go see Randy."

Ava's mouth dropped open as if she had just awoken and could see him again. He may have added, "OK?" or maybe she said, "OK," but it did not matter which, for he was already speeding for the front door.

As he fled he saw Evie at the kitchen entrance, a hand over her mouth like a witness to an execution.

He ran down the steep hill and walked to Branciforte Creek, which looked nothing like a creek. It had been excavated after the 1955 flood and encased in high concrete walls topped with chain-link fencing. A dribble of water slogged along in the former creek, now flood control channel, slowly moving sludge and a few dozing ducks.

Duncan listened to their muttering as the crosshatch of the links dug into his forehead. He thought about the times he'd had with his Dad: when they went fishing at Lake of the Woods, how he taught him to swim at Pelican Lake, when, while living in Moorhead, he had asked Duncan not to tell Ava that he was smoking, when he had cleaned the stinky black goop off his feet from Duncan running across a freshly tarred road, and how he had shocked him when, while watching the black and white news one evening, he had loudly cried, "Oh, no! Oh, no!" and seemed to collapse in his chair as Walter Cronkite announced President Kennedy had been killed.

The more he remembered, the more he felt something mean moving and writhing in his belly. The image of an ebony snake with dull red marbles for eyes sprang into his mind. The snake made him nervous and sick and angry all at once. It made him want to hit something. So, he threw rocks at the No Parking sign like he wanted to tear it apart until a man rushed out of his house and yelled, "Knock that off. Get out of here."

He did not want to see Randy yet. He did not want to see anyone. He wandered along the channel, listening to birds and the undulations of the breeze wagging the overhanging trees. He meandered through unfamiliar neighborhoods and barely flinched when a dog charged the fence he was walking by. When he paused at Marianne's Ice Cream shop on Ocean, he looked at the display without interest.

Duncan decided to head to the river because water always made him feel better. He walked past the bowling lawn and then to the pond, crunching along the gravel lane.

A familiar cackle made him stop and look for the source. Just above a low rise of turf wobbled the red beach ball, crew-cut head of Chuck Putnam. Duncan groaned. He was seeing the back of the boy's head, but the sadistic laugh was uniquely Chuck's. Any doubt was erased when he heard a loud slap, and that voice said, "You shoulda paid your quarter, dickface."

Duncan edged around the hillock to see who Chuck was tormenting today. At first he couldn't tell. From a car length back and slightly to Chuck's right, he saw the bully sitting on top of some kid's chest, his little jean-clad legs and tennis shoes jerking about. He sidestepped farther and saw who it was just as Chuck delivered another slap and laughed as the little boy cried.

It was that Timmy kid. Chuck's knees pinned his arms, and he said, "Yes," to something Chuck demanded.

Chuck bounced up and down on Timmy's chest. "Look at the smarty-kid crying. Boo hoo. Boo hoo." Timmy blubbered and pleaded to be let go. Chuck delivered more threats and more slaps. Inside Duncan the snake coiled tighter and tighter.

He had never met a kid as mean as Chuck before. He remembered his dad's advice when a boy had bullied him in Barnesville. He was seven then, and the other boy was older and bigger, but his father told him to confront the bully because bullies were actually weak.

He wasn't convinced that was true, but he had his marching orders. The next day he had walked a long, long way across the field at school to confront Martin, who was with two friends.

He didn't remember what he had said to Martin because his fear was like a screeching train in his brain, but it was something like, "Don't touch me. Leave me alone, or I will fight you."

Duncan had expected to be pounded. Dad's advice, while sincerely delivered, unfortunately, did not include any instructions on how to fight. He had never punched anyone before, well, except Aileen, whom he punched in the stomach when he was two. Did that count?

To his amazement, Martin had backed down and agreed to leave him alone. Dad's credibility swelled enormously in Duncan's mind, and he had walked away proud.

In the last three years, Duncan had not accumulated any fighting skills beyond what he had had to offer Martin. Chuck looked like a seasoned fighter, if an eleven-year-old boy could be so depicted. But it was also true that Chuck had been in fights, maybe many of them. Duncan had not.

None of that mattered on that cool, sunny October morning. The black snake coiled tighter and swelled larger with every abuse. Another slap and the acid of Chuck's derisive laughter singed Duncan's ears. The snake raised its head.

Chuck spattered spit on Timmy's face. Duncan was working up his courage to intervene when the gloating boy did something so shocking that, for a few seconds, he could not move or speak. Timmy squirmed wildly.

Duncan screamed, "You damn asshole!"

Chuck flinched and snapped his head around as if a spotlight had flared to reveal his crime. His alarm lasted all of two seconds. Seeing it was Duncan, he smirked and said, "Shut up, hobo. You're next."

"Get off him! Get off him! Get off him!" Duncan barked and advanced. That got the bigger boy's attention. He rose, stepped over and in front of his prone prisoner. "C'mon, garbage boy."

Duncan charged. He hit Chuck with outstretched fists just below his collarbones. Chuck tripped over Timmy and fell hard on his back. His head bounced on the lawn. Duncan followed on top of him, and his right fist, which was raised high, slammed down onto Chuck's nose. Instantly, he was on top like Chuck had been on Timmy, except Chuck's arms were free.

He swung wild overhand fists at Chuck's face. Most of them missed, but they came so fast and connected often enough that the damage was considerable.

Blood gushed from Chuck's nose, and his lower lip was split and bleeding. Despite this, he was fighting back hard, but Duncan barely felt the multiple strikes to his face and ribs.

Chuck managed to knock Duncan off several times, but only briefly because he would leap back on, all while whirling his arms and fists like the Tasmanian Devil from the Looney Tunes. If an adult had been present, they might have found the performance funny.

Chuck didn't. Duncan's crazy barrage was relentless as he yelled and sometimes growled like a dog. Panic sprang into Chuck's eyes. Blood that had gushed from his nose and lips was smeared on his face and shirt.

When Chuck knocked him off for the fourth time, Duncan stumbled in the remount and accidentally slammed his head into Chuck's left cheekbone. The red-headed boy's eyes glazed; he began to cry. Duncan got a clear shot and popped him in the mouth.

"Stop it...stop...stop," he pleaded softly, or did it only seem muffled compared to the roar of Duncan's rage? He continued his inept punching and scored more often as Chuck seemed to tire.

In likely desperation, Chuck heaved him off one last time and took off running. He sprinted after him. The heavy kid ran surprisingly fast. He headed over the footbridge that linked the park to River Street. Duncan stopped midway. Chuck dodged a honking car as he crossed the street and disappeared around the bank.

Duncan felt rooted there, chest heaving, and his limbs were weak. He slowly unclenched each fist; it was painful. The black snake abruptly vanished like incense smoke before a breeze. He did not know how long he remained there, dazed and wondering what he'd do if Chuck returned. A voice brought him back.

"Duncan?"

He turned to find Timmy and Randy standing at the park side of the bridge. Neither one said more, but they stared with big, marveling eyes. He walked over to them and stopped close.

"That was the bossest fight ever," Randy said. "Wow."

Timmy's face was scratched and red from the slaps. His torn shirt was pulled out. His hair was a mess, and snot dripped from his nose. But he wasn't bleeding or visibly bruised.

"You stopped him," he said in a faint voice.

"You crushed him. You made him run. You made him cry. Man-o-man, that was great!"

Duncan trembled.

"You OK?" Randy asked.

"Don't know, yeah, I guess, yeah. Shaky. Shaky."

"You stopped him," Timmy repeated with more strength.

Duncan checked himself. His hands and arms were smeared with blood. Chuck's blood. His right forearm had a nasty turf scrape from wrist to elbow, with blades of grass embedded in it. He hurt everywhere: his head from the impact on Chuck's cheekbone, his jaw from unremembered counter-punches, his ribs and hands like they'd been whacked with a mallet. His jeans were soiled with large, dark grass stains. And one of his rear pockets was nearly ripped off.

"Mom is going to kill me," Duncan said.

19

R andy said his mom could clean up some of Duncan's disaster so he would not look so bad when he went home. The two started toward his house. After a few steps Duncan realized that Timmy was not following. He stopped and looked back. "You should come with us. Mrs. Kelly is really nice."

Timmy looked younger than usual. His eyes seemed to look through Duncan, and transient tremors flitted across his face. He gazed across the river toward downtown, and in a slow, weak, flat voice Duncan could barely hear, he said, "Mom is shopping and will come looking for me."

"When?" asked Randy.

To Duncan's surprise, Timmy pulled out a large pocket watch and studied it. "An hour or so, I think."

Duncan hoped Timmy wouldn't cry. "Come on, Randy's house is just a couple of blocks away. You need to get cleaned up. You'll be back before she gets here."

"Yeah, come on," Randy said.

The corners of Timmy's mouth lifted fractionally. His eyes gleamed at Duncan, and his face lost its boy-abandoned-at-the-mall look. He carefully tucked in his shirt, finger-combed his hair, and lifted his chin. "OK."

The three walked across the park. Reaching the sidewalk, they dodged past a man and a little girl getting out of a truck parked at the curb. The child pointed and said, "That boy's bleeding, Daddy."

The man opened his mouth to say something, but Duncan ran. Randy and Timmy followed. Out of sight, they slowed to a walk,

"How did you get into the fight, anyway?" Randy asked.

The little boy to Duncan's left, vivid red marks broadcasting the impacts of Chuck's big hands, flecks of grass in his hair, and two lurid scratches down the right side of his jaw, appeared to shrink at Duncan's glance. Duncan shrugged and struggled with what to say, finally settling on, "He was picking on Timmy again. I got mad."

Their steps counted out the seconds. When nothing further came, Randy flashed a baffled look of, AND?

"Let's just get to your mom's," Duncan said.

They entered through the back of the house. Randy let the screen door slam and shouted, "Mom! Mom! Duncan's hurt."

"I'm not hurt."

"Mom! Mom!"

Margaret appeared at the kitchen entrance, gasped at the sight of Duncan, and said, "Oh my, you're bleeding. What happened?"

"I'm not hurt. Shut up, Randy. I'm not bleeding. It's not my blood." Those assertions were mostly fudges, as the scrape on his arm had just dripped blood on the floor, and he ached in about a dozen places.

Margaret frowned. "Well, come on in, let's take a look." And then to Randy, "What happened?"

Alan rushed in with Cheryl at his heels as Duncan and Timmy took seats at the kitchen table. Randy said, "Duncan got in a fight with Chuck at the park. It was bitchin'. Duncan beat him, beat him bad. Chuck was crying and he ran, and he chased him over the river and it was so bitchin'."

Margaret wrung a wet cloth at the sink and shot her son a stern look. "Watch your mouth, Randall."

She pulled a chair over, sat, and began wiping blood and dirt off Duncan's face. "Why were you fighting?" she asked in a tone that suggested she did not think it was bitchin' at all.

No answer sprang to his mind except *I was mad*, which seemed a stupid thing to say.

Into the impatient silence, Timmy said, "My fault. Chuck was bugging me. He hit me a few times." He glanced at Duncan, mumbled, "I'm not good at fighting," continued stronger, "Duncan stopped him."

Margaret carefully watched the smallest boy as he spoke, and then she examined Duncan's face. She cleaned his arm and appeared to be considering what Timmy said. The whole Kelly family was quiet, and although it must have been evident that there was more to the story, no one pressed the boy, not even Alan, who could usually be counted on to goad the vulnerable.

After a minute or two, with nothing but the soft sounds of her cloth wiping the evidence of the fight from Duncan's body, she said, "I see. Who is this Chuck kid?"

"Chuck Putnam," Randy said. "He's a sixth grader, picks on a lot of kids at school."

Alan spoke up. "Chuck Putnam? You beat Chuck Putnam?"

"Yeah," Duncan said as Margaret began working on his hands.

Respect showed on Alan's face. "Chuck's a tough little turd," he said, then smirked. "For a sixth grader."

"You know him?" Margaret asked.

"A little. I know his brother, Ted, good fighter."

"Hmmm...Cheryl, go get the iodine out of the medicine cabinet."

To Duncan, she said, "I don't approve of fighting." She glanced at Alan, "But if you were protecting your friend, that's different." She gestured at Timmy. "Are you going to introduce me?"

Duncan had not thought of the boy as his friend, so he hesitated a moment, then said, "Timmy. We have arithmetic together."

Cheryl returned with a small vial of red liquid. Opening it, Margaret said, "This is going to sting, but we don't want it getting infected." Duncan winced as she dabbed. Cheryl watched with a scrunched face and flinched at every application.

"Duncan rescued me," Timmy said.

"Uh-huh," Margaret replied. "How are you doing? Are you hurt, too? I'll do you next."

Timmy's cheeks were red, and a snot drip hung from his nose, but there were no apparent injuries. "I'm OK," he declared loudly.

Duncan and Timmy locked eyes. And he saw the injury written in the boy's eyes, eyes that cried out, *please don't tell or I will die.* An instant understanding was reached; neither would ever talk about the worst thing Chuck had done to him. With the slightest of nods and with but traces of pained smiles, it was done like a handshake contract.

Margaret finished with Duncan and noted that he would have quite a knot on his head. She cleaned up Timmy, which he accepted with gratitude.

Randy launched into a detailed story of The Fight, speaking in marque letters and giving a blow-by-blow account. Cheryl and Alan listened without interruption. Duncan thought that Randy's version made him look better than what he remembered of his fight. He felt oddly shy and proud simultaneously, as he was painted as some super tough guy.

Margaret was amazing. She told the two boys to go into Randy's room and to get out of their clothes so she could do some spot-cleaning. When done, Duncan found she had not only cleaned his clothes but had stitched up his pocket too. She replaced the lost buttons on Timmy's shirt. There wasn't much she could do about the grass stains or the blood on his shirt, but Duncan hoped that, given it was an old shirt, Ava would not mind too much.

Alan and Cheryl hung around for the cleaning and Randy's repetitive dramatization of The Great Fight. At the end of which, Alan said, "You're tougher than you look, Russkie." His smile took the sting out of the gibe, and Duncan basked in praise from someone he saw as a real tough guy.

As Alan turned to leave, he added, "You better watch out for Ted. He may not like it that you kicked his brother's ass."

Duncan tried to hide the gulp he took.

The Kellys were about to have lunch, and although Margaret invited Duncan and Timmy to join them, Duncan found he wanted to leave, and Timmy said he had to meet his mom.

"I'll go with you," Duncan said.

The two boys walked in silence for a while. As they neared the park, Timmy spoke in a smooth, even voice, "My dad says I have a small body but a big mind and a big heart. He says that, of the three, the last two are the important ones. I wish I could beat up guys like Chuck, but I know I never will, at least not with my fists. Chuck got a D in arithmetic. A D. I got..."

"An A, I know. You always get A's."

"Yeah, an A. And you got a B. You could get A's too."

Duncan shrugged. Timmy continued, "I believe my dad. I will win with my mind and heart. Chuck won't. Oh, there's Mom."

Across Dakota Avenue, Duncan saw a woman in a cantaloupe-shade swing dress. Her oval head was topped with neat, light-brown curly hair. She stood near the concrete snake sculpture, searching the faces of every boy in the park.

"Come on, meet my mom."

"Naw, I better get home."

Timmy's face dropped perceptibly. "OK," he said.

An awkward moment stretched as neither seemed to know what to say. Then Timmy cleared his throat and, in a rather precise and formal manner, said, "Thank you, Duncan."

Duncan nodded rapidly; he couldn't wait to get away. "Sure, OK, uh, see you at school."

20

A few months earlier, while running home from the beach in his bare feet, Duncan had stubbed his big toe so severely that it split the nail, dripped blood for blocks, and hurt almost as bad as a whack from the belt. As he hobbled up Ocean Street, he dealt with his disaster by imagining he was a great and powerful giant. His every step shook the earth. His head pushed clouds aside. The puny humans had reacted by dropping an atomic bomb on his toe. The hundred-kiloton blast only annoyed him. Sure, it hurt, and yes, they split his toe open, but he laughed at the pain. And he made the humans pay by crushing whole armies, batting jets out of the sky, and obliterating faraway cities with his terrible roar. Call him Dunzilla.

In a Morehead school library two years before, he had read an astronomy book speculating on aliens living on other worlds in an infinite universe. He had taken the book's illustrations as fact and was awestruck. Since then, from time to time, when the night sky was clear and black and dazzling, with its thousands upon thousands of stars, he would stare into it feeling an unspeakable longing to go out there, to meet those other beings and to travel forever and ever among its awesome wonders.

Like many boys he was an avid comic book reader. His heroes were The Thing, Superman, Daredevil and the Hulk. They battled bad guys like Lex Luther and Doctor Doom, and he was thrilled at their every triumph.

Thus, what was it like for Duncan to go from despised hobo to feared hero all in one day? He had returned from Randy's to his Nana's with trepidation tempered by being totally spent. Despite Margaret's extraordinary efforts, the evidence of what he had done was written in the abrasions on his hands, the wound to his arm, the lump on his head and his mostly ruined clothes.

When he walked in, Ava was ironing a blouse in Evie's living room. She seemed startled by his appearance, recovered, and asked him what happened. He confessed that he'd been fighting. After a few long moments examining him, during which he steeled himself for the worst, she asked,

"Did you win?"

"Yes."

Her eyes glowed, and a trace of a smile lifted the corners of her mouth. "Good," she said and turned back to her work.

Evie tut-tutted and fussed over his injuries. Keith looked on in apparent worried wonder. His sisters asked in near unison, "What happened to you?"

"I beat up a kid from school."

"Why?" they harmonized.

The whole long story filled Duncan's mind, but all he felt was tiredness. He settled on, "He deserved it."

"Why? Why?"

"He just did."

Ignoring further questions, he went to his cot, laid down and fell asleep almost instantly.

Ava woke him sometime later and announced they were going shopping. She drove him to the Shoe Outlet on Pacific and let him pick out what he liked. He chose the most expensive pair; it cost five dollars.

She did not make any more attacks on his father. She did not say how she suddenly had money for shoes. Of course, he was pleased, not perplexed, because ten-year-old boys rarely pondered how adults got their money.

By the Monday following his fight with Chuck, he'd had time to absorb the praise from Randy and Alan, and even little Cheryl, Timmy's gratitude, and Margaret's sober respect. Ava's oblique esteem gave him new pride; he saw the shoes as a reward. Duncan swelled with the knowledge of what he had done—he had beaten the big bad bully that all the other kids feared. He strode onto the Branciforte Elementary school grounds that morning with new shoes and a new attitude.

Randy met him at the front entrance. He examined his head bump, scabbed arm and many bruises. "You look tough."

Randy's admiration spilled over as they walked down the hall. He proclaimed to friends and quizzical strangers, "Duncan beat Chuck!" For emphasis, he smacked a fist into his palm. "Bam!"

Heads turned. There were exclamations of wonderment and questions galore. In Duncan's mind there might as well have been garlands of flowers dropping from the ceiling and blasts of trumpets echoing off the locker-lined walls of the Branciforte version of ancient Rome's Forum, announcing the arrival of the conquering hero.

Then the usual Monday world intruded, and he was sitting in Mr. French's geography class deflecting his question, "What happened to you?" with the ever-reliable choice of children throughout time, "Nothing."

The drone of lectures allowed Duncan's mind to drift, and it occurred to him that he would run into Chuck at recess. Doubt insinuated its way into the shining glory of his greatness like a lone thunderhead closing over the midday sun. What if Chuck was not cowed but angry at his improbable defeat? What if he wanted to fight again? Duncan's prior rage seemed a distant thing. He felt like Dr. Jekyll, who could barely remember what Mr. Hyde was like.

He was relieved to find that while doubt nibbled at his confidence, the rage had not wholly disappeared. He was still angry about what Chuck had done to Timmy, and he hated how Chuck had made him feel. Such thoughts shoved the lightning cloud away from his sun. That day went by in a blur. He would not learn much from his classes and would get a C- on his history quiz the next day.

What he remembered most were his classmates as they stole glances at him from their desks, sometimes while whispering into a friend's ear.

Randy's performance at first recess started a cascade of Telephone, with all its exaggerations and distortions. Randy dressed up the story into an even greater drama than before, and it was in admiration that Duncan sat on a swing watching and listening as he told the rapt gathering of over a dozen kids, some of them third-graders, how Duncan had vanquished the evil Chuck.

Randy said he had run to the top of the hillock shortly after it started because he heard Duncan's shouts. His view had Timmy already up and watching nearby. He told of blows and scrambles, blood flying and gushing, and punches and kicks from Chuck that didn't faze Duncan at all. He flung himself around as he demonstrated the combatant's positions and moves and had Duncan saying things like, "Leave Timmy alone! Leave all the kids alone. I'm going to beat you into mush." Mush, really?

He remembered saying something about Timmy, but none of the other words that Randy put in his mouth. Yet, it was excellent playground theater, and his audience seemed enthralled.

Duncan could see *wow* written on many kid's faces. However, a few looked at him as if they were citizens of the freshly liberated city, wondering if the great conqueror would prove to be a worse tyrant.

Randy's story had all Duncan's blows as deliberate, his blocks brilliant, and his insensitivity to pain superhuman. The headbutt was portrayed as a ninja move.

Opposite Duncan, far on the periphery of Randy's audience, were the worried scowls of Chuck's friends: Denny, Craig and Greg. Chuck wasn't there. Later, Randy said Chuck's mother had called him in sick.

Duncan stared hard at those friends. He had never felt the same fear of them as he had for Chuck. They looked away when they saw his glare.

Timmy came over and sat on the swing next to him. "Hi."

"Hi."

Together, they watched the climax of Randy's play. Timmy pointed at Duncan's bruised face and head knot, asked, "Does it hurt?"

"No," Duncan lied.

Timmy swung back and forth. "I brought my marbles, want to play?"

The crowd was breaking up. Duncan synced his swings. "Sure. Got any steelies?"

At lunch in the cafeteria, Duncan, Timmy and Randy sat together. Randy and Timmy had brought sack lunches of sandwiches and potato chips. Timmy's mom had added home-baked cookies. Duncan was eating the cafeteria's meal: whipped potatoes, dried meatloaf, and the peas and carrots combo that appeared to have been cooking since Duncan was in the first grade. A serving of red Jell-O quivered in its dish. Each had a pint of Meadow Land milk with a straw protruding like a flagpole.

While they were debating the toughness rankings of the boys at school, with Duncan elevated to number one, three fourth-graders came to their table. Kid One asked Duncan, "I had to give Chuck ten cents every week. Do I still have to do that?"

Kid Two said, "A dime? I had to give a quarter."

"Me too," said Kid Three.

They turned expectantly to Duncan like he was The Don or something. "No, you don't have to do that anymore," he said.

They smiled, said thanks, and skipped away, chattering with relief.

Timmy's face shone with approval; Randy's was a big question mark.

Duncan grimaced and shrugged.

At the second recess, the tension was thick. By now everyone knew the story, including the teachers, who looked at Duncan like he was a mercurial rooster about to upset the chicks pecking around the yard.

He, Timmy and Randy were clustered together at the marble's plot. Chuck's hyenas were milling near the basketball court, pretending to watch some other kids play. They looked his way often and were having an animated conversation that he couldn't hear.

"You going to talk to them?" Randy asked.

Timmy looked expectantly at Duncan, said, "They're Chuck's friends."

"I know. About what?"

"About what?" Randy echoed. "You've been telling kids they don't have to pay anymore. Those jerks were in on it."

Timmy nodded vigorously.

Dang.

Then he noticed that other kids were looking his way, then to the hyenas, and then back to him, like spectators at a tennis match.

Damn.

He felt the trap of being ranked number one and wondered if it would only last a day.

"Yeah, OK."

Duncan probably only imagined the gaggle of children going quiet as he walked toward the hyenas. In reality, kids kept playing, teachers admonished, and the traffic on Water Street hummed as usual, with the occasional honk. But in Duncan's mind the stadium lights had all blazed on, the cameras were rolling, and a hush had fallen upon the gathered throng.

Denny was a thin boy, a bit taller than Duncan, with slightly buck teeth. Craig had a head of sandy blond hair that always went every which way, regardless of how often he combed it. He was shorter but broader than Duncan. Greg, who rounded out the threesome, was Chuck's right-hand boy; his round head, freckled face and big ears reminded Duncan of Alfred E. Neuman. But the way he laughed made him think of a show he saw on hyenas.

The hyenas watched him approach. It took five seconds or five hours to reach the trio, depending on the point of view. He knew he had to act tough, but how? In desperation, he latched on to the image of the Man-with-No-Name he'd seen in *A Fistful of Dollars*. When he reached the boys, he said nothing for a while because words escaped him. But in hindsight, it was how Clint would have acted.

"What do you want?" Craig sneered, his unusually high-pitched voice cracking on the last word.

He stared into the eyes of the three in turn like Clint did while frantically trying to remember what he wanted to say. It was hard to stay in character without the smoldering cigarillo to talk past and the scruffy poncho to hide his nervous hands.

"Timmy is my friend. Nobody is going to bug him again. He's never going to pay you or Chuck anything. And none of the other kids either."

Denny and Craig looked scared. *Hey, this tough guy act really works.*

But Greg was defiant. "Oh, yeah, what are you going to do about it?"

Is this when he was supposed to squint and shift his eyes from side to side before shooting them? Dammit, he didn't have a gun—time to improvise.

He leaned toward Greg and said in a voice he hoped was steely and not just squeaky, "If you don't do what I say, I'll pound you just like I did Chuck."

He did his best imitation of a death stare into Greg's rebellious eyes. But inside Duncan's chest, his heart was running around in circles, hands waving in the air, screaming, "Are you nuts? You're going to get me killed."

There was a long, long moment as Greg returned his stare. Duncan hoped his facial twitches suggested a barely suppressed maniac instead of a boy about to poop his pants. But in time, Greg gulped and looked down. "All right, we won't do anything."

"You better not." And Duncan glared at the other boys, who caved too.

"OK, we won't do nothin' either," Craig said as Denny nodded enthusiastically.

The return to his friends was exhilarating. It was like he bounced along on marshmallows, and the heavenly host sang, "For He's a Jolly Good Fellow." The stadium crowd was delirious with joy after he had hit three home runs in three seconds.

He was relieved, ecstatic, and he felt powerful. He had faked being tough, and it had worked. *Yay, me!*

Timmy asked, "How did it go?"

Duncan shrugged. "They won't bug anyone anymore."

"Cool," Randy said.

The bell rang; it was back to the books.

Before Duncan got seated, Miss Sunderland, his social studies teacher, intercepted him. "Would you come with me, Duncan?"

In the hall, she said, "You are wanted in the principal's office. Mrs. Handley," referring to the sweet, dumpy-looking woman from the main office who was there outside the classroom door, "will take you to see her."

"Am I in trouble?"

Ms. Sunderland patted him on the shoulder. "She just wants to talk to you."

"OK."

As Mrs. Handley led him down the hall, her smiles notwithstanding, Duncan worried. He had never been to the principal's office before. The principal was a tall, severe-looking woman who wore pencil dresses in solid colors and stood like she was at attention while observing the subjects in her kingdom. Only kids in trouble went to her office.

He looked up again, and Mrs. Handley smiled again. Going by the main office, the ladies within also smiled at him. Was this like how the crowd smiled before the guillotine lopped off the accused's head?

Mrs. Handley knocked on Principal Warner's door.

"Enter," a strong female voice said.

As Principal Warner rose from her big, dark desk, his escort opened the door and announced him.

"Thank you, Catheryn," the principal said.

Then she smiled. "Hello, Duncan. Please have a seat."

He pulled himself up on the large, brown leather chair; his feet barely reached the floor. The principal returned to her chair behind forty acres of varnished wood.

He tried not to slouch, but the chair was too big. She grabbed a pencil, assumed a pensive demeanor, and lightly tapped it a few times on her desk.

"Do you know why I asked you here?"

It was yet another one of those strange adult questions. How could he know? She hadn't told him yet.

"Am I in trouble?"

More pencil tapping. "Well, no, but I am concerned, and I want to talk with you about what happened with Charles Putnam."

Duncan waited.

"I spoke with his parents this morning. They say a child from this school beat their son. They say he has a broken nose and a minor facial fracture. They say Charles will not name the boy who did this, and they say they won't pursue it. When I asked why not, I was made to understand that the parents expect their sons to be tough." She gestured like such an attitude baffled her. "However, as I expect you know, it is common knowledge that you are that boy. Isn't that right?"

He could hear the heavy blade of the guillotine being slowly raised.

"Yes, ma'am."

"Now, this fight did not happen on school grounds, so you are not in trouble. If it had, you would've been in very big trouble. But it didn't."

He swallowed.

"Your teachers say you have been a good boy in your short time with us, and there have not been any fights before. I want to know why you and Charles were fighting."

The room seemed to shrink in on Duncan. His breathing shallowed. He couldn't say anything. The woman waited while his blinking made the light from her window strobe.

"Duncan?"

Barely audible, he said, "I can't say."

"What?"

Louder, he said, "I can't say."

"You can't tell me..." The woman's voice drifted off, and she seemed to study Duncan, who gripped the arms of his chair with white knuckles.

"I can't rat," Duncan said. He was thinking, *Even nasty old Chuck didn't rat. I am not going to either.* He expected to be pressured and threatened, and somehow his mother, whom he feared above all others, would be called, but regardless, he wasn't going to rat.

Instead, Mrs. Warner grew more thoughtful, said, "I see. Of course, why you were fighting is all over school. It's all the other children seem to be talking about. I wanted to hear why from you. Some of it seems, well, exaggerated. I wanted to find out how much truth is in the story."

She made a few more lazy taps of her pencil. "I won't ask you to, umm, rat."

Duncan relaxed his grip and sat up straighter but watched her carefully.

"You know, Duncan, the teachers and I, our entire staff, are here to help you and the other children. I would like you to feel you could go to them or come to me if you have any problems."

To Duncan's noncommittal gaze, she added, "I wouldn't ask you to rat, but somehow let us know if you or the other children need help."

In Duncan's mind he did not see a way around the ratting part.

She sighed. "Well, if what our teachers have heard is even half-true, we have been missing a great deal that goes on in our hallways and on the playground."

She rose and walked Duncan to the door, resting one hand lightly on his shoulder. The principal's hand hesitated just short of the doorknob. "You are not in trouble. And I will inform your teachers that you told me nothing. And Charles, when he returns to school, will not be questioned about what occurred."

Duncan relaxed and thought she was nicer than some kids said. She opened the door. "Please return to class, and please, no fighting on school grounds, all right?"

"Yes, Mrs. Warner. I don't ever want to fight again."

21

November 1964

The Duncan versus Chuck melodrama faded quickly that week. The villain failed to appear, and the bad guy's buddies avoided the hero. When it became clear that Duncan had no interest in taking over Chuck's quarter and dime extortion business, kids who had shied warily away from him by Thursday shouted hellos and smiled openly.

Rumors abounded: Chuck was in the hospital; the Putnam's had fled Santa Cruz; Chuck was running from the police.

Improbable details were spun: Chuck was seen lolling lifelessly in the back of an ambulance; the Putnam family was seen fleeing Santa Cruz in a U-Haul truck; and Duncan's favorite, Chuck was seen weeping and confessing his crimes to stern police officers while they slapped handcuffs on him.

These and other cotton candy inventions were spun and passed from boy to girl to boy to girl as the adolescent troubadours competed to weave ever more fantastic wish-it-were-real tales, the degree of truth in them mattering not at all to the avid audience.

The collective imagination flared brightly for those few days, then dimmed, and the individual flames danced away to concerns about upcoming tests, games of dodgeball, football, hopscotch and races around the playground.

Friday's lunch hour found Randy, Duncan and Timmy eating together again, as had become usual.

"Still no Chuck. Think he'll come back?" Randy asked.

Timmy paused blowing milk bubbles with his straw to hear Duncan's reply.

"Dunno, don't care."

"Yeah?"

Duncan turned his Man-with-No-Name eyes on Randy, said, "Yeah."

Randy nodded with a wry smile.

Timmy resumed blowing bubbles out of the top of his milk box.

"You want to go surfing tomorrow?" Randy asked.

"Sure, let's check it out."

Duncan asked Timmy, "You want to come?"

Timmy lit up like he was being taken to see Barnum & Bailey's Circus. Duncan noticed that the boy always seemed surprised when he or Randy included him. "Yes, that would be great!" Then he looked down at his lunch. "I don't know how yet."

"It's easy; Randy showed me. You can swim, can't you?" He had a moment of doubt as he examined his new friend's slight arms and narrow chest. "The surf can get rough."

"Oh, I'm a good swimmer; just show me how."

Timmy's vivid display of eagerness sparked Duncan. He asked Randy, "What do you think? Maybe he's too little for Rivermouth."

Randy made a show of scrutinizing Timmy. "You might be right. He's so small; maybe we should take him to Cowell where the waves are little... for the kiddies."

Timmy shoved his milk away, said, "I don't need the kiddie pool. I can do it."

"What if he gets smashed into the cliff?" Duncan asked.

"Or snatched by a seagull?" Randy added.

Duncan gazed into the distance and slowly shook his head as if he were imagining all the awful fates that might befall Timmy in the sea.

Randy said, "Next year might be better, when he's bigger."

Outrage flashed across Timmy's face, quickly replaced by frowning skepticism. With narrowed eyes, he said, "Yuckity yuckity yuck," and sucked on his milk. After swallowing the carton's remains, he added, "I'm going, and I will learn how, even if you won't show me." He lifted his chin and hit them with an imperious stare that seemed to make him swell in size. "I will outswim you both."

The two teasers went momentarily blank, and their lips parted before they cracked up.

"OK, OK, OK," Duncan said. "You're in."

Lunch was over. They headed back to their classes. Randy peeled off to his. Timmy and Duncan continued toward the one they shared. The hall was filled with the high-pitched cacophony of a hundred kids' banter, accented by the slams of metal locker doors.

"You want to come over after school to play my new game?" Timmy asked.

"Sure, what is it?"

"Rock 'em Sock 'em Robots."

Duncan stopped. He had seen the ads for the new boxing toy on TV. All the boys wanted one. He had been hoping to get it for Christmas. "You have Rock 'em Sock 'em Robots?"

"Yeah, Dad just got it for me."

"Wow."

The boys entered their class.

"Meet me at the bike racks, 'K?" Duncan asked, "You walk or ride to school?"

"Walked, I live," he pointed west, "over there, just a few blocks."

Later, after the three o'clock bell sounded, Duncan found Timmy already standing near the bikes. His blondish hair was neat, as always. It seemed he must go to the barber every few weeks. His hair was swept across his forehead, and the slacks and buttoned shirt were immaculate, not something one often saw on the playground. Duncan thought he looked like a kid who should be in a TV commercial or even in one of those family shows like *My Three Sons* or maybe *Lassie*. His mind dwelled on that last one, *Lassie, hmmmm*. He started toward his friend and drew up short to bend over, laughing.

Timmy smiled uncertainly, asked, "What's so funny?"

It took him a moment, but he finally replied, "Do you know you look a lot like that kid who owns Lassie?"

Timmy scowled. "No I don't."

"Uh-huh, sure you do." He chuckled and then looked off over the trees as he realized something. His laughter exploded, but he finally managed to say, through a wheeze, "And his name is Timmy!"

The smaller boy planted fists on his hips and said something Duncan could not hear over his guffaws. When he spoke again, louder, he heard him over his laughter.

"My name is Timothy," the stern-faced boy declared.

"What?" Duncan asked as he tried to compose himself.

Carefully enunciating every word, he repeated, "My name is Timothy."

"Huh? But everybody calls you Timmy."

"I know. I don't like it. My name is Timothy."

"But?"

"My name is Timothy."

Duncan's mirth dissipated as he absorbed Timmy's abrupt transformation. One moment the little guy could look and act so goofy, making faces, giggling, blowing milk and acting up. The next he was almost like an adult, serious and fierce. He had that face now.

"OK, but I've been calling you Timmy. Why didn't you tell me before?"

"Because before, I didn't know you were my friend."

"Huh?"

"I can't stop everyone calling me Timmy, but I want my friend to call me Timothy."

Duncan felt oddly privileged, said, "OK, Timothy."

The other boy beamed. Duncan unlocked his banana bike, Timothy got on the back, and they pedaled off the school grounds and up Branciforte.

For a while they rode in silence, but as they reached the turn for Timothy's street, Duncan said over his shoulder, "If I find out you have a dog at home named Lassie, I get to call you Timmy."

"Shut up; I'm going to knock your block off."

Duncan laughed. "No, I'm gonna knock yours off."

"No, yours."

"Uh-uh, yours."

"No, yours."

They continued in that vein as Duncan pedaled up the hill and were laughing uproariously when they rolled down Timothy's driveway.

22

"Mom! Mom!" Timothy called as he slammed the front door, "I brought Duncan with me."

Timothy's mother appeared through the archway to the living room. She was a petite woman in high heels, which click-clacked as she approached across the black slate tiles of the foyer. She wore a powder-blue dress with a pattern of tiny white birds ascending from the hemline to her left shoulder. She had a long white neck, chin-length blonde hair and swoop bangs. Her blue eyes and rose mouth smiled at the visitor.

"Welcome, Duncan," she said and stopped before him.

He gulped, dazzled by her beauty and poise.

"Um, thank you..."

"Mrs. Eaton," she supplied.

"...Mrs. Eaton."

She gestured with a graceful opening of her hand. "Come in. Would you like some cookies and milk?"

He nodded and followed her and Timothy down the long hall and into a spacious kitchen. The sun slanted through large south-facing windows at the far end, where a small round table and four chairs were arranged. A central granite-topped island offered two wooden stools on which she motioned they should sit.

As they perched, she brought two large brown ceramic jars over. "We have chocolate chip and oatmeal," she said. And while placing saucers and pouring two tall glasses of milk, she asked, "How was school?"

"Fine," Duncan said.

"Good," Timothy said.

She smiled and said to Duncan, "Timothy has said a lot about you. I'm glad you came over."

"Uh-huh," Duncan said, wondering what a lot was.

It seemed she was about to say more for a moment, but it passed, and she gently said to Timothy, "Your father got home early today. He's in the den, so no more yelling, OK?"

"OK, Mom."

She left. The boys munched and slurped, getting more crumbs on the counter than on their plates.

"Your mom's nice."

"Yeah."

As Duncan finished his fourth chocolate chip cookie, and Timothy deliberately made another milk mustache, Mrs. Eaton breezed in and said, "So, are there any cookies left, or am I going to have to bake more?"

Duncan felt a spasm of guilt and leaned forward to look in the jars, but she laughed and waved his concern away. "I didn't give even voracious cookie eaters like you two enough time for that."

Duncan relaxed. Timothy erased his mustache with a red napkin.

"Duncan, Mr. Eaton would like to see you. Timothy, why don't you go to your room, I'll send him up in a minute. Won't be long."

The boys looked at each other.

"OK," Timothy said and dismounted.

He followed her down the hall and through the living room, furnished in mid-century modern. And then down another short hallway, she motioned him forward and said, "No need to be nervous; Gregory just wants to meet Timothy's new friend."

They came to a closed door, and she knocked. "Darling?"

"Come in," a voice answered.

The opened door revealed a man with wavy black hair sitting behind the coolest desk Duncan had ever seen. The walnut top seemed to float above the drawers, all thin lines and unusual angles. Scattered about its surface were huge sheets of graph paper filled with diagrams, numbers, arrows, and other symbols Duncan didn't understand. The wall behind the man was floor-to-ceiling bookshelves filled with hundreds of books, large and small.

A side table supported a large, strange typewriter with a silver ball where the typing arms should have been. A leather recliner was in one corner, and tall, narrow lamps with amber shades occupied opposite corners. A thick beige carpet covered the floor.

"Duncan, this is Mr. Eaton."

The man smiled, rose, and came around the desk. He wore gray slacks and a white dress shirt with thin, pink stripes.

"Hello, Duncan."

"Hello."

"Elizabeth and I are very glad to meet you. Timothy has talked about little else; he even seems to think that you can walk on water."

Mr. and Mrs. Eaton chuckled.

Baffled, Duncan flicked his eyes back and forth between the two, looking for a clue. Then he scratched his head, ventured, "Ummm, I do like to swim and surf."

That elicited outright laughter. Duncan felt like he had got the answer wrong on Truth or Consequences. Perhaps his expression cut their laughter short.

"It's OK, Duncan, poor reference on my part," Mr. Eaton said. Then to Mrs. Eaton, "Would you give us a minute?"

She nodded and began to leave but turned to Duncan and suddenly bent over, giving him a quick hug. Her smell was that of morning flowers with a tang of hairspray. The graze of her cheek felt like fine linen, and her hair tickled his face. Then she was gone, and the door closed. He turned to face the father.

"Please, have a seat. We don't mean to make you nervous."

He took the chair at the end of the desk opposite the typewriter. Mr. Eaton sat on his own, a plush leather high-back.

"I just wanted to thank you for what you did for Timothy."

Not knowing what else to say, he said, "You're welcome."

He pointed loosely in the direction of Duncan's face. "Are all those marks and bruises from your fight with…"

"Chuck," Duncan said.

"…yes, Chuck?"

"Yes, sir."

The man nodded. "Timothy said you stopped Chuck's attack on him and gave the boy a severe beating. Is that right?"

Duncan squirmed as he reached for an answer. He remembered that black snake inside striking and striking and striking as if he could do so, wanted to do so, forever. He looked down between his shoes, pressed his lips together, and, like a confession, said, "Yes, sir."

A long moment passed, and Duncan kept his eyes down.

"I'm glad you did. Thank you for defending my son. Timothy says that Chuck is a big, mean kid. You were brave."

He did not know why it embarrassed him to be called brave by Mr. Eaton when the praise of his peers had not. Duncan nodded but felt that they were only speaking half of the truth.

"Timothy was rather vague about the attack you stopped. Would you tell me what Chuck was doing?"

Duncan pulled a deep breath and looked into the father's eyes. "No, sir."

The man lifted his eyebrows and straightened in his chair. "No?"

"No, sir."

Mr. Eaton pivoted away and seemed to ponder the response, then said, "I see. I won't press."

The man drummed the fingers of one hand on his lips, thinking, "Do you think that boy will bother Timothy again?"

Duncan thought for a while and then said, "I don't know. He's been gone all week. I guess not."

"We don't expect you to be Timothy's bodyguard. Boys should fight their own battles, but Timothy is not built for that. He's much tougher than he looks, but fighting may not be his strength."

Despite his fight with Chuck, Duncan suspected he wasn't built for it either.

"My son thinks the world of you; you're his hero. I wanted to speak with you, thank you, but also get an idea of what kind of boy you are. You don't seem proud or too happy to have beaten Chuck. That's good. The nonviolent at heart are uneasy with violence. I don't mean to grill you. Elizabeth and I are grateful you were there to protect him. You're welcome in our home, and I promise," he laughed, "no more tough talks with the dad. OK?"

An easy smile lifted Duncan's face. "OK."

"Timothy is probably wondering what's happening. Why don't you go find him." The man rose and showed him to the door, quickly giving the boy's shoulder an affectionate squeeze. "Have fun, I'll see you later, son."

He found Mrs. Eaton in the kitchen sweeping crumbs off the island. She smiled. "He's upstairs in his room."

It was easy to find Timothy's room; he just followed the sounds." Oooonnnm Oooonnnm ta ta ta ta ta ta." For a moment, he watched Timothy run around his large bedroom with a World War II fighter plane in each hand, zigging and zagging dogfight style. The plane with the cross on it spiraled into the kid's pillow. "Zuhroommm, Zuhroommm. Ka Ka Ka Ka Boommmm. Puh Kuh."

"Got him," Duncan said.

Timothy turned shining eyes on Duncan. "Yeah, the Fokker 109 is no match for the Spitfire."

"Let me see."

Timothy handed the planes over. They were finely done models over half a foot long, decals perfectly applied, and even had tail numbers.

"Cool," Duncan said.

"Let's box."

He pulled out the Rock 'em Sock 'em Robots' box from under his bed. "Do you want to be the Red Rocker or the Blue Bomber?"

"Blue Bomber."

The boys blasted away at each other's robots for over half an hour, thumbs smacking buttons, little hands jerking their fighter this way and that, going for the knockout. Each time one of the heads popped up, they screamed, "You knocked my block off!" and laughed.

Mattel should have been there shooting a commercial. They lost count of who was ahead after ten minutes. Timothy had to pee, and Duncan wandered around his room while he was out. It was nearly three times as large as Duncan's and a wonderland full of cool stuff. Shelves next to an ash desk held models Timothy must have assembled: Frankenstein, a destroyer, a submarine, the Creature from the Black Lagoon, a red Corvette convertible, plus a dozen books.

A mobile of fighter planes, prop and jets, wobbled in the faint air currents from a fishing line hanging in the center of the room. Copies of *Boy's Life* magazine, a *National Geographic*, and a black microscope were on the desk. A wall opposite the end of the bed was decorated with a poster for the film *A Hard Day's Night,* with the Fab Four's eyes peering out from under heaps of mop-top hair. A stack of comics occupied one corner.

Under the bed were a Lionel train set, two G.I. Joe dolls, a T-shirt, socks and two pairs of underwear.

When Timothy returned, Duncan was busy trying to draw mountains with the boy's Etch-a-Sketch.

"Whatcha drawing?"

He showed him and said, "This is neat."

Timothy showed Duncan stuff under the microscope: hair, spit and a fly. The fly was the coolest and creepiest thing—even uglier close-up.

Duncan picked up a book, asked, "What's Al geb rah?"

"Algebra," Timothy said. "It's math for finding out a number you don't know yet."

"Huh?"

He wrote: 7 x X= 77

Then added: 7/7 x X= 77/7 = 11, x = 11.

"Neat," Duncan said.

He picked up another book. "What's Elementary Fi six?"

"Physics, not sure. Dad says it's about the rules for how the universe works. Atoms, gravity, light and other stuff."

Duncan thumbed through the book and said, "You're so smart."

"I'm a dweeb. Most kids don't like dweebs."

"I like smart."

Another book Duncan picked up was titled *The Solar System*, and his eyes lit up. "I like astronomy. Do you, too?"

"Oh, yeah, but I just got that."

"Did you know that Jupiter is so huge it could hold a thousand Earths?" Duncan gushed.

"Wow."

"And that the sun is much, much bigger; it could hold a thousand Jupiters?"

"Really?"

'Yeah. I want to go to the stars."

"C'mon, see what Dad just got me."

Timothy took him downstairs to the empty kitchen and through a garage door. He flipped the light on. A gray tarp covered a lump as tall as Timothy in a corner. With a bit of a showman's flourish, he flung the tarp off and onto the floor. A long white tube attached to a gray metal pedestal pointed at the roof.

Duncan goggled. "You got a telescope!?" His astonishment could not have been greater if Timothy had revealed a million dollars or a speedboat.

Duncan was all over it, inspecting the tube and the heavy gray steel pedestal with three horizontal legs. He removed a shower cap imprinted Palomar Junior from the top end of the tube. "Hey, there's no lens."

"I know, it's a reflecting telescope. Look inside."

Duncan saw his face magnified in a mirror at the far end of the three-foot-long tube. "Oh, how do you look through it?"

Timothy pointed at the blunt, black eyepiece tube jutting off the top end and explained. Then he said, "I've only used it once. Maybe we could look at the stars with it together."

He may as well have been asked whether he wanted to take Timothy's spaceship to Mars.

After that, they flitted from wonder to wonder around Timothy's home. In the large, recently mown backyard, they played catch. He saw Mr. and Mrs. Eaton standing at the kitchen window, warmly smiling and chatting as they watched them play. Too soon, it was time to leave. Mrs. Eaton and Timothy walked him to the door, said goodbye and waved as he reluctantly pedaled for home.

23

The next afternoon four boys walked under the rusty old trestle that occasionally still felt the rumble of a slow-moving train. They padded down the slope of warm sand in their sneakers and flip-flops. On their left was the full river, engaged in its perpetual process of self-annihilation as it poured into the greater waters of Monterey Bay. On the right was the Wild Mouse ride, which Duncan found scarier than the Giant Dipper. The high, narrow tracks were perched on uprights seemingly too spindly for the job. The ride's sharp turns and plunges, which usually elicited screams, were quiet and felt almost lonely on that off-season weekend. The boys barely spared it a glance.

The river was bounded on the opposite side with modest white cliffs topped with rough green bushes, like decorative frosting on the edge of an angel food cake. Several houses rose above the frosting with big windows offering spectacular views of the Boardwalk, the Fisherman's Wharf a mile away, and the broad, sparkling bay. The cliff dwindled to a finger of sandstone that jutted into the water when the tide was high. Ahead, the boys could hear the squeals and cries, the whoops, the hollers and murmurs of the crowd of other kids playing among the waves.

These human sounds floated and danced over the deeper rhythmic booms and roars of waves exhausting themselves, like the billions before them, upon the obstinate shore.

As the boys walked up a rise of sand that marked the beginning of Rivermouth proper, they heard the soothing fizz and sighs of sea-soap bubbles popping in their millions.

No one spoke for a while; it was all too beautiful, too exhilarating, all too much theirs to spoil it with words.

Rivermouth, in those days, opened into a broad fan of soft sand extending under the water and beyond the promontory. Those wanting to ride waves or splash around in the foamy swash could stand in waters no higher than their chest.

Duncan glanced at Timothy and his hanging jaw with some concern. The surf was bigger than usual, maybe larger than Timothy himself. Was this too much for the small boy his first time out? He relaxed when he noticed his friend didn't look afraid but instead like a boy on Christmas morning, finding the tree surrounded by presents.

"Woo-hoo," Randy cried. "Let's get out there."

They dumped shirts and shoes at an open spot of dry sand near the water. Timothy was the only one in proper swimming trunks, blue with white stripes on the side. The others wore faded-nearly-to-white cutoff jeans. Duncan had worn his last summer, and the zipper would barely budge from the salt and sand encrusting it.

Alan was twelve, two years older than the other boys, but he could easily have passed for fourteen. He was in the lead as the four ran, splashing into the churning and receding waters. Timothy stopped just before they were about to dive and swim out the rest of the way.

"Come on," Duncan said.

"I want to watch you do it first."

"Sure, OK." He scoped the current waves and saw they were smaller than before. "Look for the next set, OK?" Duncan and Randy had explained some of the basics of bodysurfing and how sets of bigger waves would arrive sporadically.

Timothy nodded, and Duncan was off, swimming fast behind Alan and Randy.

Rivermouth was a mob of kids mixed in with a smattering of adults. Each lightly bounced on their feet as the water rose and fell. They would be standing in waist-high waters one moment, then treading up to their necks the next. They'd dive under one oncoming wave but then have to sprint-swim to catch the one after.

A continual flux of bodies raced upriver at the front of a rolling mass of white water, passing those walking and swimming out to return for another ride.

During good sets, excited chatter tinkled among the crowd, and kids exulted at boss rides taken or moaned about great waves missed. The boys laughed at lame newbie surfers and dramatized spectacular collisions avoided.

It got quieter between sets; everyone waited, bobbed, and searched the distance for an oncoming swell that promised a rush. Then cries of "Outside, Outside!" would erupt, and the experienced would jockey for position to fly down the face of the wave.

Duncan loved this. He loved gauging the approaching swell for its height and its rideability. He loved how the water rushed away from the shore to build the wave higher and higher. He loved how the sand under his feet streamed past with that flow, carving pockets. He loved the strength in his legs as he resisted the rushing liquid mass. He loved the anticipation as the wave rose behind him. He loved timing his spring forward perfectly in sync to merge with the incredible power in that wave to sometimes fall, sometimes glide down its face, but always to be there as it collapsed in an explosion of ecstasy, enveloping him in the boiling white and salty churn, with him kicking as hard as he could, arms pressed tightly to his sides and cupping his chest and belly with his arms so that he got the longest ride possible.

Just when he wondered when Timothy would finally decide to come in, he found his new friend swimming beside him.

"Hey."

Duncan smiled and said, "Hey, 'bout time."

Timothy grinned. "Yeah."

Duncan checked the oncoming swells and spit some surf from his mouth. They paddled up and over an unworthy wave. "You ready?"

"Very."

The wave came, not the biggest, but solid. Duncan said, "Remember to push off hard and…"

"I know what to do."

They sprang and swam side-by-side and were lifted, dropped, and pushed before the swash. Duncan heard Timothy yelling as they milked every bit of energy out of that wave until they stopped together in knee-high water.

"You did great," Duncan said. "You've never bodysurfed before?"

"No. I was watching how you did it."

The boys had many rides, sometimes together, usually alone. It was a fine day, and the surfing was near-perfect. No board surfers were permitted in the afternoons at Rivermouth, so only bodysurfers and a few others with Styrofoam belly boards or inner tubes were there.

As Timothy finished another long ride, Duncan and the Kelly brothers waited for the next wave. He sprang up from the whitewater, arms high overhead, and hollered, "Woo! Woo! Woo!" Then he ran back with the receding foam until it was deep enough to swim, dove in, and swam to his new friends with apparent perfect form, like an Olympic athlete. He dog-paddled when he reached the others, said, "Man! This is the best. I've never had such fun. Let's surf all day." His face shone, and he looked even younger than before.

"You took long enough to get in," Alan said. "Were you scared?"

Without a crack in the radiance of his joy, Timothy said, "Yeah, I was really scared. I'm a good swimmer, but I have always been in a pool or lake; I've splashed around here but never tried to surf before. They looked huge to me. Wow, I rode a wave!" He said it like he was announcing his landing on the moon. And he made a face like Costello running into Frankenstein in a dimly lit house. He waved his arms. "Maybe I'd drown or look stupid and have to be rescued." He brushed wet hair off his forehead and giggled.

The mouths of his friends popped open. Part of the unspoken code of boyhood masculinity was that you never admitted fear. You might feel it, might even look like you were, and your friends might, might understand that something was scary, but admit it, proclaim it? Uh-uh.

Yet, Timothy's effusive honesty made Duncan feel warm in the cold ocean waters. He smiled and laughed, too, but cast a wary glance at Alan. What would he do with this presentation of Timothy's tender belly? Was a rapier put-down coming? He feared that he would have to defend Timothy against Alan, but he knew without a doubt that no amount of rage would enable him to win.

But Alan surprised him. Instead of narrowing his eyes, which signaled the drawing of a blade, Alan laughed and smiled, too, saying, "You're amazing; you do this like you've done it forever."

"Yeah," Randy said. "No one would ever know you're a newbie."

The brothers glowed and laughed as Timothy splashed and giggled.

"Outside," Randy said.

Heads whipped around. Alan reached, put a hand on Timothy's head, said, "Beat you to it, pipsqueak," and pushed him under before swimming away.

Timothy came up sputtering and laughing and then quickly joined the others seeking positions.

A few more waves were caught, but such cold waters eventually overcome even the blazing metabolisms of ten-year-olds.

Duncan shivered. "I'm going in,"

The others echoed, "Me too."

Timothy splashed Alan, said, "Last one in is a dweeb,"

They grabbed a wave and swam hard; Randy was christened the dweeb.

24

The early morning air was crisp and sweet. Dozens of subtle scents—Jeffrey pine, Bricklebush, cedar, mint, sage, wet lawns, rich earth, clematis and wild cilantro—wafted along invisible currents like a perfume goddess had blessed the town.

Duncan was on his regular three-mile cruise to school that Monday. His orange book bag was strapped to the handlebars. He wore a light gray jacket over a pale blue shirt. His sneakers pushed the pedals in a quick and steady rhythm driven by a body that felt good and strong after a weekend spent climbing, bodysurfing, biking and walking for miles along beaches and streets.

Under that grand Avenue of Trees, he flashed down the narrow curving road that exits DeLaveaga Park. At the hard right turn for Branciforte, he braked just enough, took the turn in a low lean, and rode the controlled slide so that his rear tire flung dirt and dead leaves across the street.

"Yeah!" he said, pumping a fist to the sky.

He resumed his easy, slow ride down Branciforte and thought how surprising Timothy was. Away from school, the quiet little nerd was a totally different kid—confident and spontaneous. He talked and talked and talked but was always entertaining and interesting.

It was the interesting bit that was so interesting. One moment Timothy could be acting like the monster with carrot sticks up his nose; the next he was telling Duncan why and how an apple fell to the ground. The boy actually liked math. Duncan didn't, but Timothy's view and enthusiasm about math and science somehow opened the door to another world.

It helped, too, that the boy loved hearing about Duncan's obsession with astronomy. When he had finished waving his arms to illustrate how far a light year was, Timothy gushed poetry about the gap between an electron and a nucleus.

Before he had left on Saturday, they went to his backyard to play catch. Between baseball tosses, Timothy's vivid explanations enabled Duncan to see the third player in the game. His name was gravity, and he was bending their throws into arcs.

Why that was so fun and cool to Duncan would have been hard for him to explain. When they had returned from looking at the telescope, he had been flabbergasted to see a portrait of Timothy on the wall.

"Is that you?" Duncan had asked.

"Yeah, Mom painted it."

He lightly touched the textured surface. The boy on the canvas was a lot younger, maybe seven. He was leaning against a tree with tall golden grass behind him and, behind that, a river. The slightest of smiles showed on his lips.

"Your mom did this?"

"Yeah, she paints all kinds of things, people, plants, the ocean."

He took Duncan to what he called her studio, a bedroom-sized cluttered room behind the garage at the back of the house. Through white-painted French doors, there was access to a small brick patio that offered a view of the yard and the town beyond.

Timothy had moved to Santa Cruz not long after Duncan had. Before, they had lived in a place called Santa Clara. His mom began painting before Timothy had been born. His dad worked for a company called IBM at their Advanced Research Center. It sounded neat and mysterious, and Timothy tried to explain what Mr. Eaton did—he exuded such pride—but all Duncan understood was that it had something to do with something called data and machines that added and subtracted faster than people.

Timothy had said, "Dad says one day machines will be able to think."

"What? Like a car will think?"

"I don't know, but I believe Dad."

Mr. Eaton still worked there, but they had moved to Santa Cruz because Mrs. Eaton wanted to be close to the ocean. Maybe that was a small part of the bond Duncan felt with Timothy. The boy had grown up over the hill, as he referred to Santa Clara. He had friends there; then suddenly he was in a new town, and his friends could have been as far away as Morehead was to Duncan.

The Eaton's were an affectionate family. Timothy got frequent hugs from his mother, who might pick him up and kiss him on the cheek. He would laugh joyfully and run into his father's arms when the man got home from the long commute over the hill.

Their goodbyes and hellos to each other sometimes embarrassed Duncan: I love you, Mom! I love you, Dad! How's my beautiful boy? Be safe out there, my fine son.

It could have sounded saccharine; it could have seemed affected. But it wasn't. Their expressions erupted naturally and quickly, and they were not lingered over or milked.

And Duncan wasn't excluded; he was always greeted warmly. Later, he would realize that it was precisely because their statements of love were so genuine that he squirmed.

All this turned over in his mind as he slowly rode down the long sidewalk leading to school, singing "A Hard Day's Night."

As he belted out, "...been barking like a dog," Duncan slammed to a stop. A teenage boy on a bike blocked his way.

"Hey, music boy. Where you going?"

He heard a bike screech rubber on the sidewalk behind him and turned to find Chuck Putnam on his banana bike.

He sucked in a sharp breath.

Chuck looked bad. His face was swollen and ugly, with extensive yellow and black bruises. His malicious gleam amplified his ugliness. But it was a surface thing. Beneath that, in the eyes, fear showed.

The teenager didn't look much like Chuck. He wasn't a ginger, and he wasn't fat. He had black wavy hair and wore a black leather jacket.

Ted. Crap.

"Don't even think of running," Ted said.

He was scared. Everything about the teenager was big: big shoulders, big head, big hands—even bigger than Alan. Duncan could barely think. His impulse was to dart off the walk into the street, but he knew he'd never make it. They were at an empty intersection just blocks from his school. A lone car passed, and he had an impulse to yell for help, but it seemed ridiculous.

"Get off the fucking bike."

He did and let it fall to the pavement. Ted and Chuck got off, too, but set their kickstands. He was trapped with this huge teenager in front and Chuck in back. He looked around for an adult.

Crap, crap, crap.

"You hurt my brother. Nobody hurts my brother, 'cept they pay." Ted advanced a step and then stopped. To Chuck, he said, "This is the kid who attacked you?"

He didn't hear a reply, but Chuck must have nodded.

"Really? You said he was bigger than you. He's smaller. Look at him, so scared he's shaking."

"He jumped me, didn't fight fair."

Outrage quelled Duncan's trembling. "That's a lie. I did not jump him."

Ted brought hard eyes back to Duncan. "If you didn't jump him, how could you have beaten Chuck?"

Asked that way, it did seem improbable. How could, how did he beat Chuck?

Before he could answer, Chuck said, "Just pound him. He cheated. He's crazy."

A flicker of annoyance crossed Ted's face. "How did you, little music boy, beat Chuck?"

Desperation was like a vice crushing his chest. He had to answer. He had to say something, maybe even what he wasn't supposed to. But if he didn't, he knew by the look in Ted's eyes that the beating he'd get would be bad, really bad. He tried to swallow and couldn't. He looked directly into Ted's scary eyes and blurted, "I was mad. He was hurting Timothy, my friend; he's a lot smaller than even me. He was hitting...."

"Wait, what?" and Ted looked past Duncan to his brother. "You didn't tell me any of that. Were you hurting his friend?"

"I didn't know he was his friend. It don't matter..."

"Shut up," Ted said, then to Duncan, "Go on."

"He was sitting on him and slapping him, laughing. Timothy was crying." He hesitated and swallowed that stone that wouldn't go down before. "He did something really awful, and I told him to stop. Then we fought."

"Look kid, I've got to get to school too. What supposedly awful thing do you say Chuck did that made you attack him?"

Duncan dropped his eyes. "I'm not supposed to say."

Ted moved a step closer. "Fuck. You better say, and you better say right now." Then his eyes narrowed as he tipped his head back. "Unless maybe you're lying."

It all gushed out: "I'm not lying! He hawked a loogie up and spit it into Timothy's mouth. He hit him in the balls and told him to swallow it."

Ted's face went slack, and his lips parted. He stared hard over Duncan's shoulder. "You did that?"

"I didn't punch his nuts; I just grabbed them."

Ted made a face as if sniffing sour milk and said, "You grabbed his nuts? You made him eat your snot? You little shit."

Ted moved close; Duncan flinched. Ted raised a placating hand and placed the other on Duncan's right shoulder.

"Look, I get it. You can't let someone do that to your friend." The big kid quickly scanned the area, leaned closer, said, "I would've done the same thing." In a blink, Ted's right fist slammed into Duncan's solar plexus.

He doubled over and fell to the ground, unable to breathe. His head and shoulders landed on a stretch of weedy, long grass, the rest of him on the sidewalk. He spastically opened and closed his mouth like a trout that had been flung into the bottom of a boat.

Ted crouched over him. "You're going to be OK; I just knocked the wind out of you. Try to relax; you'll be able to breathe soon."

Ted patted him, talking softly and gently while Duncan gasped for air.

"You see, I do get it. I don't blame you, but I promised my brother. We Putnam's stick together," then louder and directed away from the boy on the ground, "even when one of them is a total underhanded lying disgusting fuckhead."

Each gasp brought more air. His belly hurt, but he could breathe a little.

"That punch is the only price you'll pay for beating Chuck. He's not going to do anything to you, not bother you, not say a fucking thing to you." Then louder, "Right, Chuck?"

Duncan did not hear an answer.

"He's going to leave you alone. You're going to leave him alone. Right?"

He nodded and managed to say, "Yes, and Timothy and Randy."

"What?"

"Timothy. Randy. Leave them alone."

Ted laughed. "Yeah, yeah." Then to Chuck, "You're going to leave his friends alone too, right Chuck?"

The answer was a mumble.

Ted shouted, "What?"

"Yeah, yeah, OK."

"One last thing," Ted said as if warning him of impending vomiting, "Chuck gets to hit you."

To his brother: "C'mere, you get to kick him once. Just once. Hurry up."

Duncan couldn't see Chuck but heard him approach from directly behind. He tensed and cupped his hands over his genitals.

"Hurry up,"

He was breathing easier but now held his breath. The kick came. It was just a tap on his butt. He barely felt it.

"OK," Ted said. He helped Duncan up, guided him to his bike and lifted it for him. Duncan shakily mounted the seat and grabbed the handlebars for support. Chuck had returned to his bike and stared across the street.

"Chuck," Ted called, "ride with me, and hurry the fuck up. I don't want to be late again."

Chuck pedaled past but didn't look at Duncan, who stared at his school in the distance. Just before Ted rode off, he looked at the immobile Duncan, frowned, and said, "Sorry, kid."

As the two Putnam boys rode down Keystone Avenue, he heard Ted say, "I should've punched you, not him. You never hit a guy in the balls. Never."

25

December 1964

"You want to see something neat?" Duncan asked.

Timothy was carefully placing a blue Ford Thunderbird across the railroad tracks. He looked up, said, "Yeah."

Duncan put his hand on the transformer, ready to twist the knob and send 10,000 tons of locomotive steel on its way to a collision with destiny.

"Let's do two," Timothy said.

"Yeah, better."

Timothy positioned a gaudy green Chevy Impala next to the Thunderbird and faced it the opposite way on the road crossing the tracks.

"In the Impala we have the Jamison family. Mr. Jamison has stopped to talk with..." Timothy hesitated.

"Buck," Duncan supplied, "his buddy from work."

"Little did they know," Timothy continued, "that the old tracks, which haven't seen a train in years, have just been reopened."

Duncan turned the knob a notch, and the Lionel locomotive plus three coal cars, four boxcars, two oil cars and a caboose began to move.

Timothy continued to narrate:

"The Jamison kids start yelling and fighting.

"Mrs. Jamison tells them to shut up.

"Buck tells Mr. Jamison that Unitas will take the Colts all the way."

Two curves away from the intersection, Duncan cranked the knob full over, and the train accelerated.

Timothy:

"'He started it,' little Bobby says."

"No, you started it, big brother Timothy says."

"You're putting yourself in the car?" Duncan asked.

Timothy shrugged. "I will miraculously survive."

Timothy: "Their little sister pukes, throws a doll at the battling brothers and begins to cry.

"Mrs. Jamison yells for the kids to shut up.

"Mr. Jamison ignores his squabbling family and tells Buck that Jim Brown is the greatest running back ever."

Duncan: "The huge train is flying at 100 miles per hour. Nothing can stop it. The conductor blasts the horn."

Timothy: "Oh no, no one can hear it over the screaming of the Jamison kids."

Duncan: "The train is coming around the final turn."

Timothy: "Mrs. Jamison yells, 'Ralph, a train is coming!'

"'Oh no!' says Ralph."

"'Oh no!' says Buck."

"The kids scream louder. Both men try to start their cars.

"'I'm out of gas,' yells Ralph.

"'I am too!' yells Buck.

"Everyone screams; everyone tries to get out of the cars, but they can't; the doors are stuck."

Duncan: "The conductor sees the cars across the tracks and blasts the horn again and again."

Timothy: "Everyone is screaming and pounding on the windows."

"Boom!" the boys shouted as the Lionel #49 smashed both metal cars off the track and into the wall.

"Great one," Timothy said, and they dissolved into laughter.

"Hey," Timothy said after he recovered. "Want to do a school bus this time?"

"Maybe when we get back. I want to show you something."

"OK, what is it?"

"It's a surprise."

On that brisk December day, the trees outside Timothy's bedroom window waved wildly from the blustery wind. Low gray clouds scudded across the sky. It had rained heavily the night before. The boys left the debris of a morning spent playing scattered about the room, gathered their clothes and bounded down the stairs.

Mrs. Eaton was on the couch in the living room reading a book, legs curled up on the cushions. As they ran for the front door, Timothy called, "Going out, Mom."

"OK," she said. "Do you have your coat?"

"Yes, Mom."

Outside, they got on Duncan's bike and headed down the hill.

"How did you survive the wreck?"

"It was a miracle."

"What kind of miracle?"

"The miracle kind."

Duncan scoffed and laughed as he turned onto Branciforte. The trees dripped from the storm, and yellow leaves were scattered over the street and yards.

"How come you don't have a bike?" Duncan asked. "You have everything else."

"I did; it got stolen."

"Oh. Bummer."

"It wasn't a cool bike like yours. Dad says he'll get me one of those soon."

"We'll be able to ride together; that'll be so great."

After the end of Branciforte, they rode to the beginning of the steep hill and decided to walk up. They remounted, rode a little way, and then Duncan said, "Close your eyes until I say open them, OK?"

"How come?"

"Be a better surprise."

"OK."

Timothy leaned forward, put his head between Duncan's shoulders and hugged him. The twisty road exited the cover of the thick canopy, and Duncan took a right down the short road he'd visited several times before and stopped.

"All right, open your eyes."

After a moment, Timothy said, "Wow, those are..."

"Tanks," Duncan said.

A car passed on the main road, heading into the park. They got off the bike, walked up to the chain-link fence, and put their fingers through the links.

"They're huge," Timothy said.

"Look at the size of those guns."

"Come on," said Duncan, and he led the other boy around to the far side of the enclosure past trees and out of sight of the road, where they could see all six of the behemoths.

"Look at those tracks. I wonder how much they weigh."

"Let's go in and see if we can get inside one," Duncan said.

"What? Is it open?"

"Naw, but we can climb the fence."

Timothy looked up at the seven-foot-high fencing, then left and right and could see that the trees and thick brush entirely hid them.

"But the sign says keep out and no trespassing."

"So, no one's around. We can be in and out in no time."

Timothy turned a baffled face to Duncan, said, "You want to break into an army base?"

"National Guard, not Army. Anyway, it's not a base; they just store them here. We wouldn't hurt anything."

"Uh."

Misunderstanding Timothy's hesitation, Duncan said, "It won't be hard to get in. I'll throw my coat over the top so we don't scrape ourselves. Easy. I'll go first."

Timothy's face flickered with emotion; he scuffed his feet back and forth in the short grass. Did he have to pee?

"Uh."

"What's the matter?"

"I can't do that."

"Why not?"

"It's wrong."

It was Duncan's turn to be perplexed. He examined the fencing and the beckoning tanks as if an answer lay there.

"I don't get it. We won't hurt anything."

"Mom said I would know whether I was doing the right thing if I wouldn't hesitate to tell her what I had done. I couldn't tell her I did this."

Duncan frowned. Anger rising, he said, "I don't tell my mom anything."

To which the other boy did not reply.

This was supposed to be a special adventure he had saved to do with Timothy. Now, it was spoiled. Wrong? What the hell? He wasn't going to break the tanks, just look at them. Angry, he said with a sneer, "So, what? Are you afraid?"

Timothy lifted a solemn face to him, said, "Yes, I am. I don't want my mom and dad to think I'm a bad kid."

Taken aback, Duncan could think of nothing to say for a while. He didn't think it was bad, but clearly Timothy did. Somehow, it just wouldn't be that fun if he went in by himself. He glanced at Timothy's earnest, waiting face and felt his anger and disappointment fade.

"Would it be wrong if we walked around the fence so we can see everything?" Then he added, "From outside?"

Timothy brightened. "That'd be great."

They spent half an hour caressing the machines with their eyes. Those monsters of war looked and felt exactly like what they were. Hard. Mean. Threatening. Powerful. They were thrilled by all of that.

On the way back, Timothy asked, "When can I come over to your house?"

Duncan hesitated, said, "My mom doesn't want any visitors."

"How come?"

Duncan struggled to reply. "I don't know."

"I wish I could. Would you ask her?"

Duncan thought some more. "Sure. She'll say no, though. We don't have a nice house like you do. I don't think she wants anyone to see it."

"Oh."

26

Mr. Eaton crouched at the telescope on a cold night. He repeatedly peeked through the finder scope, which was mounted on the side of the main telescope, then nudged the steel pedestal a little one way or the other. Then he peeked again.

Duncan and Timothy were wrapped in their coats and wore soft caps. They heard him say, "Almost." Nudge. "Uh-huh, almost." Nudge. "There!"

They were in Timothy's backyard. Behind them the windows of the house were darkened by heavy curtains. The neatly trimmed lawn sloped toward the back and toward the northwest. From that hill they could see the lights of a few distant houses that peeked above the redwood fence and utility shed. Above, the stars sparkled, and a crescent moon hovered over the western horizon, chasing the recently set sun.

Mr. Eaton plugged a long, heavy extension cord into one dangling from the telescope mount. Duncan heard a faint hum. He made a sound of satisfaction, rose, and said, "OK. It's ready. Come closer, boys, and I'll explain how to use it."

When they stopped before him, he continued, "You know that the Earth is a big ball spinning in space. And that is why the sun appears to rise and set, and the stars slowly move across the sky. The clock drive in the mount cancels that motion and keeps whatever you look at centered. That's where the humming sound is coming from, a motor that tracks the stars."

"Do you think we'll go to the moon?" Duncan asked.

Mr. Eaton scratched his chin, said, "Well, if we can keep our rockets from blowing up, I think so. The president has committed us to do so, but it is a great and difficult mission; it is probably the greatest undertaking in human history. But look, I want you to understand that with all this talk of going into space, don't forget that you are in space. The Earth is like our spaceship, and it is moving very fast."

"It is?" asked Timothy.

"Yep. We are spinning in," he pointed east, "that direction at a thousand miles an hour."

The boys' jaws dropped.

"And the whole earth is moving around the sun in the same direction at almost 70,000 miles an hour."

Duncan's face scrunched up. "I don't feel like I'm moving."

"That's because we are moving with the Earth. I would even say it is truer that we are the Earth."

"We are the Earth," Duncan repeated. He looked up at the stars and tried to imagine moving at such fantastic speeds.

"I'm going inside for a while. As I said before, let your eyes get dark-adapted. You should look at the moon first before it sets."

Mr. Eaton pointed at a small table. "There are the binoculars; don't drop them. Look around with them first. When you find something interesting, try looking at it with the telescope." He turned on a flashlight that glowed dull red from the cellophane rubber-banded to its lens. "This will let you see without destroying your night vision."

When Mr. Eaton reached the back door, Timothy called, "Thanks, Dad! Love you!"

"Love you too, son." He went inside, and they were alone.

"Let's look at the moon," Timothy said. He moved the telescope such that it appeared to roll over in the odd way it had while moving along axes that mirrored the Earth's. Timothy looked, and Duncan could see the tiny image of the moon reflecting off his right eye.

When his turn came, he gazed through the eyepiece and was instantly absorbed in another world, one where the harsh light of the sun slanted low across thrusting mountains in high relief that cast long shadows across gray-white plains. The scene wavered in the scope but was mostly clear and crisp.

Through the binoculars Duncan saw stars beyond number, much more than he could see with just his eyes. Along the Milky Way the stars were as thick as scattered glitter, and he wondered how far away it all was.

They took turns, and their wonder was so great that their conversation became simple:

"Wow, look at this."

"Look at this."

"What is that?"

"To the left of that bright star."

Mr. Eaton returned and showed them the Pleiades, a star cluster that dazzled like blue diamonds scattered on black velvet. He showed them the Orion nebula, with its wispy gray light and bright center, where he said stars were being born as they watched. Next, he showed a broad smudge of light that he said was the Andromeda Galaxy, so bright in the middle that it spread faintly out to fill the entire view.

"It's a galaxy like our own," he said. "It contains hundreds of billions of stars."

Duncan hung on every word Timothy's father uttered. His eyes drank in every image with such thirst that the light felt like nutrients to his soul.

"How far is all this? How far does it go?" Duncan asked.

"Hundreds, thousands, millions of light years," he answered.

"But where does it end?"

"It is infinite."

"What is infinite?"

"There is no end. It goes on and on and on forever."

For a long time Duncan said nothing. He passed on looking through the telescope, choosing instead the binoculars so he could scan the sky, like looking through great magnifying windows to the heavens beyond.

He lay on the grass, disregarding the cold ground that penetrated his back.

This never ends.

Then he stood up and scanned the sky, soaking in the vast vision and was surprised to feel the brimming wetness of his eyes.

Beautiful.

As if Mr. Eaton sensed Duncan's emotion, he rested a gentle hand on his shoulder and said, "I call it glory."

Without a further word, Mr. Eaton went inside. Timothy called him over to see the double cluster in Perseus.

In hushed tones, the two boys discussed stars, planets and galaxies. Timothy explained the setting circles on the mount, how right ascension and declination were like latitude and longitude on the Earth and why they needed a finder scope to locate objects in the sky.

Soon, they grew tired and lay back on the lawn, creating their own constellations.

"That looks like a snake," Duncan said, pointing.

"Yeah, and that's Donald Duck."

"Donald Duck?"

"Yeah, see the bill and the big feet?"

"No."

"That's an ice cream cone."

A shooting star flashed across the speckled dome.

"Ooooh," they both said.

"That's Doctor Doom," Timothy said.

"That's Bugs Bunny," Duncan said.

"Where?"

"He's between the Silver Surfer and Doctor Doom. See," Duncan pointed, "he's small, but right there are his ears, and the line of stars above are his eyes."

"Oh, uh-huh."

"Do you think Bugs could outsmart Doctor Doom?" Duncan asked.

"Of course, Bugs can outsmart anybody."

"What's up, Doc Doom?"

They were laughing when Mrs. Eaton pushed back the sliding glass door and said, "Boys, come inside. It's time for bed."

"Can we stay out just a little longer?" Timothy asked.

"No, it's late. Come on."

As they slowly walked back to the house, Duncan said, "That was better than fun."

Timothy giggled. "Yeah, better than fun."

27

January 1965

The Saturday newspaper was spread out all over the kitchen table. It was mid-morning, and Duncan and Timothy were working their way through heaping bowls of chocolate and vanilla and strawberry ice cream while one searched for a movie.

"Here's one," Timothy said. "*Kitten with a Whip.*"

"Is that a Western?"

"Don't think so. It says *she's what they call a real smoky kitten... The kicks she digs... The swingers she runs with... and the guy she...*"

"Hey, ick, that sounds like a kissy pic."

"Yeah, look at the picture."

Duncan leaned over, pointed to a part of the ad, and wrinkled his nose. "Is he pulling her clothes off? Kissy pic! What's that one?"

"*The New Interns.*" Duncan sat back down to carve another chunk of chocolate delight out of the bowl.

Timothy continued, "*They save lives with a passion... And make love with abandon!*"

"Nooo. Aren't there any westerns?"

Timothy imitated Groucho Marx's bobbing eyebrows, said, "Well, there is the new James Bond movie, *Goldfinger.*"

Duncan leapt out of his chair and grabbed the paper. "What? It's out? Hey, you had your hand over the ad."

Timothy laughed and, with exaggerated seriousness, said, "Did I? I thought you'd want to see the kissy picture."

Duncan froze halfway to sitting back down in his chair. "You think I want to see kissy pictures?"

Timothy's eyes danced above his broad smile.

Duncan smiled and nodded. "You're just pulling my leg." Then he sat down, reached for the vanilla, and said, "Good one."

He heard the front door open, and Elizabeth said, "Of course you can borrow it, Alice; let me get it for you."

He whispered, "Will your mom let you see it?"

Timothy's eyes danced again, and with a trace of a smile, said, "Watch."

Elizabeth breezed into the kitchen, again looking perfect, in a knee-length white dress with black polka dots, followed by a white-haired woman in a dark blue calf-length dress. She was short and plump, with eyes that warmed when she saw the boys.

"Duncan, this is our neighbor, Mrs. King. Alice, this is Duncan, Timothy's friend."

"Hello, Duncan."

"Hello."

She glanced at the bowls and the half-empty cartons of ice cream. "I guess you boys like your ice cream, yes?"

Timothy and Duncan glanced at each other with tacit agreement about the odd questions adults tended to ask.

Elizabeth was searching for something in the cupboards. Over her shoulder, she said, "Have you found a movie you want to watch?"

"Maybe." Timothy turned his attention back to the paper. "There's *Kitten with a Whip*."

Bang. Clang. Boink.

"Or *The Farmer's Other Daughter*.

"*Kitten with a Whip? Farmer's...?*"

Mrs. King slowly turned a puzzled face upon the boy.

"Says *she's dirt poor and needs money. It's got the right kind of action...in the barn... in the bedroom... In...*"

Elizabeth ceased rummaging and whirled around, said, "Hold on there; let me see that." Her knitted brow matched Alice's.

As he pushed the paper toward his mother, he said, "Duncan says it looks like a kissy picture, but there aren't any westerns..."

As she shook her head and read, Timothy ventured, "There is a spy movie called *Goldfinger* at the Rio."

"Those other movies are not for you boys. *Goldfinger*?" She hesitated, searched the page for it, found it, and nodded. "Yes. Yes, much better you see that."

"OK, Mom." Then to Duncan, "Want to see that?"

"I wanted to see a Western, but that would be OK."

Alice King's eyes glinted with amusement, and then she looked down and pressed her lips together, repressing a smile.

Elizabeth Eaton returned to the cupboards and found what she was looking for. As she led Mrs. King out, she asked, "When is the show?"

"At three," Timothy replied.

"OK," she said.

The two women's chatter faded down the hall. Timothy dug a mass of blushing frozen milk out of his bowl, winked at Duncan, and filled his mouth with it.

28

Early June 1965

A creek ran through the woods that would become Harvey West Park. It burbled around red and gray stones, forming eddies where small silverfish twitched when Duncan and Timothy approached. The gully through which the water flowed was decorated with large, sheared boulders and Manzanita bushes with vivid green leaves and red bark. Rough forest slash covered the ground and added to the complex perfume of decaying leaves, drying branches, bark and the life-rich waters of the creek, which sparkled from sunlight penetrating through the waving leaves.

Duncan wore tan shorts and a green T-shirt, while Timothy wore his typical over-dressed-for-the-woods outfit of creased gray shorts and an ironed short-sleeved dress shirt.

Duncan lobbed a rock the size of his fist high into the air, and as it plunged into the pool, he narrated, "And a mountain falling from the sky destroys the fish civilization." A less than impressive plonk and splash was followed by a handful of stones Timothy threw into the ripples as he commented: "Meteors as big as skyscrapers finish off any survivors."

"Kuhspoosh. Kuhspoosh. Kuhspoosh," Duncan said.

They ran to the pool and found the fish were gone.

"Let's go eat," Timothy said.

They climbed up to a big flat rock where they'd left the lunch Elizabeth had made for them. Sitting side-by-side, their feet hanging over the rim and between bites, Duncan said, "We've got a whole great summer ahead. No more school."

"I like school."

Duncan gently pushed him. "That's why they call you a dweeb."

"Yeah." And he laughed.

"Soon they'll call me a dweeb, too, if I keep hanging out with you."

"They already do."

"They do not."

"Behind your back."

"Uh-uh."

Timothy grinned. "I guess not, not yet anyway."

They chuckled.

Duncan grabbed a stone and flung it hard at a distant tree. Timothy cheered the crack of impact, "Yeah, good shot!" Then, "I'm not coming back to Branciforte."

"What?"

"They're sending me to Twin Lakes Academy."

Duncan shook his head. "What? Why?"

"Because I'm bored. Dad says I need more challenges. It's for gifted kids." Timothy rolled his eyes.

"Damn." Duncan threw another rock at the same tree but missed; asked, "Where is it?"

"Off Seventh."

"Going to hang with all the other geniuses, huh?" He threw a stone at nothing.

"I'm not a genius."

Duncan gaped at him and laughed. "Shut up. Weren't you telling me about calculus last week? And I didn't get it. Soooo, you are too a genius. You're the smartest person I've ever met."

Timothy blushed.

"Except, maybe your dad."

"I don't want to be a genius; I want to be at your school."

Duncan closed his eyes and lifted his chin so the dappled sunlight could play on his face. He picked up a rock but dropped it. "You couldn't go to my school anyway."

"What do you mean?"

He stared at the stream for a while and said, "We're moving."

Timothy jumped up to face Duncan. "You can't move! You can't! Where are you going?"

"Ben Lomond."

"Ben Lomond? That's too far."

"Yeah, I hate that we're going."

Timothy's eyes shimmered. "But we're having so much fun. I'll never see you."

"Mom says we can come down on weekends."

Timothy sat. Neither boy spoke for a long time. They tossed stones and fiddled with twigs; then Timothy sighed and said, "You better."

They spent much of that afternoon exploring the woods. They looked under rotting logs and poked at the revealed bugs, chased quail, and got into a rock-throwing competition for distance, which Duncan won. They discovered a giant oak tree that they deemed worthy of climbing. Timothy called it the King of the Forest, and indeed it was. Its trunk was so fat that four boys with outstretched arms would be needed to surround it. Its long gracious branches, like the arms of a giant, extended in every direction.

They crawled up the leaning knobby trunk to the lowest limb. From there they worked their way higher and higher until they were at least thirty feet above the grassy floor. The limbs had gotten shorter and thinner, and soon it was a dizzying distance to the ground.

Timothy ascended higher and perched himself on a narrow limb. Duncan worried it might break. Clutching a few sprigs, Timothy declared, "You have to see this; I can see the ocean."

Duncan rose from his branch to join him, but a big black bug flew at his face just as he reached for the next limb. He flinched, slipped and fell but managed to grab the limb he'd been standing on, scraping his side as he dropped.

Timothy screamed his name. Duncan winced from his scraped ribs. He had snagged the branch with only one arm and reached for it with the other.

"Help."

Faster than Duncan could believe, his friend hopped down from branch to branch to branch like he was a bird. He stopped one up and studied what he could do.

Duncan looked down at a fall that now seemed like a mile. He looked up. "I've got to get my leg over the branch."

Timothy came down to lay extended on Duncan's branch, wrapped his legs around the limb and pressed his feet on the trunk. He reached an arm out, said, "Swing it, I'll catch it."

Duncan was on the edge of panic. His grip was poor; his side hurt, and a broken twig was gouging his triceps. Every time he moved, it dug deeper. "Shit, shit, ow. OK."

His first two attempts failed and scared him more because the effort made him swing wildly back and forth.

"Come on," Timothy said. "Almost."

"Don't let me knock you off."

"Just try again. I'll get you."

Timothy caught his foot on the fourth try and grunted as he helped get Duncan's leg over the limb. With much further straining, the two got Duncan close to the trunk and on top of the limb. Perched there and grasping a higher adjacent branch like he could crush it to powder, he whistled and said, "That was close."

Timothy stared intensely at Duncan, looked down and released a breath he seemed to have been holding. "Can you go down?"

Duncan relaxed his grip. "Hell yeah, let's get out of this tree."

Planting his sneakers on solid ground had never felt so good to Duncan. All the savage tension in his body faded as Timothy inspected his injuries.

"You ruined another shirt. Bad scrapes. You've got some blood here." He indicated his arm.

"I don't care. I'm not broken or dead."

Timothy only nodded.

"You saved me. You could've fallen helping me. I would've been really mad if you fell."

Timothy looked into his eyes, said, "We're friends, aren't we?"

Duncan smiled. "Yeah, friends. Let's go home."

They walked through tall green grass for a while, their feet carving a path, saying nothing. Then Timothy grabbed Duncan and wrapped his arms around him. His golden hair tickled Duncan's neck. "You're more than my friend," Timothy said, and after a few heartbeats, he whispered, "I love you, Duncan."

Duncan stilled and said nothing as the surprisingly fierce hug continued. Then Timothy relaxed his enveloping arms, lifted an earnest, hopeful face, and asked, "You love me, too, don't you?"

He frowned and blinked and tried to smile, but he could only manage, "Well, we're friends."

Those beautiful eyes searched his. "I know, but don't you love me?"

Duncan looked away and took a breath. "We're friends, best friends."

It was as if Duncan had slapped him. Timothy jerked a step back.

"You don't love me?"

He squirmed but could not answer, finding it hard to meet Timothy's gaze.

The smaller boy seemed to shrink visibly. Head down, he turned and walked away.

Duncan's feelings and thoughts roiled inside him. *Love, Timothy? I've never told anyone that I love them.* He couldn't recall anyone in his family saying "I love you" to him or anyone else either. He knew his dad did not love him. He supposed his mom did, but she never said it. He loved his sisters but certainly wouldn't say it to them. He loved Keith a lot, even though he tormented him sometimes. And he loved Nana. But he didn't say it, felt shy about ever saying it.

No one had ever hugged him quite like Timothy had, not even his mother or father. No one had looked at him with eyes like that, so open, so vulnerable, so willing to risk being crushed. He did not understand it.

He watched Timothy get smaller and smaller, the boy's head hanging like a cord had been snipped, about to reach the rarely used dirt road they had walked in on. He couldn't stand the feeling that he was hurting Timothy.

I can't lie about this. Do I love Timothy?

The boy disappeared past some trees lining the road. Duncan ran after him and caught him past the curve.

"Wait!" he called.

Timothy stopped and turned a sad, desolate face to him. For a few seconds Duncan could still not speak, and then he swallowed, said, "Yes, I love you."

The boy's face blazed like the birth of a new star. But the question lingered in his eyes.

"You do? Really?"

Duncan's face flickered with discomfort, but he shrugged and smiled, said, "Yeah, yes. Yeah, I do." He paused, adding, "But don't make me say it over and over."

Timothy laughed and hugged Duncan again in that fierce way. Duncan matched the boy's embrace.

"OK. OK. Enough, let's go home."

They strolled down the road for a while, and then Duncan said, "It's good you're going to a different school. If you blabbed this to anybody, I'd have to fight every boy and half the girls."

Timothy chuckled. "Maybe, but just the assholes."

"I don't want to fight anybody, so keep it to yourself, all right?"

Timothy sobered. "All right."

They continued, and near Encinal Timothy said, "You were sure clumsy falling off that branch." He glanced sidelong at Duncan.

"Clumsy? A big old bee flew in my eye."

"Yeah, yeah, blame it on the bug."

"But it did."

"Yeah, yeah." But Timothy was smiling broadly.

Duncan began to protest further, caught the look, snorted. "I'm easy, aren't I?"

"Yep."

29

July 1965

On that warm, sunny Sunday morning, Duncan sprayed gravel as he accelerated up the driveway from his home. He hit the asphalt, popped a wheelie and rode on just his rear tire for at least fifty feet. When he slammed the front wheel back onto the pavement, he stood on the pedals and cheered his new distance record. He wasn't on a leisurely ride like when he was going to school. No, he was eager to get to Timothy's house so they could spend the day at the beach and Boardwalk. To his surprise, Ava had given him five dollars for rides and the arcade. For once, he had money and did not have to feel like the poor boy hanging out with the rich kid.

To Duncan, Timothy was fantastically rich. He might as well have been a prince. His friend had enough toys and games to stock a store. One day, while looking through Timothy's *Sky and Telescope* magazine, he saw an ad for his telescope. It cost over $200.

His father drove a Mercedes, and his mother a Jaguar. Their house was like a palace to him. Although neither Timothy, his mother, nor his father had ever made him feel less worthy by word or deed, he was sometimes embarrassed and shy as he tried to hide the worn knees of his pants and the shabbiness of his shirts. They never seemed to notice, and he was always greeted with smiles. No one asked why Timothy could not visit Duncan's house.

And it wasn't just the house and cars and toys and the fine, modern furniture. The whole Eaton family was rich in intelligence and education. Yet here, too, he never felt condescension from them.

He raced through the park loudly singing as he liked to do whenever alone. Today, it was a medley of "Satisfaction," "King of the Road," and "Hey, Mr. Tambourine Man."

He turned for Timothy's street while imitating Mick Jagger flapping his lips. He sped up the hill, spied Mrs. King in her flower garden, and waved to her, but she was busy greeting another old woman who was giving her a hug, and she didn't wave back.

Unusually, parked cars lined both sides of the street outside the Eaton's. He would have raced up the driveway, except it was jammed with vehicles he didn't recognize. He dismounted at the curb and carefully threaded his bike between them, leaving it in front of the garage.

Excitedly, he bounded up the few steps and banged on the door. All was quiet for a while, and he was about to knock again when someone said from behind the door, "No, no, I'll get it."

The door opened, and a woman stood there in tawny, wrinkled slacks and a blue blouse. It took him a moment to recognize Mrs. Eaton. Her hair was mussed, and her skin blotchy; she wore no makeup.

He ignored the oddity of seeing her so disheveled. "Hi, Mrs. Eaton," he said with a smile.

She didn't return the smile. It was as if she looked through and past him without a trace of recognition. Then she appeared to focus, frowned, asked, "What are you doing here?"

"Well, Timothy and I are going to the Boardwalk today..." he felt compelled to add, "...and Mom gave me five dollars."

She did not answer immediately, and Duncan wondered if she had forgotten. He heard an odd tapping sound and saw that her jaw trembled. She took a long, deep breath like she was desperate for oxygen, looking everywhere except at him. Alarmed and confused, he saw her swallow, and in a voice that was barely a whisper, he thought she said,

"I can't."

Her eyes seemed to search the porch awning, the door molding, the sky beyond and almost anything but Duncan's face.

Each time louder, she repeated,

"I can't,"

"I can't,

"I can't."

Then she called, "John! John!"

Timothy's uncle came running down the hall. "What is it, Liz? What?" And he looked down at the boy as she said, "It's... Duncan." She looked at her brother with eyes both empty and beseeching. "I just can't."

Elizabeth walked away without looking back. Mr. Baker released a breath like the last exhalation of an old balloon. In a drawn face, the man's eyes seemed to consider the boy. Then he went down on one knee so they were face to face, which made Duncan's heart pound. He could hear the murmurs of unseen people behind the man.

Slowly and softly, Mr. Baker said, "Duncan, I have some bad news." He sniffed. "There's been an accident; Timothy was hit by a car." The uncle gulped and looked away momentarily, and Duncan stared at his pockmarked face, unable to blink. The man's eyes found him again, and in a voice seemingly filled with every ounce of gentleness he could muster, he said, "He's...he's dead."

Duncan's eyes were forced closed by the eruption of an icy black void within. The shocking cold of that darkness shriveled his organs, sending a spike of pain through his guts.

He heard himself ask, "Timothy's dead?"

Lightly, so very lightly, John placed a trembling hand on his shoulder, his voice cracking as he answered, "Yes."

Duncan opened his eyes as the sounds of muffled weeping reached his ears. And as the wind struck his brain, it brought a numb mindlessness such that he could think of nothing more to say, nothing more to ask. He stared open-mouthed at the coffee stain on the man's knit shirt.

A female voice from inside the house wailed, "No...No...No...," and there came a piercing crash of shattering glass. The brother jumped erect, called, "Elizabeth?" and turned away, hesitated, then turned back, knelt for a moment, and said, "Please go home, son. I'm so sorry."

Then he closed the door.

Left standing there, he gazed at the warped reflection of his face in the brass plating. He heard a new, strange sound from inside. It reminded him of something that happened months before.

***

There was a Jack Russell terrier that lived in a house on Branciforte. Most days, when Duncan was riding his bike back home from school, it would charge out of its little yard like it wanted to bite him. It would chase him for almost a whole block with, to him, demonic eyes and teeth and so fiercely that it was nearly comical. Almost. Sometimes he would stop, and the dog would stop and bark until Duncan resumed riding. After weeks of this he was angry, scared, and fed up with that tireless defender of eighty square feet of green grass.

Duncan always crossed over to the opposite side of the street, but it didn't deter the dog, who always seemed ready. Did he wait all afternoon for Duncan's appearance?

Then one cold day, Duncan decided he would not run from the dog and instead see if he could whack him or scare him or something. Sure enough, the dog charged out of his yard on cue, but this time, it was right in front of a speeding pickup truck. Duncan watched in slow-motion horror as first a front wheel and then a rear wheel rolled over the dog's hindquarters, crushing the bones like in a pneumatic vise. The truck did not stop. The dog's mashed lower half seemed nearly stuck to the asphalt. The terrier pointed his head at the sky; the crazed eyes bulged like from tremendous internal pressure, and the forelegs quivered and jerked the flattened, bloodied back half of its body back across the street. From its throat, rapid gunshot-like blasts of pure agony echoed off the walls of the houses: "Harwl! Harwl! Harwl!"

***

A sound so very much like that came from inside the Eaton's home. Even though it sounded nothing like Timothy's mother, even though it sounded inhuman, Duncan knew it was hers.

He could not move until after that unbearable barking slowly faded away to an excruciating silence, and then he quietly walked down the steps. It seemed there was nowhere to go, so he shuffled across the driveway and sat on the edge of the red brick wall topped with a deep-green hedge bordering Mrs. King's property. He knew she was talking to someone, but he was not paying attention because he had just noticed the bent wheel of a Sting-ray bicycle next to the garbage cans. It was attached to a mangled frame, and the banana seat hung broken and drooping from one bolt.

Mrs. King raised her voice, "...but he didn't even slow down. Poor Timothy came flying out of the driveway, yelling something, and right in front of Jackson's truck. He didn't have a chance to brake."

Her companion asked something. Mrs. King said, "Probably not, probably on impact. Small mercy, I guess, dying so quickly. Poor Timothy, he was such..." Then, nothing but faint crying sounds penetrated the hedge.

Duncan got his bike and walked it to the sidewalk. Several times, he tried to get on but found he couldn't. So he walked it down the sidewalk, away from Mrs. King's house. He did not want her to see him; he did not want anyone to see him.

He would have large gaps in his memory of that day. He went to the new harbor and watched the boats bobbing in their berths. He went out on the breakwater with its huge boulders and gigantic jacks-like jumbles made of concrete.

It was then that he first saw what he believed was Timothy. He had been out on the point yelling, his voice being swallowed by the rhythmic roar of crashing waves. "Why were you so stupid?" he demanded again and again.

A shape appeared over the water, not ten feet in front of him. It glowed, a vertical blur like a wisp of fog lit from within. Seeing it, he asked in a voice too low to be heard above the surf, "You are so smart; how could you be so dumb?"

He began to repeat himself but was interrupted.

"Mistake," sighed a voice.

"But we were going to the Boardwalk. We were going to the roller coaster and we were going to eat taffy and we are friends, and I...and I..."

"Sorry."

The sound of laughter made Duncan turn. A young couple holding hands approached. When he looked back, Timothy was gone. His eyes filled, and a dark mass of something rose inside his chest. He crushed his teeth together and thought, *Choke it.*

He would next remember being on the wharf, wandering around, looking at flats of dead fish, listening to the screeching of seagulls and the whining casts of a few fishermen hoping for a bite. The glow that he was sure was Timothy appeared and disappeared. He looked at it each time with a desperate longing that did not make him stay.

"Choke what?"

"Huh?" he asked the bearded man, baiting his hook.

"You were saying, choke it."

When he did not answer, the man asked, "Are you all right, boy?"

Unable to answer that either, he ran to his bike and rode away.

Next, he wandered on the beach, watching people surf weak waves, but all he truly saw was Timothy, both as a laughing, joyous memory and as the phantom that came and went. They talked some, or so it seemed, but mostly it was like Timothy was just there. When he vanished again, and the black mass rose, he clung to his magic incantation like it might save his life.

Choke it. Choke it.

Later, he went under the Boardwalk and lay on the dank sand, smelling the uniquely mixed odors of spilled beer, spent cigarettes and carnival fast food. This was years before the sand rose so high, and access was boarded over, when couples might sneak into the shadowed recesses to smooch or smoke a joint.

He must have slept, for he woke a long time later, shivering and crying. It was getting dark. The phantom of his friend was not there. Angry, he slapped himself.

Choke it.

Choke it.

Choke it.

Choke it.

It seemed a miracle that his unsecured bike was still where he'd left it on the Beach Street side of the Giant Dipper. Hungry and exhausted, it occurred to him that he was supposed to be home hours ago. He pedaled slowly along the river and over the bridge, not looking to go home yet because he had to see someone first.

After the sun had set, he sat on his bike outside the Kelly's house, looking at the lit-up windows and listening to Aretha Franklin singing about respect, probably from Cheryl's radio. He did not want to go inside, so he went to the side of the house where Randy's bedroom was. Getting off his bike, there in the shadows, he peered in and was lucky that Randy was there. He tapped on the glass until his friend came over, lifted the window and looked out at him in surprise.

"What? Why are you out there? Come on in."

"No, you come out."

"Why?"

"Just come out, OK?"

Randy shrugged. Soon, he heard the screen door slam out back, followed by the swishing of Randy wading through tall grass. Randy asked in the dim light of street-lamps and his bedroom lamp, "What's going on?"

Duncan couldn't answer at first, but as the other boy asked again, he said, "Timothy died."

Randy gasped but said nothing until, "This isn't some awful joke, is it?"

"No, car hit him." He heard the flatness of his own voice.

Randy burst into tears, surprising Duncan because he did not know if Randy had liked Timothy. He continued to cry and ask questions that Duncan could not answer. Duncan wondered at how dead he felt, how unmoved he seemed like he was reporting the weather.

Margaret called from the back door. He touched Randy's arm, said, "I gotta go. Mom is going to kill me."

Randy stared from a tear-streaked face.

"I wanted you to know, but I'm not telling anybody else."

Margaret hollered, "What's wrong? Where are you?"

He pedaled up the Soquel hill. Duncan knew he wanted to see Nana. He coasted down the drive and stopped when he saw his mother's car parked outside, the hot engine ticking in the night. He set his bike down on the porch. A sharp and angry voice penetrated the thin walls. With a sigh, he opened the door. Ava and Nana were standing in the living room, Nana's face full of grandmotherly concern, Ava's full of fury. She turned that face upon him before he could close the door.

"There you are. Where have you been? What have you been up to?"

"Nothing," he said. "Playing."

Her fury surged. "Playing? Mischief more likely. Do you know how late it is?"

With one hand on the open door, he did not answer. It was obvious how late it was.

"Dinner was hours ago, and you are out roaming around with no concern for me or anyone else."

He knew he should and normally would be afraid; Ava's fury was a terrible thing to behold, but he felt like a husk, even more numb than before. So, he just listened and knew what was coming.

"Close that door and get over here. This is intolerable."

He obeyed.

She declared, "Bend over the chair. I'm getting the belt."

"Must you, Ava?" Nana asked.

"He has to learn."

He lay over the big, rounded arms of the brown leather reading chair, his face close to the seat cushion. He heard noises in Nana's bedroom, probably Ava searching for a belt. From the bedroom, Nana said, "But, Ava..."

"No. He can't just do as he pleases."

Footsteps announced their return. He didn't look back over his shoulder. He just waited, not caring.

The first lash of the narrow leather belt surprised him, and he flinched but made no sound. The second was harder, but her aim was off, for it struck his lower back instead of his bottom. He flinched again but remained quiet.

Inside, within the dead, dull emptiness, he felt the rise of that black mass forcing itself upwards, like molten obsidian, like a threat.

Choke it.

Another blow snapped across the back of his legs. Another flinch, but he still made no sound.

The strikes came quicker and harder. Was she frustrated? Inside the husk, the black swell rose and fell like a monster wave at night on a storm-driven ocean. Over and over, he made the monster fall back,

Choke it.

Choke it.

Choke it.

From his mother's point of view, he must have seemed like a slab of wet clay that took blow after blow without a cry, without evasion, and without protest.

What he focused on, as if they weren't coming from him, were the glistening gems of his grief collecting on the seat cushion. They refracted the light from the floor lamp overhead. Yet another diamond dripped from his eyes each time she struck him until Nana cried, "Enough, Ava. Enough. Please stop. Can't you see?"

Ava stopped.

He wiped his eyes with the backs of his hands and rose without permission. The husk looked at the boy's mother. He glanced at the belt dangling from her right hand, turned without a word, and walked the short distance over to the door to the attic, opened it, and left, again without permission. That was the last time she ever hit him.

Upstairs he found his bare army cot. He lay on it in the dark, seeing the rough walls and open ceiling dimly lit by light from the one bare window. Timothy reappeared as a brighter, broader presence. Duncan didn't say anything to him, and Timothy didn't speak in his mind. That was OK. It was enough that he was there. After a while, his eyes closed, and he slept, comforted, certain that he was loved.

30

Ava had woken and taken him home later that night. On the drive he had sat as far away from her as he could, pressed against the door, head on the window, watching the world go by. He knew she wanted to ask him questions; reflected in the glass, he could see her frequent glances. Yet, she ventured nothing, and he was relieved not to be pressed.

A couple of days later he sat on their front porch in the morning light, using a comb to remove the thousands of fleas that infested their poor cat. As he dragged the black tines through her black fur, he could see the nasty hordes of bloodsucking creatures running toward her tail. Midnight looked up at him with eyes both grateful and desperate.

He heard the screen door close. Ava sat down beside him on the step. Duncan kept his attention on Midnight.

"I got a call last night from Mr. Eaton. They're worried about you."

Duncan forced another battalion of vampire specks off the cat.

"I'm sorry... about Timothy. He was... a wonderful boy."

Another stroke of the comb froze halfway along Midnight's spine. He turned a sour face on his mother.

She swallowed. "Death is a hard..."

He dropped the comb, stood, glanced at her, and walked away.

"Duncan?" she said.

But he did not stop, and she did not tell him to. Later, he wondered if he would have if she had so ordered.

Perhaps she thought he was angry or distraught. Maybe she was shy because she had beaten him. The truth was that he had walked away for none of those reasons. Though he was bruised and ached in many places, he did not care about the beating.

How could Ava say Timothy was wonderful? She didn't know him at all. He wasn't even welcome in their home. And the mere possibility of revealing the depths of his pain to her made him want to run. He did not want to hear soothing words from her. Even discussing Timothy with Ava felt like it would sully his memory and mourning for his friend. He walked away to prevent that; he walked away to be with Timothy.

So far, his friend had only appeared to him when he was alone. He believed that if he went somewhere private, Timothy would find him. So, he had taken to wandering in the woods of the DeLaveaga Park. He would talk to his friend as if he were there, and sometimes, sometimes, he would suddenly appear as a faint glowing cloud that hovered nearby, unaffected by the breeze.

He felt him more than he saw him. Timothy's presence was like an arm across his shoulders. That touch radiated warmth and joy and sad kindness, staying with him while he poured his heart out. Timothy listened as he gave voice to his hurt and loneliness but also as he shared about music and his sisters, Randy and Alan. His phantom friend rarely said anything, but Duncan always felt nestled in a cocoon of understanding.

But after several more days of this, he became frustrated and yelled, "Why won't you talk to me?"

Nothing happened. He asked again and again. Nothing happened. Angry, he stomped away over forest slash.

"Hard," a voice whispered in his mind.

Duncan stopped and turned toward the glow.

"Hard." It was a shout.

"Oh," Duncan said.

After that, he was content; Timothy's presence was enough. Then, a day came when he did not appear, not on the following day nor the next. And on another afternoon when Timothy still did not show, he fell asleep on the grass in the shade of a tree.

He had a wonderful dream; he and his friend were playing in those very woods. They laughed, and they ran, and Timothy smiled at him. And then, for a timeless, silent stretch, Timothy looked deeply into his eyes. His look carried a final message.

He awoke and stared at the needle-covered branches, knowing he would never see him again. After lying there for a long time, he stood, brushed himself off, looked around, and, voice breaking, said, "Goodbye."

31

August 1, 1965

The Findlay's '57 Chevy, pulling a small, enclosed trailer, rolled to a stop in the driveway of a dark red wood-framed cottage. A lone apple tree with twisted limbs and a hint of future fruit occupied a front yard that matched the modest size of their new home. It was dripping hot, and the kid's doors flew open as they sought to escape from the sweatbox they had been riding in for the past half hour.

Before Duncan could escape to explore the backyard, Ava called, "Everyone grab a box. Let's get this trailer unloaded."

Doors slammed. Ava unlatched the trailer doors and swung them open. A wave of roiling heat swept over Duncan. She handed boxes to his sisters. Little Keith stood behind Duncan, waiting to help. Duncan found the biggest, heaviest box, one filled with cans of vegetables, bottles of oil, vinegar and a bag of flour. He huffed as he lifted, turned and offered it to his brother.

"Here ya go, Keith."

The slight boy's extended arms dropped to his sides, and he recoiled as if the box might bite him.

"Don't tease," Ava said. "Take it in yourself."

Duncan laughed.

Ava handed Keith a pillow. "Here you go." The five-year-old brightened and followed Duncan up a few steps into the house.

The family made short work of that last unloading trip from their old house into the new. It was a cute place, shaded by large trees, like nearly all the homes in that village.

When they left the city and drove up Graham Hill Road, they entered the forested world of the Santa Cruz Mountains, with its thick canopies of evergreen and deciduous trees.

Ben Lomond was spread along the banks of the San Lorenzo. In those days, the river was often full and home to steelhead trout and coho salmon. That was long before the drought would shrink it to a dribble of nasty water.

Duncan liked their new home. He and Keith got the rear bedroom, and he had the top bunk of their new bed. His sisters got the front bedroom. Ava would again be sleeping on the living room couch.

Aileen had not wanted to leave her friends at Santa Cruz High. Imperturbable Shona had taken it in stride, neither complaining nor seeming to be excited. Duncan was glad they had left Santa Cruz. Of course, he would miss his friends at Branciforte. He would miss Randy and the ease of popping over to visit the Kelly's.

But he was glad they had moved because he was afraid. He was prone to crying for no reason. So far, he had been by himself for each incident but had been alarmed to find tears dripping down his face. And one time, when the surge of pain hit him especially hard, he had only just made it to the bathroom without being seen, flushed the toilet, turned on the water full blast and then sobbed into a towel. Repetitions of *Choke It, Choke It,* eventually enabled him to regain control—but he left the bathroom shaken by his weakness.

He felt like a plump water balloon. All it took was a tiny poke, a fleeting thought, a remembered scent and the water might gush out. It was embarrassing.

Thus, the prospect of returning to Branciforte as a sixth-grader, big tough Duncan, slayer of bullies, to be seen bawling at his desk or out on the swings at recess was just too horrifying to consider.

He hoped he would be safe in Ben Lomond and at his new school, as he would not be reminded about Timothy everywhere he looked.

***

A few days before they moved, he had gone to the Kelly's. Cheryl was out in the yard. Margaret greeted him as he entered the kitchen and asked how he was.

"I'm OK. Where's Randy?" he had answered in a high-pitched squeak.

She said her sons were at the market. In an uncomfortable silence to Duncan, he felt her tender eyes search his face for a few moments. Then she came to him and, without a word, lifted him off his feet, put his head on her shoulder, and tightly wrapped big, long arms around him. She said nothing, just held him and held him and held him, rocking gently back and forth like a great tree in a warm breeze.

It took a while, but the broken glass in his heart finally melted, and then he soaked her shoulder with an outpouring from that ever-refilling balloon while she hummed and said his name over and over. She put him down at exactly the right time and patted his face dry with a kitchen towel.

"Would you like a slice of pecan pie?"

***

After unloading, Ava made the kids a lunch of tuna fish sandwiches, potato chips and milk to wash it down. He noticed her gazing his way with concern. She had been doing that a lot lately, but they never talked about anything, and each time he saw her, she would look away.

Duncan swallowed the last of his milk, asked, "Mom, can I go down to the pool?"

"All right, just make sure you are back before dark."

Dressed only in his shorts and flip-flops, he walked the few blocks to Ben Lomond Park singing "Help!" by The *Beatles*.

He heard the people in the park before he saw them. The laughter and the screams of kids at play danced in the hot air through tall, lush trees. As he ran across Mill and scooted between the cars parked out front, he caught the rich odors of hamburgers, steaks, hot dogs and corn on the cob sizzling on grills. He dodged a squadron of plump bees buzzing over a 55-gallon drum trash can full of their treasures: soda bottles, meat scraps, Popsicle sticks and ketchup-smeared paper plates.

He went through the park gates and stopped in awe. The pool was enormous, about sixty feet across and four hundred feet long. There were kids, lots and lots of kids, splashing, swimming, running and climbing—loosely observed by a minority of adults. A slope of coarse sand and dirt, plentiful with trees, declined to a broad concrete coping on the north side of the river.

A group of girls sat there, dangling their feet in the water, giggling and chatting, their voices high and tinkling like wind chimes.

Some were warming themselves after swimming. They lazed on towels in the hot shade or the hotter sun. A redwood-stained restrooms building sat next to the dam end.

Two hundred feet upriver was a kiddie pool surrounded by redwood latticework, with over a dozen tykes splashing about and being watched by half a dozen mothers.

On the pool's far side was a steep slope that was nearly a cliff. It was covered with scrub and large trees thrusting out at odd angles, their full leafy limbs providing shade to the river below. A giant tree extended one long, thick limb horizontally, halfway across the pool. A man swung from an attached rope suitable for securing a ship to a dock. At the apex of his arc, he let go with a yell and plunged into the dark gray water.

Duncan made his way past picnickers and sunbathers, flipped off his thongs and stood on the coping next to the girls, who paid him no mind.

A boy and two girls were floating in their black inner tubes. An older man was swimming upstream with silky strokes and that repetitive head-turning-for-air rhythm of a professional. Duncan dove into the cool water, which felt warm after two summers in the ocean. He swam to the coal-headed inner-tube boy and said, "Hi, I'm Duncan. I just moved here. Who are you?"

The smaller, younger boy turned his chipmunk-cheeked, happy face on him. "Eddy. Are you new here?"

"Yeah."

"Me too."

"Can I try your tube?"

"OK." Eddy slipped over the side.

It took a few tries wrestling with the contrary rubber, but he finally got his butt in the hole and used both hands to propel himself backward while the other boy dog-paddled alongside. He settled on slowly spinning around in a circle. On the fifth orbit, Eddy pushed him to speed it up. Soon, he was digging into the water and upping the tempo. Eddy pushed harder and quicker each time, and they were both laughing until he braked and said, "Whoa, dizzy."

"My turn."

Roles were reversed, technique improved, and Eddy soon spun faster and laughed louder than Duncan had. Eddy's dad called him to eat lunch, and Duncan was left to find new friends.

He swam over to three boys who peered over the dam. The four hung onto the edge and watched the thin, silvery waterfall of river overflow like it was magic.

There were dozens of boys and girls in the park; he wanted to meet them all. He swam to first one group, then another.

He got out and ran up to two boys playing Jarts. Introductions were made, and Billy and Tony snagged a fourth boy, Greg, so that they could play as two teams. All was going well until Duncan's errant toss of his red-finned spike missed the circle by ten feet and nearly impaled someone's dog. The owner shouted angrily; the game broke up.

Moving on, Duncan greeted two boys near his age, sitting on the sand next to the kiddie pool. Half of the little ones screeched with delight; the other half screeched with complaint about irritants only they recognized. Their parents hovered, exuding love, patience, weariness and a fair amount of boredom.

Upslope from the boys, who were still dripping from the pool, were two teenage couples. The girls' boyfriends seemed exceptionally intent on rubbing suntan lotion thoroughly into their bikini-clad bodies.

"What's New Pussycat?" blared tinnily from their transistor radio.

"You just moved here today?" one of the boys, Kevin, asked from his prone position on a rainbow-striped towel. He squinted up at Duncan, shading his eyes with one hand over the long sun-bleached hair that swept across his forehead.

"Yeah."

"I got here last year."

Kevin's friend said his name was Frank. He was a tall, thin boy with wavy, carefully parted brown hair with a tangle of rebellious strands like a little dog's tail hanging over his forehead. He had a somber, nearly mournful resting expression.

"I was born here," Frank said.

"Really?" Duncan asked.

"Yeah," Kevin said, "here in the park." He tilted his head to glance at Frank, who sat behind him. "Right, Frank?"

"No, not right. That's a dumb joke." Then he flashed his big smile, revealing two crooked buck teeth, and said, "At home...in a tree." Then he laughed goofily.

They talked about the flicks they had seen and the swimming pool in San Jose, and Duncan told them about how great bodysurfing was in Santa Cruz. They watched a man swing out on the rope high over the river and drop fifteen feet into the water.

Kevin was a year older than Duncan. He had a cocky, confident air about him and a little smile that showed a perfect line of white teeth. Duncan asked about his scuffed knuckles. He claimed they were from a fight with another boy whom he got in a headlock and pounded until the kid cried uncle. Frank seemed to have heard it before and looked away at the tykes in the kiddie pool as Kevin bragged.

Mid-story, Eddy walked up chewing on a hot dog in hand, black-framed glasses on his face. "Hey," he said.

"Hey," Frank answered. "Kevin's regaling the new kid with his headlock story."

"Again?" Eddy said as his chipmunk cheeks lifted in a grin.

Duncan wanted to ask what regaling meant, but Kevin replied, "It's true, and he had it coming."

Kevin challenged Duncan to swing off the big rope with him. And he did, though he face-planted on his first try. Kevin smiled and nodded when he returned to try again despite the painful splash. Duncan felt he was being evaluated, which goaded him into an afternoon of rope-launching, diving and swimming competition with the bold boy and his friends.

Kevin took them to see a Scottish castle upriver, which was super cool, even if it was only a house made to look like one. When they got back to the park, the sun was kissing the treetops.

They dipped in the pool one last time to cool off and headed to Highway 9. As they parted for home, Kevin asked Duncan, "Hey, my dad got me an archery set, and we're going to shoot targets tomorrow. Want to come?"

As Duncan hesitated, thinking he had never shot arrows before, Eddy said, "Yeah, come."

Frank echoed the invite.

Duncan smiled, said, "OK, yeah, sure."

32

August - December 1965

The Ben Lomond Pool was great, but Duncan ached to be in the ocean. He bugged Ava so often to take him to Santa Cruz that her exasperation broke through one day, and she had erupted, "I'm not your chauffeur!" Despite or because of his pestering, he got to see his SC friends half a dozen times before school started.

The boys never talked about Timothy. Duncan had found that if he did not talk about or think about him, the tears stayed down somewhere deep, deep inside, and he could feel safe from the shame of looking weak. But he had moments, moments like while visiting the arcade or when assaulted by an unavoidable memory, that he almost broke in front of his friends.

Sometimes, Duncan scared himself. He had never been shy of taking risks, but lately he had become dangerously and impulsively more prone to doing so. He would feel an abrupt, near frantic compulsion to dart into danger like when, not long after Timothy had died, he had dashed across Water Street in front of a bus, causing the poor driver to brake hard, barely avoiding hitting him. As the driver belatedly laid on his horn, the freaky urge vanished, but at the time, in that instant, he was unsure that he had wanted the bus to miss.

***

In late August, while walking under the trestle with Randy and Alan, he announced he wanted to dive off it.

"Really?" Alan asked.

He ignored the question and ran up to the tracks above. At that time, no walkway was attached to the trestle for crossing over the river to East Cliff Drive. Walking on the trestle was officially prohibited, but many people did it anyway, as trains were few and far between.

He danced over the tar-soaked ties. About two-thirds of the way across, he judged he was over the deepest channel and moved out onto the north side along one of its rusted iron crossbeams. He stopped at the end where another beam angled up over the tracks and edged around it into a diving position twenty feet above the water.

Alan and Randy walked to the river's edge to watch.

"It's not deep enough. Don't do it," Alan shouted.

"Yeah, don't do it," Randy said.

He looked away from them to the river below. He was panting, afraid, exhilarated and had a surging urge to throw his body over.

I can make it.

"You'll break your neck, man. Or your leg. Don't be a dumbshit," Alan called.

Randy walked into the river. Duncan had two hands holding the beam behind him and was leaning outwards. He could see Randy's puzzled eyes searching his own. He looked back into the water and exhaled slowly like a silent whistle.

Randy charged through knee-high water. "No, no, no, no, no," he yelled.

Randy fell at a deep spot, swam a few strokes, regained his feet, and continued. "No, No, No!" he shouted, startling Duncan until he was directly beneath him.

He raised his palms like a traffic cop and said, "Don't. Don't."

Duncan saw that the water depth didn't reach Randy's waist. His exhilaration evaporated.

"OK," he said.

He carefully returned along the tracks and met them below the trestle. They walked toward Rivermouth.

"Were you really going to dive, dumbshit?" Alan asked.

"Naw, I was just goofing."

Randy glared doubtfully.

"Goofing?" Alan said.

"Yeah, did I scare you?"

"Not me; it's your neck." But Alan's face said something else.

They walked further, and the boom of the surf increased. Randy stared at the sand.

"Hey, look! Good rides," Duncan said into the awkwardness.

Randy lifted his head to look but wheeled and shoved Duncan so hard he fell. Standing over him, he said, "You scared me, jerk." And he ran on ahead.

***

School finally started, and Duncan rode the long yellow bus three miles to be taught in the new way that was all the rage in the US educational system: team teaching, open classrooms, and New Math. It was interesting, confusing, exciting, and dang strange. He tried to learn in a building with three merged classes totaling over seventy kids, some ahead of him, some behind him. Multiple teachers worked in a very large room created by removing walls. They taught mathematics, language, reading and history, but only some were learning the same subjects at the same time.

A real stopper for many of the kids was the concept of bases. The eyes of half the class glazed over when Miss Reynolds explained that Base Ten, the one they knew, was only one mathematical base. There was also Base Sixteen, Base Eight, Base Five, and even Base Two. She said we only use Base Ten because we have ten fingers.

A girl named Nancy, distress clear in her voice, asked, "But does anyone have only two fingers?"

Duncan loved the idea and did not care if it had any practical use, but Miss Reynolds assured him that Base Two might be the most important one to understand because of computers. He suddenly envisioned being with Timothy and his parents in their home. Abruptly, he declared he had to go to the bathroom, and she let him.

In November two men from NASA visited and told hundreds of kids gathered in the auditorium about rockets, Sputnik, weather satellites, Apollo, and going to the moon. They brought a huge model of the Saturn V rocket and space capsules and even demonstrated how liquid fuel rockets worked.

At question time, he asked if people would soon live on the moon. The tall, sparkling blue-eyed man assured him that we definitely maybe would.

***

Even though it was still hot outside, the dam at the park pool was removed on September 1, and the river was free to flow normally. When not visiting Santa Cruz, doing chores or learning new math, he would hang out with Kevin and sometimes Eddy.

That fall Ava became convinced that the kids needed more iron in their blood and began to serve weekly liver suppers. Aileen and Shona's seats were on the kitchen side of the table. Duncan had the precious window side. A typical meal might be mashed potatoes, Brussels sprouts and a slab of brown fried flesh that only a week before had been filtering toxins out of the blood of some poor calf that would never grow up to be a source of hamburger. The revolted looks on his sisters' faces indeed mirrored his own. Keith was exempt from participating in the weekly food torture for some reason.

These dinners dragged on for hours. Ava consumed hers, repeatedly proclaiming how delicious it was, while he and his sisters quickly ate everything except the liver. Their first strategy was to pretend they were eating it. They cut it into smaller and smaller pieces and strategically moved each piece around their plates to create the illusion of progress.

Repositioning the sickening, slimy, mealy masses failed to deceive Ava. "You're going to sit there until you eat it all," she declared—often.

So, they demanded ketchup to help it go down. *Heinz to the rescue!* he thought. But it took a lot of ketchup to overcome his gag reflex.

He had a big advantage over his sisters. Being on the far side of the table, he could slip pieces of liver into the napkin he held in his lap, which could then be stuffed into his pockets for later disposal. But usually, it was warm enough for the kitchen window behind him to be open, and he would flick liver chunks out into the bush there every time Ava was not looking.

His sisters scowled at the unfairness of it all, but they never finked on him. One time, Shona dumped a handful of pieces on his plate. He scowled but then grinned. All was fair in liver avoidance.

Despite these evasions, they eventually stuffed down quite a bit of liver. But did Ava really have to give them portions covering a third of their plates? Eventually, they just seemed to wear their mother down. Ava would get up from the couch after watching a show like *Twelve O'Clock High* to declare, "You still aren't finished?"

After the ketchup ran out, the three complained loudly and incessantly during a dinner that dragged on until nearly midnight. Apparently clear that her opinion about liver was not shared, Liver Nights did not return.

However, the flowering bush outside Duncan's kitchen window the following spring looked exceptionally vibrant, with brilliant red flowers and shiny green leaves.

33

December 23, 1965

High on a ridge overlooking the enemy base, Commando Team Tiger hid in the scrub under a weak winter sun. Lying prone on the sandy ground, Colonel Kevin scanned the complex below through his father's binoculars.

Lieutenant Frank whispered, "Whatya see?"

As Sergeant Eddy crawled forward, Sergeant Duncan pushed the plastic combat helmet out of his eyes and echoed, "Yeah, what do you see?"

"Looks bad, boys. There are two heavy tanks and several armored trucks, and steel bunkers guard the command center. I can't see how many of those Viet Cong bastards might be hiding inside."

"Sounds bad," Eddy said.

"Yeah, it's bad," said Kevin.

"Do you think we can take it, sir?" asked the Lieutenant.

"Can we?" asked Sergeant Duncan.

Doing his best John Wayne, Kevin said, "We must, men. We are all that stands between them and the city behind us. If Ben Lomond falls, America falls, and then we will be slaves under the boot of the godless communists."

"Gosh," said Eddy.

"Let me see," said Duncan.

Kevin passed the binoculars to him. "Careful, my dad will be pissed if we scratch 'em."

Duncan studied the base spread out one hundred feet below. The Colonel was right. The place was a fortress with big, armored vehicles and towers of steel with dangerous protrusions that could be cannons or missiles. The whole wide area was a wasteland of once beautiful American land scoured clear of all life. A poisonous-looking pond of yellow water lay like a barrier—or maybe a trap.

"Yeah, it'll be tough," Duncan said, returning the binoculars.

The mission, Kevin's idea, almost did not happen because of a conflict over their respective ranks. At first Kevin wanted to be a general and said the three other boys would be privates.

Eddy said, "Whoever heard of generals leading commando teams?"

After much arguing, Kevin conceded the point but would not accept anything less than being a Colonel. No one minded him being the leader, partly because the adventure was his idea but mostly because he was generously arming the team out of his impressive collection of toy weaponry.

Kevin chose the *Oh Wow* weapon, a machine gun that fired plastic bullets and made rat-a-tat-tat sounds. Frank got the M1 carbine that Duncan wanted, while Eddy got the Chicago mob Tommy gun. Duncan got the cap-powered Colt 45 with a holster. He almost complained but then decided it was a very cool gun. And it floated through his mind that he might be getting the best weapon after all since his gun would be strapped to his belt while the other boys would have to lug their mean-looking armaments over what Kevin said would be two miles going up and down hills through the forest. So, he accepted the pistol like a concession but was secretly pleased.

Frank got stubborn and would have quit unless he was made a Lieutenant. Kevin had offered Major, but no one was clear which rank was higher. Whatever, Frank preferred Lieutenant anyway.

Eddy and Duncan refused to be less than sergeants.

Tiger Team had headed west out of Ben Lomond on Glen Arbor Road and then went cross-country until they got to what seemed to be the beginning of a new housing development. They avoided the few houses and had hiked up to a spine of yellow-white sandstone. Behind them sat the development, and before and below was their objective.

Their descent had been steep and through occasionally thick clumps of bushes and small trees.

"What do we attack first?" Duncan asked.

"Gotta be that bunker," Kevin said.

It wasn't precisely a bunker, but it was formidable—a nearly eighty-foot-tall steel exoskeleton with ladders and walkways that supported an interior of bulbous metal chambers and piping. Five hundred feet to the north of it lay another similar structure, and between them were dragon-like monstrosities of metal and rubber angling into the sky. Huge piles of moved earth rose like conical mountains, and the armored vehicles were strategically placed between them.

At the bottom of the slope, the team gathered behind the last bush to confer before entering a battle zone with no cover.

Duncan pulled his pistol. Eddy and Frank raised their guns. Kevin let his machine gun dangle and chewed gum.

"Your orders, Colonel?" The lieutenant asked.

"Kill the Cong. Take that bunker. Meet at the top." As an aside, Kevin handed Duncan the binoculars, said, "Hey, would you carry this? My gun's too big to carry both. Don't break it."

"Did you see any watchmen, I mean sentries?" Eddy asked.

"No, let's go. Charge!" he yelled.

The first bunker was the toughest. Hordes of rabid Vietnamese attacked, only to be mowed down by Kevin's and Eddy's machine guns. Frank and Duncan picked off those they missed with amazing accuracy. Bullets by the thousands flew around Team Tiger, but they made it to the towering bunker with only minor wounds.

The commandos charged up the zigzagging stairs and blasted the remaining defenders at each level.

"Pew, pew, pew,"

"Ke, ke, ke, ke, ke,"

"Kakung...Kakung...Kakung"

And just because it sounded cool, they added the whistling sounds of dropping bombs, followed by short pauses and then raspy, growling imitations of explosions, with much hand-waving.

Up and up they went, roaring and firing until they stood triumphant on the upper deck of the perforated steel walkway, where a single narrow steel bar railing, with open space beneath, protected them from falling. The three boys raised their weapons and cheered their victory. Three boys?

"Hey, where's Frank?" Duncan asked.

"Frank?" Kevin called.

"Down here."

They looked over the railing and saw him two floors below.

"What are you doing?" Eddy asked.

"I'm guarding in case any Cong attack us from the rear."

"Oh, uh, OK," said Eddy.

"He's scared of heights," Kevin said.

"Really?" Duncan asked.

"Yeah."

Duncan considered teasing Frank immediately but decided to wait for a juicier time later.

The plan was to move on from the first bunker to attack the rest of the encampment, but, for Duncan at least, the mirage of the Viet Cong base dissolved before his eyes and became something far cooler—what it actually was. The other boys must've felt the same, for they shifted readily from warriors to explorers when Duncan said, "Check it out. Have you ever seen a truck that big?"

The main battle tank returned to its scarred yellow dump truck form.

"Those wheels are as big as my dad," Kevin said.

"Bigger even," said Eddy.

From the base of their tower soared a conveyor, its rubber tongue reaching away and angled upwards to nearly their elevation. Several eighteen-wheel silver-bellied trucks were haphazardly parked. A front-end loader, an excavator, another shorter tower like theirs and a white office trailer were planted around that wasteland of sand. Huge conical piles, a compressed road, the hills behind them and underlying the trees and brush Duncan could see was the same fine white sand the plant was built on.

Next to them was a sick-looking yellow-brown pond with a frill of scum at its edges.

"C'mon," said Duncan.

Wow and *oh* and *cool* and *look at that* was the extent of the boys' expressions as they investigated the wonders all around them. They climbed all over the dump truck; Duncan got into the cab and was dazzled by the array of dials, knobs, switches and levers. Kevin joined him, and together they looked for a key to start it. Each wanted to be the first to drive that monster around the plant.

When it was clear that there was no key, Duncan was only slightly disappointed. Having never driven anything bigger than his bicycle, the prospect of driving a truck twenty times bigger than Ava's car was a scary, if still exciting, proposition. Hiding his relief, they moved on to the front-end loader. Kevin tried to climb up and into the raised bucket, but he banged his ribs in the attempt and almost fell.

One silvery trailer truck had big holes on top. The boys climbed the narrow side ladders and stared over the edge into the cavernous interior.

They played with echoes:

"Hello lo lo lo lo."

"Who's in here, ere, ere?"

"The ogre of the truck. Bwaha ha."

"Bwang!"

"Eddy likes girls."

"Hey."

Frank blatted a long, loud, resonant burp, to which they all cracked up.

The white trailer was impenetrable. The only door was locked, and its porthole window was translucent. Duncan gave Frank a lift to look in one of the windows.

"What do you see?"

"Nothin', just desks and papers."

"Can you get the window open?" Duncan asked.

Frank struggled as Duncan kept the boy's foot planted in his joined hands. "Naw, locked tight."

"Damn."

Tired, the boys took a break at the base of a crescent-shaped pile of fine pale sand.

"I'm hungry," Frank said.

Kevin passed out the Payday bars they had bought. They munched and gazed about the conquered domain.

Eddy said through the peanuts and nougat, "This place is bitchin'."

All agreed: Bitchin'.

"How'd you know about this place?" Duncan asked Kevin.

"Dad brought me over when he needed to talk to a guy."

"Where is everybody?" Frank asked.

"I think they've got Christmas break like us," Kevin said.

It was getting late, and Kevin said they should head back. Duncan wanted to check out one last thing: the conveyor. When they had returned to their tower at the bottom end of the conveyor, he said, "I'm going to climb it."

Eddy scrutinized it. "Yeah?"

All metal struts and rough rubber belting suspended on a fulcrum point lifted the far end at least fifty feet high. Thick steel rollers underlaid the belting.

"You sure?" Eddy asked.

As an answer, Duncan climbed up the supports until he stood awkwardly on the belt. It had an undulating concave surface covered in grit. He could see a narrow walkway on the far side, but reaching it would have meant climbing down again. Walking up the belt was more fun, anyway.

"Who wants to come with me?"

All the boys shook their heads.

"Kinda dangerous. What if it starts moving?" Frank asked.

Duncan scoffed. "It won't start by itself."

"Well, hurry up, daredevil; I want to get home before dark," Kevin said.

He got down on all fours and scampered up the middle, confirming that the grip of his sneakers was sure and that he'd figured out how to move on the oddly shaped surface. Halfway up, about thirty feet in the air, he considered continuing on the safer route of the walkway but nixed the idea.

He glanced back. Kevin had his arms crossed, a bemused look on his face. The other two squinted at him like they were staring into the sun. The higher he got, the more his heart pounded. Two feet to his left was a drop-off. There was the walkway to his right, but it would still be a hard fall. Falling backward would be as bad or worse than falling over the side. An urge to look brave came over him. He turned a little and waved to his friends before continuing.

Nearing the top was like coming up that first and biggest hill on the Giant Dipper. He could not see anything past the top but the sky. The higher he went, the narrower the conveyor seemed.

A few feet from the top, he crouched lower and crawled to the rounded end of the belt, which curved away and under him. It was a long way down to the remnants of a pile of sand below.

Carefully, he turned so his feet faced down and slowly rose to stand tall. He raised his hands in the air. His friends cheered.

Out of the corner of his eye, he saw a dust plume rise over the long entry road to the sand plant. From behind a high, brush-covered mound, a blue pickup truck appeared.

"Ack," he said to himself.

"Someone's coming," Duncan yelled. "You guys go. I'll catch up."

The boys hesitated and then took off running. It took a minute to figure out how to get down quickly without breaking his neck. He sat down with hands behind, feet in front, and scooted down. He was low and out of sight unless the driver came close and from the side. At the bottom, he planned to dart inside and go behind the tower. But when he reached the base of the conveyor, he could see that the risk had lessened. He heard the truck door slam and peered over the edge to see a man walk up to the trailer and enter.

When he found his friends at the top of the hill, his pants were dirty, and his hands were scuffed, nearly raw, but he was smiling.

On the way back, they relived their adventure, bragged about their daring, and shared their wish-I-get-for-Christmas.

Kevin laughed as he briefly wrapped one arm around Duncan's neck and said, "You like walking on edges."

34

Memorial Day Weekend 1966

The high school marching bands were impressive as they strode up Pacific Avenue, backs straight, instruments blaring, and uniforms crisp and brilliant in their school colors. Duncan, Randy, Alan, and a new kid, Lee St. James, squeezed through the crowds lining the street for an unobstructed view.

Duncan liked the bands. When he was five, he had watched entranced as John Philip Sousa's bands marched in *Stars & Stripes Forever*. Yet, the whacks on the drums, the proclamations of the horns and the twirls of the batons were not why the boys had come to wait in front of the Del Mar Theatre for the parade. They were seeking the first glimpse; they were listening for the telltale sounds. They edged into the street, craning their necks.

"I think I hear 'em," Randy said.

"Yeah?" Alan asked.

Then Duncan heard it too: a rattling, roaring, thumping racket approaching from the south. The first of the monsters appeared behind the last of the woodwinds.

The boys pointed and screamed,

"Tanks! Tanks!"

They rumbled up the city's main commercial avenue with all the self-enforced restraint of a big, powerful man attempting to amble. The three beasts approached in a line, and the clacking of their treads pierced Duncan's ears, and the deep-throated rumble of tons of moving steel on pavement vibrated his chest.

Then they were right in front of the boys, and the belching stink of their growling engines hit Duncan's nose like perfume. None of his friends tried to speak above the din. They gawked. And he drank every detail of those massive machines, their turrets facing forward and their guns raised like salutes.

Too soon the tanks pounded away toward Mission Street, and the boys lost interest in the parade.

"Let's book," Lee said.

Lee was a tough-looking kid with curly brown hair, a prominent nose and a hint of freckles splashed under his eyes. Just that morning, Randy had introduced him as Lee, but the boy quickly added "St. James" as if it were a title. His eyes shone with equal glints of wounds and flint, but he quickly smiled, laughed and teased.

"I want some food first; let's swing by home," Alan said.

"Yeah, but I want to check out the new comics," said Randy.

"Me too," Duncan said.

On the way over the Soquel bridge to comic heaven at Village Center, they debated:

"Nothing could stop one of those tanks," Lee said.

"Another tank could," said Alan.

"What? A Nazi tank? No way, not an American tank."

"Yeah?" asked Randy.

"Yeah, that's why we beat them," Alan said.

"My mom says the Germans had powerful armies, but they blew it by attacking us," said Duncan.

The other three boys nodded as if he had said something profound.

"I wish we could ride in one of those," said Alan.

"Me too," Randy said.

"Me too," Lee said.

"I want to drive one," Duncan said.

Alan laughed. "How could you drive one?"

"Dunno, but I want to."

"That'd be boss," Lee said.

"Yeah, really cool," Randy said.

"Yeah, but you wouldn't even be able to see out of the tank. You saw the men driving with only their heads sticking up," Alan said.

"I'd sit on something."

Alan laughed again. "What, on a pillow? Stack of books?" He chortled.

Duncan glared at him as the boys entered the grocer, said, "Oh yeah, at least I could get in the tank. Your fat head wouldn't fit through the hole."

Alan raised his hands and made bug-eyes. "Oooooh."

Miss Foster, a checkout lady in the nearly empty store, looked up from her station as the door chimed their entrance. "Welcome back to the library," she said. It was her joke whenever they came since they often spent long stretches reading, leaning against the magazine rack, or sitting on the floor, but they also bought multiple comics nearly every time they came by.

"Hi, Miss Foster," said Duncan, Randy and Alan.

"Hi, boys!"

They descended on the two spinnable comics racks like wolves on a downed deer. He found what he wanted on the second rack: Fantastic Four, "The Coming of Galactus." He began to devour what might be the coolest story ever. He especially loved the new character of the Silver Surfer. But as he wondered how The Four could ever defeat someone as powerful as Galactus, he noticed a paperback book on the third rack. The cover had a black cross inside a white circle, the ends so bent it was like it was spinning. The title declared: *The Rise and Fall of the Third Reich—A History of Nazi Germany.* He put his comic down and lifted the book from its slot. *Whoa, so thick.* He flipped through it. 1600 pages. No pictures.

What he knew about World War II came from the few movies he had seen where the Nazis or the Japs always got their butts kicked and from Ava, who spoke about Germany as a power that would rise again. His father had fought in the war but not against the Germans. He had been in the Navy fighting Japs, but he never talked about it.

The author's opening words: *Though I lived and worked in the Third Reich during the first half of its brief life, watching at firsthand Adolf Hitler consolidate his power as dictator of this great but baffling nation...* made him forget, for the moment, the wonder of Galactus.

He found the price, $1.65. That would buy a dozen comics. He browsed through the dense pages and fondled the two bills in his pocket. He added the comic and moved to the register. Miss Foster raised her eyebrows as she rang it up. "Is this for you?"

"Yes."

"Well, well, from comics to tomes, that's ambitious."

He did not understand what tomes meant but got the gist. "Uh, I just want to read it; I think I can."

She smiled. "Good for you. That's more book than I read. Don't really like war stuff."

"Uh-huh."

He didn't have to wait long for his friends to line up at the register. He read his new book as Miss Foster took each boy's money.

As they walked the short distance to the Kelly's house, Lee asked, "You bought a book instead of comics?"

"Yeah, I guess," then he added, "I did get this one." He showed Galactus.

"That's an expensive book," Alan said. "You got anything left for the arcade?"

"Twelve cents."

Alan laughed. "That'll last you about five minutes. You'll have to watch us play."

Duncan shrugged.

"You spent all your money on a book?" Lee asked. "You a bookworm?"

"He is not. Let me see," Randy said.

He handed him the book.

"Cool marking," Randy said. "What is it?"

"Nazis put it on their flag," Duncan said.

"That's bad,"

"Totally bad," Lee allowed. "But maybe you'd rather read than surf."

"He would not," Randy said.

Duncan laughed and then dead-eyed Lee. "See you in the water, gremmie."

Lee St. James volubly defended his bodysurfing abilities as the other boys laughed and entered Kelly's home.

35

June 1966

Several days later, at 3 a.m., Duncan was in his upper bunk reading. Below Keith's breathing was a rising and collapsing rhythm of small waves. His brother, able to sleep in an instant, had not seemed to mind these nights of having a lamp on as Duncan had devoured the story of Nazi Germany's rise to power.

Dashing through the sky on his cosmic surfboard, the Silver Surfer comic lay on his dresser, unread. The drama in his new book was greater than anything he had ever imagined.

But after days of this, he had finally had enough of the machinations of crude, brutal, clever men and decided it was time for a swim at the pool despite it not being that warm. He left the house in a T-shirt, shorts and sneakers. After he jogged across Highway 9, he ran into his friends. Their hair and shorts were still wet from swimming, and all were bare-chested.

"Hey."

"Hey," The three kids said at once.

"Where you been?" asked Eddy.

"Santa Cruz."

"Oh."

Kevin seemed posed; his arms were crossed over his chest, head tilted back, face suggesting its usual, vague challenge. And something else, like a girl waiting for you to notice her new perm.

Puzzled, he looked from Kevin to Frank to Eddy and back and asked, "Where did you get the jewelry?" They were each wearing chrome-plated necklaces.

"It's not jewelry," Frank said.

"It shows we're in the same gang," Kevin said.

"Gang?"

"Yeah, we three, same gang, want to join?" Kevin asked.

He did not know what a gang was for but said, "OK."

"Whoa, it's not that easy," Kevin said.

Not easy? They were his friends. Wasn't he already in the gang?

Frank asked Kevin, "He *is* in the gang, isn't he?"

A brief sneer appeared on Kevin's face. It was like a wire pulled up the left side of his upper lip. "Still has to prove himself; we agreed on that."

"Prove what?" Duncan bit off each word.

Eddy said as if reading his mind, "You don't need to prove anything. We all know you're tough."

Duncan frowned.

Kevin said, "Still has to do it."

"Yeah, OK," Frank said and turned to Duncan. "We agreed on an initiation thing for gang membership."

Something in Duncan's expression prompted Frank to quickly add, "Which will be easy for you; it's just something we agreed to."

Kevin, his face a smirk, seemed to study Duncan.

Duncan shook his head, asked, "What do I have to do?"

Kevin touched the symbol around his neck, said, "Get one of these."

"How much does the necklace cost?"

"You don't buy them," Kevin said, "and they aren't necklaces; they're dog chains."

He looked closer and saw the necklaces were made of thick chrome-plated flattened links. "Oh, so how do I get one?"

"You steal it," Kevin said.

"Steal?"

"Yeah," said Kevin.

Every answer Kevin gave seemed to imply that Duncan might chicken out. He answered that with a question: "Where?"

"The drugstore has them," Eddy said.

"You'll do it?" Kevin asked.

"Sure."

"Yeah?" Frank asked.

"Sure."

"When?" Kevin asked.

He looked at the annoying boy, said, "Now."

Kevin leveled his head. "Really?"

"Sure."

Duncan turned to go to the drugstore, but Eddy stopped him with a touch. "You're going to do it now?"

"Yeah."

"Uh, great, hey, something else, it matters how long the chain is. The longer, the more daring you are."

Duncan narrowed his eyes. "Why?"

"Harder to steal and not get caught," Kevin said.

He thought about that, said, "OK," and walked away.

He felt their eyes on him as he went down Main Street toward the Mill Street corner. *Nobody's more daring than me.* Still, stealing? It would be his first time. He bit a nail as he continued his tense, nonchalant, affected stroll. The Man-with-No-Name would show them how daring he was.

He stopped outside the store, glanced back to the corner and saw the boys watching him. He quickly wiped moist hands on his shorts and opened the door. The brass chimes hanging from the handle clanged like bells in a cathedral. He jerked and resisted the urge to run.

An older woman at the register, waiting on a younger woman, glanced at him as he entered, then returned to speaking with her customer. They laughed. Duncan found the magazine rack and grabbed one.

With quick glances around the store, he searched for the chains. Dang it, he hadn't even asked. Dumb. He returned to his pretend reading of the magazine and suddenly noticed the title of the article: "Playtime Pinafores for Little Girls." What!? He checked the cover: *Woman's Day.* His ears burned, but his furtive looks about the store found not observers aghast at his unmanly reading preferences but his target. They were in plain sight, not far from the register, but thankfully on the away side. He replaced *Woman's Day* with a different magazine and sauntered to the chains. With effort he managed not to whistle an I'm-Not-up-to-Anything tune.

Two more customers arrived during his forty-foot journey. He studied the chains while the adults exchanged pleasantries and queried about prescriptions. They hung in various lengths from long hooks arranged by size. The longest hung below his waist. He quickly checked if anyone could see him; all were out of sight, and the clerk had her back turned, reaching for something on a shelf. In one move, he put the dangling end of the longest chain into his pocket, reached up, lifted the other end off the hook and guided the whole length into his shorts. It was done in a couple of seconds. He pulled his T-shirt down to partially hide the bulge of that lump of metal and made for the door, trying to walk naturally.

"Young man," a woman called as he neared the door, "Were you going to buy that?"

It was like a thousand sirens went off all at once. He turned, stared at her, and asked, "What?"

"The magazine, are you going to buy that?"

"Oh, yeah, sorry, forgot." And he moved toward her without feeling his feet.

She unrolled it. He was relieved that the cover showed Alfred E. Neuman on stilts with his pants down instead of a woman twirling a parasol. "Oh, *Mad Magazine*, my nephew likes this."

Duncan mumbled, "Yeah, it's funny."

"He thinks so too. That'll be thirty cents."

Did he have any money? He reached into his right pocket like he expected the cash to be there and was relieved beyond words to find some coins. He had already been planning to plead, *oops forgot*, and, *I promise to get it*, but was able to place two quarters on the counter.

She cheerfully gave him change, and he found himself outside on the sidewalk, not remembering walking out the door. His friends were still at the corner. He summoned the Man-With-No-Name again, walked casually toward them and even stopped to look in the restaurant window.

He joined them around the corner and pulled up the chain. It was much longer than any of theirs.

"Wow," Eddy said.

Kevin grinned and nodded while patting him on the back. His face had lost all traces of its prior condescension or challenge. He stepped back, folded his arms across his chest, studied the chain and Duncan, smiled and said, "Fuckin' A."

36

"Are you coming up?" Duncan said into the telephone.

"Yeah, tomorrow. Me and Lee," Randy answered.

"Cool. Your mom bringing you?"

"Naw, she doesn't want to. Going to hitch." Randy tossed that off like it was nothing, but Duncan heard the suppressed excitement.

"You're going to hitchhike? Wow, ever done it before?"

Randy hesitated, and the line crackled. "No, but Lee has. He says it's easy; just put out your thumb, and people will give you a ride."

"Great, maybe I can hitch down to see you."

They arranged a time to meet at the park pool.

The next day, Duncan, Frank, Eddy and Kevin sat at the park on top of a redwood picnic table under a big tree. Their wet shorts dripped as their hair dried in the warm shade. They watched a lanky young dude push his squealing girlfriend off the coping into the water. The boy-man laughed as she sputtered. The boys lazed and listened to music from other people's radios. Randy and Lee appeared at the table before their hair could dry.

"Hey," Randy said.

"Hey," Duncan replied. Introductions were made. Kevin's response to meeting each of his friends was a simple upnod, which Duncan thought was really cool. "How was hitching?"

"Easy."

Lee nodded. "Yeah, just like I said, we got a ride in no time. Pick a spot, put out a thumb, and here we are." It was like he thought he had invented hitchhiking. Still,

Duncan was envisioning a whole new world of freedom. He could go to Santa Cruz whenever he wanted to.

"What's with the chains around your necks?" Randy asked.

Duncan's chain was so long that he had it double-looped. But it was heavy and, for some reason, now felt ridiculous. He always took it off before he went home and then hid it.

"Means we're in the same gang," Kevin said.

"Looks tough," Lee said.

"Can we be in the gang?" Randy asked.

Kevin started with his whole you gotta steal one to belong speech, but Duncan interrupted, "Can't we just make them members for today? Randy is my best friend."

The boy shone at the declaration.

Duncan did not wait for a reply, rose, and took off his chain. "Here," he said to Randy, "you can wear mine if you want." He put it over his head.

Neither Kevin nor Frank contested the breaking of the sacred initiation procedure. In less than a week, none of them would wear their chains.

When the boys had had enough diving, swimming, dropping off the big rope, and unleashing cannonball splashes on the unsuspecting, they sat on the sand in the sun listening to somebody's transistor radio playing "Louie, Louie." The song was of great interest to the boys mainly because of its pulsing rhythms and baffling lyrics, which someone sang as if a banana was stuffed in their mouth. Did it contain secret meanings? It was suggestive, but of what?

"It's about sex," Kevin said.

"It is?" asked Eddy.

"No, it's about going on a trip," Frank said.

Kevin scoffed, "Yeah, maybe a trip to Sexville."

Duncan thought about the song. The only words he could make out were:

Louie, Louie...

Fine...something...girl,

Blah, Blah, Blah,

Think

give it to

Take her

And lots more *Louie, Louie, Louie* over and over.

"He said something about going over the sea," Frank said.

"It's about fucking," Kevin said.

Duncan felt himself blush.

"Well, if it's about that, why can't we hear all the words? Maybe it's nonsense." Lee said.

"That's why it's about sex. They have to muffle the words; otherwise, they wouldn't let it play on the radio."

This pronouncement had a great impact on the boys. It was like wisdom from someone who clearly knew. And it had the power of irrefutable logic. That and all the boys probably wanted to believe it was about sex. He found himself wondering if Kevin had already had sex. *Could he? Maybe. He's twelve, a whole year older than me. Is that when you start having sex? How else could Kevin be so sure?* Before he could ponder further, Kevin said,

"Hey, you guys want to go somewhere?"

"Where?" Eddy asked.

"Up to the Lodge. It's really cool."

He tantalized them with descriptions of a palatial hotel and a dining room with a river running through it. That's all it took, and the six boys were off. But first they stopped at Dickinson's Market for snacks to eat on the way.

As the boys made their way up Highway 9, they feasted on dessert, which for most of them were candy bars. Kevin munched on his usual Payday; Lee pulled on red licorice; the rest opted for Snickers and Almond Joys, except Eddy, who splurged on pink Snoballs.

"How far is the Lodge?" Lee asked.

"A mile, I guess," said Kevin.

"Maybe three," Eddy said.

"Three miles?" Lee said. "We should have our bikes."

"It's not that far," Kevin said.

"Let's try hitching," Lee said, and he stuck out a thumb as they continued walking.

No cars pulled over as the boys made their progress in loose double-files. The two-lane highway had only a few spots to pull over. The forest crowded the road, guardrails prevented plunges to the river, and the junctions of many driveways and roads would require abrupt stops for the few drivers who might consider picking up six boys. A pickup truck was their best hope, as they could all fit in the back.

"What do you think the bravest job is?" Randy asked Duncan beside him.

"I dunno." But he thought for a while, then, "Astronaut, I guess."

"Yeah, I think so too. Would you want to be an astronaut?"

"Oh yeah."

"Even if the rocket might blow up?"

He thought a bit, then, "Yeah."

"Me too."

"I'd do it too," Eddy said.

"Me too," several others chimed.

"Risking death is worth it for such an adventure," Kevin added.

"To go to space, see Earth from way up there," Randy pointed to the sky. "Wow."

"Gotta be brave," Kevin said.

"Bravery is all," Randy said, like quoting a line from a movie.

There was a chorus of yeahs.

"Astronauts are the bravest," Eddy said.

"What about soldiers?" Kevin asked.

Duncan heard something in his voice that made him remember that his friend had a cousin fighting in Vietnam. Eddy, who must have known this too, said, "Yeah, soldiers have to be really brave, getting shot at."

"What about cops?" Duncan asked.

"Cops aren't brave," Lee said. "They've got guns."

"The crooks have guns too," Duncan said.

"Yeah, I guess, but not as brave as blasting off in a rocket."

No one argued with that. They continued to toss the idea around.

"How about skydivers?"

"Or lion tamers?"

"Being in a submarine?"

"James Bond, he fights all those bad guys?"

"Yeah, but he's not real."

"I saw a guy dive off a hundred-foot cliff on TV," Kevin said. "That's pretty brave."

"Yeah, wow,"

"Racecar guys go over 150 miles an hour. That's brave."

"Scary fast."

"How about going under the ocean in a submarine?"

"Or climbing mountains?"

For a while the boys marched quietly up the road. Duncan told Randy, "You know those tanks from the parade?"

"Yeah."

"I know where they are, up at DeLaveaga."

"You saw tanks?" Kevin asked.

"Yeah, three of them at the parade, but there are six behind a fence in the park."

"Cool."

"I want to drive one."

Kevin scoffed, "No one's going to let you drive a tank."

"Not let; I want to sneak in and take it."

The boys had reached a curve and dip in the road where there was an unofficial turn-out. Duncan's pronouncement made them stop and face him.

"You want to steal a tank?" Eddy said.

"Not steal, just drive it around for a while."

The mouths of his friends went slack in unison. Seeing their lack of enthusiasm, Duncan had what he thought was a brilliant idea. "There are six tanks and six of us. We could each have our own tank!" he declared as if he were offering them their own country.

A few gazes lifted to the clouds; the others managed to blink in slow motion.

"It would be easy to get over the fence. We just have to figure out how to start them. Wouldn't that be cool? We could drive anywhere we wanted, the park, down roads, through trees; we could take over Santa Cruz!"

This proposal to snatch forty-ton tanks and use them to conquer a seaside town was not firing his friends' imagination as he had hoped. He tried harder. "We'd have to be brave. It would be so fun. Who could stop us?"

"Uh," Randy uttered.

"They'd shoot us," Eddy said.

"Nobody's going to shoot a kid. Besides, we'd be in tanks. We'd be invincible like The Thing." His voice had become loud and strident as if he were impersonating Mussolini on a balcony selling the glory of conquering Albania. His visions of power and triumph and maybe even of a lifetime supply of ice cream soared in his head as he reached a crescendo, raised both arms in the air, and declared, "We could do it tomorrow!"

His audience, mouths still agape, stared through him like he was a mirage. Whatever the case, that long moment stretched and stretched, and no one moved. Duncan waited for the ovation.

Then a truck downshifted, engine roaring up the grade.

Kevin said, "Hey, I want to get to the lodge."

They woke as a group, and a few shook their heads. Then they turned and walked away. Puzzled, he watched them go until Randy glanced back and waved him to come along.

37

Kevin called on a Thursday morning, a few weeks before Duncan's twelfth birthday. "Hey, meet me at The Scuz in about ten, OK?"

"K."

All the boys knew the gas station on Highway 9 and Main where they could take a quick piss. The bathroom was rarely cleaned, and the walls within were a collage of scrawled offers for male-on-male sex meetups, phone numbers of women he was assured would provide a good time and poetry about poop. Illustrations of what was possible and impossible to do with genitals complemented the advertising. Duncan made sure he used his own toilet before he left.

Kevin lived in a house on a hill, deep in thick woods, not far up Love Creek Road. He was the only child of parents Duncan had seen just once. He was waiting at the corner, dressed in blue jeans and a faded green T-shirt. A sweep of sandy blond hair crossed his forehead. He gave him an upnod greeting, which Duncan returned.

"C'mon, I want to show you something."

They crossed the Nine, which had sparse traffic and headed down to the place on the river where Kevin had taken him to see the castle. Along the way, Duncan asked, "You want to go surfing later?"

"Yeah, your mom taking you?"

"Naw, thinking of hitching."

"Yeah?"

"Yeah." It would be his first time hitchhiking since the boys had done it returning from the Lodge. The thought of doing it alone made him nervous. He would feel better with company, especially Kevin's, for his self-assurance was bolstering.

Kevin gave him a friendly smirk. "Yeah, let's. Maybe we can go to Mexico if we get good at it."

"Mexico?" He didn't quite know where Mexico was; it was just somewhere south and very far away.

"Yeah, they've got long beaches down there. It's where my mom and dad honeymooned. They showed me a movie they took."

"How long would it take to get to Mexico?"

Kevin thought as they ducked through the brush on the large undeveloped lot north of the park. "Couple of hours, maybe."

"I'd have to be back before dark."

"Yeah, let's get to Santa Cruz first."

They pushed through more bushes, and Kevin found a squat, big boulder at the edge of the narrow end of the pool. A line of tall, full trees screened the spot. They sat on the flat rock. No one could see them unless they happened to be swimming upriver. Kevin reached into a pocket and pulled out a blue package with a white swoosh on it and the word Newport above it. "You ever smoked before?"

Duncan recalled the fire he and Randy had started and decided that did not count. "No."

"I have. You want to try?"

He looked around and saw wet dirt surrounding the rock, and the brush and grass were lushly green. The river was two feet away. "Sure."

Kevin extracted two slightly bent, squished cigarettes and a book of matches. He handed one white-papered stick to him. Duncan put it between his exaggeratedly puckered lips and waited.

Kevin tore off the match, lit and cupped it even though there was no wind, bringing a flame to the Newport. "Suck on it."

He did. The end glowed red, and a sledgehammer of hot smoke hit his lungs. He coughed it out violently as Kevin patted him on the back and laughed. "I should've said sip. You'll get used to it."

He lit his own, took a slight drag, coughed a tiny puff of smoke but retained most of it, and then blew a stream like an expert. Duncan lifted his own back to his lips.

"Just take it in your mouth first. Then try little puffs deeper."

He nodded, pulled gently as advised and let it out without coughing. "Tastes like burnt candy." And even though it also tasted like a dragon had shit on his tongue, he wanted to do it again.

Smoking was cool. Half of the adults smoked; many teenagers smoked; his dad smoked three packs a day, but his mom never smoked; movie stars like John Wayne,

Sean Connery and Audrey Hepburn smoked; doctors smoked; and beautiful women and debonair men looked happy smoking, at least in the ads. Smoking was clearly cool. He just had to keep trying until his body agreed.

"It's a menthol cig." The abbreviation slipped off Kevin's lips like he'd been saying that for years. "See." He pointed to the back of the pack, which proclaimed Newport Tastes Fresher and Menthol underneath.

They sat on the rock in the pleasant, clean air, listening to the river's burbles, the crackle of burning tobacco with each draw, one boy's intermittent coughs, and the other's pleased professional exhales.

"Where'd you get these?"

"Swiped 'em from my mom. She won't miss them."

Duncan was gradually able to take more smoke into his lungs and finished the cigarette. Kevin congratulated him. He managed a wan smile as he suppressed the urge to vomit. "Don't feel good."

"Yeah, it'll get better. Should've had you smoke only half, but you were puffing away like you liked it."

"I do like it." He swallowed to suppress his rising gorge.

"It might be the menthol making you sick. We'll try regular cigs next time."

"Sure. No menthol, but can I have one of those for later?"

38

By late June he and Kevin had made several hitchhiking trips to Santa Cruz. They readily got rides from friendly people, women and men, who may have been both charmed and alarmed by the vision of two boys with their thumbs out at the side of the road. Duncan quickly became an accomplished smoker, although he did not smoke that often. He hid the smoking and the hitchhiking from Ava and his brother and sisters.

Cigarettes were expensive for a boy who only occasionally had money; It cost twenty-five cents per pack. And they could not just walk into a store, look up at the clerk, and say, "Give me a pack of Winston's." However, they could buy them from vending machines, which were everywhere, and at gas stations, restaurants, and movie theaters. But in the early going, they were wary of being seen popping coins into a cigarette dispenser out of fear an adult would intervene.

Randy and Lee took up smoking right away, but Alan and Eddy did not. The boys smoked out of sight when they could. Once, on the wharf, a fisherman had looked over from his pole and said, "What are you boys doing smoking?" They did not reply, and he did not rise, only scowled.

They had not talked about it, but they all seemed to realize that adults who were not their parents were no threat. They might disapprove, but they would not do anything. So, the boys became bolder, even flaunting their new habit and ignoring the disapproving or worried looks while keeping their distance.

The main limiter on smoking was money; with hitchhiking, it was time. When Duncan and Kevin hitched to Santa Cruz, he had to worry about returning in time to avoid revealing he'd been hitchhiking. Although it was normal for him to be gone all day, he knew Ava assumed he was somewhere in Ben Lomond, off doing boy stuff, not ten miles away, riding in a stranger's car. When he showed up at the Kelly's, Margaret assumed he was visiting his Nana. He did not correct her.

Randy and Alan began hitching to Ben Lomond. Each such journey was an escapade for them and all the boys. They talked excitedly about the rides taken and the friendly and sometimes strange people they met. Smoking and hitching were thrills, their secret adventures.

He read *The Rise and Fall of the Third Reich* whenever he was home. One late afternoon, he put aside his book. Ava was off somewhere. He said bye to his brother and headed out the door. A thought flitted through his mind that he knew what Ava did each day about as much as she knew what he did.

He wandered down the Nine and paused to watch a regular at Henflinger's bar perform his usual feat for the entertainment of a few fellow drinkers. He was a large, round man with the Santa face of an alcohol devotee. He stood on the front deck, carefully positioned a beer bottle cap between thumb and middle finger, raised it to eye height, and snap-flicked it like a UFO toward a tree near the road. He was quite good; the caps would sail ten, twenty, sometimes thirty feet if there were no wind.

Continuing to clear the book from his brain, he looked for friends and found Kevin and Eddy in the park. Eddy's seventeen-year-old brother, David, freckle-faced in blue jeans and a green t-shirt, and two of his friends, Victor and Billy, similarly attired, were there. He had met them a few times. They never bugged the boys.

As he approached, he heard David say, "We just need someone small to go under and pass them out."

"Not me," said Kevin.

Eddy saw him and waved. Duncan acknowledged with an upnod. Kevin turned and upnodded back.

"Hey, maybe he'd do it," said Billy.

"Maybe," David said. "Hey, Duncan, you want to drink some beer?"

He paused, looked at the troubled faces of his friends and suspected there was more to this than free beer. "Sure."

"We just need help getting it."

"OK."

Kevin frowned. "He means they want help stealing it."

"How?"

Seemingly encouraged, Victor said, "From Lou's, they have cases of it stacked up behind the place."

David added, "You're small enough; you could crawl under the fence if we hold it up for you."

Victor said, "Just pass a few through, then crawl back out."

He looked at his friends. "Why won't you guys do it?"

They did not answer. Billy said, "They're scared of getting caught."

Duncan looked at Kevin. "Is that why you won't do it?"

It was the first time he had seen the brash boy look uncertain. He mumbled, "Chains are one thing; breaking into a restaurant is something else."

David jumped in before anyone else could speak. "But you're not afraid of anything, are you? That's what Eddy and Kevin say. Right, boys?"

They answered with reluctant nods. Duncan's pride rang like a gong. "No, I'm not scared."

"So, you'll do it?" David asked.

"Sure."

The three almost-adults smiled widely. "Great!" Victor said.

It was deep dusk; the lights in the park were on. "We better wait until it's fully dark," David said.

Feeling bold, Duncan asked, "Anybody gotta cigarette?"

David laughed. "Hey, look at the little man." His friends laughed, too, in a friendly way. Victor reached into a shirt pocket and came out with a box of Camel's, opened it and offered them. He and Kevin grabbed a smoke. Billy flicked the flame into life from his Zippo. Everyone, save Eddy, lit up and lingered in the dim light, blowing clouds.

There was an unspoken tension as they smoked. David eased it by talking about the caper. He pointed at a dull-white Mercury Comet parked on the street, said, "That's Victor's car. We can park it behind Lou's. There is nothing but trees and bushes back there, but we can get right on the main road easy," he snapped his fingers, "like that. They've got cases of beer behind a chain-link fence, one little bulb lighting it. We can hide in the bushes. You'll be able to slide right under. We'll be there holding the fence up. Pass us the beer; we'll pull you through. Be done in seconds."

"OK," Duncan said, but a shiver of nerves hit him.

"You sure, Duncan?" Eddy asked.

He took a drag and blew it to the sky. "Sure."

Not long after, David deemed it was dark enough. "We'll drive over to where I said. You three walk over and head behind the restaurant into the trees. Meet us there, OK?"

Duncan nodded. "OK."

The three teens walked up to the car and got in. Duncan mashed his cigarette into the dirt. Kevin kept his, and they started moving.

"Make sure you can easily get back out before you go under the fence," Eddy said.

"Uh-huh."

"This isn't the same as swiping dog chains."

"Hey, shut up," Kevin said, "you trying to spook him?"

"No, it's just..." But Eddy did not finish.

"Duncan's sure, so don't mess him up. You're still sure, right?"

"Uh-huh."

But he wasn't, not really. He had said yes without even seeing the place. Now, he was going to swipe some beer that he cared no more for than he had that dog chain. It wasn't the beer. It wasn't the chain. He did not know what it was, but he knew he felt excited as they walked past the front of the restaurant. The sounds of diners and drinkers followed them up the street.

It was dark directly behind the restaurant; they pushed through a wall of scrub at the sidewalk's edge. Ahead was a loose line of trees reaching high into the night. To their right, the glow of a dim, bare bulb illuminated a small, fenced area no more than eight feet square. Only the back and left sides were chain-link, about six feet high. The outside walls of the building completed the box. There was a beat-up wood door at the back corner.

"Pssst." The sound came from past the trees. Without trying to be quiet, they walked toward the sound. Behind two bushes, between tall trees, they found the three teenagers. The car was only ten feet away, out of sight, below the Nine.

David pointed. "All those flats are beer." There were two stacks, about a dozen flats in the front and nearly that many behind. "The stack behind is just soda pop. I'll lift the fence. Billy will be ready to take the ones you grab. OK?"

"OK," Duncan whispered, "How many?"

The door to the storage area burst open; soft light spilled out before a swarthy man, who said, "Just one Bud?" Someone answered from within. The man took a case from the tallest stack, went inside and closed the door. Duncan's heart pounded.

"That's good," David breathed, "Probably won't come out again for a while. Let's do it."

He nodded, though it probably could not have been seen. "How many?"

"At least two. Try to get four. Come on."

Kevin, David, Billy, and Duncan crept forward, stopping at the fence, which was loose at the bottom above a deep dip that a digging dog may have created. They listened carefully for a while.

"OK?" David asked.

"OK," Duncan said.

David lifted the fence. Duncan lay down, pushed himself through on his back, and then jumped up. Panting, he paused to listen again. Reassured, he looked at his partners. David's face urged him to hurry up.

He nearly dropped the first case because it was heavier than he thought, but he grabbed the rest quickly and had four through in under a minute. On his back again, he stuck his arms under the fence. Billy grabbed him and pulled him through to his feet. David released the fence, and it rattled against the poles. They froze for a moment and then went for the trees.

Their escape was easy. No one burst out of the door. There was no chase, and afterward, they suspected the theft was not even noticed.

Behind three teenagers on the cusp of being drafted to fight on the other side of the world sat three boys in the backseat, wide-eyed, wide-smiled and casting nervous looks out the rear window for police cars and flashing lights as Victor drove up Love Creek Road. They turned off down a short dirt drive into a clearing that caught some light from a distant streetlight. Two six-packs were retrieved from the trunk. David pulled the tab on a beer and handed it to Duncan. "You did great, kid."

There were echoes of praise from the others. He took a pull of warm but delicious beer that tasted like triumph. Nervous Eddy and solid Kevin drank and laughed so much they almost fell over. Cigarettes were lit, and beers were consumed. Soon, the teenagers were talking among themselves about girls and a trip to San Francisco.

The first beer sent Duncan flying—alcohol with an adrenaline chaser. He would remember sitting on the ground with Kevin and Eddy smoking cigarettes, laughing and bragging, each getting smashed. The teens leaned against the car, talking softly and laughing at how much the beer affected the kids. The third beer sent Duncan into orbit. The teens decided they had other places to be, and they all got back into the car. Somewhere near the Nine he got out with Kevin. He remembered David giving him a six-pack in a brown bag while he said, "This is yours and Kevin's. Another six-pack is yours when you want it; just tell Eddy."

He guessed Eddy went with his big brother. The rest of that night would be remembered in bits and pieces. Kevin and he walked down dark streets, laughing and gulping down beer. Arms around each other's shoulders, they talked melodramatically about something and then giggled until they had to sit down. At one point they threw two-by-fours (where they got them, he had no idea) into the road to make cars stop. One screeched to a halt. They took off running.

He would not remember if he and Kevin drank all the beers or if they lost some of them. At some point, he lost Kevin. Then Duncan realized he was alone and back in the park as he looked down at the black water in the pool. He swayed and thought about diving in. Then he stumbled around the tiny, quiet town; only rarely did a car cruise by on the highway. Then he wove along the sidewalk on Mill Street and mumbled to himself. He was so tired that he sat on the curb and closed his eyes. He had no idea for how long, but at some point, a voice shocked him back to consciousness.

"Duncan!" It was Aileen. She was kneeling beside him on his right, Shona on his left. They nudged him repeatedly. They talked to and about him, but he couldn't follow the conversation. Then they lifted him and mostly carried him up the streets as he stumbled and faded. He remembered they said something about needing to get him into bed before Ava came home. He woke up late and felt sick.

Ava never found out.

39

July 2, 1966

The Ben Lomond and Santa Cruz boys were gathered at the crowded park that Saturday. They were taking a break from wrestling, swimming, diving and flying high on the big rope while bellowing Tarzan yodels. Sitting back among the trees, they watched the celebratory swarm, primarily teenagers, younger boys, and a minority of adults who were busy corralling little tykes, dozing on big towels, or tending to sizzling meat on grills.

Near the water, a group of teenagers had the radio up loud and were dancing and hooting as Tony Valentino laid down his "Dirty Water" riff:

Da-Doont

Doont

Doont

Doont

Da-Doont

And Dick Dodd wove a story about sitting on the banks of a river with lovers, muggers and thieves, who were deemed cool people.

Frustrated women were in his story somewhere, but Duncan had no idea why they would be so, nor did he care. Nor did anyone else appear to care.

The music growled from the radio.

It was cool.

So cool.

New.

Different.

Punchy.

Kevin sauntered over and stood before him and Alan, who sat on the ground to Duncan's left. He had that cocky, edge-of-insolence look he wore so often. He slowly pulled out a pack of cigarettes, took one, lit it, and asked, "Want one?"

It was a dare and a tease. They had yet to smoke in public in Ben Lomond. At the beach? Sure. Here, a few blocks from their parents? No. And this was very, very public.

Duncan furtively glanced around. "Sure."

Kevin nodded and smiled, handed him one and lit it.

"You two are going to get in trouble," Alan said,

He took a drag, but bold as he felt he was careful to blow the smoke down and quickly cup the cigarette in his hand. Kevin smirked at his carefulness but winked and copied him. They laughed together. Duncan felt so cool, pulling on his Marlboro, sipping from a green bottle and watching a girl dance on the sand.

"My dad just bought a new Mustang," Kevin said.

"Boss."

"Yeah, it's bitchin'. It's got a 289 V8 under candy-apple-red metallic paint. He says he'll let me drive it."

"Yeah?"

"Yeah."

"Cool."

Alan snorted. "He's going to let you drive his new car? Bullshit."

"Someday."

"When you're twenty? Right now, you couldn't see over the steering wheel."

Kevin squinted at Alan like he wanted to hit him, but Alan was unfazed and laughed at the hard boy who was a head shorter than he.

"Soon," Kevin said, then to Duncan, "Come by, I'll show you."

"After," he said.

The Troggs sang "Wild Thing" from the electronic box,

Alan poked him. "Hey, look at that girl."

"I am." And he had been. She was maybe seventeen and fun to watch. Seeing the intensity of Alan's gaze, he looked again. He saw a girl full of life and joy, laughing and smiling, dancing with a teen boy. He was a tall, lanky guy in swimming trunks. She was wearing one of those new style scanty bathing suits called bikinis. It was yellow and blue, and it looked the same as underwear to Duncan. Her semi-nakedness was surprising but did little else for the boy, who was enjoying her enjoyment as she shook to the music.

Alan must have been seeing something else, for his eyes were riveted on her every movement and shone with a hunger the younger boy did not understand. Randy and Lee wandered over.

"You guys are smoking out here?" Randy asked.

"Yeah, want one?" Kevin asked.

Randy looked around and shook his head.

"Lee?"

"Maybe later."

He and Kevin took a drag simultaneously, blew two streams skyward and laughed. As if that was his cue, a big man marched over and glowered down at them. He was muscular, trim and very hairy. His chest was like a shag rug, black with flecks of white.

"What do you think you kids are doing?" he bellowed. Heads turned. "Smoking? Do your parents know you're here?"

Lee and Randy disappeared. Alan edged away. Duncan suddenly felt seven again. He and Kevin stared up at the furious giant before them.

"Put those out right now."

"Yes, sir," was jerked from both children's throats at the same time. They squished the offensive items into the dirt. For a few seconds the man glared at the boys, and Duncan feared he might strike them, but he gave his head one quick jerk, turned, and strode away, grumbling, "Goddamn kids today... Hell in a handbasket."

They looked at each other. Kevin's mouth hung open like Duncan's was too.

"Told ya," Alan said.

Having seen the show, the rest of the guys gathered around. Lee said, "Who elected him sergeant"?

"Maybe he *is* a sergeant," Eddy said.

"Or a Colonel," Lee said, "He sure told you guys."

"You scooted fast," Kevin said.

"Yeah, well..." Lee started.

"Maybe you shouldn't push it," Eddy said, looking at his feet. "Smoking here, I mean."

Kevin began to answer, but Duncan wanted to change the subject.

"Hey, Kevin's dad got a new car." He told them about it, and they were off into a friendly argument about which hot car could beat the other. It was fun until Eddy shared about his dad's car, and Kevin asked Lee what his dad drove.

"I don't know."

"Don't know? How could you..."

Lee's sullen glare silenced him. Lee St. James was a mystery. He lived with his grandparents in a house off Seventh Avenue in Santa Cruz. Duncan had only been there once so far and was not allowed inside. He and Randy had gone over to Lee's to get him for a day of fun at the beach. Lee had burst through the screen door at the back of the weathered little house. His grandfather was right behind him. From the doorway the old man, who did not look that old, face rough with a few days of stubble, snarled, "Don't get in any trouble, you little prick."

Lee had been so angry, but he said nothing, and Randy and Duncan had not dared to say anything either until they were halfway to the beach.

At the park then, Duncan thought about his friends and the odd tensions that arose. Kevin had nice parents. The dad was a big, friendly man with thick black hair and a brilliant smile. He would put an arm around his son and talk about all the trips they would take. His mother was a quiet, reserved woman who seemed bemused by the two rambunctious males in her house.

Eddy's parents argued a lot, or at least their son said so. The dad was gruff and no-nonsense, a bit rough with Eddy, tending to tousle his hair and ask what he'd been up to, then he might break into a smile when assured Eddy had not been off robbing banks or doing some other crime. The few times Duncan had visited, it did seem the parents were always on the edge of bickering, a bark in every question, a bite in every reply. Their house was full of things: fancy furniture, knickknacks, a huge TV, a stereo console, and a double garage full of tools and recreational equipment.

Lee's parents could be dead, or maybe they had abandoned him. Randy and Alan would not talk about their missing father, except once when Randy blurted, "Mom kicked him out 'cause he's a drunk." And Duncan's father had abandoned them for reasons Ava never explained.

Despite the tensions triggered by comparing cars, the boys who had both parents and lots of things did not seem to look down on those boys who did not. And the boys without did not seem to envy those that had. They were friends, and that's what mattered. At different times, in different ways, the boys discussed what was important about their gang. It came down to three things: love of doing daring things, having your buddy's back, and never finking on a friend.

Perhaps the boys who seemed to have stable homes also had unvoiced troubles, undercurrents of pain or fear, and their lives were not as perfect as they appeared. Perhaps they felt close to the other boys because their troubles were obvious. Friendship was expressed between them by not asking too many questions. There was tacit understanding and that invisible hug of acceptance where everyone moved on to fun and adventure. That's what happened with Lee. Kevin caught that he had stepped on the big raw sore in a new friend and smoothly shifted. "I still say the Charger could beat a Mustang any day."

The other boys just as smoothly went with the diversion and were soon jeering and laughing again. Most of the teens dove into the pool, but two sat on their towels. The radio played "Along Came Mary." He thought it was a beautiful, catchy song, and he knew the title because they were the only words he understood. The Association seemed to be singing very clever lyrics, but all he heard was:

Blah, blah, blah, blah, blah, blah... And then along came Maryeeeeeee.

What does it all mean?

"You want to go back in?" asked Randy.

"Yeah, I'll finish this," he meant his Mountain Dew, "and come."

Out in the pool, the bikini girl yelled at her boyfriend to be careful. He was clowning as he climbed the far-side hill, pulling himself up by grabbing bushes that clung to the side. He reached a midway stump and got up on it. The trees that grew from this steep slope tended to lean out over the water. When they got to listing dangerously, the town had them cut down, leaving angled stumps, some of which were used as diving platforms.

The teen's stump was about fifteen feet above the water. He stood, arms raised, and declared, "Now, the amazing Charlino will dive into the cup of water." His friends, but not his girlfriend, laughed and cheered the performance. They slapped the water, chanting, "Dive! Dive! Dive!"

He did. His entry was near the edge of the pool. Half of his body entered the water, and the rest crumpled. He flopped over into the water. And then he floated face down. Most of his friends continued cheering.

Kevin said, "Uh-oh, that was bad."

Several adults who had watched from the sand leapt to their feet. Conversations stopped, the cheers faded, and the man floated inert.

"Charlie!" his girlfriend screamed.

The girl and several friends churned through the water to get to him, but another man, who was only twenty feet away, got there first. He rolled Charlie over and pulled him toward the far shore. The teen's head lolled like it was detached, blood pouring down his face.

"Ambulance! Ambulance!" yelled the man. "Call an ambulance!"

Several people ran for the street. There was a firehouse a couple of blocks away. The boys ran to the coping and were followed by the crowd. The girlfriend and his other friends reached the injured teen. The man, Duncan realized it was the Sergeant, had his body under Charlie, supporting his head. "Be careful of his neck," the man barked when the injured boy's friends reached him.

The girlfriend yelled, "We've got to get him to the car."

But the man said, "No." And then he added something about it being "too risky" and "may be broken."

It felt like hours but was probably less than fifteen minutes before paramedics from the firehouse arrived with a stretcher with black foam pieces on the side. Four medics jumped into the water with it and swam over. Two firefighters were busy inflating a large raft.

The whole park was quiet except for the restrained weeping of his girlfriend. His friends hovered nearby, faces etched with shock and fear. The raft was sent across. It was a complex operation to get the boy onto the stretcher, his head and neck secured, and then carefully lifted by four men onto the raft.

The time it took to push and pull that raft across sixty feet of calm water was agonizing. The men gently lifted the boy on the stretcher a foot or two off the raft and onto the coping while repeatedly saying, "Don't jostle him. Careful. Careful." Two police officers arrived and cleared a path to the waiting ambulance. The ground was rough, uneven and sloped up to the street. Duncan and friends were in front as they watched the paramedics carry the teen, whose face was white as an old T-shirt. His eyes were half-open, but he did not seem to see.

"Is he dead?" Eddy asked.

"He sure looks dead," Kevin said.

Alan chewed his lower lip. "Yeah, I think he's dead."

"Maybe he's just knocked out," Kevin said.

"Yeah, totally out," Lee said.

The paramedics reached the ambulance and slid him into it. The sirens wailed as they sped away, followed by multiple cars. Afterward, people gathered their things, got into their cars and left. The boys left the park too. There was something awful about looking at where the teen had been hurt. As they shuffled down Mill Street, Eddy asked," What happened? What did he hit?"

"There is a shelf under the water," Duncan said. The sandstone shelf, with black knobby growths, extended one to several feet from the edge in certain places. It was hard to see from above, and Duncan knew that Charlie had chosen the worst place to dive and then dove far too close to the edge.

The boys nodded. Kevin said, "Maybe we could hitch up to Forest Pool." But there was no enthusiasm in any of them for the idea. Whether true or not, they all suspected that they had just watched someone die. They debated it, but the more they talked, the sicker Duncan felt.

"I'm going home," Eddy said.

"Me too," Kevin said.

Duncan went to Randy and said, "I'll come down, and we can hit Rivermouth."

"Yeah, that sounds good." But his voice was flat, and they did not set a day.

Alan, Randy and Lee left to hitchhike home; the rest departed for their homes. Duncan had stashed his six-pack of beer deep in the cold water upriver as a later surprise for his friends, but he forgot all about it that day. Instead, he went straight home to his room, got into his bunk and spent the afternoon reading about Operation Barbarossa.

40

July 1966

By the time Duncan was seven, the Findlays had already moved five times. Since then they had moved another three. One night, near the end of dinner, Ava announced that they would be moving yet again, at the end of the month, back to Santa Cruz. She did not say why.

Duncan pushed potatoes around on his plate and glanced at his sisters. Shona supported her head with one hand, sighed, and shifted the location of her green beans. Aileen looked at Ava as if more should be said, but when it wasn't, she resumed eating. Keith smiled.

The move would be just a blip for Duncan. He was used to this, used to having nothing explained, used to leaving friends he had just made and used to always being the new kid at a new school with new teachers and new stuff to learn in new ways. However, this move would be less of a whiplash than ones before. He would return to his friends in Santa Cruz, and even though he would be leaving the Ben Lomond boys, he could always hitchhike.

His mom being mum about the whys and wherefores was not even unusual for that era of child-rearing in America. Parents generally did not keep their kids in the loop, nor did they try to soften the blow of upheavals with explanations. Duncan had wondered if this sudden move had to do with the argument he had heard between Betty and Ava. Betty had been critical of Ava's help in her business and the Scottish Festival, which, she said, had flopped. Ava had been defensive and angry. Their parting was one of harsh words and slammed doors. These were not thoughts he dwelled on for long. He had no say in the matter.

Some of the time that month, he hitchhiked to Santa Cruz, usually with Kevin, and sometimes Eddy would come along. Randy would call and say something like, "Swell's good." Then he would call Kevin and agree to meet at the bridge. These escapades had their tricky bits. Duncan worried Ava would be out driving and see him with his thumb out. Also, bodysurfing meant his shorts were soaked from the ocean and encrusted with salt. Getting back in time could be difficult. He always wanted to stay longer, and rides were uncertain.

***

One day at the Boardwalk, while each boy was chewing on a hot dog, Randy asked, "What happened to that guy who busted his head?"

"Dunno," Eddy said.

"He's fuckin' dead," Alan said.

"Yeah, like you know," said Kevin.

"He looked it."

"You an expert on dead?"

Alan took a big bite of his dog and chewed in silence.

"It was a stupid dive," Duncan said.

"It wasn't stupid," Alan said. "He just messed up."

"Naw, he didn't look where he was diving."

"No shit, Sherlock."

"It would be easy to make that dive if you weren't dumb."

"Easy, huh? Why don't you do it?"

Their walk had neared the arcade. The boys stopped and turned toward Duncan for his answer.

"I could,"

Alan laughed. "Sure, sure. You could, but you won't."

"Don't push him," Randy said, "that dive's too dangerous."

Duncan felt his boast taking him somewhere he did not want to go. The truth was that the image of that unconscious, maybe dead man, head bleeding and neck likely broken, was scary as hell. He could tell by their eyes that his friends saw it the same way. He did think he could make the dive. The height wasn't the problem as much as how far the shelf extended into the pool. But the vision of ending up like that man made him squishy inside.

"I'm not pushing," but then to Duncan, Alan said, "Just admit you're too scared to try it." Putting it that way was part of Alan's malicious brilliance. All the boys could recognize a line was crossed and that to back down and admit being scared was not an option.

"I'm not scared," the Man-with-No-Name said. "I could do it."

"So do it."

Duncan knew he was cornered. The Man-with-No-Name escalated. "I could. I could even do a tougher dive."

His words created a bubble of silence around the six boys. The happy squeals of children, the babble of the thick moving masses around them along the promenade and the dinging of pinball machines just inside the door were all abruptly muted behind a cottony wall of anticipation. Four heads pivoted to Alan, who squinted hard at Duncan.

Seconds passed.

"I dare you."

The air hissed, being sucked past several sets of teeth. Recklessness danced within him, and he felt exhilarated. "I might. I could. You'll see, but I'll do it when and if I want to."

It must have been clear that this was bravura and evasion. The silence became thicker. The next and obvious move was for Alan to double-dare. A dare upped the ante, but a double dare presented an unavoidable challenge. He would have to do it or totally lose face. He saw Alan was thinking about it. Randy blasted his brother with angry eyes.

The moment stretched. Alan stroked his chin. Then he laughed and poked Duncan, said, "Sure, sure, you let us know, daredevil."

The collective laughter sounded like relief. The boys spent the next couple of hours playing games in the arcade.

***

When he was not hanging with the gang, he was with Kevin or Randy. He would go over to Kevin's house to watch TV and throw a baseball around, sometimes with Kevin's dad, who was an affable man full of praise, hugs, and advice for his son.

"Be good out there," he might say.

"Never back down from a fight."

"If you want to achieve anything worthwhile, be prepared to work hard."

"Nobody ever got anywhere expecting life to be easy."

While the father was energetic and even boisterous at times, Kevin's mother was gentle and sweet. She was less than a foot taller than her son. Her smiles and the music of her voice contained so much love for Kevin that simply being within the penumbra of it made Duncan feel blessed. When he and Kevin would go to leave, she would embarrass her son by holding him by the shoulders and kissing him on his forehead. "Be careful," she'd say. Kevin would groan, "Mom!" She would smile and release him, but before Kevin got out the door, he would look back to say, "I will. Love you too."

Kevin no longer swiped his mother's cigarettes. There was a vending machine across from Randy's house, a green box about the size of a big suitcase attached to the outside wall of the hamburger joint. No one could easily see the boys when they slipped over to it, popped in a quarter and selected from about a dozen brands.

One day, sitting on a log out of sight of his house, Duncan asked, "Do they know you smoke?"

Kevin exhaled. "Dad does, not mom."

"He doesn't mind?"

"Not too much, just says to keep it to a few a day."

"Why not your mom?"

"He doesn't want me to upset her. What about your mom?"

"No way."

"Yeah."

"Your dad's cool."

"So is my mom, but it would bug her to know I'm smoking."

***

It became habitual to tease Duncan whenever the boys got together; whether at the beach or the pool, someone asked, "When are you going to dive off The Stump?"

He would answer, "Soon," pause like he was thinking deeply, then say," Maybe, but soon."

Everyone would laugh, yet he was hatching a plan to surprise them. On his own, he had checked the depth of the pool in various places. He knew that even dropping from the rope could mean hitting the bottom in certain spots. The shelf was of variable width all along the far side of the river. He also studied how adults dived or jumped from heights. Most were less adept than kids, but a few clearly had better techniques and form. One man could slide into the water with barely a splash.

One day, past the middle of July, all the guys met at the pool. They walked down to the edge. Alan asked the question.

"Soon, I'm thinking about it." It was a slight change, but the boys still laughed. He let them dash off to dive into the water, but he waited and thought.

Today.

And he felt that wild exhilaration that he loved. Randy waved for him to come in. He ran, leapt, tucked himself into a ball, and blasted him with the splash. After paddling for a while, he called past Randy to Alan and Kevin,

"Soon is today! Watch this!"

"Really?" Randy asked.

Duncan's answer was to swim the fifty feet over to the other bank. He went to the shelf the man had crushed his head on. He climbed up the steep, worn paths of other people, hesitated as he reached The Stump as if he was reconsidering, then pressed on higher and higher, veering to the right.

The highest stump was a newer one from a far-leaning tree. He had yet to see anyone dive off it. It was at least fifteen feet above The Stump and jutted from the cliff side almost like a board. The cut made a nearly level platform. It was tricky getting up the trunk, but he made it and stood to look down at his friends.

Shit, this is high.

He had been up once before but had not jumped. Maybe that was a mistake. Directly below, the shelf was the narrowest and the water the deepest. To make it he would still have to leap outwards as far as he could, but he needed to enter vertically and feet first like the man he had observed.

All the other swimmers were on the far side of the pool. No one, save his friends, appeared to have noticed him. If he hit wrong, it would really, really hurt. He stared down at the target spot he had chosen. His friends were quiet. No one goaded, and no one cheered. The seconds ticked by, and he feared he might chicken out.

Go now!

He bent his knees, rose, and took one short, quick bound forward to spring off the front edge with everything he had—immediately knew it was wrong. He was rotating. In the less than two seconds it took to reach the water, he flailed his arms to right himself and mentally shouted to bring his legs together, get his arms down, and breathe. He managed to arrest the sickening backward rotation, and he mostly straightened his legs and brought them together upon entry. He tried to snap his arms to his sides but forgot about taking a breath.

Bam, he hit the water hard with atrocious, laughable form. His legs buckled, and his arms slapped the water in an explosion of pain. His nuts were whacked; he felt a surge of nausea, and water gushed up his nose. He shot to the bottom of the pool, and his two feet hit big, round, slimy stones. He felt his left ankle twist.

Stunned, he hovered over the bottom with his slight buoyancy not yet lifting him toward the surface. His reflex was to curl into a ball and moan for a while, but his lungs were already screaming for air. He used his right foot to push off the river bottom and moved numbed arms in short, painful motions like a penguin signaling for help. He broke free into blessed oxygen, coughed violently and blew burning water out of his bronchial tubes and sinuses. It was hard to use his arms, but his legs worked well enough, even if his ankle twinged each time he did so.

Randy and Kevin swam hard in his direction. The other boys were close behind. In the time it took them to reach him, he composed himself enough to speak.

"Are you OK?" Randy shouted.

"Yeah, I'm fine," he croaked.

"Yeah?" Kevin asked.

"Yeah, arms sting. Didn't hit too good." He offered a fleeting smile and groaned. "I think my nuts are in my chest."

Randy and Kevin laughed. The other boys arrived.

"That was awesome," Eddy said.

"I'm going to sit for a minute." Duncan paddled toward the nearby shelf. His progress was slow, but it was not far. He sat on the shelf where the water came up to his waist. The boys sat or stood around him. They chattered about what a feat it was and asked questions about what it was like. Lee said it was great, even if Duncan had looked like a frightened duck crash-landing in a lake. They pointed to the bright red undersides of his arms and asked if it hurt. "Some," he said, wondering how long the numbness would last. He basked in their admiration. He tried to hide how sick he still felt from the blow to his balls. And he pretended he did not hurt in a dozen places.

Everyone gushed over him like he was a hero, except Alan and Kevin, who were more reserved. Alan acknowledged that his jump more than satisfied the dare. Kevin said little but appeared to study the stump above and the water below. Eventually, Duncan recovered enough to swim a little, josh and retell the story of The Big Leap. He wanted to go home but lingered, mingled and posed.

When he finally said he was done and going, Kevin came over to the coping ladder he was ascending, upnodded. "Fuckin' A, Duncan."

"Thanks."

"Crazy, but fuckin'A." The boy winked and swam toward the dam.

He stood dripping at the top of the ladder. Alan was close by, said, "Yeah, that was something, but I better be careful about what I dare you to do. People might blame me for getting you dead."

They laughed like it was a joke. He headed for home with a little limp. He felt proud, triumphant and shaken by the mystery of why he had done it.

****

More play days followed, but Kevin did not appear for any of them during those last two weeks of July.

Duncan asked Eddy and Frank, "You seen Kevin?"

"No."

He tried calling Kevin, but there was no answer. He walked over to his house, which was not far up Love Creek Road. There were no cars, and no one answered the door. He had to help pack, and more days went by. Kevin did not call him.

The day before they were to leave for their next home, he went to Kevin's again. It was up a hill at the end of a long drive that sashayed through the ragged trees. This time there were lots of cars, lots and lots of cars, along Love Creek itself, at the sides of the drive and clustered before the house.

He was panting hard before he got fifteen feet up that drive, as if the air condensed and chilled with every step, becoming an unbearable icy weight. But then his feet felt fused to the earth; he could not retreat or advance. He trembled in place, and his eyes swam, fearing what might be true.

Eventually, he backed away and headed for home. He trudged slowly down the road, one hand absently playing with the grass fronds lining the side and sang "Paint it Black" by the Rolling Stones.

41

August 1966

The cool thing about Duncan's new home was that it was only a few blocks from the beach. Not the Boardwalk beach, but the little beaches like thumbprints in wet clay carved by the ocean into the cliffs along West Cliff Drive. Many of them disappeared during high tide.

They lived on a short street just off Woodrow Avenue, and it took only a few minutes to get to the cliffs that overlooked the bay. The surf tended to be rougher there. The bigger beach at the end of Woodrow was often strewn with seaweed. People would stroll upon its sands, but Duncan did not like it because it often smelled of sewage—a large pipe that carried Santa Cruz's effluent crossed that beach and disappeared into the sea.

Their house was small like their prior houses. The boys shared a bedroom, as did the girls. Ava slept in the living room on the couch—a big old hideous thing upholstered in gold velour. There was a detached garage and a small, ill-tended front yard with a pitiful, unloved fruit tree. The large backyard was overgrown with grass and had trees needing pruning, all bounded by rusting wire fences.

The house had one tiny bathroom sandwiched between the two bedrooms. The kitchen/dining area had an old stove with gas burners on one side and a cast-iron woodstove on the other. The rent was $105 per month.

The neighborhood was all single-family wood-frame homes, which had sprung up after 1900 when a tabernacle had been built at the center of what would later be called the Circle Neighborhood due to the circular street layout.

What mattered to Duncan was that he was back in Santa Cruz, near the Boardwalk, bodysurfing and Randy. The Santa Cruz boys were spread out across town. Duncan was on the west side. Lee was on the east side, and Randy and Alan were in the middle. The Kelly's house was their usual meet-up place.

Soon after breakfast, Duncan bolted out of his bedroom, passed Ava in the kitchen and announced, "GoingOverToRandy's."

She was pouring a cup of coffee, said, "MmmmHmmm."

He mounted his bike in the front yard where he had left it, cruised over to Randy's and found him in the garage oiling the chain on his new bike. It wasn't a Sting-ray. Margaret had bought it used, and she and her son had fixed up the older, classic bike that declared Panther on the chain guard.

As they set out on the two-mile ride to Lee's, Randy said, "He wants to show us a new surfing spot."

Their friend lived with his grandparents at the end of a stubby street off Seventh Avenue. Duncan and Randy coasted down it, their fat tires crunching over dead leaves. Duncan was in stitches over Randy's story about how Cheryl had ended up with two marbles stuck up her nose. Lee's grandfather answered the front door, cutting their laughter off like jerking the stylus from a record player.

"Well?" he asked, his face showing more glare than greeting.

Duncan tried to stifle his laughter as Randy straightened, brought both feet together and said, "Hello, Mr. Nelson. Can we see Lee?"

"May, not can; what have they been teaching you at that school?"

Randy swallowed. "May we see Lee?"

He was not truly a big man, but to Duncan, he was huge. He was dressed impeccably in a crisply ironed short-sleeved shirt, creased casual slacks and polished black shoes. He looked north of fifty. On his right arm was a tattoo of a mean-looking bird with the letters USMC below it.

"Humph." The man looked at Duncan. "And who are you?"

"Duncan, sir."

"Duncan who?"

"Findlay, sir."

"Where do you live?"

He told him.

"What is your phone number?"

The odd demand took him aback.

"Come on, I want to be able to call your parents if you turn out to be a troublemaker."

He told him. Mr. Nelson did not write it down. "Now, I will tell you what I first told Randy. I won't tolerate any hoodlum activity. I expect his friends to walk the straight and narrow. If you're into mischief, there will be hell to pay. Do you understand me?"

Duncan gulped. "Yes, sir."

"Good, you better. Boys should have fun, but wrongdoing is out. You got it?"

"Yes, sir."

"All right then." He called over his shoulder, "Come out here, Lee."

He must have been just inside listening, for he appeared immediately. Mr. Nelson let him pass, and the three friends hesitated on the stoop.

"Which beach did you say you were going to?" the man asked Lee.

"The one at the end of twenty-six, sir."

"Uh-huh."

Duncan thought the man knew very well where they were going, and the question was a test rather than for information.

"May I have some money for the arcade, sir? We'll be going there after surfing."

"Hmmm." He went inside for a moment and returned with a couple of quarters. Lee stared at the coins placed in his palm with transparent disappointment.

The grandfather said, "It'll have to do. I don't want you spending all afternoon banging ball bearings around and wasting time."

Duncan wondered what summer was for if it wasn't for having fun and wasting time. Lee appeared to know better than to argue. "Thank you, sir," he said.

"OK, go on then. Have good fun."

On impulse, Duncan said, "Pleased to meet you, sir. We won't get into mischief."

The grandfather brightened, and a hint of a smile appeared, quickly followed by a questioning cast to the eyes, but he said, "Nice to meet you, Duncan Findlay," and he closed the door.

Quietly, the boys got on their bikes and rode out toward Capitola Road. As they turned onto it, Lee snorted and said in a high-pitched female voice, "Pleased to meet you, sir. We won't do mischief." In his normal voice, he asked, "What the hell, Duncan, you getting ass-kissy?"

"No, he just kind of pulled it out of me."

Lee scoffed.

"Well, *you* were all yes, sir, and no, sir with him too."

"Yeah, it's hard not to be. He'd kick my ass if I wasn't."

"Kind of a mean guy," Randy said.

"Tough," Duncan said.

"Grouchy," said Randy.

"Grumpy."

"Yeah, grumpy grouchy gramps," Lee said. The boys batted that back and forth and laughed for over a block.

The new surfing spot was another two miles from Lee's place. The waves were primarily three-footers, but the break was sweet, and they got many good, long rides before some boarders showed up. Not getting run over by a ten-foot surfboard was one thing, but etiquette was more important. For the most part, the surfers treated each other with respect. They did not ruin anyone's ride by getting in their way, and although bodysurfing was not seen as "real" surfing, the boarders were friendly and mostly let them get their rides. And the boys were in awe of the boarders—each wished they could afford a longboard like the men and teens rode—they dreamed of surfing Steamer Lane. More boarders appeared as the day wore on, and Lee said, "We should go. There's no spot where we won't muck up a ride."

***

The casino arcade got a lot of action from the boys. When the ocean was too calm, and they had even a little money, they went to that land of pinball machines, ski ball and mechanical baseball.

Lee made it obligatory that they first tried the electrocution game. Inside the west entrance was a red metal box with two copper handles. For one cent they could play who-can-stand-it-longest. Only Lee, Randy and Duncan would do it at all. Alan would shake his head and say something like, "Naw, you dumbshits can get your brains fried, not me."

There was not much to the game except courage and endurance. The player put a penny in the slot, deposited it with the turn of the knob, grasped the solid copper handles and felt the surge of electricity go into hands and arms. The volts or amps or something like that grew in intensity the longer you held on. A gauge showed 0 to 500. 500 what, it didn't say. Randy or Duncan would go first, but Lee was the acknowledged king, and he would always go last.

Duncan found the experience scary, but he did it anyway. The second the coin was accepted, and as he gripped the smooth, cool handles, it would buzz like a transformer, and his hands and forearms would stiffen from the current. As the seconds passed, the force of those electrons increased, and both his arms became as rigid as iron. He never went as high as 500, usually quitting around 300. It actually didn't hurt much, and the words on the box suggested it was good for one's health, but Duncan doubted that. He pulled his curled fingers off as Randy and Lee cheered and then jeered him quitting.

Randy usually held on longer, but the king was a maniac. It was like Lee enjoyed it. He would hold on right to the maximum current of 500 and keep going as his arms and upper body shook. A crazy grin was fixed on his face until something clicked off to stop the current. It was always the machine that quit, not Lee.

42

October 1966

On a warm Sunday afternoon, the day before Halloween, the boys held a strategy meeting at Mrs. Kelly's. Randy and Lee sat cross-legged on the floor in the bedroom. Alan lounged on the bed. Duncan had grabbed the one chair. All the eyes sparkled with anticipation.

"Does everybody have their grocery bags ready?" asked Duncan. There were murmurs of assent. "Double-bagged with good handles?" After a few moments of rustling, he received nods and thumbs up.

"OK, this is a contest to see who can get the most candy tomorrow. Fruit," the three kids facing him wrinkled their noses, "does not count."

"How about cookies?" Randy asked.

Alan and Lee shrugged. "Yeah, cookies count, and anything sweet that isn't natural. Salty crackers or chips won't count."

"What about pie or cake?" Alan asked.

Duncan showed him his *say what* face. The other two appeared to ponder the answer. Finally, he said, "That'd be pretty weird, but if anyone dumps a slice of cake or a piece of pie in your bag, I guess we'd have to count it." With a smirk he glanced at the other boys and asked, "Anyone think Alan could go all night without eating a pie or cake put in his bag?"

All laughed except Alan. "OK, so it's what's in your bag at the end of the night that counts." Then to Alan, "Smears of chocolate on your face won't count either."

Randy and Lee laughed harder. Alan flipped him the bird but then laughed too.

"Your mom says sunset is around five, so let's all be here at 4:30. Curfew is at eleven, so we'll have six hours to grab all the candy we can." There were moments of reverence as the gang envisioned bags full of peanut butter cups, KitKats, Snickers, candy cigarettes, Lemonheads, M&M's, Almond Joys and Banana Splits.

"I'm going for two bags," Lee said.

Randy gawked. "Two bags?"

"Why not?"

"Nobody has ever gotten one bag before. How are you going to get two?"

"Because I'm clever."

"What?"

"You'll see."

"We can get more than one full bag?" Randy asked Duncan like he was a judge or something.

Duncan kicked the question to the room, and they debated the nuances of candy victory for over ten minutes. They ended up agreeing that so long as the boy could carry it back by himself to the Halloween command post, i.e., the Kelly house, the total pile was what mattered, in or out of the bag or bags. Duncan reviewed the planned route moving through the better neighborhoods, the tone of which vaguely resembled Sherman's march to the sea.

"You should be a general," Alan said. The others chuckled.

"Yeah, General Duncan, the candy conqueror," Lee said.

More laughter.

"Remember when he wanted to grab those tanks and conquer Santa Cruz?" Randy asked. The boys howled.

"Yeah, yeah, and it would be easy," Lee said, rolling his eyes.

Duncan allowed an embarrassed smile and waited until the laughter subsided, then he said, "Yeah, yeah, yeah, but...but imagine how much candy we could get if we showed up in tanks?"

Six eyes drifted off to stare into space at the vision. With a gleam in his eyes and a waggle of his brows, he added, "Trick-Or-Treat!"

Lee and Randy collapsed in laughter.

Alan chuckled, said, "Yep, General Duncan." And he mock-saluted.

***

The next day was the hottest Halloween in Santa Cruz history, over 90. The boys went out, bags in hand, in short-sleeved shirts and executed Operation Chocolate Bar. For all their avarice, they were respectful as they went door to door. None wore costumes. This had a lot to do with a lack of money and a little to do with a lack of interest. The kind and welcoming adults appeared briefly taken aback by the lack of costumes and perhaps by the size of one boy who looked sixteen even though he was fourteen. They quickly recovered and offered plates and bowls containing the desired treasures. Only a few times did anyone comment on the lack of parental chaperones.

They began by moving quickly from house to house, excited and determined to win. The prize: a handful of candy from each of the other boy's bags—and of far greater importance, bragging rights.

After an hour, as the dark deepened, they slowed to a leisurely pace, laughing and chattering as they knocked on doors, rang bells and grabbed excessive handfuls of delights. They were quick, but a few adults were quicker and insisted they only take one or two items.

Many kids prowled the streets, and the overall effect was of one big party. Some of the elaborately attired criticized the boys with comments like, "Nice costume, doofus." The boys did not care because their bags were filling; they had each other, and the night had that magical sparkle of hilarity and joy in the warmth of a summer-like night.

As they scoured the neighborhoods south of the new university, UCSC, and their nearly full bags grew heavy, Randy yawned, and Alan said, "Still no pie," which brought the expected chuckles.

They compared hauls on a sidewalk in front of a mansion-like house with an impressive display of goblins, ghosts, and a dozen candle-illuminated pumpkins guarding the walk. Lee had a full bag, and two pockets were full too. The rest had nearly full bags.

"How did you do that?" Randy asked.

"Told you, I'm clever."

Randy twisted his lips, said, "But we all went to the same houses."

Alan solved the mystery for his brother. "Put your hand next to his." Randy raised his palm out. After a moment, with a grin, Lee placed his against Randy's. His was much larger—even compared to Alan's hands.

"See," Alan said, "every time we got handfuls, he grabbed more. That's all."

It was getting late, and the candy take was getting slimmer, so they headed back, hitting new houses as they went. All that night, they played no tricks: no soaping of car windows, no toilet paper rolls thrown over trees, and no eggings.

On the way back to the Kelly's, they ooohed and aaahed at Halloween yard displays. They boasted of their bounty. Alan was already making massive progress through his bag.

43

December 1966

"Lee says the waves could be super big," Randy said over the phone.

"Yeah? How does he know?" asked Duncan.

"Boarder at school said there's a big storm coming in off the coast. Bunch of high school guys are planning on doing Steamer tomorrow."

"Wow, want to do Rivermouth, or maybe 26?"

"Can't; we're going to Watsonville to see my cousins."

"What about Lee?"

"Naw, he bitched about it probably raining, but really it's his Gramps has him doing chores 'cause of that D he got."

The line hissed for a few seconds. "I miss surfing," Duncan said.

"You goin'?"

"Maybe, take a look."

"Wish I could."

"Yeah, me too."

***

The next day was a Saturday. He got up late, went into the backyard and checked the sky. A few dark puffs were moving slowly in from the west with hints of more, farther away. But it was sunny, cool but not cold, and he wondered if it was all just a story.

After breakfast he went to the bathroom, put on last summer's worn cutoffs, and stepped into full-length blue jeans to cover them. He stuffed a bath towel into his bag and grabbed a light coat.

On his way out, Ava asked, "Where are you off to?"

"Going to look at the waves, supposed to be big."

"All right."

He mounted his bike and rode out of his yard. At Woodrow he decided to skip swinging by Steamer Lane. The wind was picking up, and bigger, darker gray puffs crowded the blue above. The possibilities called to him, and he wanted to get to it.

In later years Santa Cruz would grow enormously. Traffic would be dense year-round, not just in the summer. There would be bike paths and lots of Do-This and Don't-Do-That signs everywhere. The ice-plant-draped cliffs would have their dirt paths paved over and lovely wood fences would be erected to interfere with people falling over the edge. There would be one-way streets and widened bridges, trees planted by the score on Pacific Avenue as the beginning of turning it into a Garden Mall. Preserving the history of Santa Cruz would become important, yet on that December day, he was part of that history. To him, what would be deemed precious in the future was only everyday life.

There were few cars on the road; even Beach Street was virtually deserted despite it being Saturday. There were a bunch of cars on the wharf and a few strolling people on the beach and the sidewalks. The clouds had grown thicker and the breeze steadier. The signs of the burgeoning storm excited him. He pedaled along the backside of the Boardwalk. All of the rides were closed.

He found a metal railing to lock his bike to and hurried to see the Rivermouth end of the beach. Walking past the Giant Dipper, he stopped at the top of the stairs that descended to the beach. The boom of the surf was louder than he had ever heard before, and the expanse of the whitewater was broader than he had ever seen. The beach was empty, and the waves carried no riders.

Beyond bitchin'.

He scrutinized the scene. The river was full and rushing into the sea. The breeze blew steadily into his happy face. The tide was ebbing. The waves were at least eight-footers, breaking left to right, and were of that perfect roller-crusher blend.

Lee and Randy are going to be green when I tell them.

He yelled as he ran over the sand, "Charge!" and laughed.

He was again dashing along a precious path of history. The beach of that day would not last. It was only half as wide as it would become. Nearer the sea, it declined gradually under the water as a long, broad, smooth slope of sand shaped by the San Lorenzo. It was perfect for good breakers.

The air temperature was barely higher than the water, yet he shed his outer clothes quickly. At the water's edge, he hesitated. At twice his height, the waves were big to him. The swash was a roiling foam-crowned whiteness. The backwash was being sucked to its source with evident power. A few spatters of rain made his cheeks twitch. The wind lifted his hair off his forehead. He looked around: one guy was walking west on the Boardwalk, and a man and a woman, holding hands, were far down the beach, nearing the wharf.

Three summers of virtually living at that beach, endless hours bodysurfing everything it had to offer, from gentle squeakers on calm June days that barely enabled a ride to roaring crushers that slammed him into the backwash, had instilled in him a sense of invulnerability. So, his hesitation was not from fear but respect and awe for the epic conditions.

Excitement and the heat-generating brown fat of youth warmed him in the cold gray sea. For half an hour, he enjoyed an abundance of ridable waves. He passed on four-footers he once would have been thrilled to take because he knew a six-, eight-, or even a ten-footer was not far behind. With no one else in the water, he could cut across the waves and do flips and spins with abandon. He was like a dolphin, leaping, slashing, rolling and plunging while shouting with joy. He even exulted when he misjudged a wave and was sent tumbling. Each ride ended with him swimming back out for more.

At one point a man watched from the promontory. He did not stay long, for the onshore breeze had increased, and sporadic, if light, rain came more often. The bigger waves made picking good positions and better timing of his takeoffs more critical. And he had to be careful not to let waves of that size break on him.

After a half hour of sprint swimming and dog paddling in water that was often too deep to touch bottom, he was cold and tired but reluctant to stop. The pleasure of a warm towel and a hot lunch called him.

One more.

He had to wait as the surf had dwindled to those uninteresting fours. As he paddled and bounced off the bottom, he vaguely noted that his position had gradually moved farther from shore. He was well past San Lorenzo Point when he saw something outside. It reminded him of a daydream fantasy he sometimes had while lounging on the cliffs looking across the bay. Over toward Monterey, he would see something long and blue-gray that looked like a giant wave. He had imagined it was an enormous tidal wave that would roll over all of Santa Cruz. It was only a distant fog bank, but the illusion got him every time.

Hundreds of hours of bodysurfing had honed his judgment of oncoming swells, their size, and where they might break. It took him only a few moments to discount a fog bank. The sky was overcast, but the rain had paused, and the onshore breeze was clearly stronger by the way it sent foam flying off the wavetops and stirred the trees onshore. When he realized that the oncoming mass could not be fog but was an actual swell, he felt the first stab of fear since he had begun swimming in the ocean three years before. He could not gauge the size of it, just that it was huge. Foam along the thin, breaking top of it lifted and flicked into the air.

How can it be starting to break way out there?

With only his head and neck above the water, he said, "Oh no."

He had a clear vision that if he let that wave break on him, he might die. Trying to surf it was too terrifying to consider. He panicked. He swam toward the oncoming monster. And as he did so, the swell lifted the buoy that defined the limit for boats approaching the shore. The vision of that buoy lifted so high chilled him like the water had not. He swam toward the rolling mountain like he was fleeing a shark. The boy weighing 95 pounds and the swell massing 3000 tons closed on each other at 20 mph.

I have to get over it. I have to.

They met as the monster rose like Neptune himself, the sloping face of the water mountain quickly approaching vertical. It was like being sucked up a cliff. He frantically swam up that rising face, his astonishment mixed with terror. He just made it over the top, his feet briefly catching on the breaking crest that threatened to pull him back over.

He gasped and breathed a sigh of relief, only to see that the monster god had a bigger brother. Unable to think, he raced toward the next swell. He again flew up the watery cliff face and down the backside.

It shocked him how far from shore he was. As he saw another gigantic wave coming, he noted that he was steadily moving out to sea.

Am I in a rip?

He could not answer as panic drove him toward the next one. He got over that one more easily and had a moment to confirm that he was indeed in a riptide. Rips were the bogeyman to the boys; they sucked you out and under the sea. He knew nothing about how to get out of one; the boys had agreed that to be caught in one was to drown. He knew that lifeguards rescued over a hundred people every year from riptides at that beach.

But there were no lifeguards that day. He could see little of the beach, and no one stood on the cliff, but he knew that even if they were there, they would not hear his yells for help over the immense roar of those freak waves.

It occurred to him that he was going to disappear. His mom, sisters, and brother would not know what had happened to him. And then, as the *Kraken of Swells* approached, he felt exhausted. Sprint swimming and a few minutes of panic had drained him. His arms ached and felt rubbery. He was so cold.

There was only one chance. He had to ride that oncoming, giant wave into shore. His prior conviction that doing so would kill him was replaced with its opposite. But was he already out of position? Did he have anything left to swim fast enough to catch it?

There really wasn't a choice.

He swam shoreward as hard as he could before the lifting water, sure that if he failed, he would drown, knowing that even if he succeeded, he might drown as well. He stroked and kicked with everything he had left. The water rose behind him, and he felt an exhilarating and frightening slide backward up…and up…and up.

He kept his focus forward. He felt the water as a living thing. He was lifted high and saw the churning whitewater ahead and below and the empty beach beyond.

For a second, pure awe shunted aside fear, and he yelled out the ecstasy that replaced it,

"Oh Yeah!"

He tried to cut down the face, to buy seconds of control, but it closed quickly, and he did his best to thread through the stunning explosion, to ride the churn toward the beach, toward deliverance.

But soon he was lost and buried under the turbulence, tumbling over and over and over with no sense of up or down. The heavy overcast sky made it even harder to see where light was, where air and life were.

He remembered to rely on floating upward, lifted by the big gulp of oxygen he had taken at the last second. He felt like a ragdoll being shaken every which way by a mad, invisible dog determined to separate his limbs from his torso. He reached out with those limbs for air or sand, whichever would tell him where up was.

Just as his lungs' demands for oxygen grew desperate, the fingers of one hand grazed the bottom. He twisted, pushed with his feet, and pulled with his hands for the surface. He broke through quicker than he feared as the swash was rapidly thinning and calming. It was still a churning cauldron of foam pulling away from the beach, impeded by the oncoming whitewater.

His feet finally found purchase. It helped that the following wave was much smaller. For the last fifty feet, he swam and pushed with his feet through the powerful, sucking swash until he could firmly stand.

He was relieved to see his clothes were only damp on the small hillock he had unconsciously left them on, surrounded by dark, soaked sand from the rush of the big waves. He trudged across the wet, glad to dry and wrap himself in the big green towel. The rain had stopped, but the sky was much darker. The surf was back to how he had found it.

The next thing he knew, he was lying face down on the grit, wrapped in the towel. He must have slept because he awoke to a croaking noise and the painful awareness of his chilled flesh. His eyes opened into slits, and he found a seagull staring at him from three feet away. The gull was big and white with yellow feet, and it cocked its head such that one of its eyes bored into him with evaluation.

To Duncan, that predatory stare was trying to decide if it was safe to make a play for one of his eyeballs. It was a look that also asked, *Is it dead or at least too weak to stop me?* He was eager to help the gull reach the correct conclusion, so he closed a hand around some sand and flung it a foot or two toward the bird.

"Uhn," he said.

The seemingly disappointed but uncowed bird fluttered a few more feet away, then turned and resumed studying his prospects for a big meal. Duncan sat up and shivered as he looked around the still-deserted beach. He had to get out of his wet shorts to get warm. He took them off, not caring about being naked, and was never so glad to be back in dry, warm jeans, a T-shirt and a jacket.

He slowly pedaled back the way he had come, distantly thoughtful, feeling like someone who had stepped off railroad tracks one second before the Santa Fe Freight had roared over his spot at 100 mph, leaving him standing there in the concussive blast of that 2000-ton bullet's passing.

When he got home Ava did not seem to notice the smell of the ocean on him, not the wet bag holding his shorts and towel or his tousled sandy hair. He ate something, went to his room and quickly fell asleep.

The following Saturday, he got together with Randy and Lee. He regaled them with vivid stories of riding great waves and great wipeouts too. They oohed and aahed and had just the amount of envy he had imagined.

Amid their enthusiasm over his great adventure, he nearly blurted the story of his escape—but it caught in his throat. He could share his daring and determination—but not that other thing. He could express his risk-taking and rapture—but not the feeling he had as his last chance to live rose mightily behind him. No, he wouldn't, couldn't share that.

44

May 1967

Memorial Day weekend had special significance that year due to the war in Vietnam. Every week, over 200 young men, mainly between the ages of eighteen and twenty-three, came home in body bags or aluminum coffins. Despite this fact, or perhaps because of it, support for the war was high. And observances of Memorial Day events were well attended. Yet, antiwar protests had grown in both size and frequency.

The grim reality of the war and increasing civil rights protests affected the boys very little. It was a background noise from adults talking. And the boys had a few years yet before they would need to worry about being drafted to fight in a struggle that the government still claimed was going well.

Eager to get to the beach, Duncan left his house on a pleasant morning, undeterred by the massive crowds that would surely choke the roads and the Boardwalk and offer stiff competition for waves to ride. He was walking down Woodrow Avenue, only a few blocks from his home, when a voice called, "Hey, Duncan!"

He stopped before a little yellow and white house, astonished to see Kevin behind a low, white picket fence in the front yard.

"Kevin?"

"Who do I look like?" he asked with a trace of that familiar cockiness.

Duncan shrugged. "I thought you had…" But his voice faded away.

"Thought what?"

"That, uh, you'd, uh, left. I came by before we moved down here. You weren't there."

Kevin looked away. He had a baseball in one hand and a glove hanging loosely at his side in the other. "Oh, well, yeah, I guess we did leave."

"Oh." He brightened. "How did you get here? It's great. Do you live here?"

Kevin smiled. "Yeah, think fast," he said, lobbing the ball at Duncan, who snagged it out of the air.

Kevin laughed. "Just checking. Where do you live?"

He pointed. "Couple of blocks."

"Trippy, how did we both move from the same town to another one and end up next to each other?"

"Yeah, trippy, but so cool."

The other boy nodded, face shining.

"Well, you going to let me come in so I can say hi to your mom? Is your dad here?" Now that he had gotten over his shock at Kevin's sudden appearance, he felt a burst of happiness. But Duncan had never seen one person's face transform so quickly from vitality and gladness to the dark, sagging visage Kevin's became.

The boy's gaze fell to somewhere deep within the ragged lawn. After some seconds, Kevin said in a low, distant voice, "I don't live with," he took a deep breath and looked off toward the ocean, "them anymore."

"You don't? Who do you live with?"

"Foster parents."

Duncan had heard a boy up at San Lorenzo Valley Elementary referred to as a foster kid, but he did not understand what that meant. "What happened?"

A blaze that seemed a mix of pain and anger lit the previously drawn face. "I'm not going to talk about it, so don't ask." Perhaps to soften it, he added, "OK?"

What else could he reply except, OK? Kevin shrugged off whatever deep trouble he felt. The glow and the spark were instantly back.

"Yeah, I'm glad to see you too, Duncan. Come on in and meet Mary."

Kevin's foster mother was bringing in laundry from the dryer in the detached garage when the boys entered the kitchen. Mrs. Davis was a tiny woman in tapered pants with a matching sky-blue and white checkered sleeveless blouse. Her little feet wore golden thong sandals. Her chin-length black hair flipped gracefully along the line of her delicate jaw. He learned that she was a nurse who usually did the night shift at the hospital. Her arms were wiry. She looked at Kevin with great affection and expressed pleasure at his chance discovery of his friend.

She was not very old for an adult. The eyes were a bit sunken with tinges of gray underneath. She had a worn air, but she put her laundry aside to ask light questions about Duncan and offered strawberry Kool-Aid from the fridge.

Halfway down his tasty glass of red water, Duncan asked, "I was going to the beach. Can Kevin come with me?"

It felt weird to ask this woman, who was not Kevin's mother, for permission. He almost blurted a question about the actual parents but stopped before it could escape his lips. Still, it was so hard to suppress the need to know what happened such that Kevin was separated from that lovely, loving woman and that kind, wise father. The apparent tension in Kevin at his side helped him bite his tongue.

"I guess so, but I'd like you to meet Mr. Davis. He'll be back later this afternoon. He had to check on a job."

"I'll bring Duncan back when we're done surfing."

Mr. Davis, whose first name was Leon, was a carpenter and, as Kevin would tell him, built houses. He was also a contractor who supervised a small group of men. Kevin's bedroom was at the front of the house, and there he changed into blue-green swim trunks that looked fancy compared to Duncan's worn-out cutoffs. It was messy as a boy's room ought to be, with a football, a bat, dozens of comics, a few books and clothes scattered about. A forty-five RPM record player dominated his dresser, and a poster of a concert by the Rolling Stones was pinned to the wall. Several dozen 45s were strewn next to the player.

Duncan looked closely at the poster with its headshots of Jagger, Jones, Richards, Wyman, and Watts. "You went to this?"

"What?" Kevin glanced over once he had his T-shirt on. "Naw, see, it was in Massachusetts. I ain't been there. Can't you read? No, my... It was a gift."

"Oh, very cool."

Kevin put on his sneakers. "Yeah, Stones are tough."

The boys slipped out without saying goodbye to Mary, who must have been in the garage. They walked down Woodrow singing the Stones's "I Can't Get No Satisfaction," making exaggerated Jagger lip movements and playing air guitars,

The day was warm, and the sky was clear. The beach was a throng of happy sunbathers, waders, swimmers, bodysurfers, inner tube floaters and skimboarders. The waves were only fair, and the two aggressively jockeyed for position on the best ones. They laughed, cheered, and were lost in that timeless place of nuthin-but-fun that stretched into the middle of the afternoon.

Hunger and cold finally drove them out onto the hot sand, where they pooled their money to buy a couple of hot dogs. The Boardwalk could be a torment when you are twelve or thirteen and have no money.

Exciting rides like the Rock-O-Plane, Tilt-a-Whirl, Wild Mouse and the Giant Dipper were all around. Auto scooters, the Fun House and the rubber ball bazookas

(Duncan's favorite) called to them. Everything was exciting, but each lasted just a few minutes, and what few coins adolescents might muster disappeared quickly.

"If I was rich, I'd do everything all day long," Kevin said.

"Me too."

"I'd ride the roller coaster fifty times and blast those clowns into the next county."

Duncan laughed. "We could set records."

"Yeah."

They walked up and down the long Boardwalk amongst the thick crowds, the odors of suntan lotion, sweat, ocean life, hamburgers grilling and cotton candy spinning, filling their noses. They found they had enough for two games of pinball before heading home.

***

Leon was talking with his wife when the boys came through the door. He said something about needing to fire someone named Jackson because of the stupid mistake he had made. Leon was a startlingly big man. Well over six feet, he radiated the physical power of a man who had lifted tons and pounded thousands of nails. His jeans were coated in fine brown dust. Heavy leather boots protected his large feet, and his white, blue-striped short-sleeved shirt was stained and sweat-soaked. His weathered, craggy face boasted faint blue eyes, and his head was topped with dirty-blond ragged hair. He had powerful forearms thick with golden bleached hair and a single tattoo of a snake on the right one. His hands were big and rough and marked with old and recent abrasions.

For all his daunting presence, he greeted Duncan warmly. "Mary was telling me of the serendipity of Kevin seeing you."

The big word meant nothing to Duncan. Leon continued, "I'm happy he can have a friend here after having to," he glanced at his foster son, "leave Ben Lomond."

"Yes, Mr. Davis, me too."

He was relieved when the pleasantries were over. In Leon's presence, he felt compelled to be careful with his replies.

In Kevin's bedroom, Duncan picked up the football and said, "He is really big," as he tossed it up and down.

"Huge."

After a moment, Duncan asked, "Do you like them?"

Kevin straightened the 45s on his dresser and said without looking at him, "They're OK."

45

June 1967

In June the fog often hung low over the town. The heavy, damp air discouraged getting into the cold water, and the surf was usually small then, anyway. The boys would congregate at the ever-patient and generous Mrs. Kelly's. She must have liked the boys because she let them hang out for hours in bedrooms, in the yard or sprawled around her living room while they watched television.

Sometimes, she fed them; sometimes, she shushed them; and sometimes, she simply watched them with a bemused, satisfied smile. And she put them to work cutting grass, washing dishes, taking out the trash or cleaning up in the garage. None of the boys complained; it was clear to all that they were getting the better part of the bargain.

Big events happened that month: Israel defeated the coordinated forces of three Arab nations, the annual Miss California Pageant was held at the Boardwalk, attended by thousands of eager men pretending to be interested in what the swimsuit-clad beauties hoped for the world, and China detonated its first hydrogen bomb in order, they said, to frustrate the nuclear blackmail by the Soviet Union and the United States of America.

Since things that went boom interested the boys, Randy asked his assembled buddies in the living room while they waited for a movie to start, "What if the Chinese fired a hydrogen missile at us?"

No one replied right away. Was it dread? After all, only a few years before, President Kennedy had barely averted turning the world into a fused ball of molten glass. Or were they boggled by the vision of the biggest boom of all?

Duncan said, "Well, if they fire a missile at us, we'll fire an anti-missile and stop it."

He had Randy's attention.

"Of course, then they'll fire an anti-missile missile to stop that, but," and Duncan raised his outstretched hands to demonstrate missile-on-missile action, "then we'll fire an anti-anti-missile missile."

Kevin's eyes crinkled. Randy chuckled.

"The Chinese will fire an anti-anti-missile missile-missile." Lee, Kevin and Randy laughed. Alan snorted.

"And of course, we'll do even better and let fly an anti-anti-anti-missile-missile-missile." This went on for a while, with further anti and missile appendages being added, interspersed with dramatic pauses, simulated explosions, and his hands being used to represent swooping missiles smashing into each other until Randy was rolling on the floor.

He concluded: "And since the Chinese don't have any of those, it'll be," he vocalized a long explosion sound while his hands waved around high over his head, imitating a blooming mushroom cloud, "all over for China."

The boys cheered and clapped and hooted. A bemused-looking Margaret, lingering on the periphery, shook her head and said, "Bunch of silly kids." But she grinned before she turned and left.

***

TV watching ranged from cartoons to Westerns to movies, usually war films, mythology stuff like *Hercules* or *Clash of the Titans,* to what Margaret called swashbucklers. *The Adventures of Robin Hood, The Three Musketeers,* and other movies in that vein brought cheers from the boys. That Saturday, while watching *The Black Swan,* Margaret observed, "You kids sure love tales of derring-do."

"What's derring-do?" Duncan asked.

She thought for a bit. "Being brave in the face of danger."

"I'm brave," said Randy.

His mother smiled. "Yes, you are."

"Me too," Alan said.

Her smile faded a bit. "Yes, but don't make it all about fighting."

"Duncan is brave," Randy said.

She nodded. "Yes, I'm sure you're all brave boys."

"Nobody wants to be a coward," Kevin said. "You gotta be tough."

"And love adventure," Lee said.

"Love doing daring things," Duncan said.

"Derring-do," said Randy.

Alan nodded. "Derring-do."

The others murmured, "Derring-do" like it was a motto. Soon, they were up fencing with pretend swords and shouted over and over,

"Derring-do!"

"Derring-do!"

"Derring-do!"

"To derring-do!"

While the TV commercial extolled the virtues of Pop-Tarts, Margaret said, "Of course, real derring-do is being brave for others." But it did not seem that any of the boys heard her.

46

July 1967

A unique perfume permeated the Boardwalk beach scene. It was not Estee Lauder or Aramis or Coty, not Faberge nor English Leather. It was the combined scents of sea air, baked sand, fun sweat and massive quantities of suntan lotion.

Suntan, not sunscreen.

People, especially women and girls, went to the beach to get beautiful golden tans. Lotions were slathered on to accelerate the tanning process and to achieve a lovely tone. A couple of brands had recently started offering SPF versions, but their numbers were tiny, only 2 to 5, not the virtually opaque values of 30, 45, or even 60 in the future.

The purpose of the low SPF's was to inhibit burning while getting a tan. Thus, the beach had few umbrellas and no tents or other sunshades. The epidermises of thousands of daily beachgoers thirstily soaked up the UV rays to look beautiful... and it felt great. The surge in skin cancers resulting from all this fun, fun, fun in the sun, sun, sun jolted public consciousness much later.

The boys never applied suntan lotion. There was no need and no interest. Daily bodysurfing had given them all the deep tans that the weekend sun-worshipers could only dream of. And their hair, longer now, as was the trending style, was rich with the golden blond tones that the sun god bestowed, except for Randy and Alan, whose obsidian-black hair stubbornly refused to fade.

The boys sat on the sand smoking Marlboros and Camels, not talking about much. They were in a relaxed and pleasant state after hours of wave riding. Kevin and Lee tossed a baseball back and forth. Closer to the ocean but still on Trestle Beach, four older teenagers threw a football, yelling and calling routes. The tallest one ran for a pass and looked over his shoulder for the ball instead of where he was going. He ran into Lee, knocking him down. The big teen stumbled but did not fall. Lee leapt up, rubbed his head where the teen's forearm had smacked him, yelled, "Hey, watch what you're doing."

The football had sailed over the teen's head and landed in the river. He stopped his pursuit of it, turned, and snarled at Lee, "Shut up turd," and with a blow to his chest, knocked Lee flat. "Stay out of my way."

The whole gang ran to Lee's defense. Duncan thought that if they had to fight these guys, they would get creamed. Alan, the farthest away, surprised Duncan as he raced past them all. He stood before Lee and got right in the face of the intended receiver.

"Back off," he said.

The teen retreated two steps. "What does it matter to you?"

"He's my friend. Don't pick on a smaller kid."

Lee was furious, called the guy an asshole and moved to charge. Kevin snagged him, held him and said, "Not yet, not yet." Duncan and Randy had Alan's flanks. They glanced at each other, ready for a brawl they were very likely to lose.

The big teen hesitated and seemed to evaluate Alan. There was a chance that the face-off would fizzle, but then one of the big teen's friends said, "Kick his ass, Steve."

Alan may have been big for his age, but he was still just fourteen. Duncan thought the other guy was sixteen, maybe even seventeen. And Alan was big to a twelve-year-old boy like Duncan, but he was still smaller than Steve and had a face that looked his age. Plus, his extra pounds suggested a plump softness that may have been deceptive.

Steve stiffened, stepped forward, and said, "You and your punk friends better get off our beach."

Duncan, on Alan's right, could see his friend's face. At that moment, the boy had an icy stillness about him. He made no reply, just raised his fists and assumed a boxer's stance. He stared hard and unblinking into Steve's face—and waited.

Steve's buddies appeared confused by the challenge. What did they see? Four small boys with anger and a touch of fear in their eyes and one bigger kid who was calm and ready.

"Come on, Steve, pound him," one of his friends said.

Trap closed; Steve advanced. Alan remained still and watched. Steve swung a sweeping right at Alan's head, which he quickly ducked under. He sprang up, planting a stinging left jab on the other guy's mouth, and followed it with a smashing overhand right to Steve's left eye. The teen crumpled and fell on his butt. Alan quickly advanced to stand over him.

Steve's friends took a step forward. Kevin and Lee ran forward to complete the line, with Alan at its center. Steve's lower lip was split open, and bleeding and his eyes were glazed; Duncan thought he would pass out.

Superficially, the odds still sucked; they bordered on the ludicrous. Those big, strong teens should have been able to roll right over them—but for Alan. Duncan was fascinated by what he saw. His big friend radiated much more than confidence—he seemed eager. Duncan believed that he wanted Steve's friends to attack. He wanted to fight them. Even if he lost, he would relish the battle. His look said, *Come on, so I can hurt you bad.*

Steve's guys must have seen that too. One dude frowned and said, "This just went too far. Let us help Steve." The punched teen lay flat, staring into the bright blue sky.

Alan thought for a while and then said, "OK, but all of you get out of here." He and the boys took a few steps back, but Alan kept his fists up and warily watched as Steve's friends helped him stand. The likely concussed teen mumbled something unintelligible. They led him away toward the main beach.

Alan was surrounded and showered with praise:

"That was so boss."

"Thanks, Alan, you're so tough."

"You sure sent them running."

"So cool."

"So bad."

Alan glowed, taking the praise as his due. He looked at his blushing right hand, which had already started to swell. He shook it but smiled. "Ow, hit bone."

Kevin said, "Pussy that he is, that dickhead may call the cops. Maybe we should go."

Everyone agreed that was smart. They followed Alan over the Trestle Bridge and, all the way to the Kelly's house, poured praise on him like he was Muhammed Ali.

47

At the stairs near the Rock-O-Plane, Duncan and Kevin leaned on the railing and looked out across the sea of bodies at the feeble waves collapsing on the shore. They had walked up and down the crowded Boardwalk for over an hour, dodging around hairy men and thin girls, aching to play, but they had spent the last of their coins at the arcade. They were hungry and thirsty, and Kevin bitched intermittently about how much fun they could have if only they had money. Duncan was getting sick of it and was thinking about going home.

The background sights and sounds to all Kevin's complaining were the giddy screams of Giant Dipper riders, the cheery tunes of the carousel's organ, the smells of grilled hamburgers, hot dogs, gunpowder and oil from the .22 shooting booth, and the happy laughter of those with money who were slurping their drinks and licking chocolate-covered ice cream cones.

They were even out of cigarettes. Gratefully, Kevin had not bitched about that for at least five minutes. Instead, they commented on notable characters in their field of view.

"Look how small that guy's suit is; it's tinier than a girl's bikini," Kevin said. The hairy-chested man posed with arms akimbo midway on the beach like he was the centerpiece of a department store display. The aroused bulge in his crotch was barely covered by the blue spandex briefs that may have been two sizes too small. It was impossible to unsee, so Duncan changed the subject.

"I saw a girl's titty pop out last week."

"Really? Cool. Were they big kazongas?"

"Naw, not too big, but nice. Just saw one. I think a wave broke her strap."

"What did it look like?"

"Pretty, she had a big dark nipple standing up on white skin, but she screamed and covered it. They bounced when she ran off." He paused to contemplate the vision of the girl's beauty and the nascent feelings it stirred.

Kevin joined him in that syrupy silence until a few minutes passed, then said, "You see that guy walking away?"

"Which guy?"

"Black trunks, just dodged the runaway baby."

Duncan searched and found the likely person, a trim young man with short hair about thirty feet from the water. "Yeah, what of him?"

Kevin pointed. "He put his wallet into that pile of clothes. I'm going to go grab it."

He looked sharply at his friend, said, "Come on, really?"

"Yeah, no shit."

"How?"

He shrugged. "I'll just take it. It'll be a caper. Wanna help?"

Duncan found the afternoon suddenly exciting. "Sure, doing what?"

"Come down with me. Wander away a bit, but keep your eye on him. I'll get close to his stuff, be lying around changing position, you know, getting closer. I'll look to you for the all-clear. Tug on your ear if it's safe; make a fist if he's coming back."

He considered the plan and asked, "OK, now?"

"Yeah, now."

"Wait, what should we do after you get it?"

"Hmmm, just walk back up on the Boardwalk. We won't run, but we'll go separately, OK?"

"OK."

"Follow me, but if we lose each other, meet at the trestle."

"OK."

They descended the few sandy, worn wooden steps. Duncan veered to the right. The man's small pile of clothes was isolated from other beachgoers, at least fifteen feet from the nearest person. Kevin lay down ten feet away from the target. Duncan strolled slowly and aimlessly nearby, watching the man wading into the water as a small wave broke before him. Kevin was three feet from the pile in just a few casual moves. He looked at Duncan. The man was swimming out past the breaking waves. Duncan pulled his ear.

Kevin scooted, belly down, next to the clothes and, in two seconds, found the wallet, which disappeared under him into a pocket. Duncan looked away and followed when Kevin got close to the stairs. There was no pursuit, but they ran anyway once they were in the crowd. At a passageway to the Beach Street side of the Boardwalk, with no one momentarily around, Kevin took the wallet out, removed the cash and dumped the billfold into a trash bin. They ran down to the river and then upstream from the trestle, out of sight.

"All right!" Kevin shouted.

"We did it!"

Kevin took the cash out of his pocket and counted three fives and three ones. "$18," he said.

"That was fun!"

Kevin handed Duncan two fives. "Your share."

"That's too much."

"You can buy my Dipper tickets."

"OK."

The two kids laughed in giddy relief and triumph. They congratulated each other on how slick they had been.

"I want a hot dog and potato salad, a Coke and an ice cream sundae," Kevin said.

"I'm getting a cheeseburger, fries and a banana split."

"And taffy."

"And cotton candy."

"We'll ride the Dipper till we puke." They paused; perhaps Kevin shared Duncan's realization that, given their feasting plans, that might not take long.

"That was so easy," Duncan said.

"Yeah, we have money."

"We could have a lot more."

"Yeah."

"Fun."

"Derring-do."

"Derring-do!"

They headed back to the Boardwalk to splurge. Duncan was filled with the warmth of their comradery, the thrill of a well-done caper, and the power of money. Concern for the wallet owner did not enter his mind. It was the beginning of their crime spree.

48

July/August 1967

In one way Duncan and Kevin's daily lives did not change much during most of that summer. They still went over to Randy's. They usually went to the beach. They surfed, played pinball, explored, hung out smoking cigarettes, joked and horsed around. But in another way, everything was different.

They continued their capers, taking turns being the snatcher and the lookout. They took several wallets each week. They were careful, never rushing or pushing if it didn't feel right. They chose lone men who left their stuff far from other sunbathers. If those men believed doing so gave added security, the truth was the opposite. Few paid attention to a small pile of clothes far from them on a beach with hundreds of people.

Capers were done whenever they saw a good chance. The first few wallets had less than twenty dollars each, but they scored when it was next Duncan's turn to snatch. At their usual place, he counted the money.

"Whoa, $96."

"Damn, we're rich."

That day, they went on every ride they could: the Giant Dipper four times, the Carousel three times, the Fun House, Scrambler, Wild Mouse twice, bumper cars, Rock-O-Plane, Tilt-a-Whirl and the Cave Train. They even did the Ferris Wheel, which was less boring than it looked, and the Autorama, which was more boring than it looked. They dropped three dollars blasting targets at the Bazooka stand. They played miniature golf, whacked the balls all over, and didn't keep track of the number of strokes. They spent five dollars at that tricky basketball game where the hoops were extra small; a stuffed rabbit worth about fifty cents was their reward.

They ran from place to place for hours, eating hot dogs, burgers, multi-scoop ice cream cones, tacos, and fish and chips (Duncan liked the former; Kevin hated the latter). Their young metabolisms burned the food like jet fuel. At the end of the day, they still had over fifty dollars.

As the weeks went by, they began gifting more and more stuff to their friends: packs of cigarettes, food and roller coaster rides, but not too often and not too extravagant. Kevin thought they should keep their capers to themselves; Duncan agreed. Yet, one day after another big score, more than seventy dollars, Duncan could not temper his exuberance after Kevin had gone home. He felt like a king. He felt clever, and there was a wodge of bills in his pocket to prove it. He treated Randy to all the rides, snacks, desserts and fried cuisine the Boardwalk offered. They laughed and cheered; it was so good to be back playing with him.

Later, at Trestle Beach, Randy asked, "How come you have so much money?"

He knew he was not supposed to say but was bursting to tell. With only a moment's consideration, he said, "Been lifting wallets."

He answered Randy's big eyes by bragging, "It's easy, just gotta be a ninja, sneak up, grab it, and slide away. Easy."

"You and Kevin?"

He thought hard about how to answer. He, Randy, and Kevin were close friends, but even so, to admit Kevin's role was solidly in fink territory. "*I've* been taking wallets," he said.

Randy nodded his understanding.

"He's stealing wallets!" a loud, squeaky voice behind Duncan said. They twisted to look over their shoulders. Two small boys were close by.

Where did they come from?

Duncan recognized one of the kids, Paul, as a frequent skim-boarder. He did not know the other boy.

Shit.

"What are you, an eavesdropper? I'm just storytelling. Go away."

They jumped like they'd been poked and ran off out of sight. It annoyed Duncan that he had been so careless, and he worried about it for a while but then decided it was no big deal.

The capers continued. The gang was extra happy when he and Kevin splurged on their friends. Randy was in the know, but he said nothing. Lee asked no questions. Alan took any gifts with thanks, but one day after they had all walked out of that little ice cream shop down from Shopper's Corner, he leaned in close to Duncan's ear and whispered,

"The fruits of wicked ways."

Alan waggled his eyebrows, laughed and licked the cherry scoop at the top of his cone. Duncan accepted the compliment by taking a big bite of vanilla and laughing with him.

Those were great days for the boys. The main problem was that they couldn't buy merchandise. For thirteen-year-olds, they had a lot of money, but they could not come home one day with a new bike, a surfboard or a record player without facing the question *where did you get that?*

Near the middle of August, Duncan and the gang, except Kevin, were hanging out at Trestle Beach after another session of enjoying three-foot waves. They smoked more often now, and he had one in his hand.

"The new Mustang is bitchin'," he said.

"Totally," Lee said.

"The Cougar has a bigger engine," Alan said.

"The Mustang looks cooler."

"To you, maybe."

Duncan laughed, took a drag and blew it out his nose. Debating the virtues of cars they could not afford and were years away from being able to drive was their part-time sport.

"Hey, Duncan!" a high-pitched voice called. He whipped his head around. In the shade, under the trestle, a young female cop stood in her pressed blue uniform. She smiled at him with a little glint of gotcha.

Duncan swallowed.

She did not move, just motioned for him to come to her. He dropped his cigarette as if he might be arrested for it. He glanced at his friends, tried to raise an easy, brave smile, and failed. He slogged through the sand and up the slope to her spot under the tracks.

"What's your last name, Duncan?"

His pulse pounded in his neck. "Findlay, ma'am."

"I am officer," and she said something that sounded like Flebooskee or Flebowska, but he was not really listening, "...and I need your help with something. Can you come with me?" He did not answer because his jaw felt welded shut. He glanced back at his buddies.

She asked, "Do you have anything you need to bring with you?"

He nodded and pointed at his stuff.

"You can go get it to bring with you, OK?"

Again, he only nodded and walked what seemed like a mile there and back. Neither he nor his buddies said anything. He already felt like he was wearing clothes with stripes on them. When he returned, she said, "Put on your flippers."

She walked him down the slope toward the street where her police car sat. There were no flashing lights or anything else dramatic, but the sirens in his head more than made up for it. She opened the door. "You need to get in the back." Contrary to his expectations, she did not put handcuffs on him.

"Am I being arrested?" he asked, fighting the nausea in his guts.

She cocked her head, studied him, and said, "No, my sergeant just has a few questions to ask you."

He slid into the back where the doors lacked handles. She slammed his and got in front. The radio squawked something unintelligible. As the car rolled up Beach Street, she was confusingly friendly.

"Did you have fun in the water?"

"Yes, ma'am."

"Yes, it's a lovely day. Are you looking forward to going back to school?"

One of those adult questions.

"I guess."

"Where do you go?"

"Mission Hill, ma'am."

"You can call me Janet, OK?"

"Uh, OK."

"I guess you live on the west side?"

He had to think; he wasn't used to looking at the city like that. "Yes."

She asked what street he lived on; caution reared within him.

"Almar," he lied.

"Got a house number?"

He had to think some more and realized he did not remember his number. "No, um, Janet."

She said nothing but clicked her turn signal and took a left. They were headed downtown, and she let him sit and think as they crossed the Laurel Street Bridge. He slouched low, afraid to be seen in the back of a police car. They parked on the Locust Street side of City Hall, a building he thought too beautiful to include a police station. She walked him past the sign that declared City Hall. She led him down a brick walkway and past a small blue neon sign sticking out from the wall, buzzing with one word: POLICE. She took him past a counter with a gruff-looking cop sitting behind it, who looked at him with displeasure. They walked between desks to the sounds of telephones ringing and police talking in mild voices, and she soon ushered him into a small office. The sun streamed through high windows to light the opposite wall.

A potbellied man with gray hair at his temples and black wavy oiled hair on top sat at a desk. He got up as they entered.

"Duncan, this is Sergeant Graves."

Duncan felt he was being appraised as the man took a moment before, not unkindly, he said, "Take a seat, Duncan."

He sat in a gray office chair. Its worn arms and buffed seat testified to hundreds of prior suspects. Janet stood before a four-drawer metal filing cabinet next to the door. She seemed relaxed, but her faint smile wasn't comforting. The sergeant presented a bland face to him. The moments stretched until Duncan shifted in his seat.

"Some kids have been stealing wallets at the beach. We think you might be able to help us with that."

The thumping of the artery in his neck accelerated like the drums on a Roman galley switching to ramming speed. But as there was no question, he said nothing.

"You can help us with that, can't you?"

His rapidly blinking eyes gave the light in the room a strobe effect. "No, sir."

"No?"

He shook his head.

Janet said, "You know, Duncan, when I picked you up and said we had questions, you didn't even ask what it was about." The gotcha glint was back. "Like you knew exactly why we'd be questioning you, you out of all those other kids."

"So, you do know, don't you, Duncan?" The sergeant said.

He had to piss, and he was biting a thumbnail, but there was only one path. "No, sir."

That hint of a smile vanished from Janet's face. The sergeant shook his head, looking very disappointed, and said, "Well, that's mighty odd, Duncan, because we got a tip that you are one of the two boys taking the wallets."

"I didn't do it."

As if he had not said anything, the sergeant half sat on his desktop and continued, "Seems you and another boy work as a team taking those wallets. Why don't you just tell us the truth?"

They seemed to know everything, but he answered, "I didn't do anything."

The man frowned and looked at Janet. She spoke in a way that managed to be gentle, friendly, and menacing all at the same time. "Perhaps if we spoke to your father, he could shed some light on this."

He looked blankly at her. She thought for a second, said, "Or your mother might know…"

"Don't tell my mom!" he erupted and started to cry.

She smiled. The sergeant smiled. But he did not confess.

Then the sergeant ventured, "Maybe the other boy got you into this. Maybe he did most of it or even all. We should talk to him." And then, like he was asking the time, he softly finished, "What's his name?"

It was a mistake.

He had been on the verge of breaking; full-on blubbering was seconds away, but he was suddenly clear that he had almost been tricked into ratting out Kevin. He could have betrayed him before he even realized it. Anger flashed, but he hid it. His pulse dropped, and he wiped the tears from his eyes with the backs of each hand.

"I didn't do anything, and there isn't any friend."

Of course, the police were not stupid. They saw the change. They hardened and tried further questions, which went nowhere. They were not mean or grossly intimidating. There were no hot lights in his face, nor yelling or threats. They treated him gently, like the boy he was. To everything they asked, he said, "I didn't do it," or "No."

Finally, when it seemed everyone was repeating themselves, he said, "I want to go."

The questioning stopped. The two police regarded him silently for a while. The sergeant said, "All right, you can go."

Shakily, he picked up his things from the floor and walked the few steps to the door. In front of Janet, he asked, "Are you taking me back?"

She looked down on him, said," No, Duncan, I'm not. It's not far. The walk will give you time to think hard about what you said today."

It was agony leaving the police station as if the eyes of every officer followed his every step, and he feared they might arrest him before he could get out, but when he reached sunlight and his feet touched the Center Street sidewalk, relief filled him, and he almost cried again.

I have to find Kevin.

49

August 1967

Duncan slid a dime down the gullet of the payphone. "Is Kevin there?" he asked Mrs. Davis.

She said yes, and he listened to her retreating steps, followed by the opening of a door, and faintly heard her call, "Duncan's on the phone."

He was only a block from the police station he had left minutes before. He had repeatedly looked over his shoulders as if a whole team of cops might be tailing him.

"Hey, Duncan."

"Hey, uh, look, I gotta talk to you. Can we meet?" The words jumped all over each other.

"Course, what happened?"

"Don't want to say on the phone." He heard his panting and tried to calm down.

"Not on the phone?"

"Look, I'll explain; just meet me at the arcade, Lee's machine. I'm downtown and walking. Can you come now?"

Kevin was quiet for several long moments, then, "Sure, I just finished a bunch of chores Leon had me do. I'll bike down in five, OK?"

"Great, see ya."

"See ya."

During the half-hour walk to meet Kevin, he replayed the whole interrogation several times. He only looked back once and found empty sidewalks and a few civilian cars. After running across Beach Street, he opened the arcade door and saw Kevin standing before the two copper handles. His friend upnodded.

"C'mon," Duncan said as he passed him and, without looking back to confirm Kevin was following, threaded a quick, winding route through the blooping and dinging machines. He went out the door and across the promenade, Kevin trailing, and then down the steps and over the sand, keeping close to the building until he found a spot far from anyone. He sat down and leaned against the wall. Kevin dropped next to him. They looked at the wharf and the bay beyond.

"The cops picked me up."

"Damn, figured that might be it."

He told the whole story in detail and finished with, "They don't know anything about you, and I didn't rat you out. And I won't."

Kevin recoiled as if sniffing rotten fish. "Shut up, I know that."

Duncan smiled and nodded. "OK, but somebody did."

They thought for a while. Near the water, a teenage girl and boy bounced a red, white and blue beach ball back and forth in high arcs.

Kevin said, "Maybe somebody saw us."

"Yeah, but they wouldn't know our names."

"Maybe, maybe the rat only knows you."

Duncan chewed his lip. Then he remembered. "Shit." He told him about telling Randy and the boys who had overheard.

"Randy wouldn't rat, not in a million years," Kevin said.

"I bet it was that kid, Paul. I think he is like ten or something."

"Yeah, I know who he is, always yelling."

"Yep."

They were silent for a long time as the murmur of the waves and the brilliance of the ocean appeared less pleasing to Duncan.

"Are they going to arrest me?" he asked.

Kevin blew air past his lips and frowned. "Maybe."

"My mom'll kill me."

"Doesn't sound like they can prove it, but they might arrest you anyway."

He felt sick. "I'll go to jail?"

"Juvie."

"Jail for kids," Duncan said as if it was just as bad.

"It's not terrible."

Duncan looked his question at Kevin, who said, "When," he hesitated and looked into the sky, "I couldn't be with my parents anymore, they held me in Juvie for over three weeks until they found foster parents for me."

"Leon and Mary?"

"Yes."

"What's it like?"

"They *do* put you in a cell. Most of the time, I shared one with other kids who came and went. The adults tried to be nice, but there were lots of rules. They let us go out into the yard sometimes; there are games, and some meals are eaten together. It's small. I was bored all the time."

Kevin pulled out a fresh pack of Marlboro's, whacked it several times to pack the tobacco tight, and gave one to Duncan. They smoked in the sun until half done.

"If they take you to Juvie, watch out for the older boys. Some are seventeen or eighteen; they look like men, and the ones I saw were big and mean."

"Thanks." He took another drag and released it.

They smoked silently for a few minutes, each lost in his thoughts.

Then Duncan asked, "See that guy in the Hawaiian shorts?"

Kevin searched. "Walking toward the wharf?"

"Yep." With a nod, he said, "His stuff is over there."

Kevin looked at him. "You want to do it now?"

"Yes, I'll take it."

"It's my turn."

"Not this time."

Kevin studied him. Duncan put out his cigarette in the sand and rose to go. "I'll take it, but we shouldn't meet up right after. Just go home, OK? I'll give you your share next I see you."

"Why?" And Duncan knew he meant, why do it now; why do it at all?

His face hardened, and he spat on the hot sand. "They threatened to tell my mom."

He did not creep up on the man's clothes. There was no stealthy faux ninja bullshit. He walked straight at it. When he got within ten feet, he looked back at Kevin. His friend flicked a confirming glance one way and then slowly pulled his right earlobe.

After a few direct steps, he sat down cross-legged at the target. He didn't check who was watching or not watching. He partially unrolled the pants, found the wallet and put it in his back pocket. And he didn't turn toward the Boardwalk, where he could lose himself among the crowd, but instead went toward the water. Once on the dark, wet sand, he strolled down the beach toward Rivermouth. He was going to get his bike, which he had left near the trestle, and then he'd slowly ride home.

50

A couple of nights later, Margaret brought the boys back from watching The Dirty Dozen at the Skyview Drive-In. Her treat was to chauffeur them there and to suffer two hours of watching savage criminals be trained to be savage soldiers and then unleashed on the Nazis with machine guns and grenades. For the duration, her charges shouted, clapped, chortled, and overall made lots of noise. Each boy, save her sons, had to pay their share for the show and snacks.

Back at her house, they piled out of her station wagon and decided they wanted ice cream, but Margaret had had enough. She dragged herself inside as they headed up Ocean Street toward Marianne's, an ice cream parlor that stayed open late, especially in summer.

Kevin and Duncan shared some of their wealth so everyone could get whatever they wanted. After the boys got their orders, they went outside to hang out in the parking lot, where they could talk loudly and relive more scenes from the movie.

Duncan was last out. He was carrying a double scoop of Mandarin chocolate and French vanilla. As Alan chortled for the third time over how easily the big guy, Posey, got tossed by Major Reisman, Duncan noticed a police car slowly driving by. He tensed, but it continued up Ocean and out of sight, so he relaxed.

It was a warm night, just a few weeks before they would have to return to school. They were having fun, had money, and all felt grand. Of course, everyone asked him about his run-in with the police, but he made it out to be no big deal. And despite their suspicions about what he and Kevin had been doing and why he and Kevin had so much cash to share, they did not press when he claimed he was in the clear.

Lee embarrassed the gang by repeatedly asking patrons of The Grog Shop if they would buy the kids some beer. "Get lost, boy," said one old guy as he opened the door. That was a typical response, but their brush-offs did little to deter Lee.

Duncan found it odd that a liquor store and an ice cream parlor shared the same small parking lot. One was bright and cheery; the other was dark and mysterious as if going through the door was to disappear into a hole.

These reflections were interrupted by the slow passing of what he thought was the same police car. It crawled north, and he felt his heart drop. He looked over at Kevin, who was sucking down a chocolate milkshake and verbally sparring with Alan about the movie. The big guy was attacking the most massive banana split Duncan had ever seen. Double scoops, double fudge, double nuts and extra-extra cherries. Plus, whipped cream. There was a banana in there somewhere.

But Kevin had seen the cop car, too, and they tracked it until it went out of sight. They met each other's eyes and reached an unspoken understanding. They mirrored the slightest of frowns and the smallest of nods.

He reached into a pocket, turned to Randy, said, "Hey, hold this for me, OK?" He handed him a wodge of bills equaling about forty dollars. Randy fingered through the cash. It was a lot of money for a thirteen-year-old, worth eight pairs of good shoes, 130 gallons of gasoline or 160 packs of cigarettes.

He stuffed the paper into his jeans, asked, "All right, but why?"

He opened his mouth to explain but hesitated, then said, "I think we'll see in a minute."

"What are you talking about?"

His reply was cut off by the sudden blast of red and blue flashing lights from a police car that darted into the parking lot from the side street The Grog Shop fronted. He whispered in Randy's ear, "I'm pretty sure that's for me. Go ahead and spend half of that on anything you want."

"Really?"

"Yeah, really."

The driver's door opened, and a big male officer got out. Duncan again leaned close to Randy's ear. "Oh, and watch out for any cops that pretend to be nice to you."

Randy appeared briefly mystified but then pursed his lips and nodded. "I will."

The passenger door opened, and the silhouette of a much smaller person showed. He didn't have to see her face to know who it was. The officers slowly made their way over as the boys, several Grog patrons and a few dozen ice cream customers stared.

When they got close, Officer Janet said, "Hello, Duncan."

He did not reply. The other officer, a man who towered over him, said, "Duncan Findlay, you are under arrest for..."

At that his ears filled with a roar like the whitewater of a great river, and he could not hear the rest of the sentence. He did hear an order to turn around, and his head drooped at the touch of cold steel cuffing his hands behind his back.

For an agonizingly long time, the officer carefully searched his pockets and his waistband and felt up and down his legs. He came out with a few coins and a black plastic comb. A flicker of disappointment seemed to transit Janet's face.

While doing his search, the officer told Duncan he did not have to talk to the police, but if he did, it would be used against him. This rather casually delivered speech was new to the juvenile policing system. His truncated version of what would later be well-known as the Miranda warning was based on a Supreme Court decision little more than a year old. It took another Supreme Court decision just three months before his arrest for it to apply to juveniles.

Those two decisions, and California's progressive approach to protecting juveniles, required a radical change to a system that saw the Juvenile Court as a surrogate parent, which was given wide latitude in how it and the police handled juvenile accused. It took time for the machinery of the juvenile justice system to make the changes. Despite the rulings, great latitude would still be allowed in how long minors could be incarcerated, which would affect Duncan.

The officer wrapped his big hand around Duncan's right bicep and slowly led him away to the car while his friends gaped and the growing crowd stared. It seemed an eternity until he was allowed to slide into the back seat of the patrol car. After the door slammed shut and while the officer stood guard outside, he saw Officer Janet talking to each of his friends and writing in a small notebook. Her questioning did not take long, and soon, both officers got in. The beacon lights were extinguished, and they left his friends behind. The cops were silent as they drove down narrow back streets away from Ocean. He looked out his window at the houses going by and asked, "Where are you taking me?"

"To the Juvenile Hall," Janet said.

He did not ask further questions, and they did not offer information. Soon, the police car drove under a Highway One bridge, and they stopped at a brightly lit building with floodlights on its roof, surrounded by a high chain-link fence topped with slanting barbed wire. It was much smaller than he had imagined.

A man came out, unlocked the gate, and all three took him up a short walk to a narrow porch and into a small office. The man sat down behind the desk, and he and the officers stood while he wrote down answers to questions. Not much was asked of Duncan except his full name, date of birth, address and phone number.

Janet did not react when he admitted that he did not live on Almar. While he did not know the number, he told them its location. Officer Janet affirmed that he was there pending investigation.

Duncan asked, "What's pending mean?"

The officers did not answer, but Mr. Taylor, the Juvie supervisor, took a breath and looked solemnly at him. "It means you've been arrested on suspicion of theft and will be held here while the police gather evidence to prove guilt."

He might have only just turned thirteen, but he quickly translated this. Kevin was right; they had nothing.

"For how long?"

"That's up to the Court. A judge will decide in a few days."

He translated that too. Maybe a very long time, but he said nothing. The three adults talked among themselves for a while. It was like he wasn't there. Then, the officers signed some papers and left without saying anything to him.

Mr. Taylor motioned toward one of two gray metal chairs with green vinyl padded seats. "Please have a seat, Duncan."

After he was seated, he said, "As the head supervisor of this facility, I do not make judgments about any boy's guilt or innocence. And many boys, and some girls, come here for reasons other than being accused of a crime."

Duncan thought of Kevin.

"We are more of a way station for kids in trouble." He paused, then, "It will likely feel like a jail to you. You will have to spend some of your time in a cell, and when you eat and sleep and how you spend your time here will be according to our rules and decisions. But we see this as a temporary home for our boys. You will have play time, time to read, be outside, learn new things, and be with the other boys. How you got into trouble is perhaps something you can think about." The man paused again, but Duncan remained silent.

"All right, next, I will get you settled in for the night. You will take a shower and be given new clothes. Afterward, I will take you to your room. Are you hungry?"

He wasn't but said, "Yes, sir."

"It's late, but we have egg salad sandwiches and some tomato soup." He did not ask if Duncan preferred anything else. He continued, "You will be confined to your room for," and hesitated as if resolving an inner debate, "tonight and two more nights. After that, if you behave, you'll be on the same schedule as the others, which I will cover later. Any questions?"

He stared at the floor and shook his head. He missed his friends already.

"All right then, come with me." They went through a door into the room he had seen through the window. Mr. Taylor called it the rec room. There was a folded-up ping-pong table to one side and an empty red brick fireplace. "We have our meals here."

He noticed that the window to the office was mirrored, so he could not see through it. He was taken down a hallway, and they passed heavy-looking doors with small windows. He was ushered into the bathroom, shown where the towels were, and given toiletries.

"Take a shower. I'm taking your clothes. They'll be cleaned and returned to you when you leave us. Your new clothes will be on that stool."

After the shower he put on the provided underwear and a faded blue jumpsuit that he guessed was the standard inmate outfit. He was allowed to eat in the kitchen, which looked like any kitchen in an average-sized home. He brushed his teeth and was shown to what Mr. Taylor called his room. It was a cell. It was small, with just enough room for a metal-framed twin bed, tiny desk, a bench, and four steps of pacing room to bleed off a bit of that caged animal feeling.

The walls were solid concrete, not softened by the pastel green paint. Surprisingly large, the window had eighteen narrow panes of translucent wire-reinforced glass. There was a single bare light in the middle of the high ceiling. He did not see a light switch.

"Meals are at 8:30, 12:30, and 6 o'clock. Yours will be delivered to you until you can join the other boys. When you need to use the lavatory, press that button," he pointed, "and someone will open the door for you. I will leave the light on for a half-hour so you can get settled."

His delivery had the monotone drone of a message given many times. At its end, he seemed to soften. "I know this is hard. Although you are confined, I and our entire staff are here to help you on to a better life. This could be an opportunity." He offered a glimpse of a smile, to which Duncan did not respond. "All right, good night then. Try to rest."

The thick door closed. He heard the loud clack of a lock being engaged. It took only a short time to complete the inspection of his cell. The only interesting discovery was the graffiti on the walls. They were the inked declarations of inmates before him:

Billy B. 6/3/66

Tom Davenport was here 01-14-63

Jack R was here 5/19/61

Jack R was here 8/1/62

9-29-64 CDT says

MM misses Annie 07•17•67

NEXT STOP SAN QUENTIN BITCH

Stop crying pussy

There were barely legible messages under thinly applied paint; one said: Fuck the cops.

And a mysterious one near the bottom of the wall: Watch out for the rabbit.

There was nothing else to read, no radio to listen to or TV to watch, only a couple of pencils and a pen on the desk. So, he lay down and stared at the ceiling until the light went out. Sleep took a long time to come, and he woke with a jerk from a dream where he had been falling through roiling black thunderheads until he smashed into the jagged rocky earth. A later dream had him running from dogs he could not see but only hear.

Daylight filtering through his windows woke him the following morning. He buzzed to get out, peed, and much later, breakfast was brought to him by a plump-cheeked woman who called herself Mrs. Dunlap. She also brought in magazines and books. He thanked her, and she smiled. He ate quickly, and after she had taken his tray of dishes away, the door was locked again.

He read horrifying things about the war that never ended and about riots and protests in many places around the country. He looked at pictures of sports cars and pretty girls, read about how to make a campfire and how not to get lost in the woods. He read about the Summer of Love in San Francisco with pictures of longhaired men and women speaking about love, peace, and dropping out. They smoked marijuana, smiled a lot and went on trips via LSD Airlines without ever leaving their barely furnished bedrooms. He read all the magazines and looked at all the pictures, and it was still two hours until lunch. The books did not interest him. Bored and angry, he slid into a sloppy musical babble, which he performed for the panes of glass, mixing lyrics from songs by Buffalo Springfield, The Doors and Jefferson Airplane.

Then he fell back on his bed, grunted and began to think. If Mr. Taylor had been able to look into Duncan's mind, he would have likely been disappointed by the drift of his cogitation. It went something like this:

Juvenile hall. Why do they call it that? This isn't a hall; it's a jail. Juvenile jail would be honest. It isn't a home either, whatever that man says. Pending investigation? That means they don't have shit. They have nothing except what that rat boy said. I don't even really know him. So why did he rat? What's he got against me? There's nothing to investigate. It's not like we kept the wallets, just the money; we've spent most of it. SOOOOOOOOO... nothin'. Even if they track Kevin down, he won't blab. Randy? No way. None of the other guys either—it's not like they know anything anyway. There's nothing to investigate except to ask a few boys questions they either won't answer or don't know. How long will that take? A day or two? So, why am I in here?

He flipped a pencil back and forth between his thumb and first fingers.

Why? There's no chance they can get proof, so why?

It's like I've been convicted, but I haven't.

I could be in this jail for weeks, and they don't have to prove a thing because they're still investigating. Janet was so friendly, wasn't she?

Yeah, right.

I must've fucked-up with her. She thinks I did it. Just suspicions is all. So why put me here for weeks maybe without...

Like a starburst firework exploding in his brain, he got it.

Punishment. This way they can punish me without proving anything.

He threw the pencil at the wall, said out loud, "Fuckers."

Pending could mean weeks, months even. Kevin was in here for three weeks, three fucking weeks, and it sounded like he did nothing wrong at all. Fuckers.

There was still an hour and a half until lunch.

It was hot in his cell. There were the faint sounds of voices penetrating the massive door, but he could not make out a word. Desperate, he returned to the books and opened *To Kill a Mockingbird* because it was about kids, even if the main one was a girl.

Lunch came and went, and he snarled at the food bearer. He met Mrs. Taylor, who delivered dinner. She was taller than her husband and wore thick glasses. Her inquiries about his well-being were met with a sullen glare, which she countered with chipper observations about the weather. No way would he be nice to the people keeping him locked in this hotbox. He cracked open the bottom portion of the window to let in a dribble of cool air.

A long, restless night was abruptly headed off when he reached a new level of clarity.

They can't keep me in here too long without proof, and proof won't happen. Mom will kick their asses. This isn't scary. I'm just in a room getting fed, and all I have to do is wait it out and not be a dumbass who confesses.

He laid back, content, and thought that being in Juvie might be really cool. Then he soured a little, realizing he had two more nights in solitary. But maybe it would be fun. He would have stories to tell when he got out. He just hoped his mom was not mad at him. He figured she would visit soon. It was all stuff to look forward to.

51

At his first breakfast with the other inmates, about twelve in all, who sat at two long foldable tables, Mr. Dunlop introduced him to the assembled motley group. The youngest boy looked no older than seven; the oldest was maybe sixteen. Most were around his age, some older, some younger. He was surprised that there were two girls. They sat across from each other at the far end of the second table. The youngest was thin and shy, with straight strawberry-blonde hair and bangs that hung into her eyes. She could not have been much more than eleven. She kept her head down most of the time, but she had looked at him once when he was introduced, and her gaze disturbed him. How could someone so young look so old, and how were her eyes so vacant yet so full of pain?

The other girl could not have been more different. It was hard to guess her age, somewhere between fourteen and seventeen. She was loud and brash with short black hair like the Beatles had three years before. He might have mistaken her for a young boy if he had only seen her face. But she was cute and curvy with breasts that were too big for her jumpsuit. Her banter was edgy, and she talked while she chewed.

As Mr. Dunlop said, "This is Duncan, he..." She burst in and said, "Yeah, more meat for the cage." She ignored Mr. Dunlop's admonishment and laughed as she slapped the table.

Another young boy sat next to the youngest. They darted nervous glances at the older kids like they might get hit at any second. A few boys said hi, and the rest returned to their meals. Now that his solitary confinement was over, his cell door was unlocked like the others, and he could have wandered around the small space, played games, or talked, but instead, he retreated to his room, closed the door, and read his book until dinner.

Mr. and Mrs. Taylor hosted the dinner. They served roast chicken, mashed potatoes, and peas, followed by chocolate pudding. The beverage options were milk or water, but the tough girl asked for a beer. A new kid was said to be doing his solitary, and one of the kids from breakfast was away from the table.

"What did you do?"

Duncan turned from his pudding to the source of the question on his right, a teenager with coarse, short brown hair and sharp eyes. "What?"

The teenager held out a hand. "I'm Richard, Duncan."

He shook.

"What did you do to be here?"

"Nothing."

Richard scoffed, "Weird how everybody says that."

"What did you do?"

"Nothing," he said with a laugh. It's my parents who did stuff—so much stuff that the cops decided I'd be better off here." He waved a hand about the cheaply appointed room and locked doors, adding, like he was quoting, "Safe from an injurious and neglectful home life."

"How long have you been here?"

"Almost five weeks."

"You've been in jail for five weeks because of what your mom and dad did?"

The cavalier sheen splintered for a moment. "Yeah, supposedly, this isn't jail for me. They only have me locked in for overall security and consistency in the application of the rules." Again, it sounded like a quote.

"But why? You didn't do anything."

"They have nowhere else to put me. I'm headed for a foster home, but it seems there aren't many who want a fifteen-year-old."

"Damn."

"So what did you do?"

"Why do you think I did anything? Maybe I'm like you."

"Nope, the foster limbo boys don't get a night of solitary, let alone three nights like you got."

"Oh, well, nothing."

"C'mon, what did you do?"

The other inmates had gotten up. Some went to their rooms, others to the meager entertainment options. Into Duncan's silence, Richard pursued, "What do they think you did? I won't tell."

"Yeah? I'm in here because of a rat."

"You calling me a rat?"

"I don't know you."

"That's fair. But I'm not a rat; I don't tell the adults a thing. I bug everyone for their stories. Helps me not go nuts."

"The rat told the cops I stole some stuff but didn't."

"OK, I've done bad too; I just didn't get caught like you."

"I'm not caught. I didn't do it."

"Uh-huh, you can't leave, can you?"

"You can't either."

Richard laughed." OK, OK, good. The other thing I try to find out is how smart the new boys are. You're not a dumbshit. Wanna play chess?"

"Don't know how."

"It's easy, I'll show you."

"OK."

His inquisitor got a cheap wooden chess set off a shelf, brought it back to the table and put himself on the opposite side. Richard patiently explained the game. All the pieces were there except a black rook, which had been replaced with a gray stone from the yard. While they played, Richard gave him a rundown on their fellow inmates: "Norman and Rodney, the two young ones, are waiting for foster parents like me, but they've been here less than a week. Willie and Glenn are little toughs. Willie's fourteen and has been in and out of here for a year or more. He'll end up in CYA; he likes burglary and vandalizing."

"What's CYA?"

"California Youth Authority—kid prison."

"They have a prison for kids?"

"Teenagers. More than one. Hard places."

Duncan worried whether he could be sent there. As if he were reading his mind, Richard said, "They only send hard cases there. Repeat criminals, violent assholes, not little thieves like you."

With some heat, he said, "I didn't do anything."

"OK, OK, I'll try to remember that."

"What about the big girl?"

"Connie? She and her boyfriend robbed a store. She's proud of it. The guy's nineteen. She drove the car, and he held up the place. She's going to need a new boyfriend."

Duncan moved his queen deep behind enemy lines. Richard took it with his knight. "Dumb move, but you'll learn."

"What about the young girl? She can't belong here."

"Yeah, no shit, right? I don't know; she wouldn't talk to me, doesn't talk to anyone except Connie, I guess. Anyway, all that Connie would say before threatening to bust my nose was, 'She was used nasty by her daddy,' then she promised me that if I asked Lisa about it or even spoke to that little girl, she would hurt me so bad I'd need a hospital."

Duncan's guts rolled over as he grappled with what Connie might have meant. What occurred to him, like seeing gargoyle shadows in the night, was something so horrible he didn't want to look. He pushed a pawn for no reason. Richard's bishop swooped in.

"Checkmate."

Perhaps Richard felt the same, for he immediately set up the pieces for a new game. "You're kinda lucky. You've got your room to yourself. This place had been crowded until a few days ago."

"Which cells do the girls have?"

"They don't, not this side anyway. I'm not sure, but they may have a room in the staff area."

They focused on the game for a while. "You're already getting better. In the early part, you want to develop your pieces and focus on controlling the center."

"I like it."

"Me too. Check."

"Dammit."

Richard laughed.

He managed more resistance, but the mate was inevitable. The other kids had wandered off. A young man in crisp slacks and pressed shirt came out of the office door and said to get ready to return to their cells. "Call me Carl," he said.

He and Richard went down the same hall. The other boy's cell was three doors down from his, near the lavatory. He hesitated before he went into his room, said to Richard,

"They put Lisa in jail. Isn't that wrong?"

Their shepherd stared down the hall. Richard took a long breath and slowly released it, said, "Yeah, I think so, yeah." And he walked away with Carl.

52

Over the next few days, new inmates arrived. Some left. Richard stayed. Connie and Lisa stayed. The two youngest boys went. A new young kid, nine or ten, came. He was becoming familiar with the diverse types of inmates. Some were already charged with crimes like malicious mischief, vandalism, car theft, or burglary. They were being held in Juvie Jail, awaiting a court date and a decision on what to do with them.

Others were there because they had been removed from their homes due to their parents being drunkards, violent criminals, or for being just plain neglectful. Those kids were in the limbo land of waiting for a foster parent brave enough to help a damaged child. So far, Duncan had not met anyone with his status—being held on suspicion while the police worked to build a case.

He was getting used to the routine. Cheap but OK meals were served by the clock. The boys were given chores to do each day—he had pushed a reel mower over the grass in the front and back yards. It had been nice to be outside, but the smallness of the plot and the tall wire fence with its discouraging barbed wire and locked gate made pushing the mower feel like pushing a car.

Out back there was a play area with a single basketball hoop, a swing set, and a large lawn to run around on or throw a ball, but it was not big enough to have a real baseball or football game. For some reason, although Duncan was athletic and did well in football and baseball, he totally sucked at basketball. He learned they also had classes in Juvie during the school year but would not start for a few weeks.

Mr. Dunlop did hold a class in first aid. Eight boys, including Duncan, attended. At one point a new boy, Russell, who looked about sixteen, said to another new boy, Scott, maybe fifteen, "Hey, you could bandage yourself up when you whack your head on the steering wheel of the next car you steal."

"I ain't going to crash any more cars."

"You did that last one."

"So?"

Mr. Dunlop asked, "Why did you take the car?"

Scott shrugged. "Just hate walkin'."

"Where did you learn to hotwire a car?"

"At CYA camp."

Russell deadpanned, "Yeah, can learn a lot at CYA."

All the boys laughed.

"With getting caught and injured, do you think you'll ever steal another car?"

Scott, who had unruly curly brown hair and a cluster of ugly red pimples on his face, scratched an especially prominent one, thought for a moment, and then said, "Well, if I get tired of walkin', I might."

The room roared. The only person who did not was Mr. Dunlop; he looked thoughtful.

The two married couples, who served as supervisors, lived on site. Initially, Duncan distrusted them as people, like Officer Janet, who pretended friendship but were really out to punish him. Yet he soon came to believe they were genuinely kind and cared for their charges, even when the boys got lippy or acted out. They listened to complaints and never yelled at or demeaned the kids. The inmates of any duration referred to them as "our Hall Parents."

Duncan was not ready to go that far. Hall Jailers was more like it, even if they were nice. Every day he was faced with locked doors and barbed wire and having to ask permission, sometimes even to pee.

It was after dinner on his sixth day when, angry, he asked to speak with Mr. Taylor. Carl unlocked the office door and let him in to see the man looking out the front window. He turned a gentle face on the boy and asked, "What's on your mind, Duncan?"

It took him a moment as his forehead creased in aggravation. Then he asked, "Why am I still here?"

The man stood straighter. "The police are still investigating."

"Still? There's nothing to investigate."

"A judge has given them more time."

"He has?"

"Yes."

"I want to go home."

Mr. Taylor moved a step closer to him. "Of course you do, Duncan, and I hope you can soon, but that's not up to me. It's up to the police and the court."

He chewed on the inside of one cheek and shook his head. "Why won't you let my mom see me or talk to me?"

Mr. Taylor jerked at the accusation. Duncan glared at him. The man appeared to struggle with how to reply. He took and released a long breath, sagged a little, and said, "I'm not preventing your mother from seeing you."

"But it's been six days. Is it the police?"

"No, it's not the police."

"I don't understand."

"Please sit down, Duncan."

He took the same chair he had sat in when he first arrived. Mr. Taylor sat behind the desk and clasped his hands in front of him. He swallowed, nodded as if to himself, and said, "This is a stressful time for you, and I expect it is also for your mother. There was a hearing with the judge about your case two days ago. I believe she attended. The arrest of a child can be a tough thing for a parent. She may be busy; there may be demands on her time by the court. Of course, I cannot say."

"Mom would be here if she wasn't being stopped."

Mr. Taylor took his time deciding how to field that, finally said, "In all my years as head supervisor of this place, it has always been the policy to encourage parents to see their children unless the court orders that they cannot. There has been no such order in your case. All a parent needs to do is call to make an appointment. We would happily make it happen." He took another long breath as if gathering strength to say the next words. "But it is also my sad experience that very few parents come to see their children here."

It was a lot of carefully crafted words, like wrapping layers of squishy pink foam around a dagger. Duncan felt the point anyway.

"You're saying she could come, but..."

There was no question, and the man did not interrupt, but the gravity in the room pulled at his face.

"...but that's bullshit!" Mr. Taylor did not object to his language. "She would... she would..." And his voice faded away.

The gray-haired man remained silent and still, like the greatest kindness he could offer was to allow Duncan time to process the truth on his own. Duncan stared at the desktop under Mr. Taylor's hands for a long time, and when he finally raised glistening eyes, they looked past the man and through the window into the rec room. He nodded and, in a voice that was little more than a whisper, said, "I get it. I get it." He turned his eyes to Mr. Taylor's. "I'd like to go to my room now." It was the first time he had not called it a cell.

They rose and moved toward the door. Mr. Taylor said, "You can call her, you know. Would you like to? I would give you privacy."

Duncan looked back at the green desk phone for a few moments and then shook his head. "No."

With one hand on the boy's shoulder, Mr. Taylor opened the door, said, "I'm...good night, Duncan."

"Good night, sir."

53

Duncan hated the 9:30 p.m. lockdown. The Hall Parents tried to be kind. They would patiently listen to anything the inmates had to say, but they were also rigid about the rules. He was locked in his cell on time every night, and no dawdling was allowed. Then, a half-hour later, the lights went out—much too early.

There was no TV, but the radio would be on for a few hours a day, sometimes playing rock 'n' roll, but other times, ick, music that belonged on the *Lawrence Welk Show*.

They kept the kids busy with chores. He had washed all the windows, pulled weeds, watered the grass and mopped the rec room and hall floors. Every inmate had to make their bed and keep their room clean. Connie helped in the kitchen, and she chatted freely with Mrs. Taylor, who, despite looking like a grandmother, never blanched at Connie's occasionally coarse language.

He was thankful he had not yet been given the lavatory cleanup job, which had fallen to Russell and Scott. It was a big, yucky job, for it had a large shower for several boys at a time, two toilets, two urinals and two sinks. Otherwise, he did not mind the work; he got outside, which made time pass.

One day, he, Richard, Scott, Russell and Connie sat in the far corner of the play area, swapping juvenile crime stories.

"Why did you throw a rock through the window?" Richard asked Russell.

"Wanted to see it shatter. It was so huge; what a boom it made!"

"You're looking at my tits again."

Duncan flinched; Connie was talking to him. The boys laughed. He quickly looked away.

"You *all* look, but this one stares like a calf hoping it's time for breakfast."

Scott fell over laughing, and the rest of the guys roared. A surge of blood heated Duncan's face. Connie pulled the zipper down on her jumpsuit and exposed mounds that were barely constrained by a tight white T-shirt; she said, "Look, let's get this out of the way. I know they're big and beautiful, and it's too much to ask that you don't glance occasionally but knock off the staring. Here," she looked around the yard and found no adults, "take one last good long look, boys." She cupped each breast and bounced them up and down as she smiled.

Scott sprang to a seated position; the four male mouths dropped. Duncan felt he was glowing like the stoplight in a one-intersection town. Then, he lost his self-consciousness. His mind froze, not only at the sight of that rhythmic bouncing but from the impact of her pure, scary sexiness.

Connie laughed. "How old are you? Twelve?"

"Thirteen." He did not add that he had only been so for a month.

"Bet you haven't even been kissed yet. Your mom doesn't count."

His tongue felt frozen. She did another quick survey of the yard. "Let's fix that," she said. She scooted across the circle until she was knees to knees with him, leaned in and kissed him on the mouth.

It was not a peck.

She put one hand lightly behind his head and planted a long, slow, lingering kiss. Her lips were plump and tender and caressed his. She tasted like the barbecue chicken and strawberry Jell-O they had had for lunch. He closed his eyes and was utterly lost in feeling. Later, he would credit Connie with kick-starting puberty for him.

After a while she pulled gently away. He did not open his eyes; he was floating in a new bliss. The boy's laughter brought him back to earth, but there were shimmers of envy about them.

"Hey," Scott said, "I haven't been kissed yet either." Richard and Russell tittered nervously.

"Yeah, right, well, too bad, 'cause no one else in here is getting a kiss from me."

He felt a tinge of embarrassment, but it was instantly relieved by her sparkling eyes and playful smile. Then, she transformed from sweet and sexy to stern and mean.

"No more staring by any of you, or I'll punch you in the face. Hard. Got it?"

Duncan nodded rapidly. The others hacked up yes answers.

***

The joviality of the inmates at the Santa Cruz Jail for Risqué Boys and Girls took a nosedive that afternoon with the arrival of Billy and Hank. They were ushered into the rec room by Mr. Dunlop and a police officer, which was a new wrinkle. Before, only the supervisor on duty took the new boys back. But the officer entered last and stood like a guard dog as they were led back to the showers. He did not stay, but his lingering was like a statement that they were not to act up or else.

Billy and Hank spent that night and two more in the strong cells, which had toilets and sinks. Duncan almost forgot about them, but at their first breakfast with the rest of the inmates, he remembered what Kevin had warned him about.

They sat down across from him and Richard. Mr. Dunlop went into the office. Mrs. Dunlop was busy in the kitchen. Little glasses of orange juice and empty, thick stoneware plates that would soon receive scrambled eggs and toast were on the tables before each inmate. The smaller of the two was at least a head taller than Duncan. He glared out of pop-eyes at Richard and then at Duncan from a face where nothing seemed like it belonged. Big ears stuck out nearly perpendicular to his skull. Big purple lips and a big nose were mounted above a chin that one had to search for. The black mop on his head looked like it had not been cut in months.

His partner was still bigger, and his eyes passed over the boys like they were not the food the snake sought. He had muscular arms and neat, long brown hair streaked with gold. A close-cropped strip of beard circled his face like the chinstrap on a Nazi's helmet. He had an unsettling way of looking around the room, barely turning his head. To hide his nervousness, Duncan sipped orange juice.

Richard extended a hand over the table. "Hi, I'm Richard. This is Duncan."

The two men, at least they seemed like men to Duncan, allowed that hand to hang in the air. Pop-eyes snorted. "What are you two, the Welcoming Committee?"

The other guy laughed but said," Now, now, no need to be unfriendly. I'm Billy; this is Hank." He did not move to shake, and Richard's hand retreated.

Hank ignored the boys and studied the room. And Billy stared past them at the mirrored glass of the office as if hatred could bore holes in it. Duncan considered changing tables, but something told him that would be a mistake. He was saved by the arrival of Mrs. Dunlop and Connie bringing in the food. The eyes of the new arrivals snapped onto Connie's body.

Hank elbowed Billy." Look at that. Damn, maybe it was good we got caught."

"Fuck yeah," said Billy.

Connie's eyes flicked toward the pair and then quickly away. Mrs. Dunlop drew herself up and said, "Stop that. There will be no use of that word here. You understand me?"

Duncan suspected that her palpable anger was in defense of Connie rather than over the word itself. The two slowly nodded but did not answer otherwise. To Connie, she said, "Be a dear and bring the toast out, will you? Then come eat with me in the kitchen."

Scoops of eggs and forks of sausages hit the plates. Waffles were stacked and topped with masses of butter while waterfalls of syrup poured down their sides. The room was filled with a happy din by the boys. Lisa was not there. The two men piled food high on their plates. He and Russell busied themselves with their meals until, halfway through, Richard shocked him by asking,

"So, what did you guys do?"

Hank looked up from shoveling eggs into his mouth. "What's that to you?"

Billy puffed air out of his nostrils.

"I ask everybody, just interested."

"What are you in for?" Billy asked.

"Waiting on getting foster parents."

"Yeah?" Hank asked. "What, did your old man kick you out?"

A wince of hurt hit Richard's face. Duncan jumped in. "The cops think I stole some wallets, but I didn't."

The two snorted in harmony. "Didn't do it, huh?" said Hank.

"He said he didn't do it," Billy said.

"I guess that makes it true, huh?"

"Yep, good 'nuff for me."

They laughed. Duncan did not protest further.

"So, what did you guys do?" asked Richard.

Duncan admired his courage and persistence. Hanks's lips curled in a sneer, and then he lifted a dripping waffle to his mouth and appeared to look right through Richard.

Billy smiled, said, "What the hell," and squeezed his partner's shoulder. "This here is one of America's premier car thieves. What's your total up to now?"

He answered past chunks of mashed waffle, "Fifteen, but the cops are only charging me for seven."

The boys looked at Billy, who said, "Burglary and robbery." He smiled like he had been awarded medals for the acts. Then his eyes slit at them as he added, "Aggravated robbery."

Duncan wanted to ask what that meant, but Richard banged him with a knee.

Billy said, "We've answered you little pukes' questions." He leaned over the table and hissed, "Now, fuck-off."

A day, a night, and a day with the two tough young men who turned out to be seventeen going on eighteen was a tense, joyless stretch. Billy was a watcher; he studied everything and everyone. His very presence was intimidating. All he had to do was walk up to one of the teens sitting in a chair, and he would get up and move without a word being said. Hank was a more obvious bully. When the adults were not around, he would harass the others by grabbing a book they were reading or bumping kids out in the play area. He said shit like, "Get out of my way, dingleberry." One time, he and Richard were playing another game of chess. Hank watched them for a minute, then reached down and scattered the pieces onto the floor. He smirked and said to Richard," There, I saved you, buttface here was going to beat you, and he's just a baby." That showed how little Hank knew about chess. Duncan had been down a bishop, a knight and two pawns. He'd had no chance of winning and, in fact, had yet to beat Richard.

To Duncan, Hank was an older, pathetic version of Chuck Putnam. His grade school tormentor at least had a purpose rooted in extortion. What Hank got out of picking on kids younger and smaller than himself, he didn't understand.

Lisa no longer came to meals; he supposed she had been moved out of jail. He hoped it was someplace nicer and safer. Connie came to meals, but it must have been an ordeal. The Two stared at her much of the time, Billy, through those slits for eyes, Hank openly, like an assault and a dare for her to object.

After lunch one day, Hank cornered Connie in a hallway. He could not hear what Hank was whispering, but Connie looked scared, making Duncan, Scott, Richard and Russell leap to their feet as one. With a hand to his chest, Connie pushed Hank and said, "Get out of my way."

She fled to see Mrs. Dunlop in the kitchen. Hank smirked, apparently not ruffled in the slightest by the rejection. Duncan felt foolish jumping to the defense of a girl who could easily kick his ass. And she could probably kick the asses of any of the other boys, too, except Billy and Hank.

She brought electricity with her. She was fun, open, honest, tough but also tender. She had lost her boyfriend, who Richard said was sure to go to real prison. She freely admitted to helping him in the crime. She laughed and played and was the boldest girl he had ever met. And she had kissed him.

That kiss lingered in his mind. Would she do it again? He did not think so, but she had left the prospect rather nebulous. It wasn't that he hoped for it exactly, but rather that her kiss had been a stroke across bowstrings that had never been played before. He wanted to understand, and another kiss might help him to know what the thrill was all about. Whatever it was, he was clear that her kiss was a gift. He liked her. He liked that she liked him. Being friends with a girl was such a new experience.

He rebuffed attempts by the other boys to tell them what the kiss had been like. He wasn't sure why, except he felt that to discuss it in the way they were asking would cheapen her gift. She acted like nothing at all had happened. He was careful not to look at her chest, which took real effort, but a few times, she had looked at him with a sweet smile like she knew something of what he felt, and he smiled back at her. Whenever he or she left Juvie Jail, he would not likely see her again, but her gift, her gift, would prove to be enough.

Another night was ending with the usual resented march to their cells, where Duncan would have to listen to that lock being secured. Mr. and Mrs. Taylor were doing the night shift. Carl, who usually assisted, wasn't there that night; he had Sundays off. Connie lingered, and the boys moved in the direction of their cells. Duncan heard a loud smack, and someone exclaimed, "Oh!"

He turned from the doorway of his cell to see Billy and Hank crouching over a fallen Mr. Taylor, delivering vicious punches to the man's head and gut. In seconds the man went limp, his jaw slack. Blood poured from his mouth and a cut over one eye.

"Get the bitch!" Billy ordered. Hank ran up the hall to meet Mrs. Taylor as she exited the kitchen. With one hand before her mouth, she shouted, "Joshua!"

Hank pushed her back inside, and he heard yells and the sounds of cookware and pans hitting the floor. A scream from Connie pierced the frozen shock of the other inmates as she charged Billy and, without slowing, punched him in the face. "Leave him alone!"

He staggered but stepped right back and punched Connie, and she fell backward to the floor. All the boys, except a couple of kids under ten, surged forward but stopped again when Hank came out of the kitchen with a butcher knife to Mrs. Taylor's throat.

"Stay the fuck where you are, or I'll bleed the bitch and do you next."

Everyone froze again. Mrs. Taylor's eyes stared through her thick glasses at her fallen husband. Russell and Scott had reached Connie and were helping her up. She appeared dazed but OK. Billy was shaking his right hand like it hurt from punching her.

"Listen," Billy said, "Hank and me are getting out of here. We're not going to hurt any of you long as you do what we say. Warden here," he kicked Mr. Taylor, "is going to wake up in one of his own cells. All of you back up over there," he pointed toward the office, "Hank, bring Mrs. Warden. Nobody needs to get cut; just don't get in our way, and you'll be fine."

In silence, the inmates clustered. Duncan felt at a loss for what to do. Mr. Taylor was bleeding and unconscious. His wife trembled in the ugly teen's grasp. Hank pushed his prisoner forward and kept the knife at her neck. He saw a streak of blood there. Billy reached down and ripped a ring of keys off the loop on Mr. Taylor's pants.

"Put her in there," he said, pointing at one of the strong cells. Hank pushed her inside.

"Give me the knife. Drag him in too."

While Hank did as ordered, Billy held the knife point-up and calmly studied the rest of them. Unlike Hank, whose eyes glowed and whose breath came in shallow bursts, he was calm. He even smiled at Connie. "Nice punch," he said.

Hank came out of the cell. Duncan could hear Mrs. Taylor crying, "Joshua, Joshua." Billy locked the Taylor's cell door.

"Now, all of you are going into the bathroom. Get moving,"

The two carefully kept their distance as eleven boys and one girl moved past them and down the hall. Duncan did not doubt that Billy would use that knife if he had to. It was crowded in the lavatory. Hank closed the door on them, and he heard the lock being turned. All the doors had locks in Juvie Jail.

Nobody said anything for quite a while. They could hear loud bangs like The Two were kicking down a door. Then silence.

"Is Lisa still back there?" Richard asked.

"No, she's gone," Connie said.

The faint sound of a door opening and closing was followed by more silence. "We gotta get outta here," Connie said, "Mr. Taylor is bad hurt; He may need a hospital."

He tried the door as if it had miraculously become unlocked. It wasn't steel like the cells, but heavy solid wood with a deadbolt lock.

"How?" Scott asked.

They searched the lavatory, but nothing was found that could break that door down. As they pondered the situation, the two youngest boys, Trevor and Sam, began to cry. Two other new kids he did not know tried to comfort them.

"The hinges," Duncan said, "if we can pull the pins, we might be able to remove the whole door."

"With what?" Scott asked.

It was another stumper until one of the new kids said, "I've got a knife." The group turned, and he offered one of the butter knives.

"Why?" Connie started, then, "Never mind," and took it from him.

It took the team what seemed like forever but was probably about half an hour to work out one pin using the knife, a metal rod from a toilet tank, and a heavy boot from one of the kids as a hammer; then, they more quickly removed the other pins. The door did not magically fall open. Another ten minutes were needed to scooch it off the hinges until it was free.

Connie was first out the door and shouted over her shoulder as she ran, "I'm calling the cops!"

He followed her. The rest of the gang clamored outside the Taylor's cell.

"Are you all right?"

"We're calling the police!"

"We'll get you out."

The door to the office was ajar. The private residence's door was broken, and clothes and furniture had been thrown about. The office was also a mess, with drawers emptied onto the floor. Pretty much everything had been tossed.

Connie was on the phone. "Yes, two guys attacked Mr. and Mrs. Taylor. They escaped. They locked them in a cell. He needs a doctor." There was a long back and forth as Connie answered questions and calmed down.

Duncan watched her. She was wonderful. She was obviously shaken but tough and clear and getting it done. She was also a young teenager, just fifteen years old, with a tremor in her voice, in jail but calling the police, anxious to help the man who locked her cell door every night.

She put the phone down. "They're coming."

"You, OK?" He was looking at the growing knot on her head.

She touched it and flinched. "This? Yeah, but I bet his fist and his face hurt more than my head."

They laughed. He said, "You're great."

She cocked her head and carefully considered him, then lightly backhanded his belly. "Don't get all moony on me. It was just a kiss." Her wink took the sting out of it. Then she kissed him again, but this time on the forehead. They laughed some more as two police cars and an ambulance appeared outside, lights flashing and sirens wailing.

54

In the rec room the next morning, the kids shouted over each other to the Dunlops:

"How's Mr. Taylor?"

"How's Mrs. Taylor?"

"Have they caught Hank and Billy?"

Last night they had watched their Hall Dad carried out on a stretcher after the police got the cell door open with a backup set of keys. Mrs. Taylor, Helen, Duncan heard her husband call her, followed her husband out to the ambulance. It was a short trip to the County Hospital, given it was right next door. Joshua had wanted to get off the stretcher, but the paramedics insisted he be carried. The police stayed and interviewed everyone. On Joshua's way out, Duncan heard him repeatedly telling the police that 'all my kids came to our aid' and 'they had no part in the escape.'

The Dunlops had shown up and made hot chocolate for all during the police interviews. It was one o'clock before Duncan got into his bed. He fell asleep with his clothes on. Breakfast had been delayed to 9:30, and the Dunlops were still there to serve them eggs, sausages, and toast.

"Joshua, Mr. Taylor," Mr. Dunlop said, "will be OK. He has a mild concussion and some bad bruises, but nothing is broken. They will keep him in the hospital for a while to make sure there are no complications from the concussion. Helen, Mrs. Taylor, is fine. She had a small cut on her neck. She's OK. The police are searching for Hank and Billy."

The general mood of the assembled teenagers was anger, not relief, and Richard seemed the most enraged, surprising Duncan because he had always been so calm and logical. "I hope those assholes go to prison forever," he said. "Why haven't they caught them yet? They could've killed Mrs. Taylor. I hate them. I hate them. I hope the cops kill them."

His words were a torrent, and neither supervisor tried to stop or correct Richard's eruption. When he was spent and quiet, tears shivered in his eyes, which shocked Duncan more than the anger. His friend sniffed, got up, left his food untouched and went to his cell. His outburst left the room in silence, but to Duncan, the looks on their faces mirrored what he felt.

We are not safe in here.

The rest of the day was subdued. Most of the kids, including Duncan, kept to themselves. Carl and a new assistant showed up that afternoon to help.

Everyone was surprised when Joshua and Helen walked through the door during dinner. There were cheers and even a couple of hugs. Joshua looked terrible. His jaw was swollen, and one side of his face was a nasty splash of purple-black and blue flesh, yet he beamed at his kids and smiled even though it must have hurt.

Duncan did not cheer. He wanted to snarl instead. He cursed Officer Janet under his breath as the inmates loudly welcomed the Taylors. He cursed them all: the police, the faceless judge, and the Hall Parents too. They had locked him up with men who could have killed him.

For what?

For suspicion.

Seeing Mr. Taylor's battered face, he thought,

Even you aren't safe here.

He thought about his mother neither calling nor visiting him in the more than two weeks he had been imprisoned. This pushed him down into a familiar sad and lonely hurt, but one so familiar it was soon shoved away and replaced by happy thoughts of his friends.

We cover for each other. I can count on them—always.

Joshua motioned with his hands to silence the kids, shouting things Duncan was not listening to. They calmed, and he said, "I am better than I look. Really. Last night was rough for all of us. Frightening, I know." He looked at his wife, whose face was a rigid mask, then said," But those boys," Men, Duncan almost shouted, "will be caught."

A young kid named Zachary asked, "Are they coming back here?"

"No, no, I've been told they'll be treated as adults and put in County," he rushed on, "but I wanted to say how proud and grateful Helen and I are to all of you. You came to our rescue, and we appreciate it more than we could possibly say."

The group took that in silence, and then Joshua addressed Connie, "I hear you came to my defense and punched Billy. And you got punched back for your courage, I see." He smiled. Connie appeared embarrassed—a first, as far as Duncan knew.

Russell wildly waved a hand and said, "No, no, no, you got it wrong, Mr. Taylor. She wasn't defending you. She was just mad that Billy had been staring at her tits."

The room erupted. Even Connie laughed. Helen frowned; Joshua wobbled a hand and mouthed to her, "It's OK."

When the room finally settled down, Joshua focused on Connie." We know the truth, Connie. We thank you so much, and I made sure certain people know what you did. It should help." He looked the other kids in the eyes for long moments and said, "We thank you all."

Duncan had laughed at Russell's joke, but his mirth faded like a candle flame at the end of its wick. He turned and walked to his cell. He shut the door, sat on the hard bed, glared at the thick concrete wall three feet away and declared,

I'm getting out of here.

He lay awake for hours thinking about how.

<h1 style="text-align:center">55</h1>

"You're going to what?"

"Escape."

It was just before breakfast, and Duncan had pulled Richard into his room, shut the door and had them in the corner near the window. Given the expression on his friend's face, he may as well have told him he was going to turn into a rabbit and hippity hop his way to freedom.

"How?" he finally asked.

"I'm going over the fence today."

"Uh-huh, over the fence... but how?"

"I'm quick; I can get over it in ten seconds."

"There's barbed wire. You'll get all cut up. It's got to be eight, maybe ten feet high."

"That's where I need your help." He explained how he would throw his blanket over the wire but also needed Richard's to cover the barbs fully. "You know how we can open our window only a few inches? Well, It's enough. I will drop mine outside, and I have those rubber-padded gardening gloves Carl gave me. I think I'll need two blankets. If you also slip yours out the window, I can do it."

Richard lost his baffled expression. "It won't work. You'll just get caught, probably hurt, and be in more trouble besides."

"I gotta go."

"Why?"

Duncan turned away and looked into glass he couldn't see through. "Dunno, gotta."

"Just wait, get out when they let you."

Duncan turned back and folded his arms tightly across his chest. "What do you know?"

"They won't keep you that long."

"How do you know they won't?"

"This place is temporary."

"Yeah? You've been here for over six weeks and didn't do anything wrong. They think I stole stuff. Maybe they'll keep me in here for months. Janet hates me."

Richard frowned. "Janet? Oh, the cop."

"Yeah, Janet will make it so they investigate forever. I gotta go."

Richard looked thoughtful, then said softly, "You're scared."

Duncan looked away. "They put killers in with us."

"Hey, they were bad but didn't kill anyone."

Duncan's eyes blazed at the other boy. Loudly, he said, "Yeah? You saw. He could've chopped her head off with that huge knife. And he and Billy nearly beat him to death." Then he quietly said, "Help me, OK? You can come too if you want."

Richard slowly shook his head but said, "OK, OK."

The door opened, making them jump. "What's all the yelling?" Mrs. Dunlop asked. "Duncan, Richard, you know very well that you cannot close your door when anyone else is in the room."

"Yes, ma'am," they said as one.

"All right, come out; the food is ready."

Breakfast was a feast: ham steaks, hash browns from scratch, eggs, plump blueberries in bowls for the waffles, real maple syrup, not the cheap other stuff, orange juice, bananas and bacon. For the first time, there were tablecloths and cloth napkins instead of paper. And Helen and Joshua were there, helping with the meal. Carl was too. The inmates goggled at the display and sat.

Mrs. Dunlop said, "As you can see, our meal today is better than what you are used to. Mr. and Mrs. Taylor proposed, and Andrew and I agreed that we wanted to say thank you in more than words. We try to make this as much of a transitional home as possible, but understand it can still be a hard place. So today will also be different than other days. There will be no chores…" The kids cheered. "and you can play the radio on any station and for all of the day if you wish." More cheering. "And tonight, the final episode of The Fugitive is on. We're going to roll out the TV and watch it together. Lights out won't be until midnight because the show starts at ten."

There were smiles all around, and the kids dug into the fabulous food. Some buzzed about how lucky they were to see how the show they had been watching for years ended. Duncan wasn't excited about the show. It was something Ava watched about a guy on the run from the police, falsely accused of murdering his wife. He was excited about the food and the fact that it would be a play day, and maybe, just maybe, that would make it easier to get away.

But it didn't; it made it impossible.

There were zero opportunities to execute his plan with all the free-roaming teenagers, adolescents and extra staff. He played chess with Richard and Monopoly with Scott and two younger kids. They had a lunch of sandwiches and soup. Duncan played basketball in the afternoon and did not embarrass himself too much. He wrestled with a new boy named Joe. He sang along with Peter, Paul and Mary happily proclaiming, with beautiful voices, "I dig rock 'n' roll music."

He ran, leapt, shouted and sang, and for two hours, he forgot about leaving. Dinner was barbecued chicken cooked on a grill in the yard, potato salad, corn on the cob, cokes, ginger ale and Sprite. Buckets of ice cream were plopped on the table. Tubs of chocolate, pistachio, vanilla and strawberry were emptied into bowls with a steady clink clack of spoons that sent scoops of pleasure to their doom down happy throats.

Later, a thirteen-inch black and white TV was rolled into the main room. The folding chairs were loosely arranged before it, and they watched Detective Gerard soften his hard heart and help Dr. Richard Kimble get justice by killing the man who had murdered the doctor's wife.

The inmates were stuffed, tired and happy. The Hall Parents glowed with the day's success and the affection they clearly felt for their charges. Smiling, Duncan gazed at Mr. and Mrs. Taylor and thought about how good they were. But Joshua's face was a shocking display of the damage that the fists of vicious men can do. And the big square gauze bandage stuck on Helen's neck told how Hank's cut was much more than a minor scratch.

The party broke up. All the inmates thanked the people who were likely the kindest jailers in the world. The boys moved toward teeth brushing and bed. On the way down the hall, Duncan touched Richard's hand, leaned in to whisper in his ear, "Tomorrow."

With a sad nod, Richard agreed.

56

There was no chance the next morning. Breakfast and lunch were back to the usual fare. Carl told Duncan that he would be trimming bushes and edging the grass for the afternoon. The overgrown bush on the corner especially needed trimming. It was also the property's only blind spot; he couldn't have asked for a more perfect opportunity.

After a gulp of milk washed down his last bite of a tuna fish sandwich, he grabbed Richard, said, "I'm bush trimming. Can you do your blanket in the next fifteen minutes?"

"Yeah, OK. Are you sure about this?"

"Yeah, yeah, remember to stand in that spot I said where I can signal you. Then draw Carl away."

"I remember."

"It'll take me a minute to sneak over and grab the blankets."

Richard frowned but said, "OK, well, good luck."

Thirty minutes later, Duncan was off pretending to clip foliage. Richard, a little too casually, meandered near his spot. Carl stood sentinel so he could see all the kids, including Duncan, just barely.

He severed a few of the peripheral branches and gave the signal. Richard led Carl away to help with the mower Duncan had sabotaged.

As soon as Carl was out of sight, he slipped around the corner, crouched below the windows and ran for the blankets. He stopped when he rounded the next corner, puzzled. No blankets. He knew he had put *his* out. Richard said he had too.

Crap.

He retreated to his bush, not knowing what to do except to resume snipping. There was no sign of Richard, but Carl appeared less than a minute later and said, "Mr. Taylor would like to see you."

He was friendly enough as he escorted Duncan to the rear door, but his heart sank. In the rec room Richard glumly sat on a chair. Carl told the teen, "He wants to see you after Duncan."

Carl opened the office door, let him enter and closed it behind him. Sitting at his desk, Joshua looked up and warmly greeted him from a swollen face. "Hello, Duncan, please, please, have a seat." As he did so, the man continued, "You know, my head hurts like a bitch." Duncan smiled in surprise at the first bad word he'd heard Joshua say. "Yes, even those pills the doctors gave me only reduce the pounding to a dull throb. But it's a beautiful day. How's the yard work going?"

"Uh, I was just getting started."

"Yes, yes, I guess I pulled you away. Well, you see, I've got a bit of a mystery. Annabelle, that is, Mrs. Dunlop, likes to sit sometimes on the far side of the building, catch a little sun, be by herself, that sort of thing. Anyway, just a while ago, she went to do just that, but, you know, she found a blanket just below your window. More amazing still, she found one below Richards's window too." He paused.

Duncan stared at him, so still he did not even blink.

"How do you think they got there?"

Duncan blinked and chewed his lip. "I can't say, sir."

Joshua cocked his head. "Can't or won't?"

He looked into the kindly eyes of his questioner and realized he could not lie to him. Besides, it seemed pointless. "I don't want to, sir."

Perhaps Joshua appreciated the nuance in the reply, for he thought for a while, then said, "You know, only a year after I took this job, gee, that was eight years ago now, we had a boy, I think he was fifteen, in on a breaking and entering charge. Anyway, he and a buddy decided they didn't like their accommodations and wanted to visit one of the boy's cousins in Idaho. Well, they snuck out one night (our security was pretty poor then) with some blankets and used them to climb the fence. Actually, they climbed *on top* of the fence. I woke up to their hollering, turned on the lights, and ran out with one of our staff, Mike (he's not with us anymore), to find those boys stuck on the barbed wire. They had a clever idea, see, to use the blankets to cover the barbs. Unfortunately, the blankets were poor at the job and barbed wire snags and lacerates almost anything. Each boy was so hooked that they couldn't move without hurting themselves further. We helped them down. One had a deep gash in a forearm about 6 inches long; it bled profusely. Their hands were punctured and slashed. The other kid's inner thigh was bleeding so badly it soaked his suit. It was good the hospital was nearby."

Joshua picked up a pen and tapped the desk a few times. "Do you think someone here may have had the same foolish plan?"

Duncan thought carefully for a while, then said, "If someone did, and they did not want to talk about it, but they did want to be sure that an innocent kid didn't get blamed, someone who would never have tried using a blanket to go over the fence and may have only dropped his blanket because a friend asked him to, and that someone agreed it was stupid, could the other kid not be in trouble?"

The light in Joshua's eyes danced, but he did not smile, probably because it would hurt too much. "Yes, I think Richard won't be in any trouble. The mystery of the blankets can remain a mystery. Do you know what the phrase 'not being born yesterday' means?"

The zag of his question stumped him, and he frowned. "No, sir."

"Well, ask your mother; she should know."

"My mother?"

"Yes, your mother will be here in a couple of hours. You are being released to her. The investigation found insufficient evidence to bring any charges."

Duncan slumped back in his chair and realized he had been sitting stiffly on its edge. "I'm free?"

"Yes," he answered in a voice deeper and gentler than before. "You are free. Isn't it good that a desperate boy did not succeed in climbing that awful fence?"

He tried to answer but couldn't right away. Something in the way Joshua said the word desperate made his throat constrict and his vision blur. He looked away, pressed his lips together, and closed his eyes tight, and a tear fell to the carpet. After a few moments, he was able to look at Mr. Taylor, unclench his jaw, and say in a thin voice, "Yes, sir."

57

The first thing he said to Richard when he left the office was, "You're not in trouble."

"Thanks."

"It's because Mr. Taylor is a good guy."

"You in trouble?"

"No. I'm getting out today." He burst into a big smile.

"Cool, that's great."

"My mom's coming to get me."

"Great, great," Richard said with a strained smile.

"Yeah, I hope you get to go somewhere good. Soon."

"Me too. Someday, I guess."

He got his clothes back, cleaned and pressed, better than when he had arrived. He went around, saying goodbye to everyone, even those he didn't know well. He gave Richard his phone number.

"In case you live somewhere close and want to get together."

Initially, he could not find Connie, but later, she emerged from the private area where the supervisors lived and hailed Duncan, "So you didn't have to escape?"

His look was a question.

"Helen's a blabbermouth, though you wouldn't know it at first."

For a while, they laughed and talked about their time "in prison."

"When are you getting out?" he asked.

"Don't know, but I've got a court date for next week. My lawyer, can you believe my dad hired a lawyer for me? Says I'll probably get probation."

"Is that good? What's probation?"

She explained. He said, "Hmmm, sounds like you'll be out, but they've got a leash on you."

"Yeah, pretty much. But I'll be out."

"Cool."

The office door opened. Mr. Taylor said, "Your mother should be here soon. Do you want to come in and wait for her? I don't usually let the parents into this section."

Duncan nodded but hesitated. Joshua glanced at Connie and said to Duncan, "When you're ready."

Connie beamed. "Well, kiddo, don't come back here, OK?"

"Yeah. No way."

"Maybe. You better not, but you seem to like going cross-country." That puzzled him, but then she said, "Never mind. Look, no more kisses, but here's a hug. Too bad you aren't older, you little virgin."

She wrapped her arms around him before he could process that. She was taller than he, and his head fit under her chin. He was squished against her bountiful body and was overwhelmed by her exuberance and warmth. She held him for a long time. And when she released him, he matched her big smile with his own—friends.

And there was something else—deep inside, where the man to be lay sleeping, an eye cracked open, and a deep voice rumbled, "Hello!"

"You lucky, lucky bastard," someone nearby said. At the entrance to the second hallway, Russell stood, looking disgusted. "Bet it's wasted on you too." He stomped off.

Connie laughed. "See ya, Duncan."

"See ya."

***

He saw the '57 blue-and-white Chevy drive up and park. Ava got out. Carl let her in at the front gate, and he watched her stride up the short walk, her face set in a look of suppressed fury.

Here it comes.

Only now was he thinking about how she would view him being arrested and in jail. He realized something surprising—he was not afraid of her. He was apprehensive. He was bracing for the storm, but he was not scared. Maybe facing police officers and knife-wielding thugs had changed him.

Joshua greeted her at the door and extended a hand. "Hello, Mrs. Findlay. I'm Joshua Taylor."

When she saw him, the fury seemed shocked out of her; she flinched, recovered, and took his hand. "Yes, my gosh, what happened to you?"

"Please, have a seat." He closed the door. "Seems I got in the way of those escapees we had a couple of nights ago."

Ava's face was blank.

"First, here's your son."

She went to him, crouched so they were eye to eye, put a hand on each of his shoulders, looked at him carefully, asked, "Are you OK?"

It was not a hug. She was not a hugger, but it was touching. He was thrown because the concern was so genuine, and he was so prepared for wrath.

"Yes, I'm fine. I want to go home."

"Good, good. We'll go home."

She turned to Joshua, who asked them again to sit. He explained the recent drama in detail, and Ava listened with open amazement, admitting she had read nothing of it nor been informed.

"How awful. Is your wife OK?"

"It was, of course, a terrible shock, and she's still shaken, but she's all right. The wound wasn't deep. The police did catch Hank and Billy, the boys who attacked us, up in Boulder Creek."

Ava shook her head and then looked closely at Duncan. "You were caught up in all this?"

He nodded.

"Your son was quite brave. He and the others resisted and then broke out of a locked room to call the police."

Connie was brave, Duncan thought.

She glanced at him, said, "Of course he would." Then, a glimmer of the prior fury returned. "I know it's not your fault, sir, but my Duncan should not have been in here. Do you know they kept him in this detention solely based on the accusation of one child? Just some ten-year-old at the beach. That and the baseless conviction of a single police officer who was far too sure of herself. They came up with nothing, and then that boy recanted and said he pointed out Duncan because the officer scared him. I was livid."

"My, my," Joshua said, "You're right; I have no say in this. The police deliver boys and girls to us to hold while the wheels of justice turn. Unjustly, it seems clear here. Duncan," he turned to look at him, "has always protested his innocence."

Duncan squinted at Joshua—how he said that made him squirm inside.

"That's right," Ava said, "he's innocent." She reached out and took his hand, which shocked him for the second time.

"Duncan's behavior during what, I'm sure," he glanced at him again, "was a very hard few weeks, was exemplary. By the way, he learned to play chess."

Ava ignored that last but glowed at the praise of her son. "That's right, he's a Scot."

Duncan groaned inside.

"Beg your pardon?"

"Fortitude is a Scottish characteristic."

"Ah,"

At the imminence of his release, he was beginning to feel awful. The more they praised him, the lower he sank. "Can we go now, Mom?"

She signed a release form, and they rose to leave.

"Duncan, it would sound rude in any other context, but I hope I never see you again, at least not here."

He smiled. "Yes, sir. Same to you."

They drove off, and Ava talked about all she had been through: the trips to court, the phone calls, and the reading of documents. Perhaps she really had been trying to get him out. He soon realized that they were not heading home. When she turned onto Broadway, he asked, "Where are we going?"

"To the home of that brat who put you in there."

If a boy's heart could accelerate from 60 beats to 160 in one second, Duncan's did. "Who?"

"Paul Raley, his family lives up on Windsor.

"Why?"

She ignored the question. The subsequent hour would be more uncomfortable than his entire time in Juvie. Ava spoke with vehemence at the injustice done to Duncan and of the low character of parents who would allow their son to frame hers. He had been prepared to assert his innocence and dreaded lying to her, but she was so convinced of his blamelessness that she did not even ask. She was so angry at what was done to him, her innocent son, implying that Paul's family should pay for what they had done.

It was pure torture.

The car crunched over leaves and fallen twigs at the side of the road a hundred feet from a big Victorian-style two-story home across the street. His mother stared at it.

"There it is," she said.

He was terrified. He envisioned her marching up to their door, Duncan in tow, and confronting Paul's family until the boy exclaimed, "He did do it. I heard him say so."

But they did not get out of the car. Instead, as the engine ticked its heat away, Ava stared at the house. Occasionally, she would repeat something previously said but mostly just stared. And Duncan writhed inside. The minutes crept by, and he felt sure he saw people looking out of those windows at the car with a woman in it staring at them. He had visions of them storming out of the house, banging on the car windows. "Hey," they would say, "what do you want? Why are you staring at us?"

After half an hour, he was on the edge of panic. The intensity of Ava's focus on the house was unceasing, even when she sometimes spoke. He did not understand what they were doing. Was this like an evil eye thing? Several times he wanted to confess, just to make it stop, but the cataclysm he thought would result from his admission kept him silent. So, he sat and sat, and she stared and stared. And each minute felt like an hour. And when the sun neared the horizon, she released her hands from the steering wheel, looked at him, smiled, and said, "There, that'll do it."

58

Duncan's return home was anti-climactic. They had dinner as a family, but his incarceration was not discussed in any depth. There were a couple of, glad you're backs, and Shona deadpanned, "How was prison?" To which he said, "OK." But there was no follow-up. Ava asserted that the frame-up of her son had failed. Aileen seemed uncomfortable, but she often did; Keith's attentive face had a what-are-they-talking-about glaze. Duncan wondered if anything had been explained to him.

It was weird to him that such a big event would be only lightly referred to. Even more bizarre was that it wasn't weird at all, at least not for the Findlays. When Ava had divorced Hugh, that calamity was discussed no more than Duncan's arrest and jail time.

There was love in his family, but somehow, it did not extend to knowing much about what each person felt or what they did in their daily lives. Instead, their love was a standing wave of empathy evidenced by accepting whatever they did, generally free of judgment. It especially meant that no one pried. Their journey through life together had been one long chain of upheavals, intimately shared in an abundance of silence.

Thus, they sat together that night in a dimly lit kitchen surrounded by their poverty, the children not even privy to whether they had enough money for next month's rent. They never discussed the father they had not seen for over three years. So why would they discuss the son who had been snatched off the street and jailed for weeks? If Duncan had thought about it, he would have been shocked to realize that, while stealing wallets, he likely had more money than his mother.

But the other thing about the Findlays was that despite all the moves, the divorce, the thin fortunes and the uncertain future, none of them seemed traumatized. Instead, they possessed calm strength; the Findlays rolled with whatever happened.

***

After dinner, Duncan called Kevin. "I'm out."

"Cool. Finally."

"Yeah, OK to come over?"

"Uh, best not. How about in a half-hour at The Cup?"

"OK, see ya."

The Cup was his and Kevin's secret place. Near the end of Woodrow Avenue, there was an indentation in the cliff face where they could sit out of sight. It was necessary to climb down a steep wall of ice plants to get to it. If it was high tide, slipping would have meant falling into the ocean and getting bashed by the waves. If it were low tide, it would have been a twenty-foot fall to the sand and rocks. The Cup and many other sections of the cliffs along that stretch of road would disappear over the next few decades from the ceaseless pounding of the sea.

He got there first and comfortably sat back into the ice plant. It was dark and warm. Small waves patted the cliff face below him.

"Pssst," he heard from above and echoed it. Twenty seconds later, Kevin sat beside him.

"Got a cigarette?" Duncan asked.

"Figured you'd be wanting."

He heard Kevin pull out a pack, followed by the snap of a lighter opening and the flare of the flame illuminating their faces. He took the offered smoke and sucked it into life. Kevin joined him in blowing white streams into the still air.

"You in the clear, or do you have to face a trial?"

"Naw, I'm clear. Insufficient evidence. They had nothing but the rat's word. Then he took it back. Three weeks, though. Shit."

"Bad?"

He told him everything that happened, except the kiss from Connie.

"That's heavy."

"Yeah."

"I talked to rat boy."

"Really?"

"Yeah, cornered him outside the merry-go-round. I thought I'd pound him, but he started crying immediately and, shit, he's like ten and blubbered so much I felt like a prick scaring him so bad."

"Maybe he should've come and taken my place."

Kevin laughed, even though that made no sense.

"He kept saying he was so sorry. Through all the weeping, I got the story. That woman cop..."

"Janet."

"Yeah, Janet Smudsomething,"

"Smudfucker."

"Smudfucker scared him much worse than I did. He blabbed your name just to get away. She pushed him about what she called your accomplice, but he didn't know my name or that we did it together."

"My mom said he took it back."

"Smudfucks questioned all of us. It sucked bad. Leon's not liking you right now."

"Yeah, he was stiff when I called."

"She came to the house, said they thought you and a friend did it. I denied knowing anything and said I did not believe you did it. She left unhappy, but Leon grilled me after. He got no more than she did."

"She went to Randy's and Lee's too?"

"Yeah."

"Crap."

"Why does she have it in for you? Seems like a lot of work for a few wallets."

Duncan finished the Marlboro and flicked the red glowing remains into the sea. "She tried to trick me, and I didn't go for it; she pushed, and I didn't crack. Three nights in solitary must've been her idea."

"Everyone had your back."

"I know. You in trouble with Leon and Mary?"

"I'm always in trouble with Leon. Mary is OK. She likes me; he doesn't."

"How come?"

"Don't know, sometimes he..." Kevin did not finish.

"I need another."

Kevin sent his first flying, and they both lit new ones. After a few drags, Kevin said, "You beat them."

Kevin likely didn't see his shrug when he said, "Sort of."

"We beat them."

"Yeah, but she made me pay anyway." Then Duncan laughed. "But it was an adventure."

"Derring-do."

They chuckled.

"Derring-do. Plus, I didn't get stabbed and…" He pulled on the cigarette, thought and released.

"I kissed a girl."

"You did? In Juvie?"

"Yeah. She kissed me."

There was a long moment which felt like Kevin was processing. "She like nine and pecked you on the cheek?"

"No, fifteen, it was a long one on the lips."

"No lie?"

"No lie."

"You liked it?"

"Yeah."

Kevin snorted. "Maybe we can snatch some more and get Janet to send you back."

"Not that much."

***

The next day they all met up at Randy's house. He was greeted with cheers; Cheryl hugged him. Margaret smiled and said she was glad he got out. Then, as the Winston tendrils wreathed her head, she narrowed her eyes at him, said, "You going to stay out of trouble from here on out?"

Hers was a face that could not be bullshitted. "Yes, ma'am," he said.

"Good, because there is no future down the road you'll take if you don't."

"Yes, ma'am." And he meant it, really meant it, at that moment.

The boys, without Lee, who had yet to show up, hung out in the garage for a while. Duncan told his Juvie story, which had them hanging on every word. He left out Connie and hoped Kevin would not tell.

Lee showed up near the end. "What happened to you?" Randy asked. Lee's left eye was swollen half-shut with blotches of black and blue underneath.

"Gramps punched me."

They were quickly on their feet, examining the damage. "Why'd he do that?" Alan asked. "He's your grandpa."

"Because he's a bastard. I was sneaking in through my bedroom window the night before last. My room was dark, and Gramps yelled, 'Burglar!' And pow right in my face. I went flying out the window and hit my head too. He's a mean fucker."

It was a while before anyone commented.

"He really thought you were a burglar?" Alan asked.

"Naw, he didn't even try to pretend too hard. Just looked at my face afterward and said, 'If you don't want to be mistaken for a burglar, come home on time.'"

Margaret put a bag of frozen peas wrapped in a T-shirt on Lee's eye and tch-thched over his story of assault by grandfather. After ten minutes, Lee thanked her and said to the audience of friends, "Let's go have some fun."

***

The five of them were getting a jump on the Labor Day weekend, a crazy time in Santa Cruz. Rivermouth was crowded, but the surf was decent. Near the water, they dumped shirts and shoes. Duncan put all his money under his stuff on the sand. As the five walked toward the water, he wondered if someone might steal it.

Naw, who'd rifle a pile of kid's clothes?

The long rides they got often required dodging tourists with their inflatable rafts, Styrofoam belly boards and black inner tubes. Lee was a maniac. He said the cold salty water stung his bad eye and gave him a headache, but he stayed in longer than anyone. After a couple of hours, they headed up to the Boardwalk.

Lee did his obligatory electrocution stint and yelled, "Yeah!" when it maxed out, let go, and declared it made his eye "Hurt like the devil." Then he popped in another penny to do it again.

Later, walking past the carousel, Lee laughed and pointed out some hippies: several long-haired men with beards, bandannas, and blue jeans and a pretty girl in a quilted skirt with mums in her hair. Hippies had recently begun showing up in Santa Cruz, spillovers from the Summer of Love up in San Francisco. That, and the Monterey Pop Festival, which happened back in June, had brought waves of them.

As they walked past the bazooka concession, Lee pointed out some other hippies. "Weirdos," he said.

"But they look happy," Duncan said.

"They're happy because they're stoned," Lee said.

"And they're really friendly."

"'cause they're stoned or trippin' on acid."

"What's acid?"

"LSD, it makes you see things and lose your mind and jump off buildings."

Duncan scoffed. "Bull."

"Yep."

"I read that some hippie up in Frisco jumped after taking it," Randy said.

"Yeah?" Duncan asked.

"Uh-huh."

"I like hippies," Alan said.

"How come?" Duncan asked.

"Hippie chicks don't wear bras."

Randy wrinkled his nose at that, but the other guys hooted. Duncan looked for the mums' girl, but she had disappeared into the crowd.

Dammit.

Later that afternoon, while bobbing in the foamy waters, waiting for a good set, Lee said, "We've got to go see that new movie."

"What movie?" Kevin asked.

"*Endless Summer.* It's a surfing flick. Russ says we'll drool." Everyone agreed to see it.

***

At 1:30 the next day, the gang was in line at the Rio Theater, a very long line.

"Hey look," Alan said, quoting, "Kiss-hungry girl ghosts looking for live lovers." He waggled his eyebrows. Duncan looked at the poster—*The Spirit Is Willing*.

"Just what Duncan wants," Kevin said and laughed.

Duncan fist-popped his shoulder and glared, but no one picked up on it as the line moved forward.

In a packed theater the five sat close to the screen, heads back, mouths open half the time, entranced at the most beautiful and awesome surfing scenes. Some of the time Duncan was bored because the pace was slow, and documentaries were new to him. Still, he was captivated by the quest to find the perfect wave and the vision of a life chasing a perpetual summer by exploring surfing spots around the world.

The film would be like nitro injected into the thin, fringe world of surfing. It, The Beach Boys, and better wetsuits would cause an explosion in the number of surfers and surfer wannabes. From California to Hawaii, Tahiti, New Zealand, Australia, and finally around Africa, the story's heroes *did* find that perfect wave.

It broke perfectly and continually along its line. It came in diagonally along a shallow break that went on and on. The movie said the ride was seven miles long. They claimed they got leg cramps from crouching during that nearly unbelievable distance. It was an incredible vision for bodysurfers used to twenty-second thrills.

After all that glory the boys boiled out of the theater with the rest of the audience, passing on the second feature.

"We need surfboards," Lee said.

"Yeah, we gotta do that," Randy said.

"And we need our own Woody too," Duncan said.

"We could drive up and down the coast, hitting every beach," Kevin said.

"Bitchin' beyond belief," Lee said.

"'cept we don't have any money," said Alan.

"And we don't drive yet," Kevin said.

"Bummer," Randy and Lee said in unison.

Alan said, "Duncan's loaded. You got enough to buy a car and five surfboards?"

Duncan made a show of digging into his pockets and came out with a few crumpled bills. "Is thirteen bucks enough?"

59

Halloween 1967

Nearly two months after returning to school, the boys were itching for some wild play. Randy and Alan had had a few rough weeks. Both had been held back and were repeating the sixth and eighth grades, respectively. Lee had been pissed that Randy could not come with him to Branciforte Junior High. Alan, a week into the school year and in a surprising moment of candor, had said, "Maybe I'm just stupid." And the Kellys were moving to a new house off Seabright Avenue.

Duncan and Kevin were in the eighth grade at Mission Hill Junior High. He liked it there and got mostly B's without trying too hard. His metal shop class was fun. They had a lathe, metal presses, stampers and a bunch of other metal cutting and shaping equipment. Three weeks into the class, Duncan was adjusting a band saw when his hand slipped, and a twenty-pound slab of steel squished his thumb.

The school nurse called Ava, and she took him to a doctor. By the time they arrived, his thumb had swollen, throbbed painfully, black under the nail. The doctor had him sit down. He straightened a paperclip, flicked a lighter and heated the tip to glowing red. When he touched it to Duncan's nail, it melted straight through in a blink, and blood and pus squirted like a geyser to hit the ceiling. That brought instant relief, and he went back to school.

Preparations were more serious for that Halloween than the last. While the prior year was all about the treats, this year was more about the tricks. Out around 17th Avenue there was an egg farm. Lee had noticed that they put flats of bad eggs outside down below a long, low building, which he said was for roosts.

"We can load up with dozens of rotten eggs for Halloween."

The boys had been awed by his genius. Rotten eggs were the tactical nukes of Halloween combat. The dead chicken babies he proposed they grab had been in their shells noxiously maturing for weeks, maybe months, rising in kilo-tonnage by the hour. The advisability of going nuclear on Halloween wasn't questioned. They only cared about how to carry them on their upcoming multi-mile candy canvassing campaign without nuking themselves.

The boys had never dressed up for Halloween, so they did not understand the implicit Halloween deal: We come to your door with cute or amazing costumes; you reward us with goodies. The boys' view of the deal was: We come to your door loaded for bear; you impress us with many great treats.

Randy was intent on doing the classic poop-in-a-bag-set-on-fire-on-the-doorstep gag. He laughed and laughed in anticipation. The boys seemed to think he meant finding some dog crap, but when the time came, only two blocks after leaving Lee's house, he went into some bushes and pooped in a small brown bag himself. The boys, who each had extremely high gross-out bars, were completely grossed out.

His brother asked, "You shit in that bag?"

Randy looked at Alan like *how else could I get poop in a bag*, said, "Yeah."

Maybe it had been Duncan's imagination, but he was sure everyone edged away from Randy at least a foot or two.

Hiding behind bushes across from a small, red brick home, they watched Randy run across to the house with its porch light on. He dropped the bag, lit it, rang the bell and ran back to hide with the gang.

It turned out that the man who opened the door was not stupid. Instead of stomping on the little blaze, he swore, looked around, went inside, and came back not with a gun, as Duncan feared, but with a pan of water to douse the flames. The man stared at the mess Randy had left and scanned with furious eyes across the street. Suddenly, the thick brush felt transparent. They ran across the vacant lot and kept going until they were in the clear.

They tricked or treated their way across Santa Cruz. They forgot their prankish intentions for a while as friendly people opened doors, let them grab desired treats, and occasionally asked, "Where are your costumes?"

Lee started the egging when he declared that a darkened house with cars in the drive was cheating. His first two lobs brought support from the remaining batteries, and at least a dozen eggs splattered the house windows and cars.

Chestnut Street descended from its intersection with Mission Street down a long hill to Locust Street. The boy's path had them up on a ridge on the west side overlooking the traffic under the cover of trees. It was deep dark in the trees, but the road was well-lit, and the cars sparsely flowed each way.

Randy flung an egg at a car but missed. Soon, the rest made their tosses. The first flurry only hit the pavement. The distance was over a hundred feet, shooting between the trees. Then Kevin stung the passenger door of a Pontiac Firebird at the bottom of the hill. It kept going.

Duncan aimed carefully, and his egg flew perfectly to hit dead center on the windshield of a Chevy Corvair coming down the hill. Dark orange slime exploded all over the glass. The car's tires squealed as they left rubber on the road, and it slid with its backend swinging into the other lane. The boys erupted in cheers.

"What a shot!" Kevin yelled.

Duncan glowed with the score. But the drivers of the cars behind it slammed on their brakes. *That could have been a bad accident,* he thought, feeling sick.

Kevin touched his arm. "Hey, we better get outta here."

All the boys ran up a little street near their vantage point. Duncan's alarm at what could have happened lasted for only a few minutes because Randy got into a fight with another teen.

It was about nothing. A boy a bit bigger than Randy, wearing a pirate's mask, bumped ahead of him on the walk to a house whose yard was full of skeletons and fake cobwebs. Randy pushed him and said, "Watch it."

The boy was with a girl dressed as a witch; he said, "Hey, you watch it."

More words were exchanged. Then Randy raised his fists and advanced on the boy. "C'mon, c'mon."

The kid wasn't shy. He made his fists. His girl squeaked.

Duncan realized that Randy liked to fight. He had been in several over the summer and at school. He won all but one, which could have been called a draw. His friend had a rage in him that could flare from the least slight. He felt that Randy's fighting was not about meanness, defense, or even winning. It was more like he had to blow off the top portion of an anger he could not express any other way.

The fight did not last long. Although the teen got in a couple of solid jabs, Randy gave him twice that back and had him on the ground in a hold while delivering punches too. He was a good wrestler. The other boy yelled, "Uncle, uncle, I quit."

For all his rage, Randy was an honorable fighter. He released immediately and grasped the other kid's arm to lift him to his feet. The two boys looked at each other. The big one was uncowed. He wiped blood off his lip and said, "You fight good."

Randy looked down. "You too. Sorry, I get mad sometimes."

The other boy thought that over for a while. "I wouldn't back off from boxing with you, but your wrestling's too bad for me."

Randy extended a hand. "I'm Randy."

"Brian," he said as he clasped the offering.

They all let Brian and his girl go ahead. She said she couldn't understand why Brian would shake the hand of "some punk" who had hit him over nothing. Brian told her to shut up and went back to talking with Randy. Brian was a seventh grader at Mission Hill, but Duncan did not recognize him. The girl was his younger sister, Marjorie. They joined them for a couple of blocks as the gang's bags inched closer to the top with candy, mass-produced pastries and homemade cookies. Then Brian had to take Marjorie home, and Duncan and Kevin said they would see him at school. Mission accomplished; the boys threw away their leftover eggs, of which there were only four. They headed back to Lee's.

Not far from Lee's house was an old cemetery. At that time, there were no houses close to it. Around 11 p.m., the five kids were walking past.

"Who wants to go in the graveyard?" Kevin asked.

"Are you nuts?" Randy asked. "Go into a graveyard at night on Halloween?"

"Yeah, that's the best time."

"Not me."

"Me neither," Alan said.

Lee was silent.

Kevin looked at Duncan. "You?"

He looked around. There was a lone streetlight about a block away and clumps of mature trees along each side of the street. The graveyard had an open entrance and a weathered stone fence one could easily get over. It was small, on enough land for a few houses.

Duncan smiled. "Sure,"

Kevin grinned, and they walked in while the others waited on the street.

"I can't see shit," Kevin said as he stumbled on a stone.

"Me either. Just outlines."

They went past a few dozen headstones until they were near the middle and found a low grave with what must have been a marble or stone lid. They sat down.

"You scared?" Kevin asked.

"No," he said, hesitated, "Yeah, some."

"Me too; I keep seeing weird shapes in the shadows."

"The ghouls are out tonight, booga, booga," Duncan said in a bad Boris Karloff impersonation.

"Shut up; let me have a smoke."

He took two out of his pack, and they lit them. "This will freak 'em out to see us casually smoking in a graveyard," Kevin said.

Duncan chuckled. "Yeah, but derring-do, right?"

"Right, derring-do."

Duncan calmed, and he felt Kevin relax as well. They smoked slowly, and he began to enjoy the peacefulness of the place and the abundant stars in the black sky. They finished smoking, and he heard Randy calling, "Hey, when are you guys coming out?"

"Want to play with them?" Duncan asked.

"Totally."

"You go left, I'll go right. Creep low and try to blend in with the tombstones. Let's make ghoul sounds when we get to the wall and jump over at 'em."

Kevin chuckled. "Great."

As Duncan advanced from headstone to headstone, there were more calls, impatient and maybe worried. Kevin started the loud moaning sounds. Duncan added to it, and someone yelped. They did not maintain their ghastly performance for long because they quickly burst into laughter.

"It's only them," Alan declared. "Har, har, har."

After they dropped Lee off, Randy asked Duncan, "Weren't you afraid of seeing a ghost?"

He reflected for a moment, thinking warmly of Timothy. "Naw, ghosts can be great friends."

60

June 1968

The Stokely-Van Camp Company had operated a cannery over on Owen Street near the boat harbor since 1933. It was one of Santa Cruz County's largest employers during the June through October canning season, packing green beans, pears and other seasonal fruits and vegetables. Ava became one of their hundreds of employees that June. As an iffy reward for graduating high school, Aileen was hauled over there to join the ranks not long after she had finished signing her yearbook.

Duncan was also given a job as a paperboy for the Santa Cruz Sentinel. They had a distribution facility on Ocean Street near Randy's first house. He became faintly aware that the family had been surviving off Nana, minimal and spotty child support provided by Hugh, and whatever work Ava could get from time to time. In addition to the child support money, Ava had asked for and received one dollar in alimony.

His route took him down Pearl Street, which was cradled between Ocean and the north side of the river. Then, he would head over to the Boardwalk and Beach Hill neighborhoods.

At first, he had groaned about getting up at 3 AM to get on his Sting-Ray and ride over to pick up his papers, then roll 'em, band 'em, and stuff 'em into the large canvas bags he would drape over his bike. But he loved to be out in the middle of the night, cold or not, in the quiet town. Few moving cars appeared, and only occasionally did a lone light shine from one of the houses.

He started in the cold black of night and finished as the sun heralded its coming with purple glows above the Santa Cruz Mountains. He loved throwing things and soon planted each paper where they wanted it. Learning the addresses was quick work.

As fun as the job could be, it also gave him money. Nana helped by taking him to Crocker Bank to open a savings account. She donated ten dollars toward his future wealth. He also got his Social Security card. With a bank account, an SS card, and paychecks, he began to feel almost like an adult, which was not as bad as that might sound.

Getting money, which he did not have to hide, inspired him to work more. He and Randy decided to offer their services to do yard work. Despite not having any tools, they went door to door near the Kelly's new home and landed weekly jobs. In addition to mowing lawns and trimming hedges, they removed blackberry bushes, which always involved a fair amount of bleeding. And they pulled weeds and plants past their prime.

Women mostly hired them. Many were sweet and kind. In addition to a few dollars, they might serve iced lemonade and chocolate chip cookies or maybe freshly baked brownies. But others wanted to ensure they got the maximum work out of the two for the dollars they might pay them. They watched out the window as if they feared the theft of a spade. Sometimes, they stood over them, supervising, and regardless, ended up disputing the hours worked. Still, the work suited both boys and getting things done together seemed like a different kind of play. Yard work and paper deliveries could be hard, but the small pay would become a problem later in the summer.

"Hey, don't do that," Duncan said to Randy. "They'll complain, and I might get fired." They were riding their bikes down Pearl at about 4 a.m., and Randy had aimed the paper not at the subscriber's porch but at the upright clay frog lawn ornament, knocking it over.

"No fun, but OK, OK."

Occasionally, Randy came with him on his route. Mostly, he just rode along, sometimes helping. The two boys riding together in a town asleep presented many opportunities for mischief. PJ's Liquor was along his route and got magazine deliveries. The twined tight, big bundles were dropped on the sidewalk in front of the store.

Since Connie, Duncan's interest in the female form, especially unclad, had been growing by the day. He was thrilled to discover that PJ's bundles often contained nudie magazines, not classy like Playboy, but mostly article-free, picture-rich ones like *Gent, Jest, Adam, Rapture* and *Peep Show.* He would carefully extract one from a bundle, like a treasure, and take it home. By the end of the summer, he had a box full.

One day on Beach Hill, Randy left him to inspect a little car parked on Cliff Street. As Duncan finished a house and was turning for the next one, Randy raced up and said, "That car has the keys in it.

"So?"

"Let's drive it."

Duncan stopped and looked up and down the street. It was an affluent neighborhood with fine Victorian houses, neat lawns and stately big trees. "We'll get arrested." Visions of a return to Juvie entered his mind.

"No, we won't; we'll just start it, drive around the block, and put it back in the same place. No one will even know."

"I've never driven before."

"I have, my mom's wagon in a parking lot."

Duncan lightly chewed on his lower lip and waited for a more impressive argument.

"Derring-do," Randy said with a grin.

He surveyed the houses along the street—all dark. He smiled and said, "OK, let me finish this last street. We'll come back. If it is still clear, let's do it."

Duncan finished in record time. They stared at a beauty of a car. It was a little red two-seater with a black soft top, wire wheels, and the initials MG on a medallion mounted in a small chrome grill. Duncan licked his lips, checking the house the car might belong to. It was dark and quiet.

"Let's leave the bikes below the wall. Once around and split, OK?"

Randy nodded. They carefully opened the doors, slid onto the black leather seats, and closed the doors with quiet clicks. His heart was banging as Randy stared at the controls.

"C'mon, you can drive it, right?"

"Uh, yeah, give me a sec."

Randy pushed in the clutch and reached for the keys hanging below the radio. The engine purred to life and must've been the smoothest, softest sounding car engine he would ever hear, but at that moment, it sounded like a tuba blatting: "Look, look, Duncan and Randy are stealing a car!"

The MG jerked forward and almost died. Duncan said, "Shit."

"I'll get it, I'll get it."

Jerk—Cruise—Jerk—Cruise. The car lurched forward, Randy shifted to second, and they rounded the corner.

"Woo hoo, this is awesome!" Duncan said.

"Totally, totally, bitchin', what a car!"

It felt like a long ride, but it was probably less than three minutes. Randy quickly got the hang of it. Midway, Duncan flipped the switch under the radio to see what it did. The wipers flipped back and forth over dry glass.

"Ack!" he said and turned it off.

Randy returned to the original spot. They got out and got gone but stopped at the corner to look back at the sweet car as light warmed the eastern horizon. Over the next week, they would drive it two more times, Duncan doing the last one, and each ride was a thrill. No one noticed. One day, the car was gone, leaving only good memories.

61

The Findlays were gathered in their living room one night with all the lights off, save one 15-watt blue bulb in a small lamp that cast its dim glow solely on Keith, seated opposite his family. They were in chairs brought from the kitchen, looking intently at the youngest. Duncan saw him surrounded by a thin, hazy glow. Faces appeared and disappeared, superimposed over his brother's. His sisters and mother said they saw the same things.

Ava had recently become a member of the Rosicrucian Order, and she was showing her children how to see a person's past lives. For some reason, the blue light enabled her to see what she called the *Akashic Record* of his brother. At one point he saw a young woman, then a man, then maybe a child younger than Keith. He thought it was far-out.

They took turns in the chair, and each time saw a parade of faces, like a slideshow, except the slides wavered as if they were peering through water. Aileen asked if they were seeing ghosts, voice taut as a piano wire. Ava said no, it's just a record, like seeing pictures in a library book. But when Shona was seated behind the blue light and an old man appeared to lean out from her body, Aileen squeaked and fled to her bedroom.

Duncan laughed.

His oldest sister had good reason to be spooked by the possibility of ghosts. According to Ava, Aileen had encountered one in Scotland when she was only two years old. She had screamed for two hours while she and her mother sat rigid with terror inside an ancient cottage with six-foot-thick walls and a fire dying on the hearth.

Ava had talked a lot about ghosts, especially Scottish ones. As he understood it, the centuries of clan warfare in Scotland meant thousands of spirits were wandering around the moors, angry and seeking vengeance for past betrayals. Duncan did not understand why people were afraid of ghosts. He figured they were just people minus bodies. It seemed odd to him that someone could not be scary when they were alive but suddenly became terrifying when they died.

He thought that living people could be frightening precisely because they had bodies. With a body, one could shoot, stab, punch, choke, drive a truck over someone, or a hundred other ways of hurting another. But ghosts could only float around acting, well, spooky. Of course, poltergeists could throw things, but how was that scarier than a living person throwing things?

He did appreciate the opportunities people like Aileen offered with their fear. He was already considering the reaction he might get later that night if he crept into the bathroom they shared and made bumping and scratching noises while moaning like the dead. He chuckled to himself as an Asian-looking woman appeared over Ava.

62

Summer 1968

For Duncan, being fourteen after the Summer of Love was like discovering a candy store filled with numerous mysterious treats. In the sex department there were a plethora of possibilities. Birth control pills and the free spirit trinity of peace, love and getting high had unleashed a sexual tidal wave across America. The offerings in that department tantalized his mind, if only he could understand what was specifically involved. The women in his magazines never answered questions.

There was also the problem of his age. While abundant possibilities were walking around on the streets and beaches, those that might be most interested, in an abstract way, were eighteen to twenty years old, maybe at best sixteen, and it seemed a reach that they would embrace the position of Professor of Erotic Arts for him.

The other physical thrills of running, leaping, jumping off high places, popping wheelies, bodysurfing and climbing had been well explored. The new thrill options displayed in the intoxication department boggled and frightened his imagination:

Cigarette smoking? Check, no biggie.

Drinking alcohol? Check, but a lot more research was desired.

Amphetamines, cocaine, LSD, hash, grass, meth, mushrooms, peyote, opium, and a bunch of stuff called downers, such as Quaaludes, Seconal and Valium, were all new and prevalent if only one knew who to know.

The hip people extolled some of these substances as mind-expanding and conducive to greater peace and love. The non-hip people, i.e., old people, said they were addictive, destroyed one's mind and society, and made you believe you could fly.

The hip people thought the non-hip were full of shit; maybe if they just got high, they would stop the war in Vietnam. Unfortunately for the hip people, the non-hip people wrote the laws and drove the police cars. In 1968, possessing marijuana was a felony with a one-to-ten-year prison sentence. And over 60,000 of California's hip people were arrested for it that year. Meanwhile, possession of methamphetamines or LSD could only result in a maximum of a one-year sentence.

The hip people generally believed that the harsh attacks on their intoxicants were actually attacks on their culture: the cool culture of sex, love and rock 'n' roll; the antiwar, peace-loving, freedom and justice-hungry crowd with fists or peace signs raised high in the air.

And there were enough lies, distortions and ulterior motives in the non-hip crowd that nearly everything they said about drugs or whatever was distrusted by the hip people.

The wannabe hipster, 14-year-old Duncan, was chomping at the bit for new thrills and awed by the offerings in the new candy store.

***

One day in June, Duncan, Randy and Kevin were tired of the beach because the waves were puny, and the fog would not retreat.

"Hey, let's hitch up to Ben Lomond," said Duncan.

At the beginning of Graham Hill Road, their thumbs had been out for only a short time before a blue-and-white VW bus pulled over. The two side doors flew open, and a long-haired, scraggly-bearded, smiling man beckoned them to enter. The three scrambled in. Kevin and Randy took the rear couch-like seat. The middle seat had been removed. The man sat on the floor in its place. Duncan did the same. Upfront, a man with short hair and twinkling eyes asked where they were going. Randy told him.

The woman in the passenger seat had shoulder-length straight brown hair and green eyes, wore a peasant blouse, and smiled at them but said nothing. As the bus struggled up the hill, the first man pulled a long fat joint out of a small bag decorated with tiny mirrors and embroidered flowers. He lit it and took a long, strong toke to make the end glow brightly. Then he offered it to Duncan.

Duncan felt his eyes widen and his pulse pop. None of the boys had tried grass yet; they had no access. He would be fourteen in a few weeks. "Sure," he said, "thank you."

He imitated the man's drag but did not hold the smoke for quite as long. He started to pass the joint back, but the man waved him to give it to his friends. He handed it to Kevin, who sucked on it and gave it to Randy, who did the same but coughed hard until the man gave him some juice. Randy leaned forward and passed the joint back to the man, who took another hit. He was about to give it to Duncan again when the woman spoke up.

"James, let's keep it to one hit for these boys; they look a little young. This might be their first time." She gazed with dreamy eyes at Duncan. He was feeling an uprising of powerful peace and a stilling of his thoughts, a slowing of time and a kind of bliss hitting him in the heart and the head. He smiled at her and thought she was beautiful.

"Yes, first time," he said.

She smiled back at him, nodded, took a quick hit, and passed it to the driver.

As they put-putted through the trees of Henry Cowell Park, he became engrossed in the textures of hair and metal and light. The pine trees' scent wafting through the open windows was like Aphrodite's perfume. All was bliss and smiles and togetherness. They were his new friends, and he loved them. Little was said, and as they took the turn at Felton onto Highway 9, small baklava squares were passed to the boys. It was the best thing he had ever tasted. And the orange juice they shared to wash it down was sweet and cascaded down his throat like an electric waterfall of joy.

They let the boys out right in front of the park. She flashed two fingers at him and said, "Peace." He mirrored her in word and gesture and then watched the bus drift away up the road until obscured by the trees.

***

In July the boys were walking from Lee's to Randy's when Lee said they should drop by to see a new boy named Charlie, whom he had recently met while bodysurfing at The 26. Along the way they approached a house they often passed by. For weeks they had talked about the guy who lived there. He was tall and fat and was constantly drinking beer. Every time they came by, he was in the front yard, a sorry-looking plot with short tufts of brown grass and desiccated earth in between. The yard was dominated by a large square wooden box about the man's height along every side and open at the top.

As they came along the curve of the street, he was there, he and three other men, drinking beer and shooting the shit. The men were loudly talking about cars, and the big guy, whose face was flushed under a head of short curly hair, was guzzling his beer as usual. He finished, burped loudly, crushed the can between two big hands and tossed it into the accumulating pile in the box. The boys debated how many cans were in that box.

"A thousand," said Randy.

"Only a thousand?" asked Lee.

"Couple of thousand," Alan said.

"Maybe, but they're all crushed, then it's at least 10,000," said Duncan.

"10,000 beer cans in that box?" scoffed Kevin, "C'mon."

"Maybe the box is over a big hole, and the beer cans go on and on."

"Well," Kevin said, playing along, "in that case, I'd say a million."

The boys ran with the idea, upping the number of cans and the depth of the hole to hold all the cans the man, who seemed to do nothing but drink beer, could produce. Lee topped the discussion with, "It's beer cans all the way to China."

They stopped in front of the house. The man had opened a new can and looked at them with red-glazed eyes.

"Duncan, ask him for some beer," Lee said.

"You ask him."

"C'mon, ask him."

"Yeah, c'mon, Duncan, ask him," Alan said.

It became a refrain. "Ask him."

"OK, sure."

The man watched him walk across the bumpy yard. He finished the beer and belched just as Duncan stopped a few feet away.

"Hi, my name is Duncan. You seem to have a lot of beer. Could we have some?"

The men discussing a Camaro's horsepower laughed, and one said, "Yeah, Dennis, give him a beer."

Dennis said nothing for a while, and Duncan was about to leave when he belched again and said, "You're a forward little fucker, aren't you? But, yeah, OK, I'll give you a beer." He bounced his just-emptied can off Duncan's head. Schlitz splashed on his face.

"Get the fuck out of my yard."

Dennis's friends roared.

Duncan walked back to his buddies as they made halfhearted attempts to stifle their laughter.

"Screw all of you," he said.

As they continued, he saw Dennis pick up the can, crush it, and toss it into the nearly full box.

They found Charlie and three other kids in the half-basement of the boy's home. They walked into the room from the door to the outside. Heavy curtains were drawn, and the only illumination came from two black lights shining their eerie rays on psychedelic posters. Neither Charlie nor the other denizens responded to their greetings. The smell of airplane glue filled the air, and the ones who had sniffed it from their reeking brown bags lay face down or slumped on the floor, unable to reply.

Lee's repeated calls of "Charlie?" only roused the boy to the extent that he mumbled something, groped for his bag, found it, and huffed it until he collapsed again. The boys retreated out the door and into blessed sunshine.

They fast-walked for a block. Duncan took rapid, deep breaths, trying to get the glue smell out of his lungs. No one commented for a long time. It was like they were fleeing in body and mind. Finally, Alan said,

"Death."

No one else had anything to add.

***

That same month, all the boys, except Alan, spent most of that day doing the usual bodysurfing and arcade play. They picked up their stuff and headed along the wet sand, letting thin whitewater wash over their feet, past the Cocoanut Grove, under the wharf and over to Cowell Beach. Under the cliffs and the looming presence of The Dream Inn, there was a party with about a dozen people listening to music, drinking and smoking.

Cowell Beach was a surfing spot for novices. Farther up the coast, visible from Cowell, was Steamer Lane. Usually the waves were small, one to three-footers, and offered little excitement. People from the hotel lounged on the beach, played volleyball and watched the boats and people on the wharf. People on the pier lounged and watched them watching.

At the party, a large radio was perched on a rock. The boys stopped to listen to Donovan singing, in his electronically quivering voice, about when the Hurdy-Gurdy man would be coming singing songs of love. A few long surfboards were stuck in the sand. A couple of girls swayed to the music. Several men were gathered, sitting on the sand facing the sea. The boys approached, said, "Hi." They got back hellos and an invite to sit.

The men were passing a large glass jug of red wine. A skinny man in swim trunks offered the jug to Kevin, whose eyes lit up as he accepted. Duncan offered cigarettes from his pack, and all accepted with thanks.

They smoked. They drank. They talked swells and boss rides. Hugh Masekela trumpeted "Grazing in the Grass" over the radio. No one asked the boys how old they were.

The men were drunk and happy. The boys were catching up. The wine went round and round until it was empty. A new jug was opened. A few surfers rode the modest waves. Someone was cooking hamburgers on a portable grill. The jug went round and round. It was terrible wine, which tasted better with each swallow. The boys smoked and laughed at clumsy surfing.

Jim Morrison had crawled into the radio, challenging whether you could make an angel sigh.

Duncan announced to the group that he wanted to try board surfing. "Can I ride one of your boards?" he asked in mushy wine words.

"Abseludely," said a guy on his left.

Duncan wavered into a nearly vertical stance and took a sinuous route to the board. He picked up the heavy slab and half-dragged, half-carried it to the water. His friends watched as he mounted, paddled, got upended by a breaking wave and driven to the shore. They cheered and laughed as he rose, sputtering and tried again.

Proper surfing requires excellent balance, a feel for the waves and lots of practice. In his wine-sodden state, he possessed none of these. He could time his paddling to catch waves, but rising from prone to standing was comical. Each attempt quickly ended with Duncan falling off the board, followed by him bodysurfing to the shore to retrieve it. Rinse and repeat.

At some point, he was out past the break, bobbing on the swells and lying belly down on the board, watching the glinting chop inches from his face. He heard yelling and looked up to see Kevin pointing to the bay. He looked and found a large swell approaching. He paddled feebly, catching it in the most inelegant way. He hung onto the board, never attempting to stand, as the wave threw him forward. He was immersed in swash, came to a halt on the sand, rose, and dragged the board over the beach but could not raise it. The owner was lying flat on his back, eyes closed.

Kevin had the quarter-full jug in his hand, took a swig, and offered it to him. "You really sucked," he said.

"No shit. You do better?"

"Hell no. I'm proud I can stand." He huffed. "Look at Randy and Lee; they nodded off while you were out there."

Kevin tapped Randy with his foot. "Hey, want more wine?"

"Uh-uh," the boy managed. Kevin laughed, wobblingly turned to Duncan, who offered the jug back to him, and asked, "Any smokes left?"

Kevin took a swallow from the jug and searched his shorts. "Two," he said. They smoked, drank in small sips, and watched, with dull brains, lounging tourists and the sea's undulations.

Duncan awoke on his back hours later with the sun hidden behind the trees. He felt terrible.

***

A few days later the boys, again without Alan, were in Randy's bedroom commiserating over the nasty effects of what Lee called "rotgut wine."

"We should buy some grass," Randy said.

"How?" Duncan asked.

"I dunno."

"Be better than booze," Kevin said.

"Yeah," he and Randy harmonized.

"I might know who to get it from," Lee said. He explained that the brothers of a kid he knew sold it.

"How much?" Randy asked.

"Don't know; I'll ask."

Later the next day, as they walked to the beach, Lee said, "Guy says we can get a lid for twenty dollars."

"How big is a lid?" Kevin asked.

"An ounce."

"Twenty dollars is a lot," Randy said.

"Maybe if we pooled our money?"

They did, and a day later, when Lee returned with the bag, it felt like a score. But the contents were primarily sticks and seeds. They smoked what they could but did not feel anything except sore throats. They took the bag to Alan.

"Is this real? We don't feel anything," Randy asked.

Alan took one look and laughed. "This is shit. You got ripped off."

"Dammit," Lee said.

"What did you pay?"

"Twenty," Duncan said.

"To who?"

Lee told him, and Alan said he knew the teen.

"Give me that," he said, taking the bag. Then he left.

He returned an hour later with ten dollars and a new bag full of buds and leaves. "That'll teach that asshole to rip off my friends and my brother."

"You can give me the ten bucks, or you guys can keep it, and we'll split the weed between us." They split the weed.

63

July 1968

On a warm midmorning, a few days before his birthday, Duncan opened the little white wood gate to Kevin's yard, went to the front door and knocked. Mary Davis greeted him with a strained smile. After a moment's hesitation, she called for Kevin. He came to the door with his head down. His foster mother laid a light hand on Kevin's shoulder. When he looked up, Duncan's mouth dropped.

"What happened to you?" he asked.

Mary parted her lips as if to reply for him but looked away without speaking.

"Let's just go," Kevin said.

They walked out the gate and headed toward the ocean. The left side of Kevin's face was swollen, his lip split and an ugly bruise was developing over his cheekbone.

"Who'd you fight?"

"Nobody, Leon hit me."

Duncan could say nothing for a while. The vision of that massive, powerful man hitting Kevin froze his guts.

"Knocked me into a cabinet of Mary's birds. Several of them broke." She had a collection of glass and porcelain bird figurines displayed in the living room.

"He punched you?" Duncan was trying to work through his disbelief.

"No, smacked me," and Kevin demonstrated a vicious backhand, "like that. It felt like being hit by a board."

"Asshole! But why?"

"Fuck if I know. Every night, he drinks. Mary's gone. He sits in that big chair of his and bitches. Called me good for nothing, even though I'm always doing chores." He brushed the hair out of his eyes. "I talked back; he leapt up and bashed me."

They walked the rest of the way to the cliffs in silence. Duncan felt torn between crying and screaming. He had never seen Kevin like this: shy, shaken, maybe ashamed. He was doing his best to understand. He knew some parents spanked their kids, maybe used a paddle. His mom used to beat him with the belt, but that was always in the context of disciplining him for bad behavior. This was different.

When they reached the cliffs, Kevin declined to go down to The Cup. They looked out on a rough sea. The waves were bigger than usual, walloping the cliffs and rock outcroppings, booming and blasting spray high.

Then he spoke like he was speaking to himself, or maybe to the sea, "I was so stunned; he knocked me several feet into Mary's stuff. All I could do was lie there, my lip bleeding on the carpet. I was dazed. He left. I heard the fridge open, and he came back with another beer. He drank slowly and stood over me, looking down. I didn't want," the boy's voice cracked, "I didn't want him to hit me again, so I laid still. Then he told me to clean up the mess and go to bed. That was it."

Duncan lowered his head. "Damn. Damn. Damn."

"Yeah, I heard him and Mary arguing later; you know she comes back after two. But I couldn't make out the words. She came into my room, sat on the bed and touched my shoulder. I kept my face to the wall. She didn't say anything...no, she did, just before she left, she said, 'I'm sorry' and kissed my head. That's all she did.

"Screw her," Kevin finished.

Duncan could not think of a thing to say. They watched the spectacular blasts of seawater on rocks for a few minutes. Then Kevin said, "Let's surf here."

"Here?" He looked down at the narrow inlet beach, a steep sand slope wedged between a cliff wall and small rock islands. He felt confident in the water, but this was dangerous. The big swells rolled in, broke quickly, and bounced off the rocks and cliffs to create overlapping ricocheting forces. They combined and disintegrated quickly.

Kevin ignored his question and started to climb down. Duncan followed. Once on the narrow beach, they stripped off their shirts and shoes, emptied their pockets, and dove in. The rides were wild. It was a challenge to find good positions. The surging water was like soup violently sloshing in a big, misshaped bowl. Catching a wave meant they had to be quick. The rides were short and intense as they were flung by crushers that broke close to the steeply rising beach.

The dynamics were constantly changing. It was rough, but it was thrilling. Kevin attacked every wave; he screamed on every ride. Duncan cheered and roared with him, but it felt forced. It felt like they were doing something other than surfing. Avoiding getting thrown against the rocks or cliffs took most of his attention.

Then he got caught in an especially nasty combo that sent him straight toward the cliff wall. He would have been severely smashed, except he managed a flip move at the last second, and his feet hit the wall instead of his head. Even so, the churn boiled around him and thrust him along the cliff face. His shoulder whacked rock, and he winced. Dumped on soft sand, he dragged himself out of the water and sat on the beach, just out of range.

Kevin ran to him. "You OK?"

"Yeah, a little banged." He showed abrasions on his arm and shoulder.

Kevin sat next to him and said, "Good."

"That was fun."

"Yeah, great pivot-move off the wall."

"Thanks."

"You lost control at the end."

"Naw, all that tumbling and bashing was deliberate."

Kevin smiled. "Yeah?"

"Sure. Are we done dodging death?"

The boy who answered had regained some of his cocky cool. "I suppose."

64

August 1968

After another day of bodysurfing at Rivermouth, Duncan and Kevin parted from Lee; Randy had not made it due to a bad cold. They wandered along Front Street with no particular destination in mind.

"Wish we had more money," Kevin said.

"Yeah, my paper route cash doesn't last long."

"I blow my allowance in a day."

"Yeah."

"I miss our wallet money."

"We better stay away from that."

"Yeah, Janet might be hiding in the Rock 'O' Plane."

They laughed.

"What's up with you and Leon?"

"Not much. I try to act nice, say yessir to everything. I go to my room and stay there when he drinks."

***

Since that first time Leon hit Kevin, he avoided going by when Leon was there—the man didn't like him either. Kevin said he had apologized the next day, "Sort of apologized," he had said, "He said he was sorry, but I shouldn't aggravate him. My attitude pissed him off; he was drunk, tired, so just be a nice boy and maybe I won't hit you. That's not an apology!" he had finished.

***

Up past the Soquel Avenue bridge, nearing Longs, Duncan said, "Let's go in; I want a Coke."

Longs Drugs was a big store. They walked through the automatic doors; Kevin said he would grab the Cokes while Duncan got a couple of Hershey Bars, both with almonds. While waiting near the registers, he noticed a woman go into an unattended checkout and punch a few buttons that made the cash drawer pop open. She inspected the money, wrote something down, closed the drawer, and went to the next unoccupied checkout station, where she repeated the process. His gaze unfocused as he was suddenly lost in thought. Kevin brought him out of his reverie.

They paid for their goodies. Once outside, he said, "I've got an idea; let's go over there." They crossed Cliff Street and found a spot overlooking the river. He told Kevin what he had seen.

"So?"

"We could open a register and take the cash."

"Somebody would see us standing around punching buttons."

"Not if we do it right. The way they set it up, there is an open path for the carts to go past the register. The cigarette display hides whoever is there, except maybe their head. There are just four buttons to push. What if you and I took turns walking through, pushing one as we go? The drawer opens on the fourth button. We grab the cash, close the door and walk out. The only risky point is when the drawer opens, but I could get the cash out in seconds."

Kevin stared at him for a while, looked at the river, then back, said, "That's really slick. Why close the drawer? Won't it make noise, take time?"

"The other registers are making noise all the time, and the last three registers are all near the door and not being used right now. Nobody'll notice. The drawer must be closed so it looks like nothing happened."

Kevin nodded. "Cool."

"Let's do it now."

"Now?"

"Yeah, I've got the buttons memorized. I'll be the one to open the drawer and get the cash, so you'll do the first button, and I'll do the last, OK?"

Kevin took a long time staring at the river, doubt clear on his face.

"Derring-do," Duncan said.

Kevin smiled at him, said, "Shit," then nodded and stood up. "Yes, derring-do."

Back inside they ambled past the checkout lanes, scoping. Duncan made sure Kevin knew exactly which buttons to push. There was light customer traffic in the store. Nervousness had him on edge; Kevin questioned him with his eyes.

"Yeah, let's do it," Duncan said.

Kevin walked through. Even though Duncan was watching for the flash of his hand pushing Button One, it was hard to catch. He waited until Kevin was clear, and then he did Button Two. Then Kevin did Three. Then he popped the last button, and the drawer opened. He emptied the bill slots but did not touch the coins and closed the drawer harder than he meant to. As he left the station, he glanced once up the outside path of the other checkouts and saw no one looking his way. Then he moved toward the exit only a bit faster than usual. Kevin joined him at the door. Once outside and out of sight, they took off running around the corner of the store. They resumed walking and made for the footbridge to San Lorenzo Park.

Under the bridge, Duncan pulled out the cash and counted it. "$73."

"That was easy."

The next day at the Boardwalk, they celebrated. They rode rides and got hamburgers with fries and chocolate milkshakes. As Kevin slurped the last of his, Duncan said, "Let's do it again."

"What? There?"

"Yeah, why not?"

"Won't they be on guard?"

"Let's go see."

"OK."

They picked a different register, but the second time was as easy as the first. But the money was more—$ 164. Over the next five days, they hit the same store twice more. They got $112 and then $161.

Under the bridge after the fourth time, Kevin said, "Fuckin' A, what's our total? Gotta be over five hundred."

Duncan thought, said, $510."

"Cool, we're rich."

"Let's play with it." He looked at some ducks paddling in the river, dunking their heads for food. "I don't think we should try it again there; I get a bad feeling."

"Yeah, me too."

***

Three days later they returned from a trip to Forest Pool in Boulder Creek. Alan, Lee and Randy had gone with them. It was a great outdoor pool with a high diving area and lots of swimmers. Their ride let them out on Mission Street, where they split from the others and headed for home.

As they reached Almar, Duncan wanted to stop at the Safeway for snacks. Inside, he noticed something right away. "Hey, they've got the same registers as Longs."

He felt sure Kevin's bright eyes matched his own. They forgot about buying snacks. It was the same perfect setup: empty registers near the exit, light traffic, easy walk-through and blocked view.

When the drawer opened, Duncan found the slots were crammed with cash. There was so much it took longer to get it into his pants. He had to leave most of the ones. He closed the drawer with a click and quickly glanced around. No one was looking from the other registers. Kevin was waiting at the door.

Then he saw the man—an old guy, maybe sixty, hands in his pockets, about ten feet back from the checkout he had just left. The man's stare said, *what-the-hell*. He flicked his own eyes away and forced himself to walk at a normal pace to the door. It opened as he stepped on the pad. He saw Kevin glance back once into the store as they exited.

To their left was the TG&Y, which sat at right angles to the Safeway. The boys went right and out of sight of the store. A large open field of churned-up earth and rock stretched away, the future home of more stores.

They ran.

After about 150 feet they jumped into a deep, dry ditch. They anxiously peered over the raised mound, but there was no pursuit.

"Whew, close. He looked right at you."

"Do you think he saw me do it?"

"Probably, I don't know; I looked away for a second, and when I looked again, he was staring at you."

"I almost crapped."

They shared a half-minute of nervous laughter and then again searched for pursuit. Nothing.

"How much?"

"A lot."

It took a while to count it all, and they kept checking to see if they were still safe. Finally, Duncan announced, "$567." Kevin whistled through his teeth.

"Far fucking out," Duncan said.

"Now we really are rich."

"Let's each buy motorcycles."

"Or a car."

"Or a plane."

"What?"

"Just trippin'."

"We better go."

They crouched low and headed further down the ditch until they came to a grove of trees, went down an alley and found the side street. They kept off Almar in case they were being searched for. Giddy laughter burst from them as they walked, and they could not stop smiling. At Duncan's house, Kevin said, "Damn."

"Yeah, see you tomorrow. Hide it good, OK?"

"You too."

65

Taking out the garbage was one of the few chores Ava had given him. It was a nasty job. She had canceled their garbage service in June. "We have to save money."

Instead of their trash bags going into steel cans for pickup, he had to take them to the storage room. When the Findlays had moved in, the garage was lined with deep plywood shelving along every wall. He would place the paper grocery bags full of their stinking contents on those shelves, starting at the rear. They were paper because plastic garbage bags would not be introduced to the American public until 1969.

The storeroom was detached from the house. He walked out the back door to the room's side door to get to it. Here, he always stopped for a minute to gather enough air to get in and out without breathing the atmosphere within. They usually had meat scraps in their trash, and the summer heat turned ewww smells into cloying icko-stinko-I'm-going-to-barf smells.

He would huff and puff until he nearly hyperventilated, hold it, fling the door open, run to the rear, push the bag to the back of the shelf to join its brothers, and then run for the exit. He would slam the door and gasp for fresh sea air.

There was one upside to that *Den of Disgust*; it was the perfect hiding place for his pile of cash. No one in his family would consider entering.

At a time when a Coke cost ten cents, a bottle of beer was a buck, a Big Mac was forty-nine cents, new Levi jeans were five dollars, the rent on their house was $105, and a new Schwinn ten-speed racing bike could be had for $129, Duncan was sitting on over $500. He could have paid in advance for three years of garbage service and still had more money than he knew what to do with. But the thought never entered his mind.

Discovery of his larceny was what he was determined to prevent. Thus, all those bills were rolled up in a sock and stuffed into the crotch of a rafter near the door.

The day after their Safeway heist, he was eager to go on a spending spree. He called Kevin. For a few days they splurged in their usual ways. Then, one afternoon, after eating lunch at Malio's, Kevin said, "Why don't we rent a boat?"

"That sounds fun. Will they rent to us?"

"Sure, why not? It's too late for today; let's come back early tomorrow."

They showed up just after 10 a.m. at the boat rental on the wharf. A big sign declared the rates by the hour and the day. "Let's do all day," Duncan said.

"$40? Sure, we can go everywhere."

They were better dressed than usual. They wore new swim trunks, bought at Richardson's two days earlier. Duncan had new sneakers. And they had Hawaiian shirts with patterns of flowers and birds on them. They approached a man behind an outdoor counter near the wharf railing.

"Hi, we'd like to rent a boat," Duncan said.

The man was about forty with deeply tanned arms and a face under a Popeye hat. He looked them over carefully. "Yeah, how long?"

"All day, please."

"That's forty dollars. You got that much?"

Duncan flashed sixty dollars.

"This a fishing trip? I don't see any poles."

"No, just want to cruise around the bay."

"Sightseeing, huh?"

The boys nodded.

"Ever been on a boat before?"

"Yeah, lots when I lived in Minnesota. Fished on the lakes."

The man nodded. "OK."

They told the man they wanted food and drink for the trip and would be right back. Twenty minutes later, they paid him. A couple of dozen boats were lined up on the wharf, tight together on their sides. A nearby winch was used to lower them to the water, where a large boat landing floated. They rented a skiff. It was twelve feet long and had an outboard motor. The skiff was like a sleeker, beefier version of a rowboat, made of wood and painted red.

After lowering it, the man took them downstairs to the landing and gave them instructions. He showed them how to operate the outboard engine. There was extra fuel in a can, plus life jackets and oars. The man pointed over the water at about the same distance they were from the shore. "See those buoys? You must stay outside them.

They're about 300 yards off the beach. Once you go past the river or the other way, past the wharf, there won't be any buoys except the one-mile buoy out there." He pointed toward Monterey. "It's a good idea to stay 300 yards offshore, buoy or no buoy. Especially watch the rocks. Got it? "

"Yes," they said.

He gave them a pamphlet on right-of-way rules and explained the contents. "Finally, be back before three. If you're late, it will cost extra."

"OK," Duncan said.

It took a few pulls, but Kevin started the motor. He eased them away from the dock more smoothly than Duncan thought he would. The man watched them go for a minute and then headed back up the stairs. Heading out on the ocean was a total thrill. The day was warm, and the air was still. The scent of the sea was rich in his nostrils, and the moist air flowed over his skin as they motored along at maybe five knots. The sea danced with sunlight from a thousand shifting surfaces reflecting the sun; they donned sunglasses. They smiled.

"This is so cool," Kevin said.

"Groovy."

"Where do you want to go?"

Duncan thought, said, "The one-mile buoy. I want to get way out there."

"Yeah, let's go." He turned the boat toward the distant shape. Their boat sat low in the water, and once away from the wharf, it seemed they were moving very slowly. It was a calm day, but Monterey Bay was always a little rough away from the shore. The boat cruised toward its destination with a rhythmic smack smack smack as it went over the chop.

"You did a lot of boating in Minnesota?"

"Sort of. I rode on my cousin's speedboat once. And I went out on Pelican Lake with my dad when I was six."

Kevin snorted. "Glad we got someone experienced along. I've never done this before."

He chuckled. "Yeah, that's cool. You're driving good."

"It's not hard."

The shore receded and soon seemed far away. A sailboat passed far beyond the growing buoy. It was a surprise when they neared it, for it was huge, with a red and white metal tower wobbling in the shifting chop. It emitted deep sighs like a nodding-off tuba player, and as they got closer, several gray seabirds flew from their perches at the top. Two seals sunning themselves on the base honked their complaints and slid into the water.

It was three times the height of the boys. They went close enough to touch it, and each leaned over to give it an I-was-here slap. Duncan took over driving, and they headed for Steamer Lane. Kevin leaned back and let a hand trail in the water.

"Leon calls you a delinquent."

"Really?"

"Yeah, Mary defends you, says the police didn't get anything."

"So, why am I still a delinquent?"

"He says the police don't arrest people for nothing."

"Shit, that's not fair. A year later, and he still holds that against me? What's a delinquent anyway?"

"I don't know, bad kid, I guess. He doesn't like me hanging with you. He thinks you'll get me in trouble, a bad influence." Kevin laughed.

"I thought you were the bad influence."

"I am. Your mom think so?"

"Naw, she's cool with all my friends."

The glow of Kevin's happiness was snuffed out like a blown candle. "You know, I think him bitching about you is really just his way of bitching about me."

"What a dick."

They had fun watching the surfers from a new perspective but were careful to stay clear of them. They went along the lovely stretch of cliffs to Natural Bridges and then headed for Capitola. He wished the boat would go faster. Along their way they feasted on beef jerky, potato chips, Mountain Dew and Hostess Cupcakes.

At 2:51, Kevin eased the boat up to the landing. Popeye seemed surprised that they were on time. They were tired, thirsty, and even a little sunburned—reflections off the water had doubled their exposure—but as they headed home, they sang and laughed and discussed what adventure they would do next.

66

September 1968 – May 1969

Duncan grew up with family stories of ghosts and the *Little People* of North Uist, Scotland. Since their move to West Santa Cruz, Ava expanded her interests to include Rosicrucianism, metaphysics, reincarnation and white magic.

He was a freshman at Santa Cruz High, and one day after school, he came home to find that the kitchen had a new function. All the shades were pulled down to keep it dark, and four pentagrams hung near the ceiling. They were constructed of strips of thick paperboard mounted on Styrofoam and were coated with phosphorescent paint that gave off an eerie blue-green glow.

Ava explained that she used the kitchen for her rituals, and the pentagrams were placed in the four cardinal directions. He was to keep the shades down so the pentagrams received as little natural light as possible and would thus shine from etheric light alone.

"OK, Mom," he had said.

She demonstrated one of her rituals, which involved wielding an imaginary flaming dagger, invoking angelic entities using multiple names of God, like Adonai and Elohim, and concluded with her stabbing each pentagram with the fiery blade.

"Cool," he had said, and he thought that if anyone could command spirits and angels, it was Mom.

School was of very little interest to him, and he began skipping it, a day here and a day there. Shona would write excellent excuse letters for him in her fine script and sign, forging Ava's name. She warned him not to push it; there were only so many times he could reasonably be sick or prevented by a family emergency.

Although he was bored by his American History, English and Geometry classes, he did like Wood Shop. They had table saws, planers, routers, lathes, band saws, and lots more in a big building on campus. He loved the smells of pine, oak and mahogany. The shrieks of powerful machines shaping beautiful boards and the sawdust on the floor felt grand. Their teacher, Mr. Bridger, showed them a safety film that demonstrated in cringe-inducing, nausea-provoking vivid details what could happen if his students were careless. They watched the tips of fingers being sliced off by the planer, a man impaled by a two-by-four kicked back like a javelin by the table saw, and a hand severed by the band saw. Properly freaked out by the film, he and the rest of the class immediately began practicing with the demonstrated instruments.

Santa Cruz had become Hippie Heaven. Long-haired men, peasant-dressed women, bead-wearing, mystically-eyed, THC-eyed, patchouli-fragranced, smiling acolytes of Make Love, Not War strolled the streets of downtown and around the beach. Pacific Avenue and a few side streets were no longer boring. Music wafted out of The Catalyst. Budding musicians strummed guitars or played flutes or lyres next to newly planted trees.

On a cold February 1969 afternoon, he was walking down a mostly empty Pacific Avenue on the hunt for a new coat. He tried one store after another but found what he wanted, a brown corduroy jacket with a white faux fur collar, at Leask's. It cost him $27, and his decision to buy it with Safeway money was reckless. What would he say if Ava asked him where he got it? He had vague thoughts about making up something but did not care what. He was cold and hated the old, worn blue jacket he had on. What good was having all this money if he could not spend it?

He left the store with his old coat in a bag and felt warm and proud in his new jacket with its collar up. He had a second mission that took his feet toward Cooper Street. Ava's interest in all things metaphysical was a constant presence at home. Issues of the Rosicrucian Digest were often on the coffee table. She spent many a long evening at their next-door neighbor's house discussing the Rosicrucian's teachings with Midge and Ted. They were long-term members of the Order and prided themselves on their knowledge of the mysteries and their professed ability to confound conventional thinkers, like Christian priests.

Ava was practicing astral projection, and the pentagrams gleamed brightly every day and night in the darkened little kitchen. She was building an etheric double, which, as Duncan understood it, would enable her to travel anywhere in the world in the etheric realm.

He sometimes spoke with her on cold winter nights as she stood before the hot stove, putting chunks of wood into it and warming her hands. Glowing faintly golden, copies of her arms hung in the air apart from her physical arms. And she was happy at the sight of it, for she said it meant her work was proceeding well.

Duncan devoured books about astronomy, science, history and science fiction. He dreamed of going to the stars. Stories by Isaac Asimov, Ray Bradbury, Philip K. Dick and Robert Heinlein entranced him with visions of worlds and beings that could be. The new teachings that Ava exposed him to spoke of esoteric knowledge and hidden worlds, not light years away but on planes of existence right in front of him, invisible except to the clairvoyant. He read her digests, asked her questions, and on the day he bought his new coat, went in search of more.

On Cooper Street he opened the door to Odyssey Records to tones of bells bouncing off the inner handle. The Youngbloods sang "Get Together" over the store's stereo system.

He wandered around looking at albums, and though he loved browsing through the vinyl, he was not there for the music.

It was an odd time in America. Such songs of love, peace, joy and brotherhood were popular even as protests against the war grew more violent. The war itself kept escalating in futile copious casualties, and less than a year before, Senator Robert Kennedy and Reverend Martin Luther King Jr. had both been murdered before the whole world.

Past all the racks at the back of the store, he found his destination. The Occult Shop was a recent addition to the record store, just a surprisingly small room with a stick of incense in a tiny pot of sand on the counter. Its fragrant smoke flowed sinuously toward the ceiling. A thin, bearded man watched him enter. He smiled but said nothing as Duncan stopped and looked around at the offerings. It was a tasteful, neat little shop with its books presented like treasures.

In addition to books, it offered Tarot Cards, yarrow sticks for divination and hand-made candles. He browsed books on astrology, numerology, Buddhism, the I Ching, theosophy and black magic. He stopped momentarily before the arresting picture of a long-haired Indian man on the cover of a book titled *Autobiography of a Yogi*. As he moved on, The Fifth Dimension sweetly sang about the coming Age of Aquarius.

He noticed an array of hardcover books on one wall, each with fine, embossed gold lettering on deep-blue textured leather. One was presented face out—*A Treatise on White Magic* by Alice A. Bailey.

Wow, he thought, picking it up.

There were over 600 fine-paper pages between the luxurious covers. He put his nose close to the pages and breathed deeply. He loved the smell of a fine book, the ink, the paper and the glue of the binding. The contents covered spiritual psychology, supernormal powers and the fifteen rules of soul control. With some reverence, he took his prize to the man, who raised his eyebrows when he saw what Duncan was buying.

"Starting at the graduate level?" he asked.

The question mystified Duncan, so he said nothing.

The man's eyes gleamed. "Perhaps you're a lot older than you look."

"It just seems like a good book. Cool."

"It *is* that. Really cool. Deep stuff." The man took his payment and gave him a handwritten receipt. "Let me guess," he said. "You're a Leo."

"What's a Leo?"

The man blinked a few times as if it did not make sense for his customer to buy this book and not know what a Leo was. "Astrological sign," he said.

"Oh."

"When were you born?"

He told him.

"Yep, you're a Leo."

"How'd you know?"

"I didn't know. I get impressions of people. You have that bold air that Leos walk around with."

"Huh."

"Maybe the next time you come in, I'll point out some books on it."

"OK."

Over the next few months, he visited the bookshop many times. His first purchase had proved challenging to understand, so he put it aside. Subsequent purchases were easier to read. He bought Charles Leadbeater's book on *The Chakras* mainly because of the fantastic pictures. He got the yogi's delightful autobiography, which read like a novel. He bought a pack of tarot cards, partly because divination was interesting but mainly because of the wild pictures on each card.

One day, he spied a gold-bound book titled *The Greater Key of Solomon the King –and – The Lesser Key of Solomon the King*. Unlike Mrs. Bailey's treatise, it was crudely produced but full of specific magical instructions and wild symbols representing spirits and demons the practitioner could control. They had names like Zagan and Baal. There were fantastic, detailed drawings of magic circles and pentagrams to be used in the conjurations.

It was so bizarre and fascinating that he bought it. The man carefully considered him when he offered his money. "You really go for the heavy stuff," he said.

Duncan had shown little interest in astrology. He shrugged. Before leaving the shop, the man said, "Be careful. Some consider that black magic, not to be played with."

"OK, thanks."

Ava did notice his new coat and asked about it. "I found twenty dollars on the street and spent it on this," he said.

She had thoughtfully looked at him, and he wondered if he would have to dig his lie deeper, but she said, "It looks nice." He had smiled and gone to his room, feeling deeply uncomfortable about how easily the lie had rolled off his tongue.

His new book was easier to understand than the *Treatise*, even though it was an English translation of ancient texts. *The Lesser Key* was about how to conjure and constrain seventy-two different demons, each with a unique ability or power, to do the conjuror's bidding. *The Greater Key* was also about conjuring, but of spirits with less dangerous natures, and via conjuring them in the names of God.

He thought the process was very complex. One had to pick the right astrological time, wear the right clothes, prepare oneself with fasting and prayers, confess sins to God, and required the creation of elaborate magical circles. There were spells to prevent a hunter from getting game and one for becoming invisible. He put it aside.

***

The guys were bored at the arcade on a Saturday in early April. "Let's go bowling," Lee said.

No one had a better idea, so they headed across the street to the Brunswick Surf Bowl on Cliff Street. He took off his new coat because the day had warmed up. After they got their shoes and balls inside the bowling alley, he dropped the coat on a chair behind the lanes.

The boys had a good time, but when he came back from a trip to the restroom, he freaked out. "Hey guys, have you seen my coat?"

Nobody had. After a frantic search and questioning of the staff, it was clear—the coat was gone. He went home, thoroughly bummed. The concept of karma was unfamiliar to him; even if it had been, it would not have mattered. At home, he sulked in his room.

Then he had an idea. The problem was that his idea required privacy, which was hard to come by in their little house; he shared the bedroom with Keith. He used the days of waiting to prepare. Using black crayons on sheets of butcher paper, he drew these images:

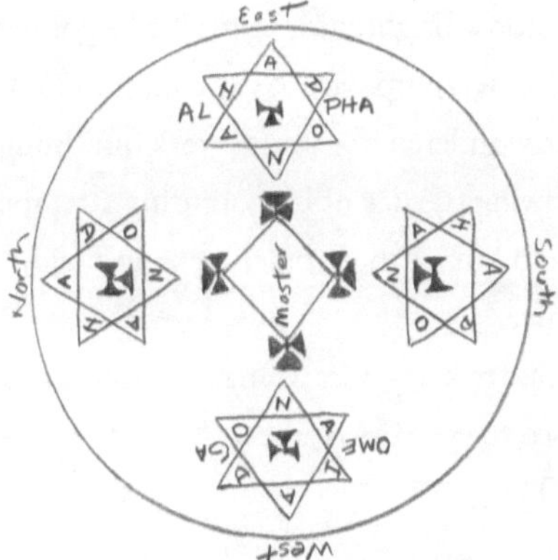

A day soon came when he had the house to himself, but he did not know for how long. In his bedroom he put the diamond symbol in the center. Each hexagram was placed in the same direction as Ava's pentagrams. The triangle was put in the east. He knew he was leaving out a lot of things. He was supposed to have a nine-foot circle drawn with the image of a coiling snake and a bunch of Hebrew written on the snake. He was supposed to have fasted, prayed, spoken softly, confessed and done an astrological calculation for the most propitious day and time.

Sheesh, it was too complicated. All he wanted was his jacket back. Surely, he could skip some stuff and get to the point. So, on a Saturday morning, a week after it was stolen, he stood on the diamond symbol and conjured thus:

"O ye spirits, ye I conjure by the power, wisdom, and virtue of the Spirit of God...

"I conjure ye by the Indivisible Name IOD...

"I conjure thee by the Name TETRAGRAMMATON ELOHIM...

"I conjure thee by the Name of God EL...

"I conjure thee by the most powerful name of ELOHIM GIBOR..."

There were many more such exhortations, including using the names of specific spirits whose nature he did not understand. They were supposed to appear to him over the circle inside the triangle. When he did not see anything on the first go round, he knew he was supposed to keep exhorting ever more passionately until the "rebellious spirits" submitted and appeared.

He worked himself into a lather, but no spirits appeared until after the fourth try when he thought a shadow shape dulled the dresser behind the triangle.

Maybe it was a trick of the light, his vivid imagination, or carbon dioxide intoxication from all his fervent exhorting, but he chose to deem it the arrival of the spirits. At that point, he adlibbed, told it about his coat, where it was taken and ordered it to bring the coat back to him. The shadow brightened, or maybe he got more oxygen, and he then skipped the self-protection wrap-up part of the conjuration. It had been fun, kind of cool, kind of silly, and he wondered if it would work but thought little more about it.

On the Tuesday following the day of his conjuring attempt, he was in Wood Shop when Mr. Bridger came to him at the lumber racks and said, "After class, go see Miss Andrews in the front office."

He walked there and said to a heavyset woman in a blue dress sitting at a desk behind a partition, "I'm supposed to see Miss Andrews."

"That's me, are you Duncan?"

"Yes."

She stood, briefly disappeared into an adjacent office, and returned carrying something. "Is this your coat?"

His mouth opened as he stared at the familiar brown corduroy with an off-white collar.

"Is it?"

"Yes, how..."

She handed it to him. "A man came in and said, 'Duncan will be needing this.'"

"Who?"

"I asked him, Duncan who? He said, Findlay."

"I mean, who was he?"

"I thought he was your father, but he didn't give me a name."

"You don't know him?"

"No, he looked like a lawyer in his three-piece suit, but when I asked his name, he repeated, 'Duncan needs this,' and left."

He stared at the jacket in his arms—dazed.

"You OK?"

He twitched. "Yes."

"Well, good, because I've got work to do. Best you get to lunch."

He shuffled out into the hall and reached into the right pocket. Yep, that piece of Double Bubble gum was there. He looked up and down the hall as if he might see the man lurking nearby, but he only saw fellow students.

Far-out.

Although he believed the jacket had been returned by supernatural power, he had no interest in doing further conjurations. It wasn't that he was afraid; it was more that he had not really believed it would work, and now, with the coat in hand, he felt cautious, aware that he was quite ignorant about what he was doing.

It was that weekend that the voices started. It began with something whispering in his left ear. He could never make out any words. Then there were more voices until it was as if a dozen or more people were with him, whispering inside his mind, and although he discerned no clear messages, the tone was urgent, insistent and seemed to want him to do something. The sounds came and went but grew progressively more frequent. He felt lost in a trance as he listened, trying to understand what it meant. When no clarity came, it started to piss him off.

"Get out of my head," he said again and again.

After two weeks of this, he had had enough. He went down to the cliffs near his home and performed a reverse conjuration, repeating power words and ordering the spirits to depart and never bother him again. To his relief and surprise, the whispering stopped instantly, and then all he heard were the sounds of the sea and living people strolling nearby.

67

June 1969

A week after Duncan completed his first year of high school, Ava got him a part-time job working at a gas station on Mission. He pumped, cleaned up and tried to avoid the owner's little dog, which seemed to have fallen in love with his leg.

He liked having the job because it gave him a little leeway to spend some of the money in his sock safe. Despite splurging here and there over the months, he still had about $300. He thought Kevin had roughly the same.

He met Kevin in front of the carousel, and they took a few rides throwing brass rings at the big clown-in-the-wall's mouth, scoring often. Next, they laughed and cheered while bashing bumper cars in a melee on a slick steel floor. And then rode The Sky Glider to meet their friends at the far end of the Boardwalk.

The boys waited in front of the Wild Mouse for a while before going on the ride. When they got off, Alan, Randy, and Lee were there.

Randy and Lee upnodded.

Alan said, "Moneybags and Warbucks have arrived."

The money had brought with it strange tensions in the gang. Last August, he and Kevin agreed that they should not talk about the heists, not because they didn't trust their friends but to protect them from the police. Janet's grilling of his friends over the wallets worried Duncan—better that they knew nothing. But they could not hide their relative extravagance from Randy and Alan, whose family was on welfare, nor from Lee, whose grandfather gave him little to nothing of an allowance. It was obvious that the two boys could buy anything they wanted, go on rides at will, and have new stuff, and Duncan had made a mistake when, in his enthusiasm, he talked about renting a boat. Forty dollars was a fortune to the other boys.

He and Kevin had shared some of the money, mostly by treating food or Boardwalk entertainments, but not as fully as they had with the wallet money. They had given half of that away. Now that Duncan had a pile of cash, he felt tighter about sharing it. Randy did not care; he was happy and grateful for anything. Lee voiced no expectations that Moneybags or Warbucks should give him anything. But Alan had taken to making little you-guys-are-rich comments, but it was done like a joke, one that he did not push.

"Surf is calling, let's go," said Lee.

"Yeah," Alan said and gave Kevin a light smack on his back. "The millionaires are holding up the fun."

Kevin winced like he had been stabbed. Alan looked at his hand in mock puzzlement, said, "Whoa, must not know my own strength." He chuckled.

"You just startled me, goober. Let's get to it."

As Kevin and the other three walked toward the stairs, Duncan hesitated.

Startled? Kevin? Since when? Maybe if a gun was fired next to his head. From a tap by a friend? No frickin' way.

He caught up but did not pursue the mystery.

Near the water, the boys stripped to their cutoffs and trunks—all except Kevin, who did not remove his T-shirt.

Lee snorted, "You going surfing in your shirt?"

"Yeah, got a little burned, don't want it to get worse."

That was a nonsensical statement to boys who were already well-tanned and spent hours in the full sun every chance they got. And wearing a T-shirt in those waters was like wearing an ice suit.

But Lee shrugged, said, "Whatever." And they all plunged into the waves.

The swells were decent, and the competition was slight. Kevin kept his shirt on, even though he looked cold to Duncan. He and Alan caught a perfect wave with Kevin and rode it into shallow water. They stood and let the sea pour off them.

"I don't know how you can swim in that shirt. You got a wetsuit under there, or what?" Alan said, and in a quick move, he pulled up Kevin's shirt, looking for the insulation, and froze at the sight.

Kevin grabbed his shirt back down, but not before Duncan and Alan had seen a mass of hideous bruises blackening his back and sides. Duncan's eyes stung but not from the saltwater.

"What happened to you?" Alan asked.

"Nothing. Leave me alone." Kevin ran out of the swash and continued up along the river.

"What the hell?" Alan said.

"I think I know; let's get Randy and Lee."

He swam out to where the two waited for another set and said, "Kevin's been hurt. Come on."

It took a while to find him. He was behind one of the trestle pillars, shivering in the sun, still covered by his slowly drying shirt.

"Leave me alone," he said.

Everyone stopped except Alan, who walked right up to him and waited.

Kevin repeated himself.

"Let me see," Alan said softly.

"Go away."

Then, in a voice so tender, like he was speaking to an injured fawn where the slightest wrong word or move would spook it into trying to flee on broken legs, he said, "Please, Kevin, let me see."

There were no tears in Kevin's eyes. His face was stone as he turned away to look across the river. Delicately, Alan lifted the shirt.

"Fuck," Lee said.

"Who did this to you?" asked Alan.

The boy did not answer for the longest time. Duncan was sure he knew, but Kevin wouldn't want him to say. No one spoke or moved until Alan let the shirt fall with the sigh of a long-held breath.

"Leon," Kevin said in a voice Duncan could barely hear.

The three waiting boys took the reply as an OK to approach. They surrounded him like a protective cordon.

"Why?"

Kevin's face of stone sagged, and his lower lip trembled when he answered, "I don't know, guess he doesn't like me."

It was Alan's poise and intense listening presence that prevented any questions or interjections. They waited and listened.

"He can be nice as a peach... when he's not drunk. Used to smack me once in a while. One backhand to the belly, maybe. He learned not to hit my face; Mary would get mad. But now he gets drunk a lot when Mary's at work. I hide in my room, waiting for him to pass out. That works... most of the time."

"How big is this asshole?"

Duncan could tell what his tough friend was thinking from the fire in his squinting eyes. "Too big," Duncan said. "He could lift your whole weight with one arm."

"A few times, I escaped out my window and came back late. But he realized one night I had gone. Next time, I got it bad."

"Like this?" Alan asked.

"No, not this bad. My ribs hurt when I breathe."

"Have you told Mary?" Randy asked.

Kevin shook his head. "Maybe she knows, but I don't think so. Maybe she doesn't want to know. He said if I told her, I would really pay."

"We should go to the cops," Lee said.

"He's got cop friends. I'm a foster brat. I might end up in CYA."

With that the boys were out of solutions. The moment dragged.

"He'll apologize. He gets all guilty when he's sober. I'll think of something."

"You could hide at our house," Randy said," Mom will protect you."

Kevin nodded, said, "Thanks." But everyone understood the flaw in that idea.

68

A couple of weeks later Duncan and Alan were sunning themselves at the usual beach. The other guys were out slicing lines down the faces of waves. To their many inquiries, Kevin reported that Leon had not hit him again.

Alan was seventeen and as big as many men. His black hair was long but recently barbered. He was muscular in his arms and legs but big in the belly. He had spent the prior school year redoing being a sophomore a year after having also redone his freshman year. Duncan thought being so much older and bigger than your classmates must be awkward.

As if he had heard his thoughts, Alan said, "I'm not good in school. Everything takes me longer to learn. I made it into junior for next year, but it was hard."

There was a breeze blowing in off the bay on that hot afternoon. The colorful sails of dozens of boats adorned the water like abstract art. Duncan enjoyed the view as he listened.

"You know what's weird, though? I can easily take apart the V-6 in the Falcon and put it back together again. And Tito says I learn fast on the job and should think about being a carpenter. But in the classroom, I'm like a dumbshit."

He heard the pain in his voice, turned to look at him, and said, "Maybe there are different kinds of smarts, all of them good. I bet some scientists don't even know what a carburetor is."

Alan laughed. "Heh, yeah, maybe so." With a little smile, his big friend mused on the idea. Duncan noticed his swollen right hand. He pointed and asked, "What happened? Did you whack yourself with that big hammer?"

Alan had a funny way of biting his lower lip like a chipmunk when thinking. As he munched, he peered in the direction of the boats. Then he reached behind into his rolled-up pants and came out with a fistful of cash. "You and Kevin have your ways of making money, and I have mine."

He guessed there could be fifty dollars in Alan's grasp. "Cool, you snatching money from Dobermans?"

Alan pumped his lip some more with his teeth and said, "Very funny. I don't know if I should tell you. You and Kevin haven't said how you got so rich."

"We aren't rich."

"No? Close enough."

Duncan waited. He could not tell; he had promised Kevin.

After more lip chewing, Alan said, "I've been surprising drunks coming out of the bars downtown. Take their money."

Was Alan joking? Duncan wished he could read his eyes, but they were both wearing shades. "You mean you pickpocket them?"

"No, push them into the wall of some alley, tell 'em to cough up the green or get hurt."

Looking down at that discolored hand, he asked, "You beat them?"

"If they make me. I knocked this one lush out with just my left jab. Man, did he crumple."

He knew Alan could be mean, but this made him a bit sick. "You have to beat them all?"

"Only did it six times so far. Half were so drunk or so scared they handed their wallets right over. This last guy, though," he raised his damaged paw, "fought back. He didn't give to a few stiff lefts, but I dropped him good with an uppercut. Broke a few of his teeth, I bet. And shoved my knuckle back. That hurt. And the idiot only had eight dollars too."

"Damn, Alan."

"No real chance I'll get caught. It's dark, they're drunk. But I do need to be careful to spread it out."

He watched Randy ride a roller all the way to the river. What could he say? Good going beating up old drunks? But Alan was confiding in him like it was a feat. Then he said the wrong thing, "I couldn't do that, hurt people like that."

Alan bristled, "I'm not hurting them for fun. Only if they won't pay."

"Still hurting people."

"Drunks."

"We get drunk... and high."

"What's your problem?"

Duncan couldn't hide his revulsion. He shook his head, said, "You're hurting people, mugging them. Shouldn't hurt people."

"What the fuck are you talking about? Getting all high and mighty on me?" Then, in a mocking voice, "Shouldn't hurt people. Bullshit. You hurt people."

"I do not."

"Yes, you do."

"Chuck had it coming."

Alan seemed baffled momentarily, then scoffed, "I'm not talking about your little boxing glory from when you were a baby."

"Then what?"

"Stealing hurts people."

"We've never hurt anyone in our heists."

"Heists, huh? Stealing. I don't know what you and Kevin did lately, but you don't think taking a guy's wallet, driver's license, pictures of his girlfriend and whatever else didn't hurt?"

"Not the same at all. We're not breaking teeth."

"So? There's different kinds of hurt."

His glare was undoubtedly lost on Alan, not just because of the shades. "Screw this," he said, removed his sunglasses, and stood. "Me and Kevin's heists are nothing like your beatdowns in alleys. We don't hurt anybody!" He was shouting, and it bothered him.

Alan smirked and laughed. "Sure, sure."

He ran and dove under an incoming wave, eager to forget Alan's nonsense.

69

July 1969

Duncan and Kevin spent much of that warm, sunny day bodysurfing at River-mouth. They mixed in so many rides on the Giant Dipper that they forgot the number.

"Twelve?" Duncan asked.

"More like fifteen."

He stopped suddenly on the Boardwalk's warm, sandy concrete to consider the enormous figure's likelihood. Finally, he shrugged, said, "Yeah, maybe. Hey, new record!"

"Let's go for twenty next time."

They arrived at their next destination, the carousel with its 73 hand-carved wooden horses, glittering lights, and mirrors. The ride had been hugely popular since it was first delivered 58 years before. Immensely adding to the experience were the tunes of the 342-pipe machine-organ, which cheerily seemed to prod the dancing horses along.

Only the outside ones would do. Leaning out from the rapidly spinning carousel, they would try to time their grab of a brass ring from the dispenser just right and then fling it in one quick motion toward the clown's maw. Blinking red lights announced a score.

After tiring of that, they headed over to Fisherman's Wharf, not to fish, eat, or tourist-watch but to explore. At the end of the wharf, there were several big, square openings in the deck with short chain-link fences around them. These were additional spaces for fishermen when the outside rails were crowded.

They stood at one of these for a while, looking at the wobbling sea. Kevin said, "Let's climb down."

Duncan looked at the fat, tar-coated pylons, asked, "How?"

"See those bolts attached to the braces? We can hang off the fence, step on a bolt, grab a board just there, step on the next bolt, grab the next board and then hang and drop to the bottom beams."

"Let's do it."

The twenty-foot-long pylons were slippery, as were the bolts that secured iron brackets and haphazard wood braces, but they were able to scramble down before anyone could notice. Once on the tarred cross-beams, they raced over the boards laughing and daring each other to dance along the next narrow beam only a few feet above the ocean. The greenish water surged against the pylons and tugged at clumps of seaweed stuck on barnacles. The sloshing of the sea seemed to harmonize with the murmurs of the people up above.

Behind one of the pylons, they startled an enormous slumbering male sea lion that honked such loud, indignant exception to their invasion of his domain that Kevin nearly fell into the cold green water. Afraid that the aggressive beast would charge and knock them off the beam, they quickly found the nearest way back up.

The sun was closing on the sea, so they headed for Randy's.

As they burst through the front door, Margaret greeted them, "Shouldn't you two be home already?"

The boys shrugged. Duncan explained, "Just wanted to see Randy. He back?"

She did not have to answer because, just then, Randy bounded down the stairs with a whoop. He hit the landing, gave Duncan a friendly punch to the shoulder, and asked, "Good?"

"It was bitchin'! Three-footers, nice curl, lots of bennies, but they stayed out of our way," Duncan said, smiling.

Randy scowled, "Damn, and I had to visit my snotty cousins."

"You can go with them tomorrow," Margaret said, then to the new arrivals, "You boys hungry? There's leftover spaghetti."

"Starving, Mrs. K," Kevin said.

They sprawled on the couch and shoveled spaghetti from the bowls Mrs. Kelly gave them while they watched *Hercules Unchained* on the TV.

After a while, the phone rang in the kitchen. Margaret answered, and then, "Yes, he's here, he and Duncan. No, no, not all day, they came in half an..." For a long minute, she seemed to be listening; Kevin turned the sound low on the TV, then, "There's no reason to be rude. I gave them dinner, and they were about to..." Another stretch was broken up with her saying, "Well...no...yes...OK...OK...uh-huh...all right then."

Margaret, all tall and bony and kind of face, entered the living room. The three boys turned to her.

"Your dad," she said to Kevin, "is coming right over to pick you up." She hesitated as if to say something more but only frowned and walked back into the kitchen.

"He's not my dad," Kevin spat and turned up the TV.

During a commercial a car honked several times out on the street. "See ya," Duncan said to Randy. Kevin jerked a goodbye upnod.

"Thanks, Mrs. Kelly," they shouted as they ran out the front door.

Leon's 1967 Pontiac Bonneville, adorned with big chrome bumpers, idled at the curb. The horn blared again as the boys dashed down the few wooden steps. Kevin laughed, said, "That was so funny when that guy wiped out into that girl."

"Yeah, knocked her on her butt, and then she slapped him!"

Cracking up, they piled onto the spacious, brown leather back seat. Duncan slammed the door. Mary was in the front passenger spot.

"Did you have a good..." Mary started, but Leon growled, interrupting, "You were supposed to be home hours ago."

"I forgot," Kevin said.

Leon turned and looked over his right shoulder at Kevin. "Forgot, huh?" he said, and then added, "What is *he* doing here?" meaning Duncan.

Kevin smirked. "He just needs a ride. You know he lives right around the corner."

In the faint light Duncan saw Leon's eyes narrow, his lips stretched into a thin line. Duncan involuntarily pulled back from the man. Had Kevin forgotten who he was talking to? His heart stomped out a new rhythm when Leon said, "You getting smart with me, boy?"

Kevin's impudence wilted, and he lowered his eyes. "No, sir," he said.

Leon drove the point home with a few more seconds of menacing staring, his thick hairy arm stretched across the seat back until Kevin bowed his head. "Uh-huh," the big man said.

He turned and shifted the massive car's synchromesh transmission into drive. The Bonneville was eighteen feet long and six and a half feet wide. A 333 horsepower V8 propelled its two solid tons. They headed over to Broadway, then over the river and up Laurel to Mission. Mary rolled her window down in the strained silence as Leon drove, letting in the warm night air. She seemed to find the passing houses fascinating. The traffic was light on Mission, and the tires thrummed as they rolled along the pavement.

Mary's voice cracked slightly as she asked, "What did you boys do all day?"

Kevin seemed not to hear; he stared out his window like he wanted to be far away. Before Duncan could answer, Leon boomed, "I don't want to hear what the little fucker and his delinquent friend were up to." The exclamation sent a strong whiff of booze to the back seat. Kevin raised his head like a gazelle hearing something big advancing through the grass.

Cool sweat erupted on Duncan's skin. The meanness, the violence and the sheer frightening power of the man had been known to him almost entirely through Kevin's reports. But that night he felt the simmering rage in the likely drunk giant—and he was trapped.

Leon turned onto Almar Avenue. They were close to home. It was a straight, two-lane residential street that ran less than a mile until it dead-ended into West Cliff Drive.

Leon mumbled something, but Duncan only caught snippets like "no respect" and "always pushing." Kevin wobbled his head, glanced over at Duncan, showed his cocky lopsided smile and leaned forward to give Leon the finger down low behind his seat. A little laugh escaped Duncan, but then he saw Leon's angry eyes in the rearview.

The man snarled, "The little shit just isn't worth it." The tank leapt forward with a screech of rubber on asphalt.

Almar was posted as 25 mph. The blacktop was uneven, with poorly done patches and unrepaired cracks. Residents' cars sparsely dotted spaces along the curbs. Barely twenty-four feet across, there were a few stop signs before it ended at a cliff thirty feet above the crashing surf, or rocks and sand, depending on the tide.

As they bounced over the railroad tracks, he saw the red line of the speedometer cross 50 mph and climbing. Mary whined that Leon should slow down, but the big man with a loud voice told her to *shut the hell up* as he raised his right hand as if to backhand her. She shrank away and leaned against the door, but the blow did not come.

The next stop sign was a red blip as they blasted through the intersection, hit a bump hard, and Duncan banged his head on the roof. The headlight beams danced on power poles, trees and fences. Kevin searched for something, probably a seat belt, but couldn't find it. They were a recent innovation, and no one they knew used them.

Holding onto the door, Kevin said, "I'm sorry, I'm sorry, I'm sorry. Stop, STOP."

Duncan didn't understand how this had turned so ugly and terrifying so quickly. Leon was grousing stuff the fourteen-year-old boy couldn't quite hear over the roaring engine and the squeaks of the shocks. The telephone poles zipped by. The flicker of dim streetlights penetrated the darkness inside the Pontiac, adding a moon-like white to the green glow of the panel that revealed Leon's savage profile.

Mary was curled in a ball, crying. The boys screamed as the Bonneville neared 65 mph. Their hands dug into the upholstery of the front seatback. The road seemed to evaporate beneath them. The headlights briefly flashed on houses, cars, fences, and a bike left at the side of the road. Ahead, Duncan knew that nothing was beyond the twenty feet of clifftop except air, rocks, and water.

He squeezed his eyes closed as he screamed. Moments ticked past, and he felt his mind lock up, go blank, and suddenly he was nauseated like when he would go briefly weightless on the roller coaster. Then he was slammed forward, and there was the shriek of tires failing to grip the road. The massive hunk of steel fishtailed wildly. The violence of being jerked back and forth as the car stuttered ahead turned into a sickening slide sideways. They hit something that made the car tilt and lift and then collapse with a bang on hard earth.

In the relative silence, Duncan felt the car sag to a rest.

He forced his eyes open to find they had crossed West Cliff and were on the dirt path at the edge close to the thirty-foot drop. A cloud of dust swirled and sparkled in the lights. The incongruously peaceful sound of small waves dropping upon the shore entered through Mary's open window. Creaks and pops and moans continued. Leon's wife gasped a sob.

He and Kevin were side-by-side in the middle of the back seat, grasping the front seat leather so hard it was bunched up into a narrow ridge in their hands.

No one came out of their homes to investigate. A young man and a woman cruised by in a convertible without stopping. Minutes passed without a word as Duncan listened to their rapid breaths—all except Leon's, who seemed to breathe slowly and steadily as he held the steering wheel with stiff, straight arms.

Finally, he edged them off the path over the short curb with an abrupt plunk-plunk-plunk-plunk of the wheels and said in a soft, even voice, so quiet, so uninflected that Duncan could barely hear but which, when he did, pierced him like an ice pick to his gut, "Never, never fuck with me again, boy."

Kevin said nothing and did not even move. Leon slowly drove the few blocks to Duncan's house as if nothing had happened. He asked Mary if there was any of that ice cream left. They rolled to a stop in front of Duncan's house, and when he started to get out, he found his hands shaking. While he tried to make them open the door, Kevin grabbed his arm, leaned over and whispered into his ear, "Don't tell your mom. Don't tell anyone, not anyone, OK?"

Duncan looked into his friend's eyes, released a shuddering breath, nodded once, and whispered, "I won't. I promise."

He managed to get out of the car but stumbled a little on the sidewalk before shutting the door. He watched the taillights disappear around the corner and chewed on a knuckle as he wondered if Kevin would be all right. It took a few minutes standing in the barren yard, looking up at a gibbous moon that had just risen, before he felt he could go inside and not give anything away. With a deep breath, he opened the front door to find Ava on the couch.

With an annoyed frown, she said, "You were supposed to be back before dark. What have you been doing?"

70

On a Friday night Duncan, Randy, Lee and Kevin went to the new Boy's Club in downtown Santa Cruz. They were putting on a dance, and the boys wanted to meet some girls. Alan wasn't interested as he had a girlfriend, Carol Ann, who sometimes sat on his lap in front of the boys, nibbled his ear and cooed like she was giving a show. Alan claimed he had been "doing it" with her for a while, usually in the back seat of his Ford Falcon.

There were a lot of teens at the club, more boys than girls, and no band but those playing on the stereo record player with big speakers. Boys and girls hugged the walls, working up the courage to get on the floor as Grace Slick sang "Somebody to Love."

Duncan sipped pink punch as he scanned the girls in the room. He and Randy made observational comments while pretending not to be nervous. First, Kevin got a girl to dance with him, and then Lee did as well. Watching them dance made him feel like a coward, and he wondered why it was more frightening to ask a girl to dance than to rob a store.

"Derring-do," he said to Randy, walking across the floor toward a girl he had been eyeing for a while. She was pretty in her white blouse and knee-length green skirt, and her long brown hair descended in waves to her shoulders. Brown eyes from beneath bangs watched him approach. Her posture was like a soldier's at attention, and he thought the petrified look on her face matched how he felt.

"DoYouWantToDance," he said. Her hesitation made his heart sink, but then she nodded rapidly, and he took her offered hand to join the growing crowd on the floor.

They started with "Jumpin' Jack Flash," which helped melt some of their tension. And really got going with "Born to be Wild" and laughed as they grooved to Tommy

James and the Shondells belting out "Mony Mony." They got totally loose, and the crowd of teens yelled and cheered to Sly and the Family Stone's awesome "Dance to the Music." Perhaps the chaperones thought the kids were getting too wild because the next song was Cherish by The Association, and he got to awkwardly slow dance with her.

Her name was Beth, and he said it was pretty because he had heard that in a movie once. She smiled. Soon she was laughing at his silly stories of beach antics and a recent fishing trip gone wrong. Her sweet laugh was like a finch's song in spring.

It's likely the dance organizers had in mind a pleasant, chaste affair. The attendees, however, seemed to see it as a make-out vector. Flash-in-the-pan couples drifted away in various directions, not to be seen again for many songs.

At a break in the dancing, with more punch in their hands serving as props, he asked, "Want to go outside?"

"OK."

He took her hand, and they strolled down the sidewalk to the rear of the club. His heart was pounding. He wanted to kiss her but was at a loss on how or when to make such a move.

"Where do you live?" he asked.

"Los Gatos."

"Oh." It surprised and disappointed him that she lived so far away. Just when he was feeling truly stupid while looking for a private place among the landscaping, a voice whispered, "Duncan, over here." It was Kevin, standing at the door of a school bus parked behind the club. He and Beth approached. The bus sat under big trees in the dark.

"If you want to make-out, come in."

He felt the heat of a blush, gratefully hidden by the shadows. He looked at Beth, and she gave a little nod. Two other couples were inside the bus: Kevin and a girl with big eyes that glowed luminously in the dark, and another boy and girl he did not know. He took Beth to the back, and they sat on the wide seat. The awkward moment stretched, and there was a great risk that he would blurt what many virginal boys might blurt at the moment of truth, "Hey, have you ever laughed so hard milk came out your nose?" or "What do you think about the Baltimore Colts?"

They both stared forward, and she was clearly waiting for him to do something. Since he couldn't think of anything to say that wasn't stupid, he took her hand and leaned slowly toward her, anxious that he might be rebuffed, but she parted her lips and he gently kissed her. He drew back to see if that was OK. It was, as her eyes remained closed and her face waiting. He kissed her again and remembered how Connie had kissed him with supple lips that reached to say something exciting. As they continued kissing, she responded; he could feel her heat and the shallow, rapid turn of her breathing. At one point, she tilted her head back as if offering her neck, and so he kissed her there several times along the white, smooth, pulsing surface. And then he did not know what else to do. He had an erection that ached, and he half-hoped and half-feared that she would find it. But he was also on a bus with other teens, so he hesitated. Beth took his hand and lifted it to one of her breasts. He gasped a little, kissed her again, and squeezed and caressed the fullness in his hand. He was sure he was being a klutz. Was he doing it too hard, too soft? Does she like this? Her answer was a sigh and a fierce return kiss. After a while longer, just as he was again wondering what else to do, and the clamor from his groin was demanding action, she took his hand and put it under her blouse and did something that exposed her breast to his touch. Then, it was he who was breathing in shallow, rapid punctuation. He fondled her, and she twitched, so he lightened his touch and felt amazement that something could be so soft and silky. Her nipple was hard, and as he accidentally grazed it, she whispered, "Oh," and so he grazed it again and again. He wanted to touch more of her, and he let his hand drift down the rising and falling satin of her belly. She was panting, as was he. He put his hand on her thigh just above her knee.

Will she let me?

He kissed her again and hesitantly moved his hand up her thigh. She stiffened and abruptly sat upright. "I have to leave," she said. She looked frightened in the dim glow of a distant streetlight, so he pulled back at the sudden change.

She stood, repeated, "I have to go," and walked quickly to the door. She pushed the lever that opened it, frowned, said, "Sorry," and disappeared,

Only then did he realize that the other couples had already gone. He remained in the back in the dark for quite a while, wondering what he had done wrong.

***

He knew Kevin was delaying going home. He used to do the same thing when he was younger, and Ava was more fearsome to him. Once he had stayed out too late, he would rush to do something else to stay out later. His anxiety would build, and he would dash off to do something else, and his anxiety would grow even more. Only when all his friends had abandoned him, listening to the calls of their own fears, would he slowly return home to face the consequences.

"Maybe he's asleep," Duncan said.

"Maybe."

They were walking along Plateau Avenue through the quiet neighborhood. Only a distant barking dog disturbed the silence. At the corner of Woodrow, Kevin said, "He started drinking again. Hasn't hit me, but he's been giving me ugly looks."

"You can go in quiet; maybe he won't notice."

"Maybe."

Soon, they stood on the walk outside his house. A dim light could be seen through the kitchen's side window. "Come in with me, OK? I don't think he'll do anything if you're there."

He thought of how Leon had nearly killed them but said, "Sure."

They opened and closed the gate with just the slightest of creaks. Kevin tested the door. Locked. He opened it with his key. The door seals parted with what seemed a loud swish, but the front room was dark, and at first, they did not see Leon sitting in the recliner.

They froze.

Leon was still, and he heard heavy breathing. Kevin eased the door closed, and they carefully stepped across the carpet to the hall that led to Kevin's bedroom. They were nearly there, and Duncan felt safety was at hand when Leon's voice boomed,

"Kevin! C'mere."

"I'm here with Duncan, just a little late."

"Kevin! Get your ass in here, now!" The command had the off-pacing and slurred intonations of the deeply drunk.

"But Duncan..."

"He can wait. Move it."

Kevin turned to comply, and Duncan moved with him, but Kevin put up a hand to say no. Duncan frowned and reluctantly mouthed, "OK." Kevin walked down the dark hall to face the beast in his lair. Duncan entered the bedroom and turned on all the lights. He left the door open and stood at the doorway, listening.

"Closer," Leon said.

He only heard snippets of a long rant: "Don't do what you're told...Won't put up with it...If it weren't for Mary, you'd be...No more fucking with me, by God...You're just a little shit who costs more than..."

Then there were a series of what sounded like questions, but he could not hear any answers from Kevin. Then,

"Answer me, or do I have to..."

"Don't hit me!"

It was the first reply he heard Kevin make.

"Don't."

Then he heard a smack like a mallet on meat and what sounded like a grunt from Kevin. There was another smack, then a scream. At first he thought Mary had come home to the brutal scene, but it was Kevin who had screamed. Duncan started down the hall.

Kevin screamed again, but it sounded like rage, not fear. He yelled, "I hate you! I hate you!" followed by another sound like someone punching a wet towel. Leon roared, and Kevin appeared in the light from the bedroom, running like he was fleeing rabid dogs. Duncan stepped aside and followed him in. Kevin slammed the door and fumbled the little slide-bolt lock into place. There was another roar from the man in the house.

"Help me!" Kevin said as he began pushing his dresser in front of the door. They got it in place as Leon banged on the door, tried to open it, and roared again,

"Open this door, goddammit!"

The boys frantically added chairs, the little desk and even piles of clothes to bolster a child's dresser. Duncan was so afraid that he grabbed everything at hand to build a barrier between them and what sounded like King Kong on the other side of a thin wooden wall.

They jumped back as Leon, in his fury, pounded and pushed against the lock. He threatened the worst beating of Kevin's life if the door was not opened NOW. Neither boy spoke. They stood side-by-side, mouths open. Duncan trembled.

There was another inarticulate bellow and a loud bang as if he had kicked at the obstruction; it burst the lock from the molding. A crack split the white paint on the door panel, and the dresser moved. Another BAM splintered the center of the door, and the dresser nearly toppled.

Kevin ran to the window, threw it open, said, "Come on, come on," and ducked out. He followed and dove into the bushes in the bed outside. He winced as a branch carved a gash across his ribs and hit bare dirt, then lawn. Kevin was already opening the gate.

They ran down Woodrow toward the ocean. He was sure he had never run that fast in his life. With silent agreement they made for The Cup and got down in the dark with sure feet and hands. Once seated, they pressed their backs against the cliff wall, panting.

The tide was high, and the surf large. The waves smashing into the cliff sent tremors through the sandstone. White spray shot up in front of them like a heavy curtain that fell and was replaced soon after. It was cool but not cold, and his shivering was neither from the cold nor the mist. They huddled there for a few minutes and said little except, "Holy shit," and "Will he come looking?"

A few cars passed by up on West Cliff Drive. In addition to the Bonneville, Leon had a Chevy Suburban that he used for work. It had one of those exterior searchlights the driver could maneuver from inside the vehicle. As they continued to hide, the lights of a car slowly coming down Woodrow brilliantly illuminated a wall of spray. Duncan had a feeling and started to rise.

Kevin grabbed him and said, "Don't, he'll see you."

The car stopped at the West Cliff stop sign, less than a hundred feet away. There it sat for several minutes. Then the headlights panned left toward the route to the lighthouse. Duncan relaxed as the engine sound diminished. Then they saw that searchlight flashing along the cliff tops to their left and over the water. Not long after, the car returned, and the light lingered slowly over the cliff top above them and onto the rocks and waves beyond. It moved on and did not return.

Even though the crashing surf was loud, and they knew they could not easily be seen, they waited for a dozen minutes and said nothing or even moved. Duncan eventually calmed and looked at the shadowed face, which he could see pretty well with his dark-adapted eyes. Kevin let out a big breath and pulled a fresh pack of Marlboro's from his shirt, smacked it over and over against one hand, compressing the tobacco more than needed. He opened it and offered one to Duncan. He took one for himself and lit each one with the steel-cased lighter he had lifted last summer.

After they had smoked for a minute, Duncan asked, "What happened?"

"He hit me," Kevin took a long drag, released, "I hit him back, right in the face."

He was astonished. "You hit Leon, you hit Leon?"

"Yeah, popped him good too, just as he was drawing back to bash me again." He sighed and said, "But it probably felt like a flea bite to him."

"Fuckin' A, Kevin. He scares the shit out of me."

"Yeah, me too. I couldn't stand it anymore, being afraid all the time. My dad...well, you just don't let people hit you. You don't."

For a long time, he marveled at his friend's bravery and the strength of his heart. His cigarette died, half-smoked, between his fingers as he saw that Kevin was at the end of a road. He flicked the acrid smoldering filter away as the other boy said something buried in the roar of the surf.

"What?"

"I can't go back."

He nodded and asked for a replacement smoke. Relit, he took a deep drag and blew a jet of smoke into the breeze coming in off the sea, where it was blasted apart like a flock of birds being fired upon.

Softly, barely audible, Kevin said as if speaking to himself, "I can't go back."

Duncan let another draw of smoke escape from his lips, said, "Yeah," and frowned, "Yeah."

"Been thinking about leaving."

"Leave? Where to?"

"Canada."

"Canada!?"

"Yeah, someplace he can't find me."

"But Canada? That seems, uh, far."

"Naw, it's not so far. It'll be easy. Just hitch, and we'll be there in no time. We could get in with no trouble. I hear Canada is great."

Kevin spoke glowingly about a place called Vancouver, like it was a golden land of freedom, beauty and safety. As he talked, his cigarette hand waved, and the bright, red dot of burning leaves traced patterns of hope in the night air.

Duncan had heard the *we* and watched the silhouette of his friend as he grew in certainty and enthusiasm. "It'll be a great adventure," he finished. For some minutes, neither spoke. Duncan gazed across the bay at the smudge of lights in far-off Monterey.

"Would you come with me?" Kevin asked, voice tremulous.

Duncan glanced at the remains of his cigarette and flicked it into the blast of the latest wave. He had already decided a minute before but hesitated before saying, "Sure, let's go to Canada."

They laughed, almost gleefully.

"Canada," Duncan said like he was saying, China.

"Canada," Kevin said like he was saying, sanctuary.

"Doesn't it get cold there?"

"Yeah, some, bring a coat. I've got it all worked out."

"When?"

"Tomorrow."

"OK, tomorrow."

"Derring-do."

"Yep, derring-do."

71

Mid-morning the next day, the two boys, in blue jeans and T-shirts, had their thumbs out where Highway One intersected Mission.

"We can't say we're going to Canada," Duncan said.

"Yeah, no shit. Where then?"

"We pick a town up the road a ways. When we get there, we pick another."

"That should work, but it's got to be far enough so we get long rides and not a bunch of short ones."

"Uh-huh, something at least fifty, maybe a hundred miles away." They agreed on San Francisco for their first leg.

The night before, they had waited in The Cup for a long time. Mist from the surf and juice from the crushed ice plant they had sat on chilled them, but they wanted to be sure Leon had given up. Then Kevin alarmed him when he said he wanted to return to Leon's and get stuff hidden in the garage. Duncan had waited in the bushes at the foot of the driveway while Kevin slipped inside. He got his money, a sleeping bag and other things he did not detail.

Kevin had slept under the portico at The Circle Church. Carrying his bag, clothes and all his money from his sock safe, Duncan found him there early the next morning. He was sitting on his rolled-up sleeping bag, sipping OJ and munching on a donut from the market across the street. They walked to the TG&Y, where they bought rain ponchos, a flashlight, a cheap blanket, and two cloth laundry bags to put everything in. At the Safeway they bought food and drinks for the road.

Duncan felt so exposed at the busy corner with the stuffed white bags at their feet. He and Kevin studied each car that passed by, fearing one would be mad-Leon.

"Let's take any ride we can get," said Kevin. "We have to get out of SC."

Duncan nodded and silently begged every approaching car, *please*.

"What if people ask why we're going to wherever?" Kevin asked.

"How about to visit relatives?"

"Good, but only if they ask."

They were saved by a long-haired guy named Bill, who stopped for them in his powder-blue Volvo.

"San Francisco?" they asked.

"Nope, San Jose."

They got in, but Duncan did not fully relax until miles later, as the car slalomed back and forth over the dangerous curves of Highway 17, when he allowed himself to believe that they were free and safe.

Without Bill asking, Kevin excitedly spun a story about how they were going to visit his dad in San Francisco. It was a surprise. They would go sailing on the bay, and Kevin added many other impromptu details neither had discussed. Duncan joined in, adding details like Kevin's father was a lawyer and how he had a big house. Kevin said he lived with his mom as his parents were separated. His eyes misted as he said it, and Duncan was impressed that his friend was such a good actor. The effusive excitement of the boy's story had the driver nodding and smiling.

Bill let them out at the 101 interchange. Kevin said they could take it all the way to Seattle. With the bags over their shoulders, they ran to a good spot on the 101 North on-ramp. They cheered, they laughed.

"We're going! We're going!" Kevin shouted over the incredible din of traffic, much thicker and faster than in Santa Cruz. Their smiles would not quit as they gyrated and danced while thrusting thumbs out to approaching cars.

Two women in a Chevy gave them a ride to Palo Alto, and three women in a VW bus got them to San Francisco. For Duncan it was a wondrous journey. He had only been to the Bay Area twice before, once when very young to visit his Nana when she lived in Richmond and then at the train station when they had arrived in 1964, but that was at night, and he had seen little. But this trip presented endless marvels, like the P3 Orion sub-hunter aircraft flying out of Moffett Field and its enormous hanger, the bay itself, cities that went on and on, the San Francisco airport, and beautiful San Francisco, all hilly and seemingly old.

"We're going to drive over the Golden Gate," Kevin said. He had seen it once, but Duncan had only seen pictures.

"Could we walk across it?"

"I guess so."

Getting to San Francisco was one thing; getting through it was another. The VW ladies confused both boys by letting them out on a street named Van Ness.

"But where's the 101?" Kevin asked.

"Van Ness is 101," said the shotgun lady.

"What?" Kevin asked, "But it's just a big street."

"Yes, it's like this for a few miles that way," she pointed north up the straight Boulevard, "then it jags left toward the bridge."

Kevin looked as dubious as Duncan felt.

"Don't sweat it," she said. "Just follow the signs. The left is at Lombard." She smiled. "Bye, boys." The bus put-putted a block and made a U-turn.

"Shit," Duncan said.

"This map doesn't say the freeway turns into a street."

Duncan pointed at a 101 sign stuck on a light pole. "Seems she's right."

They looked about. It was a sketchy neighborhood with wide, empty sidewalks in a sparse mixture of commercial and light industrial buildings. Moderate traffic zipped by in both directions. They stuck out their thumbs and did not get any takers for too long, so they began walking while thumbing, hoping for a safer-feeling area.

"Where do we say we're going next?" Duncan asked.

"Santa Rosa."

They walked over a mile before a young man and woman (Kevin called them hippies) gave them a lift in a VW Beetle. Each fender had been hand-painted, alternating blue and yellow. They would only take them as far as San Rafael. The back seat of the "Bug" was cramped and uncomfortable, but he did not mind. The Golden Gate Bridge was even more beautiful and wondrous than he had imagined. Big ships and little sailboats plied the deep blue water far below as they passed under the enormous towers.

They waved back at the friendly people waving to them from the departing VW.

"Now where?"

Kevin studied the map and measured with his fingers. "Healdsburg."

They were lucky as they got a ride quickly. The man in the Ford truck said he was going to Geyserville, close to their destination. In those days, Healdsburg Avenue doubled as 101. The man said he had a few errands to do in Healdsburg and let them out along the business stretch of the highway.

"I'm hungry," Kevin said.

"Let's find a restaurant."

"There's an A&W?"

"Something better, a real restaurant, so we can eat steak and mashed potatoes and have chocolate cake."

They walked two blocks before finding a promising sign: Lorna's Kitchen, Best Steaks in Sonoma County. The bell on the door jingled as they entered. Only three of the dozen or so tables were occupied. Instead of the linen tablecloths Duncan envisioned, it had vinyl red and white checkerboard covers. A buxom woman in a calf-length white dress approached them; she eyed the full bags they carried.

"Are you here to eat, boys?"

"Yes," Kevin said.

"Can we get steaks?" Duncan asked.

"Sure, are your parents coming too?"

"No, they told us to go eat while they did some errands. We're on our way to Portland."

"Uh-huh, steaks cost more than burgers. Did they give you money?"

Duncan reached into his pocket and produced two twenties. "Well, I guess they did. OK, pick a table, and I'll come back with menus."

They took one near a window, far from the other diners. Kevin leaned close to his ear before they sat down. "Boy, you sure lie smooth," he said.

"I don't see how it matters whether our parents are coming if we have money to pay. Besides, now that we are on our own, we better get good at lying, or some nosy adult will get us sent back."

"Right on."

She said her name was Trina as she put glasses of ice water covered in dew on the table. She then handed them menus that opened like books.

"What's the best steak?" Duncan asked.

She thought a bit and said, "Well, we have T-bones, rib eyes and filet mignon."

"Which one costs more?"

"The Filet Mignon. It's $4.95, comes with mashed potatoes or country fries, green beans and salad. At dinner hour, we have baked potatoes, but it's too early for that."

"I want that. Can I get chocolate cake?"

She looked up from her pad and pen; her mouth opened but then closed. Perhaps she was remembering the $40. She wrote Duncan's order down and looked up. "We have German Chocolate."

"I want that."

"OK."

"And a big glass of milk."

"Uh-huh, anything else?"

"Coffee."

The pen wavered. "OK," she said, wrote it down and had Duncan tell her how he wanted his steak.

"More?" she asked.

"No."

Kevin said he did not like steak and chose the barbecue chicken dinner plus apple pie with ice cream.

"You want coffee too?" she asked.

"Ick, no."

After Trina left, Kevin asked, "Since when do you like coffee?"

He shrugged. "Older people drink it all the time."

"It's bitter."

He shrugged again. "When do we get to Vancouver?"

Kevin pulled the map out of his bag and studied it awhile. It showed the Western States of America. "I don't know, I guess tomorrow."

"Cool, where next?"

"Uh, the rest of California looks like tiny towns like this one, but there's a place called Crescent City that must be bigger. It's next to Oregon." He checked a chart on the map and said, "288 miles. Let's see if we can get a ride all the way there."

"Yeah, let's keep hitching 'til we do."

"Be halfway if we can."

Trina plopped two salads on the table, each with three cherry tomatoes on top. Duncan popped a tomato into his mouth and crushed the juice out of it. He watched a young couple with a little girl in tow enter and be shown their seats. Outside, it was a warm, sunny day, and people strolled by about their business. He realized he was smiling. He looked at Kevin and saw he was too. Their smiles were small, just the corners of their mouths pushed upward by the bubbles of gladness within.

"Fuck, Leon," Duncan whispered.

Kevin nodded and smiled bigger. "Yeah, fuck him."

"We'll be in Canada before he gets over his hangover."

"Yep."

"Now we can do anything."

"Yep."

"Go anywhere."

"We're free."

"Totally."

And they were laughing hard when Trina arrived with her arms full of steaming plates. The steak was wrapped in bacon. The red-brown juices oozed out and colored his potatoes as he sliced off a bite. It was tender and more delicious than anything he had ever tasted. Kevin, his mouth smeared with sauce, raved about the chicken. They shared food and declared that all of it, even the salads, was wonderful, great and the best. The pie was thick with perfect apples, and the three-layer cake slice was tall and thick with frosting.

Duncan loved the coffee. Kevin took a sip, pronounced it very fine and ordered his own. They had refills, and as the caffeine kicked in, they chattered praises for Trina, the restaurant, the lovely town filled with nice-looking people, and for everything.

Then, with their plates scraped clean and only the salads not finished, Duncan said, "People leave money on the table."

"Yeah, it's a tip. Didn't you see when we were at Malio's?"

"Uh-uh, What for?"

"Dunno, but everyone seems to do it."

"Huh. How much?"

"Dunno." He thought a little. "I guess it depends on how much you liked the food."

Trina gave Duncan the bill, which was about $12. He put a twenty on the table and said, "I have to use the can."

"Me too."

They left their bags and found the restroom. When they came back, their change was waiting. Duncan left it all, and they carried their bags to the door. Trina went to their table and called to them, "Hey, boys, don't forget your money."

They turned, and Duncan said, "No, it's a tip; we really liked the food."

Her lips parted, and her eyebrows came together as she examined the bills and coins. She bit her lower lip as if troubled, and then her face cleared. She glowed at them and said, "Thanks, boys!"

They agreed to walk far enough away so no one from the restaurant could see them hitchhiking. "Was that enough?"

"Sure, a lot, but it was a great meal."

72

The boys sauntered up the street. Duncan's bag felt lighter than before despite the contents being unchanged. They lingered at shop windows just to linger, not because they wanted anything. He was eager to get to Canada, but the day felt too fine to hurry. Soon, they were past the shops and the hotels, and only a Shell gas station remained in the line of commercial buildings. This was good as he felt the cumulative pressure of a big glass of milk, a glass of water and three cups of coffee.

"I gotta piss again."

"Me too," Kevin said.

Business done, they returned to the side of the road. He noticed a white Ford Fairlane southbound among the light traffic because the two men within were looking at them. The car continued into the town. A light breeze stirred the large-leafed trees that crowded the few pine trees across the road.

"You think it snows a lot in Vancouver?" Kevin asked.

"Probably, it sure did in Minnesota, and that was near Canada, not in it."

"Good we're going in July, I guess. We can buy better clothes and coats when we get there."

Duncan nodded and wondered if getting a ride in Healdsburg might take longer than it had farther south. Santa Cruz and San Francisco had a lot more hippies driving around.

The Ford Fairlane passed them northbound. When the passenger glanced their way, he nodded and smiled. Not far up the road, the car turned right.

"If we don't like Vancouver, we could try Seattle," Kevin said.

"Would make it easier for Leon to find you."

"Yeah, he won't find us in Canada, but maybe we could live up there for a year and come back to the US."

Duncan did not reply. He was musing on the bodysurfing possibilities that might exist so far north when the same white Ford pulled over about thirty feet up the road. They ran to it and opened the rear door. Two young men were sitting up front. Both were white and in their early twenties. They wore tight white T-shirts and blue jeans. The driver had a bit of a James Dean thing going, including the quiff hairdo and a pack of cigarettes trapped in a sleeve. His passenger looked fresh out of the Army with his butch hair and heavily muscled arms. Duncan would end up thinking of them as Jimmy and Joe.

"Where you boys headed?" asked Joe.

"We want to get to Ukiah," Kevin said. Duncan twitched but did not question the sudden change from Crescent City.

The two men looked at each other and smiled. Jimmy answered, "Hey, that's where we're going. Get in." They did, putting their bags on the floor next to their feet. Jimmy waited for a few cars to pass and then reentered the lane.

Joe had his arm up on the seat back so he could easily look at his hitchhikers. "Why are you going to Ukiah?"

"To visit my dad," Kevin said.

"You don't live with your dad?"

"Not now, just my mom. They're separated."

"Uh-huh, where's your mom?"

"Santa Rosa."

"Uh-huh. She doesn't mind you hitchhiking?"

"Didn't tell her, just left a note."

"Uh-huh. Won't she miss you, get upset?"

"She works. I'll call once I see Dad."

"Uh-huh. Works all day then?"

"Yeah."

"Uh-huh. Does your dad know you're coming?"

"No, it's a surprise." Kevin had said that before, but it felt wrong to Duncan this time.

"Uh-huh."

Jimmy and Joe exchanged looks that said they both felt satisfied. Duncan realized he was scratching his hand repeatedly. Other folks maybe asked one or two questions, but they didn't pump them for information. It felt like Joe was checking off boxes on a list.

Joe lit a cigarette and let the smoke flow from his nose into the back seat. "Bet you boys can't keep the girls off you."

It wasn't a question. Duncan and Kevin said nothing. Joe turned to Jimmy, asked, "Whatcha think? These boys' hot meat for the girls?"

Jimmy laughed harshly, assessing the boys in the rearview like a raptor eyeing rabbits. Long, tense moments passed before he replied, "Yep, I bet the girls love'em."

"Do the girls love you?" Joe asked.

Duncan forced himself to stop scratching but started tapping a foot, but he had no answer. Neither did Kevin. Joe leaned over the seat back a bit and spoke in a soft, confidential tone, "You know what I think? I think it's your lips. You both have really nice lips, especially you," he said to Duncan. "Girls like nice lips to kiss." To Jimmy, he added, "Isn't that right?"

Jimmy coughed that same mallet on wet wood smack, said, "That's right. Girls would want to kiss those lips all night long."

Joe nodded. "I bet they would."

Duncan forced himself to stop tapping but started scratching, then stopped that too. For some reason, he dared not look at Kevin. He kept his eyes on Joe but had no idea how to answer. How he answered, if he answered, felt extremely important. Then, the tension seemed to dissolve when Joe whooped and smacked the seat.

"Relax, I'm only joshing you." To Jimmy, he said, "I got them squirming, didn't I?"

"That you did," Jimmy said as he looked into Duncan's eyes and barked a laugh that didn't change his eyes. "He was just kidding. You boys want a cigarette?"

Duncan and Kevin quickly said, "No."

They drove in fearful silence for a few minutes and entered a little town named Geyserville. Duncan released a breath he had not realized he was holding. He chanced a look at Kevin, whose return stare was like a sprinter's poised for the starting gun. He caught a look that the men on the front seats gave each other. It felt like a decision.

Jimmy cleared his throat and said, "Say, uh, I need to make a little detour to take care of something. It won't take long. That OK?"

Duncan heard himself say, "OK."

The man turned off onto a road that went south—no other cars were in sight. It felt like the time to do something had arrived. He was thinking hard for a way out.

I gotta be cool.

He made himself relax, leaned back in the seat, let his head lie back as if bored, and said to Kevin, "How does your dad like being a cop up in such a small town?"

Smooth as an ice cream sundae and just as chill, Kevin replied, "Oh, he likes it. Likes the other cops and thinks he can get promoted quicker there than down in Santa Rosa."

"You really don't think he'll be mad we hitched?"

"He'll be mad, all right." Kevin inserted a real-like laugh. "Chew me out, no doubt, but he'll be mostly happy. He likes you too."

"Cool."

Kevin pulled a pack of Marlboro's from his bag and said to the men, "OK if we smoke? We brought our own."

Jimmy squinted hard at the road, even though they were driving in shadow. Joe stared at Jimmy. A few heartbeats stomped by, and Jimmy said, "Sure, that would be fine. Light up."

Kevin offered Duncan an extended cigarette from the pack, and they lit them and blew smoke out cracked-open windows. The men were taking them on a narrow road that followed a crease between two clumps of low hills. The rough terrain held random mixes of pine trees, spring-green leafed trees, brush and rocks. The road curved west. Open grassy fields were on their left, and hills were on their right—they were driving through a wilderness.

The boys and the men smoked, the former with feigned casual ease, the latter with short, nervous puffs. After rounding a curve, Jimmy gunned the car and 300 feet later slid to a stop at a dirt and gravel turnoff.

"Get out," he said.

"What?" Duncan asked.

"GET. THE. FUCK. OUT."

They grabbed their bags and ejected themselves out of their doors. The Fairlane did a U-turn and sped away. The boys watched it disappear around the turn. He looked at Kevin, exhaling like wind sighing through trees.

"We have to get off this road," Kevin said.

"Why?"

"Any minute now, they might figure out we were bullshitting them and come back to get us."

"Oh crap, yeah."

They pushed between two large scratchy bushes at the foot of the hills and headed up the slope, running in the zigzags required by the density of trees and scrub. Far across the valley of grass behind them were a couple of houses, too far to help. He glanced over his shoulder as they ran. Occasional gaps in the forest showed the road below. Kevin had been right; a few minutes into their sprint, he spied the Ford Fairlane coming back.

"Down!" he said. They dropped and panted, Duncan telling Kevin what he saw. They could not risk looking, so they lay low and listened. A minute passed, then two, then more. Somewhere below, he heard two car doors slam. Then, nothing for a while.

"Hey, boys!" A voice that sounded like Jimmy's shouted. "Come on out. We didn't mean to scare you. Come on, we'll take you to Ukiah."

They were probably five hundred feet off the road and a hundred feet higher than the men. Their pursuers sounded like they had parked short of where they had put the boys out. Still, neither boy moved or even whispered. They waited and waited.

"It's a long hike back to the highway, you know. Don't be stupid. Come on down, and we'll be friends again. Take you to your dad."

They waited.

Unintelligible sounds of what sounded like arguing filtered through the trees. Then, one of the men shouted, "You stupid shits. We came back to help you, but OK, last chance, we're leaving."

They waited.

Doors slammed louder than before. The car engine revved, followed by a short screech of tires slipping on asphalt. Duncan looked at Kevin. He moved his head to say no. They waited. There might have been the faintest note of brakes squeaking, but he could not be sure.

They waited.

Then, from a place farther up the road, Jimmy yelled, "Fuck you!"

Car doors slammed again, and the faint sound of tires rolling faded gradually away to where they had first come. They waited a few minutes more before rising and heading further up the hill.

"Let's get to the top and see if we can see where we are," Kevin said.

It was a short, easy climb to the summit. They found a trail that might have run along the ridge line. The problem was that it paralleled the highway, which they could see a mile or two to the north.

"If we go down now, we might run into those two creeps again," Duncan said.

Kevin nodded. "Yeah."

"How about we make our way down, get closer, and see if there's a safe place to hitch?"

"Yes, if not, maybe we can find somewhere to sleep and go early tomorrow."

Decision made, they sought out routes down the rugged slope. Duncan felt his hope crashing.

How did this go from great to scary bummer so fast?

They wandered through strange woods, and it was a hard hike over rough ground with no trails. And they had no water. The one Mountain Dew from his bag was emptied at the crest.

As the late afternoon light dimmed, he wondered what kinds of animals roamed those woods. Other than birds, they had not seen any.

"Hey, look," Kevin said, pointing. The trees had thinned as they descended, and a two-story house stood in a large clearing. They went closer.

"See anyone?" Duncan asked.

"Nope."

They discussed what to do. On the one hand, it would be a relief to get out of the woods, but if anyone was home and saw them emerge, they might call the cops. On the other hand, the light was fading. It was getting too late to hitch safely. They surveyed the property from the perimeter while they stayed behind the tree line.

"Looks empty," Kevin said.

"Yeah, I think so."

"I bet their road goes right down to the highway, can't be more than half a mile. Let's sleep here."

"Get in the house?"

"Naw, we shouldn't break into anybody's house, but maybe in that would be OK." He pointed at a low, red-painted outbuilding about sixty feet from the house with a slanted roof. Next to it was a little corral without an occupant. They descended warily, and it was twilight when they reached the long shed. It was unlocked, and they stooped a little to go inside. It had a dirt floor and few contents: an old shovel, a pitchfork, a pickax, a half-full bag of fertilizer, a wheelbarrow missing a wheel and stacks of weathered boards.

"Maybe nobody lives here," Kevin said.

"Yeah."

Near the house they found water from a hand-pumped well. They looked through the windows. Though it had some furniture, the house showed no other signs of habitation. In the dwindling light, they drank water from the Mountain Dew bottle and finished off the potato chips and the Three Musketeers bars. All they had was a flashlight to see by. They put the blanket on the dirt and would use the sleeping bag for warmth.

As Duncan sat on a bag of fertilizer, he felt bone-tired and angry about something he wasn't sure about. Had it really been less than twenty-four hours since they escaped out Kevin's window? Canada seemed a million miles away from a shed with a dirt floor in the middle of nowhere.

Why did I agree to come here?

He watched Kevin take his shoes off in the glow of the flashlight and remembered why.

But he was still angry. "What did you do to be sent to Leon?"

Kevin put his shoes aside and sat cross-legged on the blanket. "I told you not to ask me that."

"We're running from Leon and were running from those two guys. Why is it such a big secret?"

"I'm not going to talk about it."

"I want to know."

"Tough."

His anger flared, flirting with that rage that might come. "What's the big fucking deal? Just tell me."

The other boy stood and clenched his fists. "It's none of your damn business."

Duncan remained seated. "But I'm your friend."

"I'm never going to talk about it. Never." Kevin shouted, and his hands remained clenched. In the dim light, they glared at each other. Duncan's frustration simmered in his guts. He looked away, turned and said, "Screw this, I have to piss." He got up, went out, and tried to slam the door, but it stuck on a dirt clod.

He peed behind a tree, no longer worried about wolves or bears. He remained outside while night settled in, loving the brilliant stars in the black sky. Finally, the cold drove him inside. Kevin was under the spread-out bag on his side, facing away. He removed his shoes and got in, pulling the covering over himself and putting his back to Kevin.

He lay in that silence until his tiredness reached up and overcame the anger and acid of their fight. He figured Kevin was asleep and was near nodding off when Kevin softly spoke,

"I didn't do anything. Remember that day at the park when you jumped off the high stump? When we split up, and I went home, I…" He paused, and Duncan heard him pull a sharp breath. "… I found Mommy on the kitchen floor. She was jerking and twitching. Her eyes all messed up; blood splattered on the floor. She had bitten part of her tongue off. I didn't know what to do. I called Dad; he said he'd get an ambulance. I held her and I talked to her as those damn jolts seized her. She couldn't hear me. Her eyes looked everywhere but at me. The jerking stopped, and she finally turned her eyes to me, but it was like she was blind. The ambulance came and Dad too…but three months later…" He was silent for a long time. Duncan listened to the moaning of the wind through the trees and wondered if Kevin would say more, then, "three months later she was dead. Cancer ate her brain."

He stopped, his breath a series of sharp, short intakes and shuddering releases, and Duncan thought that was all, but he continued, "Dad lost it; he loved her so much. I…, well, he got fired. He barely left her side after I found her. All our money went to the doctors and them taking pictures and medicines that didn't do shit except shrivel her and make her skin ugly.

"She had so much pain. They kept her drugged most of the time, but when she woke, she sometimes tried to go without the morphine, and even though I could see the agony in her eyes, she always had a smile for me. Mom was tough.

"One day, Dad got into a fight with some dude at that bar up on Nine. He said the guy insulted Mommy's memory. Cops said he beat the guy to death. But *he* said the guy fell and hit his head. They still convicted him of something called manslaughter. He is doing five years at Folsom. He won't let me see him, says it's no place for a boy.

"They put me in Juvie for a few weeks. Then they gave me to Leon and Mary." Kevin's voice sounded calm by the end. Duncan lay in the dark with him, his mind emptied of thought. Then he realized Kevin's shoulders were shaking, and his stifled weeping was a repetitive pulse of pain. Duncan's tears rolled over the contours of his face as he listened. He had an impulse to hug Kevin but hesitated. He settled for reaching out a hand to rest on his friend's back, but Kevin shrugged it off, so he lay there with him until the shaking and the staccato bursts of grief stopped.

"I'm sorry," Duncan said.

At some point, they both fell asleep.

73

Duncan woke up hungry. Kevin wasn't to be seen. Sunlight penetrated the cracks in the walls and gaps around the door, making dust beams that sparkled in the mostly dark. He found Kevin out by the well pump, munching on something and gazing toward the far side of a valley partially visible through the trees.

"Hey," Duncan said.

"Hey, found some jerky at the bottom of my sack." He offered the open cellophane bag with several pieces in it.

"Thanks." He bit off a chunk, put the rest in a pocket and splashed water on his face from the pump.

"It's pretty here," Kevin said, "not like Santa Cruz, drier, but pretty."

"Yeah, real pretty."

As they ate through the dried beef and drank lots of water, they talked about a lot of things: about who may have lived in the house and why they were not there, about whether it would get wetter the farther they went north, about which was the best rock band, Kevin said, the Rolling Stones, Duncan said, Led Zeppelin, about how they wanted to go a lot farther each day and get to Vancouver quickly, but not about their fears, not about their friends or family, and they did not talk about what Kevin had shared the night before.

"You were quick and smooth there in the car. Saved our ass," Kevin said.

"So were you."

Kevin chuckled and said, "Yeah, but I didn't see a way out until you spoke."

He acknowledged the compliment with a nod. "Let's get to Canada," he said.

On the way down the road, Kevin reached into his bag, pulled out a hand axe, and said, "If we run into those guys again, we do anything not to be taken, OK?"

He studied the weapon. It had a foot-long, burgundy-colored handle and a heavy blade with hints of rust. It could do wicked damage. He nodded and handed it back. "Yeah, no way we get in that car."

Kevin put the axe back in the bag, came out with another weapon, and gave it to Duncan. It was a small sledgehammer with an even shorter handle, maybe weighing two pounds. "You can have the axe if you want."

"Naw, that's OK. I'll fight with this."

It took nearly an hour to get to the highway. They ran across, but few cars seemed to be out. They were north of Geyserville but chose to walk and thumb toward Cloverdale, wanting to put distance between themselves and the creeps.

They were so used to readily getting rides that they did not expect to have to walk very far. Each car that approached was examined at a distance, and they were ready to bolt if it looked like *that car*. But vehicles came and went, and no one stopped.

"Maybe we look too ratty," Duncan said.

"Yeah, maybe, I'm kinda dirty."

The hours crept by, and their one source of water, the pop bottle, was empty. A car pulled over on the outskirts of Cloverdale. They ran to it, but Kevin said, "We're here. We need to eat and get stuff."

They had had their thumbs out by habit. They told the guy that they did not need a ride after all. He berated them and zoomed off, spraying gravel at them from his tires. At a gas station, they cleaned up as best they could and changed into their second set of clothes. They found a little café and stuffed themselves. They bought a couple of jugs with lids and filled them with water. They walked to the far end of the tiny town and stuck their thumbs out. Cars and trucks passed, some white and boxy like the Fairlane but without scary occupants, and no one stopped.

"Shit," Duncan said as another car leaving the town did not even slow down. "Where are we headed now?"

"Same, Crescent City, I figure."

"How far?"

"260, I think."

Finally, an old pickup truck pulled over. The man behind the wheel was a lot older than the truck. He wore a beaten, stained, wide-brimmed hat, and his salt-and-pepper whiskers looked a couple of weeks old. The truck was faded brick-red with many dings like craters on Mars, and the windshield consisted of two flat panes separated by a strip of chrome.

"Howdy, where ya going?" he asked out of a nearly toothless mouth and then smacked his gums.

"Crescent City," Duncan said.

The man looked through his windshield for a rather long time, apparently considering the momentous issue. Eventually, he said, "Well, not goin' that far, but I can take ya to Arcata."

Duncan looked at Kevin. "Is that anywhere near Crescent City?"

Kevin shrugged. The man at the wheel answered, "Be forty, maybe fifty miles short, I reckon."

They thanked him for the ride, slid onto the surprisingly comfortable cloth bench seat, and put their bags on the floor. The first thing he noticed was that the old guy was a cautious driver. He kept his speed below fifty. Other cars passed them, and it felt like they were crawling along. The second thing he noticed was that the old guy was uninterested in conversation. He mainly answered, yep, nope, or would grunt. A typical lengthy response was "still a ways" or "can't say that I have."

He and Kevin gave up after an hour. Sometimes he put the radio on, but always to country music, which sounded either terribly mournful or silly to Duncan. Kevin suggested they find a rock 'n' roll station. That was squashed with a simple, "Nope, ain't music."

Duncan decided he was not unfriendly; he would smile at them with gleaming eyes. It was just that he was quiet and maybe had no interest in talking to boys.

The hours dragged on, and the sun dropped toward the horizon. Spectacular mountains of water vapor bloomed in the sky, casting shadows on the hillsides. Shortly after the orange globe set and the clouds nearly filled the sky, raindrops began to play tunes on the metal roof and glass. Through the spattering, he saw the last of the sun's rays brilliantly lighting the slopes of low mountains ahead.

The truck's wipers were feeble and worn; they struggled to push the increasing rain off the glass. The man repetitively smacked his gums like an echo to the wipers. The metronome-like sounds pulled Duncan's exhausted mind and body into a heavy sleep.

A screech of brakes and Kevin's jab woke him up.

"This is as far as I can take ya."

He peered through the distorted, rain-bubbled windows at a two-lane road. They appeared to be at the end of a Highway 101 off-ramp.

"Here?" Kevin asked, his voice competing with the battering on the roof.

All was black except for a few distant lights and the slash of one car's headlights on the freeway. The rain had progressed from heavy to torrential.

"Yep, gotta get home up thataway," he said while pointing a limp, crooked finger toward a barely visible side road.

The boys looked at each other, their faces half-lit by reflections from the headlights and half-darkened by dismay. Kevin glanced at the rains' frenzied dance on the asphalt, looked at Duncan and shrugged *whatever*. They grabbed their bags from behind the seat, thanked the man, and stepped out into the cold and wet.

They got the rain ponchos on quickly, but they covered half-soaked clothes. The dim red of the truck's taillights disappeared behind dark water curtains. He and Kevin searched for signs to the Highway 101 North on-ramp. When they finally picked it out in the gloom, they ran. The ramp was a long curve descending from a bridge over the highway. They positioned themselves as best they could, but there was no cover. Already, they were sopping from the knees down. Not far away, but too far to walk, shone the lights of a small town. They presumed it was Arcata.

"Can you believe that old dude dropped us here when over there would've been somewhere dry to wait out the storm?" Kevin asked over the drumming of the rain.

Duncan could not bring himself to say the guy was mean, a jerk or anything bad. He just did not understand him.

Over the next half hour, two cars drove by without stopping. The rain was so heavy that he had to cup one hand over his nose and mouth to breathe. The only upside was the lack of wind. He stood in the rain for more miserable minutes as Kevin walked far up the ramp. Was he looking for cars? Through the curtain of water, he watched Kevin, and a chill filled him that was about more than the cold rain.

For the first time on this trip, he was unsure. He saw himself as small and weak, threatened by people and forces beyond him. And Kevin, shrunken by perspective, image blurred by the rain, appeared a specter fading away into the dark.

Kevin turned. A corona of bright yellow light blazed around him. Kevin angled toward the guardrail as a pickup truck rolled slowly down the ramp. They shouted and put out their thumbs. The truck passed Duncan and pulled over, brake lights glowing the red of rescue. Kevin had run, and they reached the truck together. They threw open the door, and the man inside asked, "Where are you going in this deluge?"

Simultaneously, Duncan said, "Crescent City," and Kevin said, "Portland."

"Get in," the man said.

They brought a few gallons of water with them in their clothes and on their ponchos, but the middle-aged man with his lined, concerned face did not seem to mind. "So, which is it?"

"Portland, sir," Duncan said, "I just thought Crescent City might be far enough for tonight."

"Well, boys, I can take you, but you're both soaked and cold to boot, I bet. I was going back to my house anyway. Let's get you dry, and I'll have Alice, who's my wife, give you some food and a hot drink before we go on. What do you say?"

He and Kevin exchanged looks.

"That would be welcome, sir. Thank you," Kevin said.

They drove for a few miles without speaking. Duncan was glad for the warmth of the heater. As they reached the first exit, the man glanced at their bags on his floor, asked, "What's in Portland?"

Kevin's response was delayed, but he eventually said in a tired voice, "My dad, sir. We're going to visit him."

"Yes?"

"He's a police officer. He and my mom are separated. It's a surprise." Kevin said it in a flat, obviously rehearsed tone over the noise of the torrential rain while they drove down a dark road that seemed like nowhere. Their story sounded to Duncan as phony as it was.

But the man nodded, said, "OK, we want to get you there safely. Let's go see Alice and a warm fire."

After another mile, they turned down a bumpy gravel road for a few hundred feet and stopped before his house. They ran to the door. The rain was lessening. Alice greeted them. Ernie, Alice called him, explained why they were there.

With but a moment's critical inspection of them and with a glance back at her husband, she said, "OK, let's get you into the toasty living room, and I'll whip up some food. How do ham sandwiches sound?"

"Great," they answered.

"Then some hot chocolate."

She led them into a strange living area. It was a couple of car lengths wide and three times as long, heated by three potbellied woodstoves spaced along the wall adjoining the kitchen. They had three children, two boys and a girl, who greeted them like visitors from Alpha Centauri.

Ernie excused himself. Alice fed them, and the kids watched them eat from the far end of the room. She had them remove their wet shoes and socks, which she put near one of the stoves. They visited the bathroom to change into their other pants, which were dirty but dryer.

Duncan felt happy, relieved and safe in their home. Kevin and he smiled at everyone. The three kids kept their distance and remained watchful and silent.

Halfway through his second cup of cocoa, he noticed the flashing red and blue lights outside the window. Ernie went to the front door. He and Kevin rushed to the window to see a man exiting the police car. Ernie let the officer in, and Alice flashed an apologetic look before she fled to the kitchen.

The boys didn't resist. They gathered their things, and the officer took them from the house. Ernie's last words were, "It's for the best, boys."

The officer did not handcuff them, only put them in the back. He asked, "You are runaways, aren't you?"

"Yes sir," they answered. The game was up.

He drove them not into Arcata but to Eureka and the central police station. He took them upstairs to a large room lit by fluorescent lights and filled with desks, only a couple of which were occupied. It was about midnight. He had forms to fill out. He asked many questions: name, address, age, parents' names and locations. The officer lifted his eyebrows when Kevin said, Folsom Penitentiary.

"Where were you going?" he asked. When they answered, Canada, his eyebrows went up again, and he asked, "Why?"

Kevin said, "Heard Vancouver is nice." It was flippant and clearly dissatisfying to the officer, but he did not press. Duncan volunteered nothing. It was Kevin's choice not to mention Leon's abuse.

He searched them and found the axe, the sledgehammer and the cash. He whistled and asked how they had gotten so much money. Their answers of jobs did not satisfy either, but again, he did not press. Finally, he left, and they were alone in the vast room.

Kevin started it. He looked at Duncan, and a snort escaped him. Duncan chuckled and smiled. Then Kevin laughed. So did he. Their laughter and grins bounced between them, growing in volume and width until they were howling and could hardly stay in their chairs. Several officers entered at the far end of the room, where they stayed and watched with puzzled or bemused expressions.

$$74$$

Their euphoria faded not long after the cell door clanged shut, but not because they were in a cell. After being on the road, run-ins with bad people, hiding in a shed, and the fierce storm, their inescapable room with its thin mattresses, toilet and stark interior design was welcome.

No, the high went poof when Kevin asked, "Who do you think will come and get us?"

They were sitting across from each other on the beds. Duncan thought about Ava and the 1953 Chrysler New Yorker she was currently driving, and then he scrunched his face and said, "Leon."

Kevin chewed on his index knuckle and lowered his head to stare at the floor.

"What if we told the cops here what he did?" asked Duncan.

"What are they going to do about it? Keep us here? Wouldn't believe me anyway. The cops would side with Leon, not the foster kid."

"I'd tell them."

"They wouldn't believe you either, Juvie boy. And I'll get extra bad beatings for causing trouble."

He could say nothing to that. They remained in glum silence for several minutes. Then Duncan said, "We need adult help, someone who will believe us and take your side."

"Yeah, like who?"

"Mrs. Kelly. She's good. She knows you; she'll help."

Kevin grew thoughtful and nodded. "She would, wouldn't she?"

"I'm sure."

Kevin brightened.

Duncan said, "And if that doesn't work, we'll run off again, just better."

It was late, and with some resolution achieved, they lay down to sleep. At no point had it occurred to Duncan to go to Ava.

The next morning, after a breakfast of scrambled eggs and toast, one of the officers came to their cell and said, "Your ride is here."

They were taken down a hall to another room with a wire cage. The man inside the cage gave them their possessions back and had them sign for them. Duncan was surprised that all the money was included. The custodial officer must have seen the astonished look on his and Kevin's faces as they fingered the cash.

"What? You thought we'd keep it?"

Cash in pockets, bags in hands, he and Kevin were escorted down another hall and up some stairs. With each step his feet felt heavier.

"C'mon, you two, hurry up. I would think you'd want to get out of here."

A few more stairs, and then he opened the door to what must have been the main entrance, a large room with a high counter with two police behind it, full of the morning sun. Instead of dreaded Leon standing in the lobby, Mary turned an anxious face upon the boys.

The officer had her sign something, and their escort said they could go. Mary rushed to Kevin, stooped, and wrapped him in a hug. "I was so worried about you. Are you OK?"

"I'm fine."

"Good, good." She looked at Duncan and asked, "And are you OK too?"

"Yes."

"Good."

"Is Leon here?" Kevin asked.

She grimaced, took a breath, lightly grasped Kevin's hands, and said gently, "Yes, let's go outside. We need to talk." She straightened and moved toward the door. Neither he nor Kevin followed. She turned back toward them.

"Is he going to hit me?" Kevin asked.

A hand flew to her opened mouth. "Oh, gosh, no, no, he's not going to hit you." She looked at Duncan. "No one's going to be hit. Come." And she moved toward the door again. One of the officers at the counter was busy writing something, but the other appeared to be carefully listening to their conversation. Duncan and Kevin remained rooted.

"Please, it'll be all right."

They followed her outside to an empty sidewalk. He wondered what their chances would be if they just ran. The way Kevin was scoping the area made him think he was wondering that too.

"We're parked around the corner. I had Leon stay in the car because he told me what happened. I'll want to hear your side. He's not going to hit you. There's not going to be any more hitting, I promise."

He was not convinced, and he doubted Kevin was either. Mary seemed sincere, but she had not been the one hitting, and tiny Mary wanting and big Leon complying were very different things. Yet, this was the wrong time and place to run.

"Please, come, we'll work things out. It'll be better."

After several more moments of hesitation, they followed her around the corner. A half-block down Leon stood on the sidewalk next to his 1964 Chevy Suburban. He appeared weary in blue jeans, a plaid shirt and an unshaven face. Being in Eureka midmorning meant they must have left Santa Cruz around 4 a.m. He and Kevin stopped twenty feet from the big man. Mary kept walking. A twitch of what looked like pain crossed Leon's face. He sighed, walked around the parallel parked truck, and got in the driver's seat. Mary opened the door and pulled the seatback forward so the boys could get in the back.

Leon pulled onto the street and said, "I'm relieved you're both safe."

They got on the 101 and drove along the coast past views of the bay and the spits of land just beyond. No one spoke. Leon focused on his driving. Mary wore a worried frown and kept glancing at Leon. The boys sat quietly in the back. Duncan was waiting for the big shoes to drop.

Sometime after leaving the ocean views behind, they turned inland and descended from low hills with a view of a small green valley. Mary said, "Leon, pull over. We need to talk with Kevin and Duncan."

Without replying, he turned off onto a side road and found a turnout where they had a view of the valley and hills beyond. She turned in her seat and put one arm over the back to look at the boys.

"Leon and I are separating. Kevin, you will be safe because it will just be you and me at the house. Leon is going to live elsewhere until he can get free of his alcohol problem. I should've done something when he nearly..." She swallowed and pressed her lips together, seemed to fight for control, and continued, "killed us on that drive. I'm sorry." She glanced away momentarily and said thinly, "I was scared too."

She asked the boys for their versions of what made them run away. They told her. Leon stared straight ahead and disputed nothing. Mary let them talk; here and there, she asked a question. Often, she cringed, but she let them tell it all. When they were done, she looked at Duncan, asked, "I understand Kevin running away, but why did you? Did you fear Leon coming after you?"

He motioned no with his head but did not answer otherwise. Mary studied him. He looked down.

"He's my friend," Kevin said.

Duncan looked at Mary. Her eyes filled, and her mouth trembled into a little smile. "I see."

Leon was silent through all of it until, after Mary suggested they get on their way, he said without looking at the boys, "I've promised Mary I will give up the booze and never be violent like that again. I'm joining Alcoholics Anonymous. I won't be staying at the house tonight, and not until Mary says it's OK." He hesitated, then, "and not until you don't feel afraid of me anymore."

Neither boy said anything, but Mary reached out and gave Leon's arm a brief, encouraging squeeze. They stopped for lunch at a McDonald's in Santa Rosa. Over burgers, fries, shakes for the boys, and coffee for the adults, Mary asked Kevin, "Did the police give back the money you had?"

Both boys answered, "Yes."

Mary flashed a wry smile at Duncan and said, "The police said you each had over $200. I won't ask where you got it, but I'm pretty sure you didn't find it and very sure you didn't work for it, despite what you told them."

She let the weight of her stare press upon them. Then, to Kevin, "I am going to open a savings account for you. With my approval, you can spend some of the money on important things. I don't want you blowing it. I want you to learn how to manage money and" her stare intensified, "about making it legally. Understood?"

"Yes, Mary," Kevin said.

Then she said to Duncan, "Your money is between you and your mother, but I hope you will talk with her about it, and I hope," she glanced at Kevin, "both of you grow to understand that doing wrong is never the way to get ahead."

***

The Suburban pulled up in front of Duncan's house. He had been dreading this for the last hundred miles. Ava, Aileen and Keith came out and stood in the yard, but there was no sign of Shona. Mary got out, and Duncan pushed the seatback forward and contorted himself to exit out her door. The closer they had gotten to home, the younger he had felt, until at last, he was almost a little boy again coming back to face an angry, fearsome mother. He bent low and put his left foot on the step, rose, and his other foot was halfway to the ground when he truly saw Ava.

It is amazing how quick the mind can be and how much it can sometimes see instantly. What Duncan saw was like a sledgehammer to his gut. He saw a forty-two-year-old woman with unkempt hair who appeared smaller than she had been just a few days before. He saw forty hours of desperate worrying and two days of not knowing if he was alive or dead. The word *shattered* exploded in his mind.

He realized that he had left without even leaving a note, as if neither she, Aileen, Shona, or Keith mattered. He had simply disappeared with his clothes and his money and had not looked back once.

He found it hard to look at his mother. Aileen was difficult to read; she seemed to be fighting an inner battle between sadness and anger. Keith looked perplexed. Duncan forced his head to turn to Ava and forced his eyes to meet hers. "Hi, Mom," he said.

75

"She asked me to promise not to run away again," Kevin said. It was the day after their return, and Duncan was walking with him up Delaware on their way to Randy's.

"Did you?"

Kevin shrugged. "She asked me to give her a chance. Leon dropped us off, didn't even come inside, and I haven't seen him since, just a day, but... I watched Mary pour all the booze down the sink: beer, wine, some whiskey, which I thought was a bummer." He laughed. "You and me won't be doing any drinking, I guess, while she's at work."

"Maybe not."

She tried to put the fear into me, saying again how we could have ended up dead. I didn't argue that I could have also ended up dead staying here, but maybe she saw it in my face because she again promised to protect me, even go to the cops if Leon does the least bad thing."

"So, you promised?"

"Yeah."

They walked for a while, not speaking. It was another warm, sunny, glorious day in Santa Cruz, yet Duncan felt the town looked different somehow. Smaller? He could not figure out why.

"What did your mom say?"

"Not much. She's treating me like a bird she's scared to startle."

"She take your money?"

"No, and I didn't mention it."

"I had to give mine to Mary."

"All of it?"

"She let me keep ten bucks."

***

Cheryl opened the door and loudly called over her shoulder, "Mom, the desperados have returned." Then she giggled and said, "Come in, desperados."

"Hi, Cheryl," Kevin said.

Duncan watched what used to be a little girl scamper off to see Margaret in the kitchen. For the first time, he noticed how pretty she was.

"What's a desperado?" he asked.

"I dunno."

While drying her hands with a small towel, Margaret entered the living room from the kitchen. Cheryl trailed behind her.

"Hi, Mrs. K," they said.

She did not smile or return the greeting. She stared hard at each of them, eyes flicking back and forth between them, from a sharp, intense face that seemed to have new lines. "I don't think you have any idea how worried we were."

He gulped. Alan and Randy pounded down the stairs and shouted greetings, which they stifled when they seemed to catch the tension in the air.

"And you don't run away to somewhere nearby like San Jose or Monterey but to, God help me, Canada. What the hell were you thinking?"

Her use of the mild swear word, coming from a woman he had never heard swear before, made him gulp again. Kevin, though, told her exactly what he had been thinking. He told her about Leon's abuse, their flight as he broke the door down, and why they imagined Canada would be a haven. From her shifting expressions and the horrified look on Cheryl's face, Duncan knew that her sons had kept Kevin's secret. And, clearly, Mary had kept Leon's violence a secret as well. Kevin finished by explaining what Mary was doing to protect him.

Her eyes moistened at his telling, but she did not wipe them. "Such a brutal world," she said as if to herself. And Duncan wondered how much of that world she may have seen. Then fire blazed in her eyes, and she declared, "He should be in jail."

Moments passed, and then she said, "I understand, but I wish you had spoken to me first. You have to trust the people who love you. And you," she said to Duncan, "Ava had no idea why you left. She loves you; she would have helped." He heard this assertion as if it were a new idea.

Margaret seemed to gather herself, took a deep breath, said, "Well, enough of that, let's celebrate that you made it back. I imagine you're hungry; you boys are always hungry."

She fed them bologna sandwiches, macaroni salad and barbecue potato chips. He and Kevin told stories of their journey, stories with that attractive sheen of dangerous adventures safely stored in the past. They skirted the run-in with the two guys in the Fairlane. Duncan figured they would tell Randy and Alan that later.

After thick slices of apple pie and tall glasses of milk, Alan announced that he had gotten a pellet gun, and they could do target shooting in the backyard. His gun was powered by compressed CO_2 canisters that fit into the butt of the Luger-style pistol. All the boys and, to his surprise, Cheryl, piled out the back door chased by Margaret's warning, "Don't bust any windows."

The gun was metal and heavy, and it made a satisfying whack when the lead pellet smashed into any of its array of targets: old cans, a milk crate, bottles, and a hand-drawn target of concentric circles mounted on a plank.

Everyone took turns. Cheryl was a better shot than anyone else except Alan. They cheered excellent shots and bad ones too. As he and Cheryl waited for another go and watched Randy aiming carefully at an old doll Cheryl was sacrificing, she asked, "What were you going to do if you got to Canada?"

His response was delayed by his marveling at how her long, straight blonde hair moved as she turned her head and how her blue eyes twinkled as she asked the question.

"Well?"

He shrugged. "I don't know. We were going to figure it out when we got there."

She giggled, and for a moment, she was little giggly goofy Cheryl again, but then he wondered, *When did you get so pretty*, and felt confused.

"I know," she said. "You were going to live rich as desperados."

It was a tease, but he had almost missed it as he had been enjoying the music of her voice. "What? Wait, what's a desperado?"

She smirked. "An outlaw."

"Me and Kevin aren't outlaws."

"Sure you are."

"No, we aren't."

"You steal, don't you?"

He recoiled and did not know why her use of that word stung so much. "We don't steal. I mean, it was a long time ago. We did some heists and a few capers, that's all. It was fun. We're not outlaws."

Cheryl giggled. "I think it's super cool, but whatever you call it, you're still desperados."

He was about to protest further when Alan shouted, "Hey, Cheryl, your turn."

She danced off. He suddenly worried that if Cheryl thought they were outlaws, maybe Mrs. Kelly did too.

Crap.

He argued with himself. He wasn't really stealing; they were derring-do adventures. They had done brilliant heists. And it wasn't like we did it a lot, just a few bold and brave capers. It was great fun and exciting as we outfoxed the adults. Cheryl obviously admired him for being a desperado, which bothered him—a lot.

I'm not an outlaw.

He watched her shoot her own doll in the eye.

Am I?

76

A few days later Lee said the gang could go shooting with a friend of his. That sounded fun, so Duncan, Kevin and Randy went to Jack's house with Lee. As they walked up a rise at the edge of Niman Marks Park, Lee said, "His dad has all kinds of guns; Jack will let us pick which one we want."

"What are we going to shoot at?" Randy asked.

"Dunno, whatever we find in the forest."

"Will there be plenty of trees to shoot in the forest?" Duncan asked.

"What? You want to shoot trees?"

"If that's the only game."

Lee was about to answer but stopped when Kevin and Randy laughed. "Oh, you're just joshing. Ha. Ha."

Duncan smiled.

Lee laughed. "All right, funny boy, let's go see what we can shoot."

Jack was a big, lanky teen with big teeth who took them into the basement where the guns were stored. His father's arsenal comprised at least a dozen guns: pistols, rifles and a shotgun. Only Jack was at home. He bragged about how often he went to the shooting range and how he had killed a deer once. It turned out that they did not get to choose which gun they wanted. Jack handed out his selections to each of the gang. Randy and Lee got black semi-auto pistols, Kevin a big chrome-plated revolver, and Duncan a .22 rifle.

Jack gave them brief instructions for each gun and finished with what he said was most important, "Let's not shoot each other, OK? So be careful not to point yours at anyone, all right?"

The group's energy was very high. They chattered about how boss their guns were. He was quite excited. Pellet guns and arcade .22s were nothing like this. Jack grabbed two guns: the largest semi-auto pistol and a 16-gauge shotgun.

Not far from his house, he took them up a long dirt road, and soon they were in a thick forest. Jack said, "There's a clearing up ahead where we can practice shooting."

It was a small open declivity surrounded by big trees through which ran a thin creek. They heard birds but could not see them, so they *did* end up shooting at trees. He was disappointed in his gun; it did not boom like the others, and bark did not fly off the trees when his bullets struck. But their combined barrage was loud and satisfying. Shouts and cheers from the boys as bullets hit targets added to the din.

At a pause in the action, Randy pointed. "Hey, look at that squirrel."

Out on a long horizontal pine tree branch about twenty feet up, the little creature peered down at them, chattering and barking disapprovingly.

"Bold, ornery little shit, isn't he?" Jack said. "I guess he objects, huh? Let's shoot him."

Five guns opened up on the one-pound target, and everyone missed. The squirrel darted back and forth along the branch. Bits of smaller branches were blasted into kindling. The fusillade was deafening.

Duncan took two shots and stopped. He stared at the puffy, furry creature, its eyes big, its nose twitching, its jerky erratic jogs to nowhere and was overwhelmed with waves of terror, panic and confusion.

What is this?

Everyone else kept firing; some took careful aim, but the squirrel remained unscathed. Nausea slammed Duncan. He dropped his gun and bent over, placing elbows on his knees. He rose and shouted, "Stop! Stop! Stop! Don't kill it!"

Kevin and Randy were nearest to him. They stopped first, and then Lee and Jack did as well. The sudden silence was startling.

"You OK?" Kevin asked.

On the spot, still reeling from something he did not understand, he said, "Don't kill it."

Out of the collective blank looks, one face, Jack's, scoffed, "Why not?"

He felt at a loss. How many birds had he beaned with well-thrown rocks and felt only triumph? He had even stung a raccoon or two and swelled with pride at his marksmanship. So, why?

"It's afraid. Let's just let it go..." And his voice trailed off in the face of their incredulous looks. It sounded stupid even to him.

"What are you, a pussy?" Jack asked, and to Lee, "You said your friends were tough."

"I don't know," Lee said, "but he's not a pussy."

Duncan told Randy, "I don't want to kill it."

"Oh, Jesus," said Jack, "Let's just shoot the rodent and be done."

None of his friends raised their guns, and he did not know if that was because they agreed or just out of loyalty.

"Maybe you're all pussies,' Jack said. He went to the base of another tree where he had left the shotgun, picked it up and pumped it. The squirrel had frozen, its black nose pulsing, when the gunfire had ceased. As Jack approached, it started to move, but he was fast, took quick aim, and pulled the trigger. The blast blew the squirrel and half of the branch apart. The limb sagged, and debris fell.

"There," Jack said.

Duncan lowered his head and said more to himself than anyone, "I'm going home." Then, to Kevin, he pointed at the rifle and added, "Give him his gun back, will you?"

Kevin studied his face for a moment, then nodded.

He slowly walked back to the main road. He intended to continue but decided to wait in case his friends were close behind. He heard more shots, but only a few. It wasn't long before the whole group reappeared.

As the somber and conflicted-looking group approached, Duncan struggled to understand what had happened. He had no answer, but he feared their ridicule. As for Jack and his sneering, angry face, he cared not at all. His friends greeted him without a hint of judgment.

Jack was different. He walked right up and leveled the shotgun at his belly. Duncan went still, and the round black opening of the barrel gaped like a cavern.

The other boys erupted,

"Whoa, whoa, whoa, what the hell?"

"Don't shoot."

"What are you doing?"

At that moment, he couldn't think. After seeing what the shotgun had done to a thick branch and a squirrel at forty feet, he was overwhelmed with a vision of his guts being blown out through his spine. Jack looked at him like he wanted to do it.

"You said never to point a gun at anybody," Lee said in a soft, placating voice.

Without taking his eyes off Duncan or his finger off the trigger, Jack said, "That didn't include pussies."

The seconds crawled as everyone remained rigidly attentive. Then Duncan managed to say slowly, steadily, thinly, "I'm going home."

Turning around almost made him faint. He slowly walked away, hardly able to breathe. He got about ten feet when the clattering of metal hitting the pavement made him flinch.

"We are too," someone said.

Duncan glanced and saw his friends' guns were on the ground. He kept walking, and they caught up to him.

Jack called to their retreating backs, "There wasn't even a shell in the chamber. Just wanted to see if the pussy would pee his pants."

No one said a thing until they were nearly out of sight, then Lee yelled, "You're fucking nuts, asshole!"

Jack acting like he was going to kill him clearly dwarfed the scene of Duncan's distress over the squirrel, for the former was all the boys talked about on their way home. *Psycho, lunatic, mean asshole, where did you meet that jerk, Lee,* were part of their rapid-fire conversation. Duncan did not say anything. He was just glad not to be shaking or stumbling.

Kevin stopped him with a hand on his shoulder. The others stopped too. He made an exaggerated show of inspecting the front and rear of Duncan's jeans and said, "Just checking if you pissed yourself."

Despite his heart's gradually calming but still hard thumping, he answered, "No pee, just sweaty. You want to check that?"

The boys howled. They continued their journey home. As they walked, he did not participate in his friends' banter. And while he was pleased that he could still quip like the Man-with-No-Name, he remained troubled by the mystery of his reactions.

Maybe I am a pussy; I almost got shot over a squirrel.

***

The next day, he, Randy and Kevin were warming in the sun after a bodysurfing session.

"Who's going to watch the moon landing?" Randy asked.

"Who isn't?" Kevin said.

"I wouldn't miss it for anything," Duncan said.

"But what if they crash?" Randy asked.

"I saw some scientist saying they might sink into moon dust and disappear, like into quicksand," Kevin said.

"Really?" Duncan asked.

"That's what he said."

They discussed the incredibly awesome fantasticness of landing on the moon over 200,000 miles away for twenty minutes, and then, out of nowhere, Randy asked, "Why did you freak out about that squirrel?"

"I didn't freak."

"Don't kill it, don't kill it," Kevin mimicked.

Randy laughed. Duncan wanted to sink into the sand.

"It's afraid. Let it go," Kevin continued.

Randy fell back and laughed more, said, "That was trippy."

He couldn't think of a thing to say, so he looked at his feet.

"What was freaky was Jack," Randy said. "I really thought he might shoot you."

"Yeah," Kevin said, "that was scary. Next time Lee wants us to meet a new lunatic friend, I'm going to say no fuckin' way."

"The guns were pretty cool, though," Randy said.

"Yeah, but mine kicked like a bitch, hurt my wrist."

Duncan stood. "I just didn't want to kill it, OK? I don't know why. OK? OK?"

He left them with their mouths open and tried to lose himself in surfing the crappy waves. No one brought it up again that afternoon, and when they left the beach, Duncan said he had something to do and went his separate way. At first, he did not know where he was going, but he found himself at the Sportsman's Shop looking at pellet guns. He coughed up eleven dollars for a wicked-looking black pistol and walked home thinking, *I am not a pussy.*

***

The day before the moon landing, Duncan was back at the Kelly's, showing off his new gun. All the boys were there, and they ooohed and ahhhed and praised its accuracy as they took turns shooting. Cheryl was off with friends, and he realized he was disappointed.

Nobody said anything about squirrels or being freaky. He felt better, tougher, and fierce as he blasted already perforated targets along the back fence line. Kevin and Lee left early, and soon, he got the idea that Margaret wanted some peace around her house. He had to go home for dinner anyway.

Outside on the sidewalk, in front of their house, he saw a fat seagull perched on top of a telephone pole across the street. He didn't like seagulls; they were annoying scavengers that seemed to crap constantly. And he remembered that one gull he was sure had wanted to peck his eyes out.

I am not a pussy.

He walked right under the gull, who glanced down at him with a squawk of disdain. He raised his gun, pointed it with two hands, and pulled the trigger.

Pow.

He had not expected to hit it, but to his shock, the bird croaked loudly and fell like a stone to his feet. It crash-landed, wings half open, and struggled to rise. Its distressed, raspy pleas tore through Duncan. He felt terror and pain as the creature flopped and flailed about on the concrete, unable to fly, unable to walk.

"I'm sorry, I'm sorry, I'm sorry," he said. The intensity of what he believed was the bird's fear and hurt made him panic. He had to stop its pain. So he shot it again and again and again, yet it wouldn't die. Finally, desperate, he shot it point blank in its little head, and it lay quiet as a sprawled-out mess.

He ran from the site of what he felt was a crime and didn't stop until he reached the Lincoln Street Bridge. He looked down at the sluggish brown water.

Why did I do that? It was just an ugly bird. But why? What's wrong with me? It hurt so much. How can I feel it? What's wrong with me? It was just a bird. Just a stupid, dumb bird..., but it hurt so much.

He took the pellet gun out of his pants, turned it over and over, examining it, then, with a violent shake of his head, flung it as far as he could to splash into the middle of the river. Then he walked home.

77

On the day of the first moon landing, Duncan was riveted to the tiny black-and-white TV the Findlays owned. He watched replays of the spectacular Saturn V launch from five days before and soaked up every mission detail Walter Cronkite's gravelly, comforting voice explained.

Space exploration was in its infancy. The computers used were primitive, little better than slide rules or an abacus. Yet, less than ten years since President Kennedy had committed the United States to the mission, they were on the verge of accomplishing it.

His family drifted in and out of his awareness as they watched parts of the broadcast, but when it got closer to the actual landing, at around 8 p.m. in California, they all watched, as did three-quarters of the country and a sixth of the world. Four-sixths of the world, excluding the United States, did not have TVs. At touchdown Mr. Cronkite was so moved he was at a rare loss for words, and astronaut Wally Schirra wiped his eyes.

Duncan was disappointed. He couldn't see anything through the snowy static except black and white blobs. One blob moved next to another blob. He presumed it was Neil Armstrong. Afterward, he stayed up late talking excitedly with Ava about future missions to the moon and Mars and even his dreams of traveling to the stars. She listened with kind, attentive eyes and a pleased smile. Since his return they had not talked about his running away adventure. She had not asked him any questions. No restrictions were placed on when he left or came back each day. Yet her eyes followed him when he was home, and each time he came back or emerged from a night of sleep, eyes newly tender shone with relief.

He had never found Ava especially interested in him. Yet on that night, she seemed to hang on to his every word, to be caught up in his every enthusiasm, and to encourage him to express more. After his sisters and brother had long since gone to sleep, he paused in his exuberance and looked at her. He truly looked at her and saw terrible insecurity.

A few seconds passed, and he said, "Leon was hurting Kevin. Really bad. That's why, Mom."

He felt released from the secrecy he had kept for so long because of Kevin's openness with Margaret. He told her everything: the savage drunken beatings Kevin had endured, the near-death drive to the cliff, the attack the night before they fled, and even his and Kevin's close call with the two men in Healdsburg.

And he told her what Mary was doing about it. He said Kevin had promised not to run away again, but he did not promise so himself. As they sat side-by-side on the couch, Ava did not hug him, but she did reach out a hand and squeeze his. She said, "All Mrs. Davis said was that there had been problems at home, and she and Mr. Davis were resolving them."

"Leon moved out. He's not supposed to return until he's not a drunk anymore."

She nodded. "You were lucky."

He thought about the man pulling over in the heavy rain and said, "Yeah, I guess we were."

78

August 1969

"What's the big surprise?" Duncan asked. He and Randy sat on a hillside underneath thick trees where they could see Pacific Avenue below. It was cool and private in the deep shade. Randy reached into the worn denim satchel he had brought and pulled out something in a brown paper bag. Like a magician pulling Thumper out of a black hat, he revealed a bottle three-quarters full of amber liquid. The label said Old Musketeer.

"All right! "How'd you get whiskey?"

"From my dad."

"Your dad? He's here?"

Randy rested the bottle on a pile of leaves and looked down between his bent knees. "Yeah, but I didn't want you to know."

"How come?"

"He's a drunk and a bum."

"Oh, but he gave you whiskey?"

"Sort of. I've been going over to his place now and then 'cause I can drink beer with him. We watch TV and get plastered. I swiped this after he passed out."

"Won't he be pissed?"

"I dunno, maybe, I don't care. It's not that fun getting drunk with him. He talks on and on about doing nasty sex things to women."

"Ewww."

"Yeah." He suddenly looked up at Duncan, asked, "Hey, we're still friends, right?"

It took him a shocked moment to reply. "Always. Why ask that?"

"Dunno, forget it." He played with the bottle. "Just you split for Canada, didn't say shit to me."

"Oh, yeah, it happened so fast. We would've called when we got there." But he realized he had not thought about calling at all.

Randy nodded, gave him a half smile, and said, "Yeah, I know."

"Sorry."

"Hey, I want to drink with my best friend and have fun." He opened the bottle, took a sniff and flinched. "You had whiskey before?"

Duncan shook his head but said, "Naw, except my mom and dad gave it to me when I was two, but I don't remember that."

"You had whiskey as a baby?"

He laughed. "That's what they said. Supposedly, I loved it."

Randy laughed and handed him the bottle. "The pro should have first swallow."

He wrinkled his nose at the sharp odor, took a sip and coughed as it coated his esophagus.

"Well?"

"Kinda harsh, warm going down. Here."

Randy reacted the same, asked, "What's eighty proof mean?"

"Dunno, 80% alcohol, I guess."

"A lot more than beer, huh?"

"Three or four times at least, I bet."

"Cool."

They lit cigarettes and passed the bottle back and forth. The whiskey tasted better and better. They smoked and drank and laughed. They walked the short distances of each of their memory lanes as they revisited adventures taken. Abruptly, Randy asked, "Do you think I'm stupid?"

"What? No."

"You're in high school, and I'm still in junior."

"So, it's just school."

"You know I got suspended three times last year."

"Three?"

"Yeah, for fighting."

"You won, right?"

"Yep, even the bigger guys lose if I can get them on the ground."

"What'd they do?"

"Called me stupid."

"Fuck'em."

"Yeah, fuck'em."

"This is a lot better than beer. Let's go to the beach."

They went to the wharf first. Randy kept the whiskey in his bag. They slipped into private nooks, behind fish markets and restaurants, to take more swigs and laughed at each other's tendency to weave and stumble. At one of the little fences around the openings in the wharf, Randy asked, "You and Kevin climbed down there?"

"Yeah."

"Want to now?"

"Now? Hell no. Not drunk; we'd fall."

Randy leaned far over the chain-link and stared at a seal resting on a beam below. "How much have you stolen?"

There was that stinging word again. "On our heists?"

With a wry smile, Randy stood up straight and said, "Yeah, on heists. Alan said you robbed a bank."

"We didn't rob any banks."

"Sis calls you desperados."

"Yeah, I know." He sobered briefly within his euphoric haze. "What does your mom say?"

"Mom's fair. She doesn't know anything, not really, but it's not like you hide how much cash you got. Not good anyway. I told Cheryl to knock off the desperado shit around mom. She giggles and calls you a dashing desperado anyway."

"What's dashing mean?"

"I dunno, but I think she has a crush on you."

Even high, Duncan knew not to touch that.

Randy continued, "Mom just says she hopes you grow out of whatever you're doing."

They wandered around, drinking when they could, doing their best to look "normal" and likely failing, but no one seemed to notice the two intoxicated fifteen-year-olds. Near Randy's house they grabbed kumquats off a tree in someone's yard because they were hungry. They upended the last of the whiskey on a quiet residential street two blocks from Randy's house and left the bottle on the sidewalk.

Not long after, Duncan asked, "Why ya knockin' ya own door?"

Randy's rolling laughter continued until he finally said, "Wanna see if summun home."

The door opened, and Margaret filled the entrance. Randy hung off Duncan's shoulder, unable to stifle his hilarity.

"Oh, dear," she said.

He would remember being fed pancakes, bacon and coffee. He passed out in Randy's room. Neither boy vomited. He awoke in the late afternoon feeling like crap, with Margaret sitting on the edge of the bed next to him. As she gradually came into focus and with the still unconscious Randy snoring next to him, she put a gnarly hand on his chest and patted him there while letting him come to. Under her scrutinizing grave, sad eyes, he felt embarrassed at his state.

"I don't want Randy to end up like his father." Her pats were drumbeats of emphasis. "You boys are too young to be doing these things." Pat. Pat. Pat. "Yes, you're smart, and you're quick, and you know it, but you're also reckless, so reckless. I don't want to see you get crushed." She brushed the hair out of his eyes. "Think about where you're going, Duncan." And she lightly tapped his forehead a couple of times and repeated, "Think. Think." Then she got up and left.

He lay there for a long time, looking at the blurry ceiling, wrestling with her words.

***

A few days later Mary served Duncan and Kevin leftover lasagna and Caesar salad for lunch. It was over a month since she had kicked Leon out of the house.

"So I accidentally put some wicked topspin on the ball, and it cleared the net by an inch and smacked him right in the nuts." Kevin chortled.

Mary pressed her lips together as mirth danced in her eyes and said, "Please say groin or something else, uh, less graphic."

"He did groan being hit in the groin."

Mary and Duncan smiled.

"Did he barf?" Duncan asked.

"No, I said sorry. He didn't fall over or anything. He was just used to my weak-assed," Mary interrupted, "Kevin," and he revised, "weak lobs and was not ready for the rocket I hit just by luck."

"Mr. Adams said you are learning quickly and could be an excellent player."

Kevin forked a chunk of lasagna, waved it briefly in the air, then said to Duncan, "Maybe, but four lessons, and I still blast the ball over the fence sometimes."

"You like it?" Duncan asked.

He chewed a moment and said," Yeah, it's fun."

Mary ignored her food and looked at Kevin with such obvious warmth and perhaps pride that she got him thinking about how they had changed. He realized that his view of Mary before was as a background figure, timid like the new kid at school, softly and carefully spoken like she was afraid to be rebuked. She had hovered within the aura of Leon's dominance like a half-person.

The new Mary was radiant and seemed physically larger. Her gestures and her speech were quick and sure. She had the vitality of an athlete instead of the draggy, dulled presence of a worn-out nurse. Kevin no longer did that shifting eyes thing where it seemed he was continually tracking escape routes. He smiled more and, for weeks, had not flashed that cocky sneer Duncan was so familiar with. Kevin gave Mary something else instead of the instant defiance he used to show Leon. He tried to find a word for what it was.

Finally, he thought, *Trust, he trusts her.*

As he watched foster mom and foster son laugh together, Duncan knew he didn't trust Mary, but he had some hope that she would not let Kevin down.

***

On a late August afternoon at the beach with the guys, Duncan gathered his stuff to head home. He was anticipating what Alan was going to say, like listening for that moment when the drip would hit the drain.

"Be good," Alan said.

He wanted to hit him. Ever since he and Kevin had returned, Alan had replaced *bye* with, *be good*, and only to Duncan. He turned. Randy and Lee were already on their way toward the trestle.

"Knock it off," he said.

"Knock what off?"

"The 'be good' shit."

Alan waggled his eyebrows. "Don't you want to be good?"

He ignored the question. "Stop. What's this all about?"

Alan shrugged and offered a got-me smile. Duncan had found that Alan could be quite honest if he didn't buy into his mind games. His big friend answered, "It's what Mark, my boss, says to me. I figure you need saving, so I say it to you."

"Save me? From what?"

"Sin, so Jesus will like you."

His brain locked up while he tried to decide if this was some new manipulation. Before he could reach a conclusion, Alan said, "Mark took me to his church, and I've been learning about salvation and what happens if you do wrong."

"You went to church?" He still could not decide what Alan was up to.

"Once. I don't want to go to hell for breaking commandments."

"Have you gone all religious or something?"

"Thinking about it."

"Huh, OK, you can stop bugging me to be good because I'm not going to hell and not breaking any commandments."

"You steal."

Duncan countered, "That was a year ago and was just a fun thing."

"Still stealing."

"Who did you mug last week?"

Alan sputtered, said. "How did...?"

"Your hands. They are all beat up from beating someone up. And what about the gash on your arm?"

Alan looked at his injuries, said, "Guy might've been drunk, but he put up a fight and pulled a pocketknife."

He shook his head, said, "And you're telling me to be good?"

"Mark says Jesus forgives me."

"Really? I think you're supposed to stop doing bad too."

Alan chewed his lip and said, "Yeah, that's probably so. I'm trying."

They picked up the rest of their things and walked together over the beach. Duncan asked, "Will you stop bugging me to be good? It's pukey."

"OK, I guess. You gonna quit stealing?"

"Just stop."

"OK."

***

Since the moon landing Duncan had spent many nights talking with Ava. After dinner, after watching shows like *The Twilight Zone* or *Perry Mason*, when Keith was asleep, his sisters too, or else they were out with friends, he would sit on her couch and roam subjects of science and metaphysics, old history and new hopes. He found it strange that he was eager to share with her. And he was pleased that she seemed eager to share with him and would listen to what he had to say.

After years of reflexively hiding almost everything about his life, he now voluntarily said what he did each day. True, he left out getting drunk with Randy or occasionally getting stoned. He did not smoke cigarettes around her, but she must have known for years that he did. He did not confess past crimes but wasn't committing current ones. But everything else, all the safe stuff, he told her, and since it was like having a book's worth of information dumped on her versus his prior terse telegrams, she seemed very happy.

Her sharings with him were equally safe. She did not speak of his father or her job, why she was recently estranged from Nana, nor about money or her daily struggles. Instead, she talked about her metaphysical studies, reincarnation, Rosicrucian practices and principles, and rituals she labeled White Magic. The pentagrams still glowed brightly in the kitchen.

On a night in late August, in the middle of their conversation, she said, "I have something for you."

He wondered if he had misheard her. She had already given him school clothes for his birthday, which was well past. She had never given him something except on his birthday or at Christmas.

"Really?"

"Yes, stay there." She went out the front door. He heard her open and close the car trunk. Reentering the living room, she held a six-string guitar by the neck. She brought it to him on the couch. It was beautiful.

"Wow, Mom, a guitar?"

"You have been talking so much about rock 'n' roll and how great it would be to play; I thought you'd like to learn."

He took the guitar, placed it across his thigh, and strummed the slightly out-of-tune strings. "Sure I would."

"Good. I found someone who will give you lessons."

He strummed the strings, tried cords he made up, and caressed the smooth, varnished wood like he was petting a cat. "Thanks, Mom." He noticed her satisfied face and wondered at how different things were between them.

$$79$$

September 1969

Early on a Saturday morning, Ava woke Duncan. "Kevin wants to see you. He's at the front door." He quickly put on some clothes and wondered what had happened. The Findlay policy of no-friend-can-come-inside meant his buddies usually just called for meet-ups. In his T-shirt and jeans, he went out the front door. Kevin spun around from his place underneath their little tree and shouted, "I'm gonna see my Dad!"

Duncan rubbed the last bit of sleep crud from his eyes and said, "Awesome. When? Where?"

"Tuesday, at Folsom."

"Wow, where's that?" He had never asked where Folsom was.

"Up near Sacramento."

"So, how? I mean, he just decided it was OK out of the blue?"

"It was Mary. She went all the way up there to see him. She talked him into it." Tears brimmed in his eyes, but he did not look away.

Duncan could not find anything worthy to say.

"Mary said the real reason he wouldn't let me come before was that he was ashamed. He didn't want me to see him there behind those walls, in his prison clothes." A tear dropped, and he looked away. Then, he said faintly, "I just want to see him."

"That's so great," he said, although it felt lame compared to the moment.

"Yeah, I wanted you to know. I've got to go. I just wanted you to know."

"OK."

As Kevin walked away, Duncan said, "Say hi from me, all right?"

Kevin's radiant smile was like the sun on a beautiful spring day, and he said, "I will, I will. Maybe we can get him out early." And he ran off like his feet barely felt the ground.

***

He was not having much success playing the guitar or projecting his etheric body. He'd had several lessons from a guy with a little studio near the wharf. He learned fingering and string names, some basic chords, how to hold it and the pick. Mr. Turner had him doing scales and whoop de do, playing "Home on the Range." It seemed far, far away from riffing "Purple Haze."

Etheric projection was proving a challenge too. He took baths beforehand because he was supposed to be clean. He worked on his concentration but not his visualization; lack of imagination was not his issue. Multiple times he had lain on his bed and saw the light-filled tube, and he had steadily and carefully ascended. He felt the bed rise, saw the walls around him pass, got to the top, stood, and opened his eyes, expecting to be in the etheric realm near the ceiling. Every time, he was still in his bed, looking up at the ceiling in the dark.

***

Duncan's return to school had not interfered with his talks with Ava two or three times per week. Shona intended to marry her boyfriend, and he told Ava about the mahogany hope chest he was making for her in Wood Shop. He also told her about his boxing training and put a positive spin on the guitar lessons he continued to struggle with because he did not want to disappoint her.

One late night in September, her sharing became a lecture on the metaphysical studies and practices she continued to pursue. He listened with fascination as she described how to develop powers of thought, emotional energy, psychic energy, etheric energy, powers of prayer, and how to use telepathy. She described cyclic law and how to use that knowledge.

Her enthusiasm expanded to a demonstration of several magical rituals that conjured and appealed to specific angels and God to help her. It was like he was her student, and her hopes for him were high. He felt treated like an adult. When she was done, he wanted to impress her with his own explorations. He went to his room and returned with several books he had bought at The Occult Shop, ones she had yet to see.

She picked up *The Secret Doctrine* by Helena Blavatsky and nodded. "She's the mother of Theosophy. I've been meaning to read this. You've read it?"

"A little. Kinda dense. I look up a lot of the words."

She flipped pages, pausing to read a bit here and there, and then put the book down. "I see."

She picked up *The Greater Key of Solomon*. He proudly said, "I used that to get my coat back after it was stolen."

She raised her eyebrows. He told her the story of his conjuring and the mystery man. He stood and demonstrated his ritual. When he finally sat down, she spent quite some time leafing through the book, reading aloud snippets as if to herself, "The 37th Spirit is Phenex...I conjure thee O, thou Spirit Raum...O Adonai most powerful..."

She put it down without comment and picked up *The Black Arts* by Richard Cavendish. Ava frowned. Despite its title, it was not a book of detailed instructions in such arts but rather a history of the occult. Relatively innocuous subjects like astrology, numerology and the Tarot were covered. But chapters like The Lords of Darkness, Worship of the Devil and Necromancy may have given her pause.

It was after 1 a.m. when she put *The Greater Key* on top of the other books and said, "This could be dangerous magic."

He remembered how he had fought the voices but said, "I only did it that once."

She seemed to weigh her words very carefully and said, "Good, I think summoning dark spirits should be avoided."

He had thought she would have been impressed by his studies, not worried. How was his magic any different from hers? She was so serious about this. It was just cool stuff to know. Then her demeanor changed, and she looked tenderly at him and asked, "Duncan, are you going to be a black magician?"

There was so much in that simple question, and it hit him hard.

Are you choosing to be evil? That was what she meant.

And how she asked with such sad, searching eyes showed that she felt powerless to affect his decision.

He also saw that she was trying hard not to offend him, anxious not to say anything that might drive him away again.

Mom loves me.

That realization disturbed him. He chewed on a nail and said, "I don't know; it's just interesting."

She took a deep breath and said, "Well, please think about it." He said he would, and they parted for their beds. It took him a long time to go to sleep.

***

The next day, after breakfast, he went to The Cup and sat nestled in the ice plant, watching the glimmering bay. It was cool and calm, and the sea air was sweet. Little waves caressed the sand below.

What's the big deal? he thought. *I'm not evil; they're just books. Some of it is evil, I guess, hexes and curses, demons and the devil, puh, if any of that is even real. Just fun, weird shit is all. I did get my jacket back. That was far-out. But I don't hurt anybody.* He remembered Alan saying that stealing hurts people. *Yeah, who is he to talk? He punches people and robs them; now that's hurting. Not me. Me and Kevin did heists, we had adventures, we outsmarted...* He sighed.

He lit a cigarette and smoked for a while. Then he remembered Timothy saying, "That would be wrong." He smiled widely, but then his face collapsed, tears burst from his eyes, and he could barely breathe, like it was only yesterday he had knocked on his door for the last time.

Will this ever go away?

Just as quickly, he laughed out loud, remembering Timothy pretending to be Groucho Marx with his father's glasses on and working a carrot in his mouth like a cigar.

That would be wrong; that's how Timothy had seen things. Not me.

Everything had been about excitement, thrills and adventures, not whether it was wrong. Could he do it? Could he push the edge and get away with it? It was fun to risk, fun to dare, courageous to be a boy of derring-do. *And I got lots of money too.*

The latter thought soiled his vision of noble bravery. *I guess it might hurt to have your wallet stolen. But who got hurt at Safeway?* He frowned.

Maybe somebody got blamed. It was a lot of money. Damn.

He thought of Margaret and Randy, Kevin's joyous face, an egg splattering on a windshield, Timothy telling him he loved him, the man who rescued them in Arcata, grinning predators leaning over car seats, Mr. Taylor being so kind, when he had lied to Ava after Juvie, the thrill of scoring big cash, and the joy of traipsing through the world, feeling powerful—untouchable. For years, even his mother had not controlled him, not really.

That would be wrong.

Mrs. Kelly wanted him to think. Mom wanted to know.

I should tell her.

No one was there when he got home. Two of his books were on the coffee table. He didn't see *The Greater Key*. He looked around for a while without success. Then he looked behind the couch, which was up close to the wall shared with the kitchen. It was on the floor... and something else too. To get the book, he had to lift it out. It was a poster-sized white pressboard with pictures pasted all over it. He carefully put it on the couch.

The board was covered with dozens of pictures cut out of magazines. It was a collage of images: piles of money, beautiful homes, couples walking hand-in-hand, new cars, diamond necklaces, fine women's clothes and landscapes of what he was sure was Scotland. He stepped back to take in the whole effect and wondered why Ava had made it.

Then he got it. She had explained that the Rosicrucian method of prayer was the practice of creative visualization. Precise imagining, intense concentration and the pouring of one's psychic energy into the process was deemed a higher, more effective level of prayer. He knew Ava had been doing just that in creating her etheric double. He was sure her collage was a tool to get the essential things she wanted: romance, money, freedom, and a home in the land she loved.

He got his book, put the collage back, and stood looking at the old, tattered couch she slept on with a couple of thin, folded blankets and a lumpy pillow. Terrible sadness crushed him, and he did not know why. He ate a sandwich in the dark kitchen, got money from his sock safe in their dump, and quickly left to find his friends.

***

After dinner, he watched *The Honeymooners* and *Hogan's Heroes* with her and Keith that night. His sisters were off somewhere pursuing other interests. When Keith went to bed, he stayed with her as she drank tea.

"I don't want to be a black magician."

She hesitated mid-sip, perhaps startled by the abruptness of the declaration.

"I want to be an astronomer."

"An astronomer?"

"Yes. I want to explore the universe, maybe work at Palomar or for NASA."

Her smile and evident relief annoyed him. "I like learning, but not anything evil or mean or that hurts anybody."

Perhaps his vehemence made her sit up straighter and look intently at him. "All right, all right, good, Duncan." Her face glowed and seemed to lose years of age. Her happiness ceased to bother him.

"I want to take you to Scotland; I want to take you home," she said.

"I want to go too." It wasn't true, except at that moment. He loved Santa Cruz. He loved California and America, but speaking so directly to Ava and feeling her care lifted his spirits immensely.

"Uist has the darkest skies; it would be perfect for astronomy."

"Maybe I could have my own observatory."

"Yes, you could. They may even have an astronomy program at Edinburgh University."

"Would I have to learn Gaelic to go there?"

"I'd love you to speak Gaelic, but most people speak English."

"Did you ever see any of the Little People there?"

She drank from her tea and put the cup down. "Not directly. They say you can catch them out of the corner of your eye, and a few times I thought I had, but I'm not sure."

She retrieved a photo album with many pictures of Scotland from when she lived there before he was born. In it were photos of the thatched roof house, with its five-foot-thick white walls, where she and Aileen lived for a while. North Uist was a land of few trees and looked primitive to him, but she loved it. In her eyes, it must have been paradise; in his eyes, the photos seemed like windows into the twelfth century.

She pored over the pictures with him. A few included his father, but she ignored those. "When we live there, we can help liberate Scotland from England." It was something he knew she would say, but her voice carried less conviction than at other times and seemed tired. Scotland was like a dream to Duncan, a far-off magical place that he would love to see but which was about as likely to happen as him going to Mars.

The conversation roamed over Scottish and English history, World War II, how Germany was likely to rise again, and how brave Scottish soldiers were in that war.

It was nearly 2 a.m. when they rose to go to bed. Ava leaned close and gave him a quick hug, which astonished him. He managed to hug her back, and she said, "Good night."

"Night, Mom."

80

July 1970

Duncan was alone on Seabright Beach, waiting for Michele to return from her trip to the beachside house that was party-central. Her trim silhouette had strolled across the sand, past the large group of people gathered forty feet away around a driftwood fire. Those warming themselves around its blaze laughed and murmured, drank beer, sipped wine, sipped and passed pipes while Neil Young, out of large speakers mounted on the nearby deck, sang about his love for the "Cinnamon Girl."

Shortly after sunset, Alan had dropped him, Randy, Lee, and Kevin off at a big party at a house on the beach. Only Kevin had been invited, so the rest were crashing it. But the others were now gone. Lee had been kicked out hours before because he picked a fight with some guy over nothing. Randy went with him.

Duncan stayed because of Michele.

Kevin left an hour later with the excuse that Mary expected him home. But it had more to do with the absence of unattached girls than Mary's expectations, Duncan having sparked with the one remaining.

So, as his watch pushed its hands closer to midnight, Duncan sat on a fat driftwood log gazing across black water fringed with white foam, musing on the recent past and enjoying his high.

High on Michele, not from grass or booze.

His sophomore year grades were all A's. Well, except in English, where he only snagged a B, a sweet save at the end of the semester by pulling out an A for a short story he had written about an astronaut discovering life on Pluto.

If Timothy were here, he'd be cheering, I guess. And he laughed to himself.

His guidance counselor, Miss Wood, had listened to his lofty desires to be an astronomer and work for NASA. In October, her first reply threw cold water on his flaming ambition—to even have a shot, he needed to get *much* better grades. Then she worked bellows of encouragement to build that fire back up, saying she believed he could do it and outlined an arduous path through the layers of math and physics courses required.

He took it as a challenge.

Lee's fight was not a surprise. Over the past year he had greatly increased in height, mass and belligerence. He pumped iron like he was preparing for prison. And the anger, that crazy combustible anger, had swelled too. He often hunted for fights, with Randy being sucked along—out of loyalty. It could be anywhere, anytime.

Back in April, as Duncan was leaving the Del Mar Theater with Randy and Lee, Lee hard shoulder-bumped a teen exiting with his girlfriend and claimed the other kid had done it. A bunch of stupid shit accusations flew back and forth, and suddenly, Randy and Duncan were in the thick of it, backing Lee's fight with the guy and his friends.

It was ugly.

Lee knocked his guy out as the girlfriend screamed. Randy and Duncan outfought the other two, who fled, but then a police car showed up, and they ran. Hiding from the cops under the Soquel bridge and listening to Lee crow about how big and bad they were made Duncan feel sick.

I'm not going to be a bully.

His aversion to getting trapped in some stupid fight instigated by Lee meant that he spent more and more time with Kevin. They played tennis whenever they could. A couple of weeks ago, out on the court, he announced that his dad would likely be paroled in September—that's what their attorney said, anyway. That day, Kevin could not help whacking the ball over the fence.

Alan had dropped out of school, which may have been a good thing. He landed a full-time job as a carpenter, rebuilt the engine in his Cougar, fell in love with a new woman, and became a devoted Christian. And although Duncan had little interest in Alan's religious choice, he felt great respect for him; he was a changed man. The occasional maliciousness, the manipulative streak, and the eagerness to hurt people had disappeared. His newfound faith and conviction were free of anything sanctimonious or preachy.

But a great shadow loomed over his big friend's better life, and all the boys knew it. He was 18, and the death maw of Vietnam was wide open, being fed by all the good young men America's draft could pour into it. And without the possibility of a college deferment, Alan was unlikely to avoid the call.

Kevin's life with Mary remained good. She was divorcing Leon. The man had managed to stay away for months, presumably sober, but he then began showing up at the house uninvited, drunk. Kevin said Mary kept the door locked, and usually after Leon had bitched and pleaded for a while, he would leave.

Until April. Late one night, he went farther. In a rage, he threw a planter through the kitchen window. Mary called the police.

***

Early in the summer, he and Kevin happened to go into the new Longs Drugs on 41st Avenue. Kevin had nodded toward the unoccupied registers. "Same as the other store."

"Yep," Duncan answered.

"Want to?"

Duncan shrugged.

Kevin's eyes twinkled. "Derring-do?"

Duncan thought a while but shook his head. "Uh-uh,"

Kevin laughed. "Yeah, me neither."

***

Duncan turned his head, startled out of his memories by the crackle of fresh flames and the explosion of red embers blooming upwards like a swarm of fireflies from new logs being tossed onto the fire.

And there was Michele in her hip-hugging bell-bottom jeans, white blouse and long straight, black hair kept off her face by a violet headscarf—returning to him. They would both be juniors come September, she at Harbor High. Michele loved science, French and the Grateful Dead. She didn't smoke cigarettes, said she didn't care that he did and was one of the few girls who had a surfboard, which she used whenever she got the chance. Duncan was revving to change schools, already strategizing how to convince Ava to move across town.

David Crosby wailed about almost cutting his hair as Michele sat beside him on the log, offering one of two bottles of Bud she was carrying. He took it but let it hang as he leaned in to kiss her. She kissed him back, and they both dropped their unopened bottles on the sand.

After a few minutes, the electricity of her touch still sizzling on his skin, they parted, and he was captivated by her quirky smile while the light of the fire flickered in her eyes. She looked out to sea, then to him as if to say something, back to the bay, then to him.

"What?" he asked.

"Were you ever in Juvenile Hall?"

"Uh."

"A few years ago?"

He already thought she was smart and cute. Now, he wondered if she was psychic.

"Yeah...uh, how could you know that?"

"Did you know a girl there named Connie?"

He rocked back on the log, shut the mouth he realized he had left open, and answered, "Yeah, sure. You know her?"

"She's my sister."

His mouth reopened, but he recovered with a laugh. "Connie's your sister?" He almost said something about Connie being awesome but squelched that as he considered what else she might have told Michele.

She nodded. "I just called her and mentioned your name. She said she knew a boy there named Duncan. She laughed, thinking you might be the same guy." Flashing that quirky smile again, she bobbed and finished, "Said you were cool, made being locked up almost fun."

He searched her face for any sign that she was put off by his having been in Juvie but saw only amusement.

"It's late," she said. "I've gotta go. She's picking me up in a few."

Dammit, he thought.

"Oh, OK," he said.

She stood, and he rose with her, masking his disappointment. For the first time that night, he realized how late he would be getting home, but he didn't care. He and his sisters were often absent from home—Ava no longer tried to control their comings and goings.

Led Zeppelin's "Ramble On" swirled and spiraled through the air as they walked toward the house and its dwindling crowd of partiers.

"Want to go to a movie with me?" he asked.

"Sure," she said, taking his hand. "That'd be fun."

"What would…" he started.

"Could we see *2001*?" she asked as they ascended the steps to the redwood deck.

"Definitely," he answered, not knowing where or if it was showing in town but determined to take her somewhere, anywhere, *wherever it was*, even to San Francisco.

Afterword

Thank you for reading my book.

Writing it was a rewarding experience. Memory, research, and imagination guided my typing fingers, and the characters led me through their adventures and challenges. In creating this story, I was struck by how much has changed in America in the intervening decades. I sought to capture the flavor and views of those times.

It helps to get reviews, especially as this is my first published book. If you feel like doing so on Amazon, Goodreads, or other sites, I would greatly appreciate it. Thank you.

To contact me, please visit my website, rodglasgow.com or my Facebook page Rod Glasgow – Author.

Acknowledgments

I want to thank Pam Osborn for carefully reading every version (so many) of this book. Her comments and editing suggestions were invaluable. Thank you, Gordon and Jean Glasgow, for reading an early version. Their comments were both insightful and encouraging, giving me a perspective I would not otherwise have had.

The resources at the California Digital Newspaper Collection, particularly their searchable copies of virtually every edition of the Santa Cruz Sentinel for the time period of this novel, were of great help to me in my extensive research. Another valuable resource was the Santa Cruz County Historic Photograph Collection, available online at the University of California at Santa Cruz. Plus, the multiple volumes of *Hip Santa Cruz*, edited by Ralph H. Abraham, were enjoyable reads and provided reminders and insights about the people and culture of 1960s Santa Cruz. Also, *Then & Now: Santa Cruz Coast* by Gary Griggs and Deepika Shrestha Ross provided fascinating comparative views of the dramatic changes to the Santa Cruz coastline and structures.